Acclaim for John Banville's SHROUD

"A virtuoso tale of grief, loss and salvation. His dazzling lyricism and extraordinary language resonate long after the story ends. . . . This dreamlike novel . . . glows with the subdued brilliance of its author's searching intellect. The long stretches of breathtaking prose, addictive and illuminating, are what make this *Shroud* just shy of miraculous."
—*The Oregonian*

"A ravishingly beautiful writer. His prose is clean and unfussy . . . and his images and metaphors have a visionary keenness that's almost violent; they strike the readers like blows."
—*Salon*

"*Shroud* shocks its reader. . . . It throbs along powerfully . . . until out of nowhere a beautiful sentence stops things cold. Banville's prose is thick and sumptuous."
—*Entertainment Weekly*

"Can only be called a page-turner. . . . What propels the reader's fascination and admiration is the brilliance of its art." —*St. Louis Post-Dispatch*

"Banville . . . [has] an allusive, alliterative prose style; a sly sense of humor; a meditative intelligence drawn to art and artifice; an appraiser's eye that seeks out the odd corners of beauty in this world but reserves a disdainful glance for its conventions. . . . An unlikely and affecting story of redemption."
—*Houston Chronicle*

"A work of fiction with . . . imaginative ambition and integrity."
—*The Washington Post Book World*

"John Banville is a master of narrative, language and imagery. His fictional characters . . . have daunting intellectual and individual breadth. . . . The author's gift is the taut examination of characters as they hold their own disquieted review of themselves. His prose is eloquent and his language reverberates with clarity."
—*Rocky Mountain News*

"As much potboiler mystery as it is intellectual tour de force. . . . As a meditation on the nature of personal identity, indeed on the meaning of truth, *Shroud* is a masterpiece."
—*Fort Worth Star-Telegram*

"Every sentence of *Shroud* is thrilling with Nabokovian wit, sorrow and beauty." —*The Commercial Appeal* (Memphis)

"Difficult to resist. . . . Banville has always been a sumptuous writer, but his love for the Jamesian sentence seems especially well-suited here." —*The Milwaukee Journal Sentinel*

"Almost every one of his gorgeous sentences has the brooding, propulsive power of the heavens above his narrator's lost Belgian home. . . . Banville weaves a haunting, lingering tale of a soul forever severed from its own identity." —*Seattle Weekly*

"Hallucinatory. . . . His skill at not losing us along the way is simply extraordinary. So is his prose, which, like *Shroud*, is hypnotic." —*Delaware News-Journal*

"Narratively performs the very theory it allegorizes. The story engages quite suspensefully. His diction and command of language . . . are nothing short of genius." —*The Mobile Register*

"Part mystery, part epistemological jigsaw puzzle, part black comedy. . . . We're treated, on nearly every page, to the pleasure of a formidable writer's fresh take on age-old themes: the nature of self and the limits of love." —*LA Weekly*

"I am grateful for what I discovered [in *Shroud*], grateful for watching a deeply moral writer at the top of his game, grateful for having known a literary character far more intimately that most 'real people' I have met. It will . . . amaze you." —David Prather, *Huntsville Times*

"In this mesmerizing novel, taut with intelligence, compassion and wit, Banville has once again worked his extravagant alchemy, transmuting this prose of the familiar world into the poetry of revelation and renewal." —*Independent on Sunday*

"In beautiful, lucid prose, John Banville describes a tragedy so strongly rooted in history and character that, like all real tragedies, it could not happen otherwise." —*The Times* (London)

John Banville

SHROUD

John Banville was born in Wexford, Ireland, in 1945. His first book, *Long Lankin*, was published in 1970. His other books are *Nightspawn*, *Birchwood*, *Doctor Copernicus*, *Kepler*, *The Newton Letter*, *Mefisto*, *The Book of Evidence* (which was shortlisted for the 1989 Booker Prize), *Ghosts*, *Athena*, *The Untouchable*, *Eclipse*, and *Shroud*. He won the Booker Prize for his novel *The Sea* in 2005. He lives in Dublin.

INTERNATIONAL

ALSO BY JOHN BANVILLE

SHROUD

SHROUD

John Banville

VINTAGE INTERNATIONAL
Vintage Books
A Division of Random House, Inc.
New York

FIRST VINTAGE INTERNATIONAL EDITION, JUNE 2004

Copyright © 2002 by John Banville

All rights reserved under International and Pan-American Copyright Conventions.
Published in the United States by Vintage Books, a division of Random House, Inc.,
New York, and simultaneously in Canada by Random House of Canada Limited,
Toronto. Originally published in hardcover in Great Britain by Picador, an imprint of
Pan Macmillan Ltd., London, in 2002, and subsequently in hardcover in the United
States by Alfred A. Knopf, a division of Random House, Inc., New York, in 2003.

Vintage is a registered trademark and Vintage International and colophon are
trademarks of Random House, Inc.

The Library of Congress has established a Cataloging-in-Publication record for the
Knopf edition of *Shroud*.

Vintage ISBN: 0-375-72530-X

Book design by Iris Weinstein

www.vintagebooks.com

Printed in the United States of America
10 9 8 7 6 5 4 3 2

We set up a word at the point at which our ignorance begins, at which we can see no further, e.g., the word "I," the word "do," the word "suffer": —these are perhaps the horizon of our knowledge, but not "truths."

ONE

W ho speaks? It is her voice, in my head. I fear it will not stop until I stop. It talks to me as I haul myself along these cobbled streets, telling me things I do not want to hear. Sometimes I answer, protest aloud, demanding to be left in peace. Yesterday in the baker's shop that I frequent on the Via San Tommaso I must have shouted out something, her name, perhaps, for suddenly everyone in the crowded place was looking at me, as they do here, not in alarm or disapproval but simple curiosity. They all know me by now, the baker and the butcher and the fellow at the vegetable stall, and their customers, too, hennaed housewives, mostly, plump as pigeons, with their perfume and ugly jewellery and great, dark, disappointed eyes. I note their remarkably slender legs; they age from the top down, for these are still the legs, suggestively a little bowed, that they must have had in their twenties or even earlier. Clearly I interest them. Perhaps what appeals to them is the suggestion of the commedia dell'arte in my appearance, the one-eyed glare and comically spavined gait, the stick and hat in place of Harlequin's club and mask. They do not seem to mind if I am mad. But I am not mad, really, only very, very old. I feel I have been alive for aeons. When I look back I see what seems a primordial darkness, scattered with points of cold, hard light, immensely distant, each from each, and from me. Soon, in a few months, we shall enter the final decade of this millennium; I will not live to see the next one, a matter of some regret, the previous two having generated such glories, such delights.

Yes, I have returned to this arcaded city, unwisely, it may be. I rented a place in one of the little alleyways hard by the Duomo, I shall not say which one, for reasons that are not entirely clear to me, although I confess I worry intermittently about the possibility of a visit from the police. It is not much, my bolt-hole, a couple of rooms, low-ceilinged, dank; the windows are so narrow and dirty I have to keep a table lamp burning all day for fear of falling over something in the half dark. I would not wish to be found dead here, the door broken down, my landlady screaming, and I in who knows what mode of disarray. She is, my landlady—*quella strega!*—a widow, and of a decidedly histrionic bent. She tells me this used to be the city's red light district, and gives me a look the import of which I do not care to speculate upon, widening her eyes and holding her head far back, affording me an unpleasant view into the caverns of her nostrils. I always suspected I would end up like this, an outcast, stumping the back streets of some anonymous city, talking to myself and being stared at by passers-by. Yet I chose to come back here, though not out of fondness, certainly. Turin resembles nothing so much as a vast, grandiose cemetery, with all this marble, these monuments, these gesturing statues; it is no wonder poor N. went off his head here, thinking himself a king and the father of kings and stopping in the street to embrace a cabman's nag. They lost his luggage, too, as once they did mine, sent it to Sampierdarena when he was headed in the opposite direction; forever after he could not hear that melodious place-name without a snarl of rage.

Enough of these vagaries. I am going to explain myself, to myself, and to you, my dear, for if you can talk to me then surely you can hear me, too. Calmly, quietly, eschewing my accustomed gaudiness of tone and gesture, I shall speak only of what I know, of what I can vouch for. At once the polyp doubt rears its blunt and ugly head: what do I know? for what can I vouch? *There exists neither "spirit," nor reason, nor thinking, nor consciousness, nor soul, nor will, nor truth: all are fictions* . . . So the crazed philosopher declares, swinging his mighty hammer. Yet the notion haunts me that I am being given one last chance to redeem something of myself. I am not speaking of the soul, I am not that far gone in my dotage. But there may be some small, precious thing that I can buy back, as once I bought back Mama Vander's silver pill-box from the pawnbroker's. It occurs to me to wonder if that might have been your real purpose, not to expose me and make a name for yourself at all, but rather to offer me the possibility of redemption. If so, you have already had an effect: redemption is not a word that up to now has figured prominently in my vocabulary. But then your motives were never clear to me, no more, I suspect, than they were to you. Perhaps you did indeed betray me, and someday soon a publication will pop up from the presses in an obscure corner of academe with a posthumous essay in it, by you, on me, and I shall be disgraced, laughed at, hooted out of the lecture hall. Well, no matter.

❧

The name, my name, is Axel Vander, on that much I insist. That much, if no more. Her letter was delivered to me one morning a world ago in the pleasant town of Arcady by a helmed and goggled Hermes on a bike. The message it carried was one I had been waiting for and dreading all my life, what I think of as my life, my real life. Now it had come at last, and the first thing I felt was embarrassment. It was as if I had been informed that a long-dead sibling, hardly remembered and never loved, was not dead after all, but tritely and vigorously alive, residing in a neighbouring suburb and about to pay an impossible visit. What could I find to say, at such a distance of time, to this discarded version of myself? I drank whisky all day, euphoric with terror and panic, and woke up at dead of night to find myself slumped in the old swivel chair down in my study with a burnt-out cigarette stub still in my fingers. From outside in the soft California darkness I could smell the smells that were exotic to me even yet, after so many years: eucalyptus, dust still warm from the day's sun, the tang of charcoal drifting down from the blond hills where fires had been smouldering sullenly in the grass for months. I let the letter fall to the floor and laughed the inane laugh of the inebriated. A car sizzled past on Cedar Street, going very slowly, as if its driver were counting the house numbers, and I thought of a mask with narrowed eyes behind it scanning the doors and the blinded windows. I lifted a hand and cocked my thumb and pointed a finger into the darkness where the door was. I laughed again, more phlegmily this time, and turned my hand around and stuck the pointing finger into my mouth and let the thumb fall like a hammer. I would have put a bullet in myself if . . . if what?

Pah.

I tried to rise but could not, and fell back with a clatter, the chair squealing in agony under me, my dead leg rolling like a log. I hate this leg, ineluctable companion of my failing years, hate it even more than the sightless eye that glares at me unmoving from the morning mirror, clouded and colourless as I imagine the eye of a dead albatross. That is what I am, a dead weight hung about my own neck. It will not be so for long more. Lately I have begun to feel that I am falling off myself, that my suety old flesh is melting off my skeleton and soon will all be gone. I shall not mind; I shall be glad; I shall rise up then, bared of inessentials, all gleaming bone and sinew smooth as candle wax, new, unknown, my real self at last. There is a moment that comes in drunkenness, or on the far side of it, when, as is said to happen sometimes to the afflicted in the throes of a heart attack, I seem to separate from my body and float upward, and hang aloft, looking down on the spectacle of myself with disinterested attention. It had happened now. I saw myself sprawled there, and then shift again with a violent heave, like a splayed horse trying to get to its feet, flailing about help-lessly, muttering. I reached for the bottle on the desk and drank greedily from the neck, making suckling noises. My mouth was raw from the long day's drinking. When I let my arm sweep down beside the chair the bottle slipped from my fingers and rolled with a joggling hesitancy on the polished wooden floor, pouring its heart out in lavish, glottal gulps. Let it spill. In truth, I dislike the smoke-and-ashes taste of bourbon, but early on I had fixed on it to be my drink, as part of my strategy of difference, another way of being on guard, as an actor puts a pebble in his shoe to remind him that the character he is playing has a limp. This was in the days when I was making myself over. So difficult it was, to judge just so, to forge the fine discriminations, to maintain a balance—no one could know how difficult. If it had been a work of art I was fash-ioning they would have applauded my mastery. Perhaps that was my mistake, to do it all in secret, instead of openly, with a flourish. They would have been entertained; they would have forgiven me; Harlequin is always forgiven, always survives.

I heard paper crackle under one of the castors of the chair, like a snicker of admonitory laughter. It was that letter. See: I lean, I grunt, I pluck it up and flatten it with a fist on the arm of the chair and read it yet again in the cone of gold-dusted light that bathes me in its undeserved benevolence, my old wild leaning head, my slop-ing shoulder, my rope-veined claw. The typewritten lines flicker in time to a pulse beating in my temple, and my good eye waters with the effort of keeping the words steady and in line. She was in Antwerp—Antwerp, dear God! Her studied, scholarly tone amused me. Narrowly, striving to concentrate, I speculated as to how much she might know. I had thought I had shaken off the pelt of my far past yet here was evidence that it would not be entirely sloughed, but was dragging along behind me, still attached by a thread or two of dried slime.

It came to me then, with drunken clarity, what I would do. Odd, how this random world insinuates its sly suggestions. I scrabbled among the papers on the desk and found the embossed card that had been lying there for a week and read with a rictus of contempt its curlicued and pompous blandishments. *Chiarissimo Professore! Il Direttore del Convegno considera un altissimo onore e un immenso piacere invitarla ufficialmente a Torino* . . . I had intended to decline, of course, with a curt and scornful note, but now I saw that I must go, and make her come to me there. Where better to confront my ruin, if that was what it was to be?

When I had read the letter first my first thought had been to disappear, simply to stand up and walk out of my life, as I did once before, with remarkable, with outrageous, success. It would be less easy this time; then, I was no one, now there are people—a select band, but a band—across however many continents there are who know the name of Axel Vander; all the same, it could be done. I had my escape routes mapped out, my secret bank accounts primed, my sanctuaries sealed and waiting . . . I am exaggerating, of course. But for a minute or two I did entertain the thought of fleeing, and was entertained by it. It made me feel daring, dangerous; it made me feel young. I wondered if this wielder of the poison pen, whoever she might be, had known the effect her letter would have on me: was it possible she was allowing me time to cut and run? But where would I go to, really? Whatever plans I might have put in place, there was nowhere farther I could escape to beyond this tawny shore, last edge of what for me was the known world. No, I would not do it, I would not give her the satisfaction of hearing the clump and stumble of my clay feet as I fled. Better far to confront her, laugh in the face of her accusations— ha! I would lie to her, of course; mendacity is second, no, is first nature to me. All my life I have lied. I lied to escape, I lied to be loved, I lied for placement and power; I lied to lie. It was a way of living; lies are life's almost-anagram. And now my earliest exercises in the art, my prentice falsehoods, had come back to undo me.

I woke at five in spectral rain-light, not sober yet. For a second I expected Magda to give her familiar moan of mild complaint and turn over in the bed with an oceanic heave. I reached out a hand beside me to where she was not; the sheet there had a special, faintly clammy chill that I knew I must be imagining and yet was convinced I could feel. I lay with eyes still shut and lit my wake-up cigarette, then rose and walked barefoot into the living room, my dead leg thumping on the maple boards. I am not of an apocalyptic disposition, having seen so many worlds seem to end and yet survive, but that morning I had the certain sense of having crossed, of having been forced to cross, an invisible frontier, and of being in a state that forever more would be post-something, would be forever an afterwards. That letter, of course, was the crossing point. Now I was cloven in two more thoroughly than ever, I who was always more than myself. On one side there was the I I had been before the letter arrived, and now there was this new *I*, a singular capital standing at a tilt to all the known things that had suddenly become unfamiliar. The house had a tense and watchful aspect, as if resentful of my intrusion on its furtive doings at this unaccustomedly early hour. Phantoms of shadow hung about, trying not to be noticed. A window streamed with rain, and opposite it in the room a patch of wall rippled like dark silk. I stopped still and peered into the gloom, seeking a focus; there were times when Magda was there, a palpable presence, but not now, and the shadows were shadows only. From the garden I could hear the rain beating on the leaves and into the clay, and I pictured it, falling down straight and shiny as wires through the windless dawn.

The coffee machine was still at its diarrhoeal labours when the rain stopped abruptly. I never got used to the weather on that coast, it was always too orderly, too arranged; there the spring

with its discreet matutinal downpours followed by days of seam-
less sunlight had none of the unpredictability, the flushed feverish-
ness, of the springtimes of my youth. Arcadians complain of the
climate, in their relaxed, wry way, but to me these conditions
hardly constituted weather at all, product that I am of Europe's
bleak northern lowlands with their ice storms and slanting rain
and skies of tumultuous cloud endlessly unscrolling eastward. I
took my steaming mug into the breakfast nook, easing myself awkwardly between the bench seat and the table. The drenched garden, tousled and glittering, had the abashed look of something
picking itself up after an unseemly tussle. There would be mist on
the bay for half the morning, until the sun was strong enough to
burn it off, as the weather forecasters would say. I like that phrase,
to burn it off, the figurative, brisk assurance of it. Out there on that
coast the elements are something to be patronised; even the not
infrequent earthquakes are a sort of huge communal joke. In the
first months after we moved into the house I used to love to sit like
that of a morning, looking out on my avocado tree, my peach tree,
at the humming-birds busy about the bush that I think is called
hibiscus, listening in a state of tingling bliss to the early-morning
news on the radio, impatient for the end when the risibly solemn-
voiced announcer would inform me of what the day had in store
for me, the highs and lows of temperature—never too high, never
too low—the breezes pacific and soft as breaths, the fog's standing
mirage. It was like being promised a succession of lavish and
wholly undeserved treats.

I went off to the bathroom, and when I returned, haphazardly
shaven and putting on my tie, this time Magda *was* there, in her old
grey dressing-gown with the frayed drawstring, sitting in the nook
where I had sat. She looked as solid as an armchair, with hands laid
flat along her thighs and a yard of flannel stretched between her
splayed knees, and my heart gave a sideways knock and for a second I was afraid I would fall over. This is how I best remember her
in that house, planted there in the neuralgic light of early morning,

the iron hair severely parted down the middle and the heavy braids coiled against her head like two outsized earphones, her callused feet bare, her brooding, inexpectant gaze fixed slightly off to one side of me. Today she held her face turned away a little, at a characteristically watchful angle. It seemed that she might speak, if I waited long enough. But then I blinked and she was gone, and my heart settled down grumpily to its accustomed, rocky measure. Why could she not leave me alone? She had wanted to go, I was sure of it, so why must she keep coming back like this? My coffee mug stood at the place where she had appeared, still with its faint plume of steam; it had the look of the smoking barrel of a gun.

Unnerved, I went into what was known, I do not know why, as the lounge. It was the dimmest room in the house; a lamp had to be kept burning wanly there, too, day and night. Perhaps that was the reason people were always unwilling to linger in the room, despite the sofa and the easy chairs and the invitingly jumbled bookshelves. People? What am I saying? There never were people, to speak of, except me, and Magda. We did not encourage visitors; we were not sociable; we barely knew the names of our nearest neighbours; it was how I had insisted it should be, and Magda had willingly complied, at least I think she did so willingly. I sat down on the couch, crapulent and tired and squelchy with sudden, sweet self-pity. I never feel more acutely the pathos and perils of my life as in the early morning, the very time when I should be full of renewed hope and vigour. Briefly my resolve faltered; why was I going on this journey, what did I think I would achieve? I clasped a hand under my knee and heaved up my dead leg and banged it down on one of the little tables, making the lamp-bulb jump and blink. What choice did I have, but to go?

There was a single window in the room, large and long, giving on to a narrow walkway and the siding of the next-door house. Day had fully taken hold now and the window was a big rectangle of wettish sunlight slashed through with diagonals of indigo shadow; against the gloom in which I sat it might have been a painting, garish and flat as a primitive depiction of a tropical scene. I remarked inwardly again how uninsistent was the sunlight in this part of the world, a matt radiance, unvarying and calm, that would fill every square inch of the day like a bright, colourless gas, seeming not to have its source in the sky but to shine out of the very things on which it was falling, the buildings white as sugar cubes, the pastel motor cars, the burnished, black-green trees that lined every street like so many dreamy guardians. I noted too, more immediately, the dustiness of the room. Since Magda's going I had made no attempt at maintaining the place; I was not even sure where the cleaning things were stored, though I thought surely there must be a broom, a mop, a pail . . . ? I had been under the impression that Magda had kept a daily woman, who came when I was not there, but although I waited in on successive mornings, no one turned up. Perhaps I only imagined gleaming-black Jemima, with her rolling eye and stupendous bosom and cotton-white headscarf tied in a top-knot. Then did Magda do all the household chores herself? I do not know why this possibility should be surprising, but it is. Now, with her gone, dust lay everywhere undisturbed, a fine, soft, mole-coloured fur, cut through by a pathway maze that marked out the pattern of my widowed life in the house: door to hall, kitchen to table, bathroom to bedroom. The margins of my world were disappearing, crumbling into this grey penumbra of soft dirt.

Widowed, or widowered? Is there such a word? Sometimes even still the language puts out a foot for me to trip over.

In her last years it was a mystery to me how Magda passed the time when I was not at home, as increasingly I made sure not to be. Housework was hardly the whole answer, even for one as slow-moving and deliberate as she always was. Whenever I enquired of her what she had done during the day she would take on a cornered look, holding her face at that three-quarters angle away from me and letting one shoulder droop, so that I felt I was being edged around by a large, wary ruminant. These cringing reactions of hers always annoyed me, although I could not think in what terms exactly to protest, and I would have to content myself with giving her my steeliest, white-lipped smile, drawing air in swiftly through my nostrils with a reptilian hiss that made her flinch. After these exchanges it gratified me that she would go about the house all evening heaving troubled little sighs, or being extra quiet, as if she were listening anxiously for the abatement of my anger. When we were in company together, at some unavoidable party or college reception, I could not resist making dry asides about her, inviting those unwise enough to engage us in conversation to join in my amusement at her incongruous, ill-attired, mute presence by my side. Those witticisms of mine at her expense were at least part of what made her into a public joke; through the years I had overheard her referred to variously as "Vander's Mädchen," and "Mutter Vander," and, mysteriously, "Old Eva." She did not seem to resent these petty public cruelties to which I subjected her, and would even smile a little, shyly, as if in pride at how appallingly I could behave, her large, button-black eyes shining and her upper lip protruding plumply. And of course this happy tolerance infuriated me all the more, and I would want to strike her, as she stood there amid the press of people in her overcoat and her broad, flat shoes, holding a glass of wine she kept forgetting to sip, contentedly isolated in the unfathomable depths of herself, my big, slow, enigmatic mate whom for the best part of forty years I must have loved or else I would have left.

I stood up from the couch and went into the bedroom again, where I was startled to discover that I had already packed a suitcase. I must have done it in the early hours, when I was drunk. I had no memory of it. I recalled telephoning the airline, and my surprise at being answered not by a machine but by a wide-awake and irritatingly bright human voice—I cannot adjust to the world's increasing nightlessness—but after that there was only the fuzzy, faintly humming blank of inebriated sleep. Perhaps it was more than the bourbon, I thought; perhaps my mind was going.

How would one detect the encroachment of senility, when what is being attacked is the very faculty of detection itself? Would there be intervals of respite, flashes of frightful clarity in the midst of maunderings, moments of shivery recognition before the looking-glass, goggling in horror at the dribbled-on shirt-front, the piss-stained flies? Probably not; probably I shall shuffle into senility all unaware. The onset of extreme old age as I am experiencing it is a gradual process of accumulation, a slow settling as of soft grey stuff, like the dust in the untended house, under which the once-sharp edges of my self are blurring. There is an opposite process, too, by which things grow rigid and immovable, turning my stools into ingots of hot iron, drying out my joints until they grate on each other like pumice stones, making my toenails hard as horn. Things out in the world, the supposedly inanimate objects, join in the conspiracy against me. I misplace things, lose things, my spec-tacles, the book I was reading a minute ago, Mama Vander's redeemed silver pill-box—there is that bibelot again—that I kept as a talisman for more than half a century but that now seems to be gone, fallen into a crevice in time. Objects topple on me from high shelves, items of furniture plant themselves in my path. I cut myself repeatedly, with razor, fruit knife, scissors; hardly a week passes when I do not find myself some morning hunched over the handbasin fumblingly trying to unpeel a plaster with my teeth while blood from a sliced finger drips with shocking matter-of-factness on to the porcelain. Are these mishaps not of a different order from heretofore? I was never adroit, even in the quickest years of youth, but I wonder if my clumsiness now might be some-thing new, not merely a physical unhandiness but a radical form of discontinuity, the outward manifestation of lapses and final clo-sures occurring deep in the brain. The smallest things are always the surest warning, if one but heeded them. The first sign I regis-tered of Magda's malady was the sudden craving that she devel-oped for children's food of all kinds, popcorn and potato chips, toffee bars, sherbet bags, penny lollipops.

In the street outside a car horn brayed; for me the sound of the car horn is that great republic's most characteristic call, full-throated, peremptory, with an undertone of amused mockery. I snatched up my suitcase and my stick and lurched to the door, like a long-term convict who has heard the dead-bolts shooting.

The taxi driver was a caricature immigrant from the East, bearish and taciturn, a Russian, most likely, as so many of them seem to be in these newly liberated days. He took my bag unwillingly and turned and lumbered with it down the porch steps. There are times when that entire coastal strip seems a film set and everyone on it a character actor. In the street the lush trees shone in the sun and there were bright blooms in every front yard, yet even now, in this early morning at the height of spring, the air had a musty, used-up feel to it, another effect of the general lack of weather, and no wind, and the smog that even the dawn rains cannot fully dispel. The driver did not open the taxi door for me, and I had difficulty getting into the low-slung vehicle, first throwing in my walking stick and then turning and folding my torso in half and shoving myself backwards through the door on to the seat and grasping my useless leg in both hands and hauling it in after me. Hard to be graceful when you are half a cripple. Throughout my laboured manoeuvrings, the Russian sat in front like a stone man, facing impassively forward, hairy-eared, his thick shoulders stooped. Now he shifted a lever somewhere—I never did learn to drive that country's vast and terrifying motor cars—and trod on the accelerator and the engine roared and the taxi surged away from the kerb like a stuck animal. Turning, I spied one of my neighbours standing out on his porch in string vest and shorts, watching me go, with what seemed a look of confirmed suspicion, as if he were only waiting for the taxi to turn the corner before running to the telephone and calling the authorities to inform them that the suspect bird next door had flown the coop. He is one of those indigenous, lean, tall types with greying curls and a bandit's drooping moustache. In the two decades and more that he lived beside us I exchanged no more than a handful of guardedly polite greetings with him, although once he came to the house to complain about a stray dog that Magda had taken in; I got rid of the dog, naturally. Now for the first time it occurred to me to wonder if the fellow might be a Hebrew. I thought it likely—those springy curls, that nose. Half the population of Arcady and its environs seemed to be of the Chosen, though not the kind that I was once used to; these *Luftmenschen* were altogether too sure of themselves, too pushy and uncomplaining.

We came down to the shore and turned in the direction of the bridge. I had been right, there was still mist on the bay, though the sun was steadily strengthening. The highway was congested with morning traffic, six lanes of it hurtling forward like a herd of maddened animals. I pressed my hands over my face. I was tired; my mind was tired; it is wearing out, like the rest of me, though not as quickly. And yet it cannot stop working, even for an instant, even when I am asleep; I can never quite come to terms with this appalling fact. Repeatedly now, especially in the night, I return to the awful possibility that the mind might survive the body's death. They say that Danton's severed head was heard to heap curses on Robespierre. To be trapped like that, even for a minute, to feel the system shutting down, to see the light finally failing—ah! The taxi banged over a ramp in the road and began the long scramble up the slope of the bridge, waddling along at a strained sixty, the tyres whooping and the engine rattling like a faulty air-conditioner. I leaned my head back on the greasy plastic of the seat and closed my eyes again. In the dark the old questions teemed. What do I know? Less now than yesterday. Time and age have brought not wisdom, as they are supposed to do, but confusion, and a broadening incomprehension, each year laying down another ring of nescience. What do I know? When I opened my eyes we had gained the first crest of the bridge, and the city was there before us, walking sedately up and down its line of low hills, the bristling buildings flat and featureless as in a stage backdrop at this still-early hour. A tiny aeroplane was poised on a high bank of petrol-blue smog. In all the time I lived there I was never once on the other bridge, the famous rust red one; I do not know for sure where it leads from or goes to. What do I care for mere topography? The topography of the mind, now, that is a different matter . . . *The topography of the mind*—do I really say such things, out loud, for people to hear?

A battered white car driven by a frail black youth veered suddenly into the lane in front of us, and the Russian stamped on the brake and the taxi groaned and perilously swayed, and I was thrown forward and struck my good knee painfully on something hard in the seat-back. A traffic accident, that quintessential American road show, was always one of my liveliest terrors, the intolerable absurdity of all that noise and heat and hissing steam and pain. The angered Russian began jockeying for position, and at last with a tremendous wrench of the steering wheel he pulled into the left lane and overtook the white car and opened the automatic window on the passenger side and flung out a polysyllabic Cossack curse. The black boy, a skinny arm resting on the door beside him, his long, delicate fingers drumming in time to the music thundering from his car radio, turned and gave us a broad smile, showing a mouthful of impossibly huge, impossibly white teeth, then hawked deeply and spat a stringy green gobbet that landed with a smack in the corner of the rear window by my face, making me start back in disgust. The boy threw up his Egyptian head and gave a heehaw laugh that I saw but could not hear above the traffic roar and the pounding of the radio, and shot forward gleefully in a black blast of exhaust smoke. The Russian spoke savagely some words that I was unperturbed not to understand.

From the bridge, by an exit I had never noticed before, we descended abruptly into an unfamiliar wilderness of filling stations and cheap motels and ochre scrubland. I wondered vaguely if the

Russian really knew the way to the airport; it would not be the first time one of these angry exiles from Muscovy had taken me to the wrong destination. I watched the disheartened landscape with its raked shadows fleeting past and was struck yet again by the strangeness of being here, of being anywhere, in the company of all these deceptive singularities. The Russian was the Russian with the long arms and the hirsute ears, the black boy was the black boy who wore a torn singlet and had spat at us; even I was the I who was on my way to the airport, and from the airport to another, older world. Were we, any of us, anything more than the sum of our attributes, even to ourselves? Was I more than a moving complex of impulses, fears, random fancies? I spent the best part of what I suppose I must call my career trying to drum into those who would listen among the general mob of resistant sentimentalists surrounding me the simple lesson that there is no self: no ego, no precious individual spark breathed into each one of us by a bearded patriarch in the sky, who does not exist either. And yet . . . For all my insistence, and to my secret shame, I admit that even I cannot entirely rid myself of the conviction of an enduring core of selfhood amid the welter of the world, a kernel immune to any gale that might pluck the leaves from the almond tree and make the sustaining branches swing and shake.

Here is the airport, in the morning's splintered glare, the flustered travellers lugging their bags, the taxi cabs like milling hounds nosing at each other's rear parts, the black man in the peaked cap grinning and saying, "*Good* morning, sir!" with enormous, false, emphatic cheerfulness. I paid the Russian his fare— the brute smiled!—and took my suitcase and turned on the swivel of my stick and went forward with my boatman's gait to meet a shadowy otherself in the smoked-glass doors of the departure hall that at the last moment, just as it seemed I and my reflection must meet in mutual annihilation, suddenly bethought themselves and opened before me with a hot gasp.

Fly! Fly!

She placed the two frail scraps of newspaper on the little lamp-lit table by the bed and sat back on her heels and studied them for a long moment, her hands laid flat on the table edge and her chin resting on her hands, now the news report of his long-ago death, now the side-by-side photographs of him and of the other one, all faded by time. Each breath she breathed clouded briefly the glass top of the table and stirred the fragments of sepia-coloured paper. They were brittle and light as a butterfly's wings. She felt a thrill of guilt; she had clipped them out with a nail scissors, hunched over the newspaper file, expecting the librarian to see what she was doing and come and upbraid her in guttural outrage and in a language not one word of which she would understand. She wondered again at the misprint in the caption to the photograph—*Axel Vanden*—the inexplicable appropriateness of it. How young he looked, hardly more than a boy, very good-looking, but with such an alarmed expression; it was probably just that the camera flash had startled him, though she could not help seeing fright and foreboding in those eyes. The other one, beside him, wore a grin, insolent and yet self-mocking. She picked up delicately in her fingertips the two rectangles of rice paper, which she had trimmed to an exact fit, and laid one each over the two cuttings, first the report of his death, then the photographs. The fountain pen she had bought was of an old-fashioned design, plump in the middle and tapered at the end; it had cost an alarming amount of money. Inside, there had been not the rubber bulb she had expected—the fake-antique effect was confined to the exterior—only a rigid plastic ink cartridge. It was better this way: a bulb she would have had to remove, for fear of it leaking, or bursting, but she could leave the cartridge in, it would be safe, and small enough to give ample space for her purpose inside the hollow of the barrel. This way too the pen would work, and that was good; verisimilitude is in the details, that was a lesson she had learned at the knee of a master. Now she moved the two pieces of newsprint to the front edge of the table and carefully, not daring to breathe, rolled them tightly on to the spindle of the ink cartridge, first one, then the other, face down with the protective sheets of rice paper between them, and secured them with a loop of fine thread she had teased from the hem of her blouse. Tying the knot was difficult, for the leaves of newsprint and the rice paper all kept trying to uncurl, and she had to make three attempts before she succeeded. She was careful too in screwing back the barrel of the pen; at one of the turns it snagged somehow on its threads and made a cracking noise, and she had the sensation of something soft and warm flipping over in the pit of her stomach. But then it was done. Resting fatly in her fingers the pen felt as full as a loaded pistol. To test it she wrote her name with a flourish on the pad beside the bed; the nib was too fine for her liking. She screwed on the cap again and clipped the pen into the pocket of her blouse and went and stood before the wardrobe mirror and looked at herself for a long time. Her own reflection always fascinated her, and frightened her, too, this inescapable person standing there, so known, so knowing, and so strange.

Tonight the voices in her head were silent.

Now there was nothing more to do; she had made all possible preparations. Axel Vander would have had her letter by this time, over there on the far side of the world, they had assured her of that at the post office. She had asked for the swiftest possible delivery; it had taken another dismayingly large handful of her dwindling store of bank notes. She went and leaned by the window and looked out into the night. In the square there were rain puddles, shiny and black as oil, and a line of trees, plane trees, she supposed, throwing ragged, oblong shadows across the pavement. She could hear a barrel organ playing somewhere, with mechanical and sinister cheeriness—a barrel organ, at this time of night?—and there was a faint, sickly aroma of what it took her a moment to identify as vanilla. She liked being here, in the unfamiliar city, the isolation of it. She was sure he would come. Perhaps as soon as tomorrow. He might even have set out already. She pictured him, tried to picture him, hurrying through the airport, flustered and petulant, banging his fist on the ticket counter and shouting out his name, demanding attention, insisting he must have a seat on the very next flight; he was famous for the violence of his temper. A tremor of excitement ran through her and she shivered. The only face she could put on him was the one from the newspaper cutting, with its youthful grin. He would be angry, and frightened, too, perhaps; he might offer her money; he might even threaten her. But she was not afraid. The prospect of his rage, his threats, did not alarm her; on the contrary, it made her feel calm, as if she were flying, somehow, suspended on firm air, unreachable, beyond all peril. What did she want from him? She did not know. There was something to be desired, certainly, she felt it inside her, like a vague and not unpleasurable distress; it was the feeling she imagined of being newly pregnant. She held his fate in her hands, his future; she had found him out. Yes, he would come, she was sure of it.

It was after midnight when I got into the city at last. There had been flight delays and missed connections, and the limousine that had been supposed to meet me at the airport was not there, the driver having tired of waiting and gone away. Then they told me my suitcase had not arrived, that it must have been sent on to somewhere else. At the lost luggage desk a swarthy clerk with his cap pushed to the back of his head and an unlit cigarette tucked behind his ear pretended not to understand my Italian—which, I might have told him, I learned from Dante—then shrugged and said the bag could be anywhere, and gave me a sheaf of incomprehensible forms to fill in. I threw the papers back in his face and for a horribly thrilling moment it seemed, from the truculent way he lowered his already low brow and scowled, that he might turn violent, and I took a step backwards and hefted my stick defensively. He only shrugged, however, and jabbered into a telephone, and told me someone would come, and turned contemptuously away. There was another wait then. Fuming, I sculled myself up and down the arrivals area, cutting a swathe through the press of tourists and noisy families and self-important businessmen with their slim briefcases and too-shiny, tasselled shoes. Presently a uniformed young woman from the airline arrived and informed me with a musical little laugh that yes, the *Professore*'s luggage had indeed gone to another destination, but that it would shortly be brought back and sent directly to my hotel. She had a large bust and a faint moustache and unpleasantly protrusive eyes, and reminded me of a celebrated operatic diva of the immediate postwar years whose name I cannot for the moment recall. I swore at her, and she blinked rapidly and ventured a glassy smile, not trusting that she had heard me correctly. She went off and found a taxi for me, and I was driven at astonishing speed—one always forgets how they drive here—through the humid night, into the city, where the last of the Saturday evening crowds were still promenading under the stone arcades.

Then at the hotel I found that my room had been given away. They pretended to have no record of my reservation, but from the evasively vacant look of the bald old body at the reception desk I knew it was a lie. I raised my voice, and made threats, and stabbed at the floor of the lobby with my stick. The manager was summoned, a preposterously handsome, heavy-set, ageing dandy, mahogany-coloured and shiny-haired, with the puffed-up chest of a heroic tenor—this entire business was turning into *opera buffa*—and advanced on me, unctuously smiling, with hands outspread, and assured me that everything would be arranged, everything would be fixed, in just a little while, if I would be patient. So I went and sat on a squeaky leather chair in the deserted bar, under the resentful eye of a tired barman, and drank too much red wine, and when at length I was led up to my room, on the fifth floor, a partitioned-off brown cell with a naked lavatory bowl standing in a corner, I was too tipsy and tired to complain any more. Despite exhaustion and the lateness of the hour, however, I decided I must speak at once, immediately, *now*, to the letter-writer, my mysterious nemesis, and even called the switchboard and asked to be put through to Antwerp, but then I paused and thought better of it—I would have started straight away to shriek at her—and threw down the receiver and crawled into bed, bleared and unbathed, still wearing the underwear I had not changed since setting out half a world ago.

I passed a restless night; the bed, as so often with hotel beds, was far too small to accommodate me and my stiff leg, and I was woken repeatedly by noises from outside, car horns and revving motorcycles and young men shouting to each other from street to street. Toward dawn the clamour abated and I fell into a doze, beset by violent dreams. I woke early, sweating alcohol, my brain beating, and rose and stumbled to the window and opened wide the curtains and squinted up between the beetling buildings at the dense cerulean sky of Europe.

After breakfast, with renewed fuss and apologies, I was moved into a large suite on the more salubrious third floor. The rooms were spacious and cool, with floors of black marble, silken smooth. My returned suitcase stood at the foot of the bed, wearing a shame-faced look. I have a fondness for hotel rooms, the air they have of tight-lipped anonymity, the sense of being sealed off from the world, the almost audible echo of whisperings and indrawn breaths and women crying out in helpless rapture. Reclining in a mid-morning bath I concocted a picture of Miss Nemesis: a dried-up old virgin with blue-veined talons and spectacles on a string, and a mouth, with a fan of fine wrinkles etched into the whiskered upper lip, set in bitter dissatisfaction at the lost promise of her youth, when she had worn slacks and smoked cigarettes and written that thesis on Wordsworth's politics or Shelley's atheism that had so shocked and impressed her tutor at Girton or the bluestockings at Bryn Mawr. Surely she would be easy to deal with. First I would try charm, then threats; if all else failed I would take her to the top of the Antonelli Mole and push her off. Laughing, I began to cough, and felt my tobacco-beaten lungs wobbling in their cage like heavy, half-inflated, wet balloons, and the bath water around me swayed and almost slopped over. My cigarette case, another purloined trinket from the past, was beside me in the soap dish. I lit up, small flakes of hot ash hissing around me in the water. Nothing like a good deep chestful of cigarette smoke to quell a morning cough.

I hauled myself up in a cascade of suds and immediately jarred my elbow on the edge of a glass shelf. This new pain struck up an echo in the knee I had bruised yesterday in the taxi on the bridge. I stood a moment clutching my arm and swearing. I am a bad fit with the world, an awkward fit; I am too high, too wide, too heavy for the common scale of things. I am not being boastful, quite the contrary; I have always found my oversized self burdensome and embarrassing. Before me in the misted glass of the bathroom's floor-length mirror my reflection loomed, pallid and peering. I went out to the bedroom and stood by the window looking down into the shaded defile of the street, still massaging my bruised elbow. A bus went past, cars, foreshortened people. At the corner, where an angled block of buttery sunlight leaned, a woman selling flowers looked up and seemed to see me—was it possible, at such a distance? What a sight I would have been, suspended up there behind glass, a grotesque seraph, vast, naked, ancient. I lifted a hand, the palm held flatly forward, in solemn greeting, but the flower seller made no response.

Almost before I knew what I was doing I had snatched up the telephone and asked for the Antwerp number. Waiting, I could hear myself breathing in the mouthpiece, as if I were standing behind my own shoulder. Wet still from the bath, I dripped on the marble floor, in the darkly gleaming surface of which I could see yet another, dim reflection of myself, in end-on perspective this time, like that bronzen portrait of the dead Christ by what's-his-name, first the feet and then the shins, the knees, and dangling genitals, and belly and big chest, and topping it all the aura of wild hair and the featureless face looking down.

She answered on the first ring. I hardly knew what to say; I had not thought I would reach her at once like this, I had expected delays, obstacles, evasions. Yes, she said, yes, this is she. I could not place her accent; she was not English, and yet an English-speaker. I knew from something in her voice that she had been doing nothing, nothing at all, only waiting for me to call. I pictured the scene, the meagre room in the cheap hotel, the light of a northern spring morning the colour of shined-on lead falling from a mansard window, and her, sitting on the side of the bed, head bowed and arthritic old hands folded in her lap, biding through the long hours, listening to the silence, willing it to be broken by the telephone's jangling summons. She spoke with judicious care, costively, rationing the words; was there someone with her, overhearing what she said? No, she would be alone, I was certain of that. I said that she must come to me, for I would not go to her, and there was a lengthy pause. Then she said it was a question of the fare; train travel was expensive, and it was a long way. Now it was I who allowed the silence to expand. Did she think I should pay for her to come and ruin me? Still I would not speak. Very well, she said at last, she would take the overnight express and be here in the morning, and without another word, yet not hurriedly, she hung up. I shivered; the bath water drying off had left my old skin stretched and chill. My hands were shaking too, a little, but not from the damp or the cold.

I dressed, impatiently, as always now. With the years I find these necessary morning rituals increasingly irksome. For whose benefit was I putting on this shirt, this linen suit, this tie that was too short and too broad at the end and made me look, as I could see from the mirror, as if my tongue were hanging out? The old should have a special garment, something like a monk's habit, simple and functional, and suitably presageful of the winding-sheet. I ran my fingers through the crackling strands of my unruly hair, without visible effect; I never wanted to let my hair grow wild like this, especially when it began to turn white, but I felt it would be expected of me, the famous Mijnheer de Professor from the doddery, woolly Old World. Suddenly, like a soft blow, the memory from childhood came to me of my mother wetting a fingertip and smoothing down the comma of wiry hair on the crown of my head that always a moment afterwards would spring up again. I recalled too the curiously voluptuous shiver of disgust I would experience when she was helping me into some new item of clothing, a blouse, or knee-breeches, or a crisp navy-and-white sailor suit with the pasteboard price-tag still dangling from a buttonhole. What was the cause of that inner recoil? An excess of intimacy with my mother, under the chrysanthemum-smell of whose face powder I could detect a medley of more intimate and more exciting odours? No, that is not it, I think; what made me flinch, surely, was an over-consciousness of self, the sudden, ghastly awareness of being trapped inside this armature of flesh and bone like a pupa wedged in the hardened-over mastic of its cocoon. Immediately, again, came the demand: *What self?* What sticky imago did I imagine was within me, do I imagine is within me, even still, aching to burst forth and spread its gorgeous, eyed wings?

The lift was an old-fashioned, rackety affair, the sight of which twanged another vaguely nostalgic string at the far back of my memory. I could hear it coming down from above, stopping at every floor and flinging open its gate with a noise of mashing metals, as if successive armfuls of wire clothes-hangers were being crushed between giant steel claws. When it reached me, though, there was no one in it. The lobby too was empty, the reception desk unattended. Through a partly open door behind the desk I spied the manager from last night, eating a sandwich, sitting hunched at the corner of a table on which there was a typewriter and untidy mounds of papers. He was tieless today, with the sleeves of his white shirt rolled and the collar open on a tufted triangle of bulging chest. Was he, out of costume like this and in slight dishevelment, was he, I wondered, more himself, or less? He was going at the sandwich with the concentrated ferocity of a dog that has not been fed for days. When he saw me looking he did not acknowledge me, only scowled, his jaw munching away, and leaned out sideways and pushed the door shut with his foot. I was about to walk on when there rose unbidden before my mind's eye the image of the coffee mug, the one I had left on the table in the lounge when the taxi arrived to take me to the airport. I saw it all that way away, on what was now the dark side of the world, the rim marked with a dried half moon of gum from my morning mouth, the coffee dregs turning to a ring of furry brown powder in the bottom, just standing there in the darkness and the silence, one among all the other mute, unmoving objects I had left behind me in the locked house, and it came to me, with inexplicable but absolute certainty, that I would never return there. Shaken, I faltered, and put a hand to the desk to steady myself. A clerk came out of the office and looked at me. To cover the moment's infirmity I asked for a map of the city, and the clerk opened one between us on the counter and with a show of laboured dutifulness—why do his kind always glance aside in that blank, bored way just before they speak?—began to show me on it the location of the hotel. Yes yes, I said, I knew where I was! I snatched up the map and without folding it I stuffed it into my pocket and went through the glass door and corkscrewed myself on my stick down the steps into the high, narrow street.

What did it mean, that I would not go back? Was I to die here, in this city? I am not superstitious, I do not believe in premonitions, yet there it was, the conviction—no, the knowledge—that I would not return home again, ever. But then I thought: *Home?* I walked along the street in wonderment and muddled alarm, in the unfamiliar air, smelling the city's unfamiliar smells. At the sunlit corner I came upon the flower seller. She was seated beside her stall on a folding canvas stool. She was a foreigner, another refugee, I surmised, not Russian, this time, but a native of one of those statelets wedged like boulders of basalt, though beginning rapidly to crumble now, between the straining continental plates of East and West. Her skin was a dull shade of khaki, and she was dressed in what looked to me like a gypsy costume, with bangles and many cheap rings, and a brightly coloured headscarf knotted tightly under her chin. She was young, no more than thirty, I thought, but her face was the face of an old woman, pinched and sharp. She was talking to herself, rapidly, in a low, rhythmic sing-song, a sort of atrophied whine of entreaty and complaint. I felt a jolt, as in the experience of putting a foot on to the non-existent top step of a staircase in the dark, when I saw from the filmed-over emptiness of her eyes that she was blind. She sensed my hovering presence at once, though, and fumbled a spray of lily-of-the-valley from the stall and offered it to me, her whine intensifying into a pitiful but curiously unurgent, almost indifferent, beseeching. I produced a bank note, in an absurdly enormous denomination, and she put out a thin, leaf-brown hand unerringly and took it, and stored it swiftly in an inner recess of her beaded bodice. I waited for my change, but none was offered. She sat and softly keened complainingly as before, oblivious of me now, it appeared, rocking herself back and forth on her stool. Only then did I notice that she was in an advanced state of pregnancy. Behind me a yellow-and-black tram went past, spitting big, soft, flabby sparks from its over-head connection and causing the pavement to quake. Stooping in the lee of all that force and clangour I turned and hurried on.

I dodged into the first caffè that I came to and sat at a table far at the back, as if to hide from a pursuer. My upper lip was damp with sweat and my heart was joggling from side to side like a car-toon alarm clock. What was the matter, why had that encounter so disturbed me? I recalled the old man in Paris, a distant relative on my mother's side, in his dank apartment in the Marais, pressing fistfuls of francs into my hands and reciting for me the names of people who might help me, in Lisbon, London, New York, chant-ing them over and over in an urgent murmur, as if they were the verses of the Law. Even now, half a century later, I can recall a sur-prising number of them—their names, that is, for of course I never went near the people themselves. They would all be dead by now, most likely, and their children grown up, become lawyers or doctors or big shots in the insurance business, who would not care who I was, or what I had made of myself, or how, for no good reason, I had deceived that old man in the Marais, telling him I was someone other than who I was. I lifted my coffee cup with a hand that was trembling again and sought to quell the memories welling up out of the murk of the past. *What is remarkable is not that we remember, but that we forget*—who was it that said that? I looked about me at the caffè's ornate trappings, the chandeliers, the pot-bellied coffee machines, the gleaming copper spigot at the bar from which a constant purling cord of water flowed. There were few patrons: a panting old man and his panting dog, a woman in an elaborate hat eating pastries, and a clownish, carrot-haired fellow wearing an ill-fitting, loud, checked blazer and a bright yellow shirt with a soiled collar, the wide wings of which were spread flat over the lapels of his blazer, who kept glancing surreptitiously in my direction with a faint, elusive leer. By the door three black-tied waiters loitered, exchanging desultory remarks and eyeing the toecaps of their patent-leather shoes. For a second, strangely, and for no reason that I knew, everything seemed to stop, as if the world had missed a heartbeat. Is this how death will be, a chink in the flow of time through which I shall slip as lightly as a letter dropping with a rustle into the mysterious dark interior of a mailbox? I paid my bill and rose abruptly and made for the door, again as if I were fleeing someone, and had the sensation, as so often at such precipitate moments, of having left something of myself behind, and thought that if I were to look back now I would see a crude parody of myself sprawled on the chair where I had been sitting, a limp, life-sized marionette, hands hanging and jointed limbs all awry, grinning woodenly at the ceiling.

The door, heavy and high, resisted me, and I had to lean my weight into it to push it open. At my back I heard a flapping step, and saw in the sunstruck, bevelled glass panel of the door in front of me the reflection of a grinning face looming at my shoulder. It was the red-haired fellow, the one who had been watching me while I drank my coffee. I turned to confront him, and the door on its stiff spring swung back and struck me on the shoulder, and would have sent me pitching headlong among the tables and the chairs and the legs of the waiters if Carrot Head had not grasped me by the elbow—the one I had bruised on the bathroom shelf, naturally—and held me upright. He had a large, round, high-coloured face, with a sprinkling of ginger bristles on cheeks and chin that glittered in the sunlight falling through the glass. That awful blazer was far too big for him, as were his trousers, and he wore a pair of incongruous, once-white plimsolls with soiled laces and thick rubber soles. He nodded and leered, saying something in what seemed to be dialect. I shook off with difficulty that insistent and insinuating hand, and took a step forward and let go of the door, hoping it would bash my pursuer in the face, but he avoided it nimbly and followed me into the street, still keeping up his incomprehensible patter. The only word of it I could make out sounded like *signore,* which was repeated over and over, with puzzling emphasis, while Carrot Head nodded vehemently and pointed to his own face. I turned away from him and set off along the lofty corridor of the arcade as fast as my bad leg and the uneven paving flags would allow, keeping my gaze fixed furiously ahead. Still Carrot Head would not let me go, but trotted eagerly beside me, burbling away, and leaning down and round and up to push his face in front of mine. And so we went along, by the stone archways, through alternating intensities of shadow and sunlight, glanced at by quizzical passers-by, until, at an intersection, beside a second-hand bookstall, I halted suddenly and took a step sideways and lifted high my stick in a hand white and shaking, and Carrot Head at last fell back, pursing his lips and shaking his head with a sorrowful smile and holding up placatingly a pair of empty palms.

Out of the shadows into the long piazza I stepped, and paused to stand a moment, breathing hard, waiting for my anger and disquiet to abate, still wondering what the fellow could have wanted of me. With a cold eye I took in what the guidebooks would call the panorama: the wedding-cake façades, the bronze horseman unsheathing his sword, the famed twin churches down at the far end of the square, all bathed in a honeyed, sunlit haze. I find this city no more attractive or interesting than any other I have known. Customs, legends, tales of colourful characters and events, such stuff leaves me cold; the picturesque in particular I find revolting. I do not care what battles Emanuele Filiberto won or lost, or where Cavour liked to eat his dinner. History is a hotchpotch of anecdotes, neither true nor false, and what does it matter where it is supposed to have taken place? How I used to despise those novelists whose paltry fictions it was my misfortune in the early years of my career to be forced to foist upon my students, I mean those northern worshippers of the sun-drenched south, the self-styled pagans—frauds and remittance men all—whose scenes were set on thyme-scented islands, or in pine-shaded hilltop villages, or in that steamy seaport in a disregarded corner of the Mediterranean, where the hero and his sloe-eyed mistress shared their parting dinner in a little restaurant up a side street from the harbour where the tourists never ventured, the anchovies and the bitter olives and the rough local wine, and the restaurant-keeper's wife humming something plangent, and the street arabs wheedling, and the three-legged dog gnawing a knuckle of bone, and the old poet at the next table coughing his life out over a last absinthe. As if place meant something; as if being somewhere vivid and exotic ensured an automatic intensification of living. No: give me an anonymous patch of ground, with asphalt, and an oily bonfire smouldering, and vague factories in the distance, some rank, exhausted non-place where I can feel safe, where I can feel at home, if I am ever to feel at home, anywhere.

I walked on. A stream of motor cars was flowing swiftly through the square, separating into two channels around the bronze horseman's plinth and meeting and mingling again in cacophonous disorder on the other side. The sun was being stealthily swallowed by a fat, barely moving cloud, putty-grey and burning silver all along its forward edge. A pigeon landed in front of me, descending in an awkward flurry on churning wings, like a rapid succession of violet-grey ink-blot tests. I turned again and struck away from the square, and walked through ever narrower, cobbled streets, until I came out at last unexpectedly into a wide avenue flanked on both sides with chestnut trees in flower. Here I could breathe more easily. As I passed under the first broad, high, cool canopy of leaves, it occurred to me to wonder when a tree would feel most like itself, when it would feel it had most fully achieved its true being. I mean, if it were sentient—and who is to know if we are the only conscious ones, or that our consciousness is the only kind there is?—at what stage of its yearly cycle would it say, now, *now* I am what I am, now at last I am in my total treeness. Would it be in spring's first greening, or the full-leafed glory of June, or autumn flame, or even the gnarled nakedness of winter? And to live that cycle of life within another cycle—the one from bud to bareness, the other, the longer one, from sapling to hollow stump—surely that would be confusing. Would the fall of its leaves feel like incipient death, each year? Would spring feel like rebirth? Thinking these thoughts, in that midday's green dusk, I heard, or felt, rather, a reverberant boom, as if in the distance a great sheet of pliant metal had been struck with a huge, soft hammer. Thunder? I did not think so. Some aeroplane noise? A cannon shot, perhaps, marking the midday hour? Whatever it was it disturbed me. I quickened my pace, veering off in the direction of the hotel.

Presently I realised that I had lost my way, and I had to stop at a street corner to consult the crumpled map the hotel clerk had given me. I was squinting up in search of a street name when I registered the girl, on the corner opposite, looking in my direction. She was tallish, fair, neither pretty nor plain; I would not have noticed her had she not seemed to be regarding me with a smile, knowing, not unfriendly, as if I were someone she had met long ago, in faintly discreditable circumstances. She stepped forward into the street, squeezing between two cars parked closely nose to tail. Was she coming to accost me? The prospect made my pulse quicken, and I did not know whether to wait for her or flee. Who were all these people, the flower seller, Carrot Head, now this girl, and what did they want with me? The lorry had already braked, its tyres locked and shrieking, when it struck her. I had the sense of her spinning on her toes, head thrown back and hair flying, fast and tensely graceful as a dancer. There was a cry, not hers. A burly, grey-haired man on the pavement behind her threw up one arm and said something loud and deprecating in a deep bass voice. Vehicles squawked and pulled aside to right and left as the lorry hurtled down the centre of the street for twenty yards and came at last to a slewed, smoking stop. The girl had fallen back and was draped against the side of one of the parked cars with her arms flung wide. There was blood in her hair, and a glistening, innocent-looking trickle of blood coming out of her left ear. The large man who had thrown up his arm was toiling toward her at a bow-legged run, but before he could reach her she slithered abruptly to the ground as if everything inside her had suddenly liquefied, and lay in a boneless heap. Now others were running forward, and people were scrambling out of their cars and craning to see what had happened. I turned about quickly and set off at a headlong lurch, not caring which direction I was going in, so long as it was away from there. People jostled me, pressing forward for a glimpse of the fallen girl, with vague, eager, self-forgetting frowns. I was in a sort of panic, gasping, the sweat running into my eyes, and there was a blazing pain deep in my groin. I did not know what I was fleeing from; not the girl's death, certainly, or not only that. A half-formed image came to my mind—from Bosch, was it, or Dante?—of an emaciated, gape-mouthed figure, stooped and naked, running with uplifted arms through a landscape of burning red earth, bearing another figure, its own double, lashed to it tightly back to back. At last I came to the quiet of a secluded small piazza, with cobbles and more strutting pigeons and a patch of dusty grass, all loured over by the baroque, blocky façade of a palace, the name of which I knew I should know but could not remember. Unable to go any further I flopped down on a bench of polished marble. There was no one else about. A noontide pall of lethargy had fallen on the city. That slow cloud now hid the sun, and the soft grey air and the silence calmed my seething nerves. The pain in my groin subsided.

Why such upset? This was not the first violent end I had witnessed. Was it that it was another of death's heartless demonstrations that even the young are not immune to its capricious singlings-out? No, that is too obscure. Perhaps it was simply because the girl had seemed to be looking at me, had seemed to know or recognise me, might even have been about to speak to me. But why should that make the encounter, if such it could be called, so unsettling? In certain circles, admittedly rarefied, mine is a well-known face. I am used to strangers recognising me. They will pause, the young in particular, and look at me, shyly, or with resentment, or more often just that slow, dull, witless stare, as if it is not the real me they are seeing but a representation of me, an animated model set up for their free and exclusive scrutiny. So why should the girl's attention have made me want to take to my heels? Oh, but I knew, I knew of course, why I was agitated: it was not the girl I was thinking of, it was Magda. When she was alive I could hardly be said to have given her a second thought, while now she was constantly on my mind, if only as a shadow, the solitary spectator sitting in the benches above the spotlit ring where the gaudy and increasingly chaotic performance of who and what I am pretending to be is carried on without interval. She lingers there, unwilling shade, wishing to be gone, perhaps, yet curious to see the not so grand finale, with its tumbling clowns and bowing acrobats and trained animals doing their last lap. Only in death has she begun to live fully, for me.

Strange, but try as I may I cannot remember exactly how or when we met. In my memory of it, that first, long-ago season in an unreally vivid New York is all haste and noise and sullen heat. Even in the streets I felt as if I were trapped inside a huge, smoky, deafening factory. Everything was always on the move, there was never a moment of cessation or stillness. Traffic thudded day and night along the streets above the corner basement room where I lodged; the papers on the scarred old table I used for a work desk shivered and shifted in the draught from the electric fan some acquaintance had given me, as it turned its fuzzy face and fencer's mask slowly from side to side in obdurate refusal of relief. All day a confusion of disembodied legs passed back and forth on the pavement outside the ground-level window above my table, as if there were a riot, or a disordered, shuffling marathon dance, continually going on out there. And then there was the talk, incessant, raucous, plosive with challenge or swollen with sudden declarations of sincerity and fellow-feeling. I would meet them at the end of their working day—*work* was one of the sacred words then, pronounced with breathy awe—the scrawny young men in open-necked shirts, with their flat haircuts and Zippo lighters, sweating earnestness, the serious-eyed girls in pumps and calf-length skirts clutching paperback copies of *Capital* to their chests like breastplates. The thin, sweetish beer, the charry cigarette smoke, the sudden squabbles that were as suddenly quelled, the shouts and thrusting forefingers, and that gesture of half-angry dismissal of a contrary opinion, so characteristic of the time and place, a free-wristed, sideways slap at the air and the face turning aside, with wrinkled nose and drooping lower lip: *Ndah!*—all this was intensely strange to me, and yet familiar, too, I could not think why, at first, until I realised that of course I had seen it all over and over again, for years, in the cinema, every Saturday night, when I was young. America on the screen had been more intimately familiar to me than the streets of the city where I was born and where I lived. And so, in New York, the actual New York, that was how I chose to present myself, as a character out of the pictures, a fat cigarette lolling in my lips and a tumbler of bourbon at my elbow. I even used to dress the part, in brown fedora and tight, double-breasted suit and two-toned shoes. Oh, yes, it was quite a figure that I cut. The intellectual as tough guy, that was all the rage, in those days. All I lacked was a companion, some big babe, loose and hard-drinking, and as tough as I was supposed to be. People were baffled, therefore, especially the girls, when it turned out to be sweet, silent, undemonstrative Magdalena that I chose to be my moll, my mate.

Even then, when she was still in her twenties, there was a massive, stony quality to her, something granitic and unrelievedly grey, that was curiously attractive, to me, at least. I quickly understood, when I first began to notice her, that she kept to the background not out of shyness or fear—although she was shy, she was fearful—but in order to be able to watch and listen to all that went on from the shelter of anonymity. She was unflagging in her obligingness, doing errands for the men and the bossier of the girls, fetching books for them, and packs of cigarettes, and sandwiches and paper cups of coffee; I can still see her, in her sandals and no-colour knitted dress, her hair in fat braids, coming down the basement steps in that odd, elephantine way that she had, turning sideways and lowering one broad foot on to each step and then bringing the second down to join it, her chin tucked into her fish-pale throat and her gaze fixed on whatever it was she was carrying. She was living on the Lower East Side—a placename that in those days still sounded as suggestively exotic to my ears as Samarkand or the Isles of the Blest—with a plumber, a militant Pole of simian aspect with a revolutionist's wire-brush moustache, who was said to beat her. She would not talk about him, even when she had left him and had come to live with me in my basement, bringing a bot-

tle of bourbon as a moving-in present and one not very large suitcase containing everything she possessed. Late one night the Pole
turned up in the street outside, drunk and in a tearful rage and
calling out her name, and banged on the door and would have
kicked in the window had it not been barred. I wanted to get up
and chase him away—even with my bad leg I did not doubt I would
be well able to see off the little ape—but Magda prevented me.

She did not like to talk about herself or her life; when she did
mention some event from the past her voice would take on a tinge
of puzzlement, as if what had happened had happened to someone
else and she could not understand how she knew so many of the
details. Nor did she care particularly to hear about my life before
we had met. Others, even the brashest among our acquaintances,
regarded me with a kind of wondering respect, with a holy reverence, almost: I was the real thing, a genuine survivor, who had
come walking into their midst out of the fire and furnace smoke of
the European catastrophe, like Frankenstein's monster staggering
out of the burning mill. To Magda, though, herself a survivor, I was
simply Vander—she did not care to call me Axel; it sounded, she
said, like the name of a guard dog—a man much like any other,
more volatile, perhaps, than the ones she was used to, potentially
more violent even than her Pole, but still no more than a man. She
did not remark particularly my dead leg or my blind eye, and
accepted without comment the bragging lies I told her as to how I
had come by them—my stand against a rampaging mob, the blow
I got from a storm trooper's rifle butt—lies I had rehearsed so
often that I had come almost to believe them myself. Early one
sweltering morning, though, I woke out of a doze to find her leaning over me—our bed was a mattress on the floor—with her
large, soft face propped on a hand, contemplating me in big-eyed,
solemn silence. For a minute neither of us stirred, then she
touched a fingertip to the pulpy lid of my bad eye and murmured,
"And I only am escaped alone to tell thee," and the bristles stood up on
the back of my neck, as if it were an oracle that had spoken. Who

would have expected Magda, big, slow, flat-footed Magda, to come out with something so grave, so sonorous, so biblically apt to both our states?

My life with her was a special way of being alone. It was like living on intimate terms with a creature from another species; she was to me as remote and inaccessible as some large, harmless herbivore. At times I thought there was no mystery to her at all, that she was as blank as she seemed, then at others I grew convinced that this appearance of unmoving calm that she displayed was a mask she had fashioned for herself behind which she too must be locked in frantic strategies of calculation and control, practising, like me, for a part she did not believe she would ever be able to fill convincingly. In the state of mutual incomprehension that was our life together we were forever surprising each other. She was alarmingly well read, as in the early days I had frequent and shame-making cause to discover. Already I had made myself adept at appearing deeply learned in a range of subjects by the skilful employment of certain key concepts, gleaned from the work of others, but to which I was able to give a personal twist of mordancy or insight. In everything I wrote there was a tensed, febrile urgency that was generated directly out of the life predicament in which I had placed myself; I was fashioning a new methodology of thinking modelled on the crossings and conflicts of my own intricate and, in large part, fabricated past. I could discourse with convincing familiarity on texts I had not got round to reading, philosophies I had not yet studied, great men I had never met. My assertive elusiveness, as one critic rather clumsily called it, mesmerised the small but influential coterie of savants who sampled and approved of my early pieces. Though they might question my grasp of theory and even doubt my scholarship, all were united in acclaiming my mastery of the language, the tone and pitch of my singular voice; even my critics, and there were more than a few of them, could only stand back and watch in frustration as their best barbs skidded off the high gloss of my prose style. This surprised as much as it pleased me; how could they not see, in hiding behind the brashness and the bravado of what I wrote, the trembling autodidact hunched over his *Webster's,* his *Chicago Manual,* his *Grammar for Foreign Students*? Perhaps it was the very bizarreries of usage which I unavoidably fell into that they took for the willed eccentricities in which they imagined only a lord of language would dare to indulge.

Do not misunderstand me: I have no doubt that I possess genius, of a kind. It is just not the kind that it has pretended all those years to be. I sometimes think that I missed my calling, that I could have been a great artist, a master of compelling inventiveness, arch, allusive, magisterially splenetic, given to arcane reference, obscure aims, an alchemist of word and image. Indeed, my critics often grumble at the desolate lyricism of my mature style, seeing behind it the pale hand of the poet. I take their point. Mine is the kind of commentary in which frequently the comment will claim an equal rank with that which is supposedly its object; equal, and sometimes superior. In my study of Rilke, an early work, there are passages of ecstatic intensity that world-drunk lyricist himself might have envied, while those long, twinned essays on Kleist and on Kafka are as desperate and inconsolable as any of the plays or the parables of those two hierophants of dejection. Shall I bow before these great ones? Shall I bend the knee to their eminence? Damned if I will. I hold myself as high as any of them, in my own estimation. What troubles me only is the thought of all I might have done had I been simply—if such a thing may be said to be simple—myself.

Magda was apparently as impressed by me as everyone else was, and took my poses and my brilliant pretences at their face value. If she knew I was a fraud, she did not seem to mind; seemed, indeed, to admire me, in her detached way, for my nerve and resourcefulness. There was a particular, small smile I would occasionally catch fleeting across her face when I was expounding to a spellbound company on some dense text she knew I had done no more than glance at. She *had* read Hegel and Marx, and much else beside. She could reel off quotations as by rote, for she had a remarkable memory, even if little of what the quoted passages might signify had stuck; she carried her knowledge of all those titanic thinkers like an atrophied limb, the intellectual equivalent of my useless leg. She had obediently studied the century's revolutionary texts at the bidding of the Pole, since he was not a great reader himself, but was determined they should be the perfect Party pair, he the hammer of activism, she the sickle of ideology. She shrugged, telling me this, and smiled, fondly, as at the recollection of some not entirely innocent childhood game of make-believe. Yes, she saw through us all, in her mute, intuitive fashion. Was that the reason I chose her above the others? Was that the reason she chose me? Was she my protectress, the guardian of my borrowed, my purloined, reputation? It comes to me with mournful force that these questions now will never be answered, or not by her, certainly.

She regarded the past as a sort of huge, unavoidable mistake, a whole set of wrong beginnings that had now, at last, been put right. If she had any anger for all that had befallen her it was directed not at the devisers of the vast project of destruction in which she had been caught up and from which she had barely escaped with her life, but at the very victims of it, all those who had not escaped, even her bewildered parents, her sister who had been so vain of her dark beauty, her little brother, still clutching his toy bugle as he was marched away. It was not that she blamed them for not resisting, or for being hapless and confused and self-deluding—her mother before being hustled to the trucks had squeezed her hand and made her promise to write—but for the simple fact of their having existed, of their having been there in the first place to be taken away from her in the last. She had kept nothing of them, no photograph, no document, no lock of hair, only her memories, and these she would willingly have relinquished, had she been able. That she of all of them was the only one to have survived, because her name had somehow slipped from the lists, was only another cause for baffled, mute anger.

We had been together for some months before she would tell me any of this. Late one raw November afternoon we had been to the cinema—or the movies, as I was learning to call them—and were sheltering from the cold in a coffeehouse on Bleecker Street when she began to weep, quietly, almost pensively. In the interval of the double bill a newsreel had been shown of scenes from the ruins of Europe, and the sight of those seemingly endless ranks of corpses had jogged something in her, and now she could not stop telling me what had happened to her. Sitting beside her as she talked, I held myself motionless, barely breathing; my fist, lying on the table by her hand, felt so heavy it seemed I would never be able to lift it again. Her recollections of flight and escape were fitful, lit in flashes: the sharp white stones on a mountain track; massed, dark trees moving past in the headlights of a lorry in which she lay hidden under sacking; a boy soldier at some dusty border post offering her an apple from his tunic pocket. It was as if she had made the perilous journey not in linear time, but in great leaps, from stopping place to stopping place, between each of which she had somehow been absolved from consciousness. When she had finished I had to tell her my story, of course, the etiquette of our predicament as survivors demanding it. Story is right. We had left the coffee shop by then and were walking down the street in the bitter cold and the gathering dusk, the traffic flowing along beside us through the slush like wreckage being carried on a river in sluggish spate. She leaned heavily on my arm, a dragging weight. She did not want to hear the things I was telling her, she was tired of them; she resented the burden of her tragic fate, and mine. In the light of her resistance my inventiveness burgeoned; never before or since did I spin my tale so well or so convincingly as I did that night, weaving through the lies a few, fine, shining threads of truth, as the wet white flakes fell fast around us and the huddled, faceless figures of passers-by loomed up at us suddenly out of the lamplight and as quickly vanished behind us into the dark. I could not but admire my own performance. What a fabulist I was; what an artist! And I never did tell her the real, the whole, the tawdry truth.

High in the air above me there came again that hollow booming sound I had heard on the avenue under the chestnut tree, and I woke with a shiver from my reveries. The day had cleared and the sun was hot in the piazza under a cloudless, hard, white sky. I recognized suddenly where I was: it was here that N., in the final months before his collapse, had lodged in a room in the Fino house on the corner looking out on the massive façade of the Palazzo Carignano—that was its name!—scribbling crazed letters and signing them *Dionysus, The Crucified, Nietzsche Caesar* . . . I closed my eyes and pressed a thumb and finger to them until tiny lights like distant rockets began to pop and flare in the darkness behind the lids. I am convinced my blind eye works when it is shut. I saw again, as clearly as I had seen it happen, the truck skidding and the girl spinning and the man with the grey hair throwing up his arm in that strange way and calling out as if to warn off some unwary intruder on this scene of violence and blood. I opened my eyes again and rose unsteadily to my feet, heaving myself up with both hands pressed on the crook of my stick. I was hot; I was thirsty; I was tired.

⁂

When I woke the curtains were pulled against the light of day and I thought it was still dawn and that everything that had happened since my arrival had been a dream. I lay motionless on the bed, staring into the gauzy folds of shadow about me, gripped by an obscure panic. I could not understand why I was dressed in suit and tie; I even had my shoes on, although the laces at least were undone. My right arm had been asleep and tingled unpleasantly now as the blood began to move in it again; my injured elbow ached. Slowly memory began to gather up its fragments. I had drunk a bottle of wine with lunch in the hotel dining room and had stumbled up here to my room to rest and must have passed out, felled by alcohol and the last embers of travel fever. I got myself up cautiously and sat for a moment on the side of the bed with my head bowed. Why had I come to this city? I was too old and worn to travel so far for the sake of a whim. I could have made the writer of that letter come to me in Arcady, that would have tested her resolve. I rose with a groan and went into the windowless bathroom and stood wincing and blinking in humming white light. Dandruff, caries, Doctor Baloardo's big pockmarked nose. I washed out my mouth; the tap water tasted of tin. I stood and gazed dully in the mirror, hands braced on the basin and my shoulders hunched. I had the sensation then, as so often, of shifting slightly aside from myself, as if I were going out of focus and separating into two. I wonder if other people feel as I do, seeming never to be wholly present wherever I happen to be, seeming not so much a person as a contingency, misplaced and adrift in time. My true source and destination are always elsewhere, although where exactly that elsewhere might be I do not know; perhaps it is in childhood, that age of authenticity the scenes of which I can summon up more and more vividly the farther away from them that I get. Banal possibility. Dull thoughts in a dulled mind. It was the wine, the weariness.

The taxi was waiting for me at the door of the hotel. I was late already, but I did not care; let them wait. This time the city, in afternoon light, showed me another, softer side to the one I had seen that morning. Sun glanced, white-gold, on car roofs and the windows of caffès. We passed under the Mole, absurd in its pagoda lines. I noted without enthusiasm the thickening flotsam of strolling students in the streets, and presently the grey concrete headland of the university buildings hove into view. When I saw Franco Bartoli on the steps, standing on tiptoe with neck outstretched and casting about him anxiously, I had an urge to duck down and order the taxi driver to drive on. I asked myself bitterly again what had possessed me to come to Turin, what there could be here for me except confrontation, exposure, humiliation. I alighted from the taxi and turned back to pay the fare, and saw out of the corner of my eye Bartoli trotting toward me happily, already speaking although he was still well out of earshot. He is a delicate, balding, bearded, egg-shaped little man, voluble and nervous, and watchful as a weasel. He pressed one of my hands tightly in both of his and babbled breathless welcomes which made me grind my teeth. I pushed past and levered myself up the steps on my stick with Bartoli fairly dancing about me. So good of me to come!—such an honour!—everyone so eager to see me! I scowled. "Who is here?" I demanded. Bartoli ticked off names on his miniature fingers. "Old friends," he said, beaming, "all old friends!" I almost had to laugh.

And here they were, waiting for me indeed, fifteen or twenty of them, in a wide, low-ceilinged top-floor room the four walls of which were made of sheets of smoked plate-glass bolted between rust-red girders, in the brutal modern way. They were huddled together in the middle of the large empty space where a bar had been set up on linen-covered trestle tables, all with their faces turned toward me expectantly as I stood eyeing them from the doorway. It was true, I did know most of them, the faces if not their names; I am not good at remembering names, even when I try, which is not often. I sighed, and with Bartoli bouncing ahead of me I set off across the floor, fixing my stony smile in place and bringing my stick down on the squeaky rubber tiles with deliberate force. Bartoli dived into the crowd, swirling and swooping among them like a choreographer assembling his troupe. He has the mannered and slightly mechanical movements of a professional performer. I was greeted on all sides with wary warmth. Bartoli drew me to the table where the drinks were, and when the waiter, a dark young bruiser with a peasant's hands, did not move smartly enough he seized a bottle and two glasses and poured the wine himself. "A son of the south," he said to me out of a corner of his mouth. "They live on our taxes and send us oxen in tribute." Franco is very vain of his accentless English. The waiter was watching him sullenly. He handed a glass to me and tipped his own in salute. "Hard to believe that we have lured you here at last," he said, with a sharp little twinkle. "We have invited you every year for the past seven years—I checked our records, yes—but always in vain." He was like a boxer, outclassed and outweighed, dodging and feinting, looking for an opening through which to jab an insult at me. I hardly attended him. I was remembering, with sudden, hallucinatory intensity, the summers of my boyhood at my grandfather's farm. A city child, I always registered first and most acutely the smells of the place, of flowers, fruits, and plants, and of their decay, the hot smell of horse dung, the smell of earth and excrement in the little wooden privy in the garden under the heavily scented elder tree, the exquisite perfume of the wild strawberries I hunted for in the hedgerows, the smell of mushrooms, the smell of hens and of their blood, the smell of the cat and the dogs, the smell of chaff, of oil, of spurts of boiling water, of animal and human sweat, of my grandfather's tobacco, the pungent smell of wine, and worn cloth, the smell of sawdust, the smell of my own sweat. I liked best the time of harvest, when the wheat and oats and rye were brought in from the fields to the threshing shed. It was, or seemed to me to be, a vast building, big as a church, big as a cathedral, with a lofty, arched ceiling and high-set windows through which thick beams of sunlight streamed down. The air was dense with swirling chaff, and the workmen coughed and spat and swore, shouting to make themselves heard above the constant din. The threshing machine was an enormous, complicated wooden structure, like a giant insect, the moving parts of which kept up a deafening clickety-clacking. It was driven by a steam engine attached to it by a long leather belt that terrified me as it shuddered and slapped like a thing in agony. In the shed it was always a luminous dusk, and the men moved about like ghosts, with cloths tied over their mouths. Low down at one end of the machine the golden grain flowed through an open funnel into the sacks, while, high above, the stripped and broken straw was shucked out in ceaseless, wild and somehow comic eruptions. I stood beside my grandfather, who above the noise attempted to explain to me how the parts of the machine worked. What a sense of splendour and communion I felt, before this scene of labour and its rewards! And then at midday all work stopped and an extraordinary, ringing silence descended, and we all marched off together to the cavernous stone kitchen of the farm where my grandmother served up a meal of beer and bread and eggs and thick-sliced sausage. At rest as at work the men treated each other as if they were a band of brothers, slapping each other on the back, shouting at each other across the length of the room, laughing, swearing, calling out ribald insults. I wandered freely among these men who were exhausted yet elated, too. No one paid me any particular attention; it was as if I were one of them. Then, with the help of the beer, the first artless murmurings of a song would be heard, halting at first, seeming to go wrong and lose its way, only to break out at last in an exultant cacophony that caught me up in its sweep and made my chest constrict and my throat swell with emotion. In a pause in the singing I was made to take a drink of beer, and although I hated the sour taste, which reminded me of the pigsty, I smiled and smacked my lips and held out my cup for more, and was applauded, and then the singing welled up again, and from the far end of the long table my grandfather smiled at me . . . All this I remembered, even though it had never happened. Certainly, there was a threshing machine, but I only ever glimpsed it at work, from outside the shed, which I was forbidden to enter because of my supposed weak constitution; I was kept away from the workmen, too, for fear I might see and hear things unsuitable to a child of my tender years. It was all a dream I had worked up out of my desire to be there, in the threshing shed and the kitchen, in the midst of men, a fantasy born of my longing to belong. Now through time-dimmed eyes I peered from this high place out at the city, all burned-looking beyond the smoked glass of the walls, and it was as if I had come round from a swoon to find myself among a band of survivors huddled here above the site of a vast and ruinous conflagration.

A touch on my arm made me turn. For a second I did not recognise Kristina Kovacs. It was not that she had aged very much, or changed greatly in appearance since I had seen her last, yet all the same something had happened to her. She looked not like herself but like a close relative, her own twin, perhaps, vaguer than the woman I had known, less sharply defined, faded, somehow, and somehow hollow-seeming. I could not think what to say to her, and instead leaned down quickly and kissed her on the cheek. Her skin was warm and dry, and seemed to vibrate tinily all over its surface, as if she were in the grip of a fever. She put a hand to the spot where I had kissed her and gave a familiar, dusky laugh—I am not the kissing kind—and leaned back from the shoulders to look up at me, holding her head to one side, her black eyes bright with fond malice and amusement. She exclaimed at how well I looked; she seemed genuinely surprised, as if she had come to a place in her life that allowed only of disimprovements. And yet she was no more than half my age. I wondered if she could recall with the same sweet, poignant clarity as I did that afternoon years before when she had come unannounced to my hotel room, in Budapest, or Bucharest, was it, or Belgrade? The place does not matter, only the moment. I remembered her salmon-coloured slip and the solemn way she lay down on her back before me on the bed, as if she had been felled by the awesome force of her own passion. I bit her lips until they bled, I licked the soles of her feet. Now she was asking me what I would speak on tomorrow at the conference, and Franco Bartoli popped up like a toy man at my elbow and, smoothing a hand on his fine, soft, gleaming beard, said with a roguish smirk that surely Professor Vander could have only one subject, here, in Turin . . . ? I did not know what he was talking about. "I have prepared nothing," I said. I wanted him to be gone from my side. I was picturing the sprinkle of freckles in the hollow between Kristina Kovacs's pale, mismatched and somehow melancholy breasts. Behind her now the smoky city stretched away to the mountains in the distance with their furled rim of cloud. She was still gazing up at me with that wry, intimate smile. She has, or had, a habit of moving her head very slightly from side to side, as if she were swaying in time to the measures of a slow, inner melody. I felt unwell. The sour wine had parched the linings of my mouth. I leaned out to set my emptied glass on the table and took the opportunity to elbow Bartoli as if by accident in his little paunch, which made me feel better, then stamped away from him and Kristina Kovacs with pointed rudeness and planted myself before one of the glass walls with my back to the room, glaring bleakly out over the city. Behind me the buzz of conversation faltered briefly and caught itself up on a higher, more brittle note: Axel Vander being a boor, as usual. As I had at the hotel window that morning, I imagined again how I would seem to someone looking up from the streets below, an airborne figure, suspended on an angled stick and perhaps about to plummet, a decrepit, lost archangel. Once more I experienced a burning, bile-like rush of self-pity, pure and unfocused. Kristina Kovacs came and stood beside me, a breathing presence, the crown of her head level with my shoulder. I fancied I caught a whiff of her breath, warm, brownish and bad. Together we looked out at the distant mountain ranges. "I think I have been found out," I heard myself saying, in a tone of laboured, unconvincing lightness. "I had a letter. Someone has been looking into my past. She is coming here." I glanced sidelong at Kristina, and smiling she returned my glance. "She?" she murmured, shaking her head. "Oh, Axel, have you been foolish again?"

I was instantly abashed and angry at myself. I could not think why I had confided in her. She knew nothing about me or my past, the real or the invented one. What was she to me but an afternoon of mostly simulated passion in an overheated hotel room in a snowbound city I would never return to? I have always supposed it was those few hours in bed that had prompted the belated review she wrote of *After Words*. The review was a light piece, intended to be teasingly allusive; it had struck an incongruously frivolous note amid the weighty lucubrations of *Débat*. The letter of thanks I sent to her when the piece appeared had cost me much effort. I had sought to match her sly, arch tone, but the result was unsatisfactory in a way I could not quite make out. Her note in reply was all innocence and warm affection, with no mention of our tryst. Now I wondered uneasily if perhaps she did know more about me than she pretended, about my past, I mean, my interesting past. Well, what did it matter any more? That harpy even now on her way from Antwerp would likely be the end of me. I was, I realised, looking forward to the prospect of destruction. Yes, let it come, I thought, almost gaily, I shall welcome it! All at once, in place of the anger and self-pity of a minute ago, I had a sensation of incipient weightlessness, as if at any moment I might float upward, wingless and yet wonderfully volant, and drift away free, into air, and light, the empty, cold and brilliant blue.

"I am dying, Axel," Kristina Kovacs said.

She was looking at the floor with an almost girlish air of surprise and faint shame, as if it were some passionate secret she had blurted out. "Yes, I am dying," she said, more softly this time yet with more force, testing it, impressing on herself the incredible truth of it. I stared down at her. An aeroplane passed low above the building with a ripping rumble, and an instant later its vast shadow flashed across the glass walls. Kristina smiled, and shook her head ruefully, and said she was sorry, and that I must forget she had spoken. "Tell me about your girl," she said with awful, brave brightness. "The one who has found you out, I mean. You said it was a girl, didn't you? In the past it always was. What dreadful secret has she uncovered?" She laughed, not unkindly. I gripped the walking stick fiercely in my fist. How did she think she had the right to speak to me like this? I am Axel Vander. People do not say such things to me, with such impudence. She took a step nearer and put a hand on my arm, her grip at once urgent and infirm. I knew what was coming. I drew back from her touch. The air seemed suddenly thick, unbreathable. "Do you remember Prague?" she said. Prague, then, not Belgrade, not Budapest. I would say nothing. "So hot," Kristina murmured, her gaze blurring as she smiled into the past, "so hot, that hotel room . . ." This was intolerable. I looked about. Someone must rescue me. Where was that fool Bartoli, now that he was needed? "I'm sorry," I snarled, "forgive me," and wiping my mouth on my sleeve I turned from her abruptly and launched myself out across the sea-wide floor toward the door and escape. Franco Bartoli came hurrying after me, yelping. I brandished my stick, more in threat than farewell, and plunged on, a man pursued.

When she came out of the train station the street lamps were still palely burning in the dawn light and the air was the colour of dirty water. A map of the city showed her that it was not far to the hotel where he was staying. She decided to walk. A tram came lurching along its line. She liked trams, the ungainly, earnest look of them. She waited on the pavement as it passed, her bag in her hand, her raincoat over her arm. She felt like a figure from an earlier time, with that coat and bag, her plain dress and old-fashioned shoes, the eager, untried younger self of someone who in time would be famous, famously tragic, perhaps. Often she saw herself like this, in other guises, other possible lives, and so vividly it seemed she must have lived before. She shivered a little, and put on her raincoat; she had expected it would be warmer, this far south. Later the sun would come out. She had hardly slept on the train, huddled in a corner seat in a crowded compartment with her bag under her feet and her folded raincoat for a pillow. The train had kept stopping at deserted stations, and would stand for long minutes creaking and sighing in the night-deep, desolate silence, before setting off again with a series of loud clanks. Once she had pressed her face to the window and peered up and had seen that they were racing along beside a range of high, jagged mountains, whose sheer bases came to within a yard or two of the track. She had supposed they must be the Alps. She could glimpse their peaks, sparkling and unreal so high up there in the moonlight. She remembered being in the mountains once long ago with her father; he had pulled her up a slope on a sled, and afterwards had let her take a sip of his mulled wine. In the dark hour before dawn she dozed for a while; it was less like sleep than one of those fretful night fevers of childhood, and she woke repeatedly with a start, thinking one of the other passengers had touched her, or tried to interfere with her belongings. As they were arriving at last a fat man had stood up too soon and when the train stopped he had pitched forward and almost fallen on her, and to save himself had clapped a huge hand on her shoulder, hurting her. He had smelled faintly of vomit. Now, shaky and light-headed, she set off across the broad avenue. In the piazza before her the starlings were waking noisily in the trees, and a great flock of pigeons rose up, their thousand wings making a noise like derisive applause.

She did not know what she would do when she got to the hotel. It was still early, and she would have to wait at least an hour before she could think of announcing her arrival. She would not mind waiting in the lobby, but she was not sure the hotel people would even let her come inside at such an early hour. The voices in her head started up then, as she had known they would, as they always did when she was uncertain or nervous, seizing their chance. It was as if a motley and curious crowd had fallen into step behind her, hard on her heels, and were discussing her and her plight among themselves in excited, fast, unintelligible whispers. She stopped for a moment and leaned against a shuttered shop window with a hand over her eyes, but with the world blacked out the din of voices only intensified. She took a deep breath and went on.

Dozing in the train she had dreamed of Harlequin in his half-mask. Then she had roused herself and brought out her notebook, her fountain pen. *H. the headman, his mask and bat. Maistre on the exe-*

53

cutioner: "who is this inexplicable being . . .?" Rip the mask from his face
to find—another mask. Father father father.

The phantoms behind her fell back.

And now already here was the hotel, with a laurel bush in a pot at the foot of the steps. The glass door swung open automatically before her, and she wondered if instead of approaching it at the measured pace that was demanded she had run at it full tilt would it have still managed to open in time or would she have been too quick for the mechanism. She saw herself sprawled there on the marble step, amid big lances of shattered glass, the blood pumping from her throat and wrists. It struck her how like hospitals hotels are. A young man in a smart black suit behind the reception desk smiled at her non-committally. She walked past him with her gaze fixed straight ahead and her back arched, trying to look as if she had a perfect right to be there. She had never understood exactly how hotels work, or what the rules of hotel living are. For instance, how would paying guests be distinguished from the other people who would drift in and out here during the day, casual visitors, people coming for lunch, or for assignations in the bar, suchlike? Would that young man at the reception desk know she was not staying here? She had not asked him for a key, but she might have one, all the same, might have got it earlier from one of his colleagues, before he came on duty, and taken it with her when she went out. There was her bag, of course, but it was not very big, and might be a shopping bag, for all he knew. But why would she have gone out with a shopping bag at dawn, when no shops were open, and how could she be coming back now with it full?

The lobby was all gleaming marble surfaces, with hidden lighting and a low ceiling. There was a sort of pond in the middle where water splashed among ferns, soothingly. She took off her coat and sat down at one end of an uncomfortable leather couch that she knew the backs of her legs would stick to even through her dress. A large, indifferent silence hung about her. She wondered if the ferns in the pond were real or made of plastic; they looked suspiciously genuine. She was trying not to think of the voices; often, just thinking of them was enough to set them going. The young man from the reception desk came and asked, in English, with cool politeness, if she wished for anything, some coffee, perhaps, or tea? She shook her head; she did not know what the procedure for paying would be; she imagined herself offering him money only to be met with an offended stare. He was handsome, like a film actor, dark and smooth and poised. He smiled again, this time with a shadow of irony, she thought. As he was turning away he glanced at her bag and lifted an eyebrow, in a way that told her he knew she was not a guest. She wondered enviously how he had decided. Perhaps everyone checking in was photographed in secret, and the pictures were kept in a file under the desk, and he had gone through it and not found hers. More likely he had known just by the look of her, the way she was sitting, so straight, with her knees together and her hands folded in her lap; that, and the fact that she had not gone up in the lift, to her room, the room that she did not have. She looked at her watch and sighed. A single, gloating voice began whispering in her head.

⋟

Here I am, asleep again, and dreaming. In the dream I am in an aeroplane, or on it, rather, for the cabin is open to the sky, with a metal floor and a rounded metal canopy above supported on thin steel struts. There are other passengers on board but I cannot see them, the headrests of the seats are set too high. The air is gushing against my face, wonderfully cool and mild. Far below, through breaks in the cloud, I can see fields and rivers, little puffs of green that must be trees, and houses, and highways, a whole toy world laid out and stretching off to the curved horizon on all sides. As I fly along, feather-light and free, I am myself and also someone else, and this is all right, and natural. A stewardess comes and leans over me, telling me something, but when I look up at her I see that she

has a bearded, pained face, the face of a man, gentle but not effemi-
nate, the eyes lightly closed as in death, the lids stretched like
paper or silk over the bulging orbs beneath. She is handing me
something, a folded sheet of paper, a letter, perhaps, which I try
not to accept, but she insists, still with that gentle, kindly, suffering
expression. *Signore,* she is saying, with soft urgency, pointing to
her bearded face, *signore, signore.* I push at her to make her stand
aside, the paper crackling in my hand, and try to rise from my seat,
but cannot, my leg will not let me. I know that the plane is going
to crash, I can feel it dipping out of its headlong course, can feel
the metal floor shivering with the strain. The world was rushing up
to meet me, the objects in it growing bigger in sudden, ratcheted
expansions, like a series of photographic enlargements being laid
rapidly one over the other. At last I got myself upright, my leg sev-
ering itself painlessly at the hip and releasing me, and as I hopped
bleeding down the aisle I saw that it was not an aeroplane I was
travelling in but the open back of a lorry that bucked and swayed as
it hurtled driverless through the smoke and blare of the midday
traffic. There was a cry, and someone shouted something, and I
woke, cold with sweat and clutching the edge of the mattress, my
teeth clenched and my legs tangled in the sheets.

I rose unsteadily and went and shut the window, seeking to
block out the noise of the street. It was not yet seven and already
the day was in full, clamorous swing; I thought wistfully of
Arcady's somnolent mornings. On the bedside table behind me
the telephone rang. I grew up without telephones, and have never
managed to become accustomed to the instrument, the way it sits
there, the same in every house and hotel room, ready to break out
at any moment without warning, petulant and demanding as a
wailing infant. I went back and sat on the side of the bed and
picked up the receiver cautiously, and cautiously applied it to my
ear, and for a moment saw myself as my father, with all his wari-
ness of the world's machinery. My father. How strange. I had not
thought about him in . . . how long? A voice was speaking in my

ear, from the reception desk, to inform me that *"una persona"* was waiting for me downstairs. I nodded, as if the receptionist were standing in front of me. Then I put the receiver down again, exhaling a breath. So.

I ate breakfast in my room, unhurriedly, and afterwards lay in a scalding bath for a long time. Now that she was here, now that the moment of confrontation had arrived, I had drifted into a state of lethargy and lazy contemplation. That momentary vision of my father had stirred up all manner of unexpected memories from the far past, of my childhood, of my family, of the Vander household with its many cousins, uncles, aunts. It was as if I were drowning, calmly, with my life not so much flashing before me as playing out selected scenes for me in dreamy slow motion. At length I rose and towelled myself briskly and put on my linen suit, hopelessly wrinkled now, and my stubby tie. Grimly I grinned at myself in the mirror: the drowned man dresses for his own funeral. In the corridor there was a mortal hush. The lift arrived with its clangings and mashings and I stepped into the box and descended, with one hand in my pocket rubbing a coin—the ferryman's levy!—between a finger and thumb.

Odd, that Arcady should have been the place where I ended up, so far from everything that I had once known. It was in the wrong direction entirely; by rights, I should have been borne the opposite way, like so many others, into the heart of the calamity, the toppling towers, the fire storms, the children shrieking in the burning lake. When I got to Arcady and looked back, however, I saw that everything I had done had been pushing me relentlessly toward it, as if the essays published, the addresses delivered, the honours won, had been so many zephyrs wafting me irresistibly westward, from Europe to Manhattan, to Pennsylvania, to the plains of Indiana, to bleak Nebraska—such harsh poetry in those names!—and then in a last, high leap, over the mountains and down to that narrow strip of sunlit coast where I came to rest with a soundless, dusty thump, like a spaceman stepping on to an unknown planet. Unknown, that is the apt word. The place was always alien to me, or at least I was an alien in it. The fact is, I was never there, not really. I took no part in town life, such as it was. I did not buy a car. I never went on that delicate, spindly, far-famed red bridge. Walking in Arcady's steady sunlight, that seemed trained on me always like the light of an impersonal but ever-watchful eye, I would close my mind to the present and be again in the city where I was born, and walk again in the narrow, secret streets where I walked as a child, and see again the spires and the huddled roofs and the frozen fields beyond, scattered with tiny figures at work or play, as in one of those hackneyed Dutch genre scenes of mingled labours and festivities. Oh, what would I not have given in those unvarying Arcadian days to catch even for an instant the flash of rain-light on an April road in Flanders! And yet, I should have been at ease in Arcady. There, everyone had previously been someone else, at some time, in some entirely other existence, just like me. In all the years I lived in the town I never met a single person who had been born there. *Where are you from?* Arcadians would ask of each other, and stand smiling, brows lifted and lips expectantly parted, anticipating a story, a history. They would confide the most intimate details about themselves and their pasts, and give that characteristic shrug, shrugging it all off. The future was their legend. I, of course, fascinated them. Unlike the comrades I had left behind in New York, they were not interested in me as a political exemplar, but flocked to me nevertheless, filled with curiosity and wonder, as if they were visiting some ancient, hallowed site of immemorial rituals, battles, bloody sacrifice. They would walk around me, viewing me from all angles, wishing they had brought their cameras and their guidebooks. I encouraged them, the most agreeable or at least the most useful of them, welcomed them, accommodated them, until I judged my authenticity had been sufficiently attested, and then I shut fast the gates and let the portcullis come crashing down, and stay down, its rivets rusted fast.

Magda felt even more displaced than I did in lush and leafy Arcady. She had almost liked New York, its teeming streets, the bustle and the crowds and the ceaseless clamour of human concourse. The farther west we went the more of life was leached from her. The air in those vast spaces we travelled through dried her out, hollowed her out. In Arcady the young frightened her, from the boy on his bicycle who hurled the rolled newspaper against our front door first thing every morning with vicious energy, to the under-age hoodlums racing each other on motorbikes up and down the umbrous avenues, turning the air rancid with exhaust fumes. She began to hide from the world, hardly venturing out of the house and never without me to accompany her. I cannot recall at what point exactly I realized that her mind was decaying. Perhaps the defect was there all along, a spongy patch she had been born with in her brain, that had spread steadily until all within her cranium had turned to pulp. When did she develop her taste for toy food? I would find lollipop sticks stuck to the floors, crumbs of cake between the covers of the bed, candy wrappers floating unflushably in the lavatory bowl. Frequently now I would come into the house to meet her standing in the hall regarding me with a wild, unrecognising look. I would hear her talking to herself, in the bathroom, or on the stairs, a hushed, urgent whispering. Then one morning she walked into the kitchen leaving behind her across the floor a trail of little turds as flat as fishes, and I knew the time had come when she must go.

In the hotel lobby a coach load of elderly tourists was checking in, with much complaining and bickering; they, like me, had suffered delays and loss of luggage. I paused on my stick outside the lift and looked about. Where was she, this *persona*? Two fat businessmen sat on low armchairs facing each other across a lower table, intent and watchful, as if in preparation for a bout of arm wrestling. A girl with red hair was hiding in the corner of a couch, with a bag at her feet, waiting for someone, hoping not to be noticed. A painted hag passed by, lost in the folds of a fur coat, with a pug dog in her arms. I went toward the reception desk but could not reach it for the milling tourists. I considered simply walking out the door and away, clearly I saw myself go, except that in my imagination my damaged leg was repaired, and my step was youthful, and rapid, and carefree. Even before she spoke I had sensed her behind me. It was the girl, of course, the girl with the red hair; I should have known. Tall; pale; freckles on her nose; eyes that were—what?—greeny-blue, yes, and flecked with amber. I noticed her tall girl's way of standing, one leg back, the forward knee bent, trying to take an inch off her height. She was holding her bag protectively before her with both hands on the strap, as if to ward off a feared and confidently expected assault.

"I am Catherine Cleave," she said. "I'm called Cass."

⁂

We sat in the lobby, facing each other from either end of the leather couch, the girl bolt upright with her fists on her knees, her raincoat beside her and her bag on the floor; she had the slightly dazed, disbelieving air of a refugee who no more than an hour ago had made it across the border under fire. I was irritable. The water splashing in the ornamental pond kept distracting my attention: what imbecile had thought to put ferns and a fountain there? I like things kept to their proper place. I studied the girl, or young woman, as I supposed I would be required to think of her. The aspect she presented was at once striking and dowdy. I noted the fine bones of her wedge-shaped face, the delicate, slightly inflamed pink at the canthus of her eyes, the blonde down on her arms and on her long, bare, bony shins. She was telling me in hurried and disjointed detail of a research project she had been engaged on, for years, it seemed, to do with Rousseau's children, if I recall; I barely listened. I was thinking how disappointed I was. I had expected someone far more formidable than this. She might have been a student of mine, one of the more desperate types, from the old days, when I still had to have students. So she hoped to make her name by exposing me, did she? Well, she might succeed, but at a cost, and what a cost, to herself no less than to me, I would make sure of that. As she talked, her eyes, unnaturally wide and bright, kept darting here and there over my person with a flickering, fascinated intensity, so that I felt I was being very rapidly assembled, a sort of living jigsaw puzzle. A faint, fast vibration came off her, as if there were something inside her spinning without cease at terrible, soundless speed. I interrupted the gabbled history of Jean-Jacques' abandoned brats to ask if she would like to have some breakfast and she looked at me in a sort of panic and vehemently shook her head. I felt as if I had come face-to-face on a forest path with a rare and high-strung creature of the wild that had paused a second in quivering curiosity and would in another second be gone with a crash of leaves. I knew the type. They always sat in the highest tier of the lecture hall, fixed on me hungrily, never speaking a word unbidden. I looked at the deep, shadowed cup above her clavicle and was surprised to feel my old libido rubbing wistfully its callused claws. I am afraid I always did favour the crazed ones.

When I enquired where she came from and she told me I said it was a grand place, home of many fine and famous poets. How could I, even on the telephone, have missed that burr, that brogue? I asked which hotel she would be staying at, and saw from the way she faltered and frowned that she had nowhere to stay. Good. Perhaps there would be a room available here, I said smoothly, lifting my eyebrows at her. She looked about dubiously at the marble floors, the chandeliers, blinking. But yes, I said, she must stay here, I was sure there would be a vacancy, I would go and arrange it, right away. As I hauled myself to my feet I saw with obscure satisfaction how she had to check herself from reaching out a hand to help me. At the desk she waited silently at my elbow; in her stillness she was still vibrating. Yes, I announced, turning to her, all airy blandness, there was a suite available, would she like that? Mutely she looked at me. I smiled. "Something more modest, then?" Her forehead reddened. The sleek young man behind the desk was stony-faced. I set a registration card before her and offered her a pen, which she declined, and instead brought out a fountain pen of her own from the pocket of her blouse. She bent to write, with a schoolgirl's frowning haste. I tried to read the address she was putting down, but could not make it out. Her handwriting startled me in its violent uncontrol; the spiked letters in slanting lines were like so many rows of smashed-up type. Deftly I snatched the key the clerk was offering her, and picked up her bag, too, before she could reach for it. She reddened again. I drank her blushes like sips of the most refined and precious cordial. For certain, I would have fun with this one! She turned toward the lift and I followed her. Wide shoulders, long haunches, and much, much too tall. Side by side we ascended, eyes cast upward. She smelled sharply of sweat as well as something dull and faintly medicinal; I sensed a past of institutions—schools, and more than schools; sanatoriums, perhaps? Perhaps her lungs were bad. I was not sure if people have bad lungs, any more. How widely one's musings range on these peculiar, these extraordinary, these fantastical, occasions.

The room I had got for her was small and looked out on a flat roof and a row of odd, blackened metal chimneys like the smokestacks of an ocean liner. I placed her bag on the bed. She stood with her back to the window in a defensive, folded-in stance, shoulders hunched forward around a chest made concave and her palms pressed together in front of her stomach. I said she must be tired, after the journey, and she said yes, it had been hard to sleep on the train. Then there was silence again. She had made no mention of the letter she had written to me or of its contents. I said that she should rest, and then we would go out together and take lunch. "Lunch?" she said, as if it were a word in a foreign language, her mouth slack and slightly askew, seeming to frame something further that she would not say. I flared my nostrils and snuffed up a draught of the room's deadened air, seeking to savour again the civet smell of her sweat. Old friend libido stirred anew. She, and the room, and the bag on the bed, and those ship's funnels outside, all seemed suddenly part of some thrilling, absurd adventure I had suddenly found myself embarked upon, and a thousand years or so dropped from me as lightly as a fall of scurf. "Lunch," I said, "yes!" brooking no objection, and nodded, and turned, and reversed my walking stick and hooked it on the door handle and opened the door, a gamesome gesture, and if I had been wearing a hat I would have tipped it, too. I shall soon be free, I told myself, not knowing what it might mean, and not caring.

Outside the door I paused; my hands were trembling.

I took her to the Esmerelda, thinking to impress her, but she paid no heed whatever to the mournful rococo splendours of the place, the red plush walls and sparkling crystal, the napkins of rich damask, the heavy antique cutlery. She hardly ate, only stabbed with her fork at the food on her plate without looking at it, pushing it this way and that. She had changed into a dull-coloured dress without sleeves that gave her, disconcertingly, the stark look of a recent and very young widow. She sat before me, straight-backed, her tall, narrow neck extended in a birdlike, swanlike, fashion, and although we were level eye to eye I had the curious feeling that she was somehow set above me, looking down. She had done something to her hair, had tied it back, or perhaps had just brushed it in some different way, exposing her broad, flat cheeks and the too-large flanges of her ears; the effect, I am not sure how, was of a not quite concentrated state of desperation. I had no appetite, but a great thirst, as always. I drank first a bottle of red wine thick as blood and afterwards repeated jolts of grappa, each one driven home with a thimbleful of tarry coffee that made my nerve-ends twitch and fizz. She sipped a glass of water. The smoke of my many cigarettes formed a rank cocoon around us and set her coughing. We were seated at a window looking on to a narrow, deserted street, with a crumbling church opposite. So many times in my long and infamous career have I sat like this across from some girl in a restaurant, cigaretted, sinisterly smiling, an arm negligently thrown over the back of my chair, holding myself up before her awed and admiring gaze like a gobletful of the rarest fine old vintage. Now here I was, doing it again, even in my senescence. I was telling her about the first winter when I lived in New York, sequestered in that basement room on Perry Street where in the summer I had feared I would die of the heat and now thought I would never be warm again. Magda showed me how to roll up newspapers to make fuel for the stove. I was working all day and half the night, no let-up, giddy with excitement and fatigue. "I knew what the thing would be called before I had put down a word," I said. "*The Alias as Salient Fact: The Nominative Case in the Quest for Identity*. I could already see the dust jacket, with the title in big bold lettering above my name in more modest twenty-four point." I chuckled, and drank my grappa, and felt with masochistic satisfaction the sulphurous, oily liquor lifting another layer of membrane from my tongue; surprising, the semblance of assuagement such tiny pains, willingly suffered, can bring to one's sense of self-loathing . . . Ah, but how cold it was in that room. I would sit wrapped in a blanket with only my face and my writing hand free, my brain buzzing from the barbiturates I ate by the hour. The wind coming in from the river keened in the window frame and tiny balls of soot rolled across the page where I was writing. I had tried to work in the public library, for the warmth, but had been driven out by the presence around me of so many other mendicants who were too much like myself, haggard and sighing, picking their noses and surreptitiously eating sandwiches out of brown-paper bags. Then the thing was published, and at once, as in a fairy-tale, like Cinderella in her pumpkin carriage, I arrived. "Such things were possible," I said, "in those days. One book could do it. Of course, everyone read it"—I waved a hand lazily—"and everyone thought I was speaking directly to him. Or her." I caught her eye and smiled disparagingly. Do you know those smiles, that make the flesh of your face seem to crackle like cellophane from the effort?

She watched me, motionless, her knife and fork suspended; her suddenly going still like this brought a small shock to the air between us, as when the refrigerator, that has been throbbing to itself unnoticed, all at once falls silent, with a lurch. "You convinced them," she said. I shrugged. "It was the times," I said. "Identity was the general obsession, then; identity, and authenticity, all that; the existential predicament, ha ha." Yes, yes, I convinced them. Most of them. Shiftiness: which one of them was it said that moral shiftiness was the most striking characteristic of every line that I wrote? I did not know the word, and had to look it up. "After that everything changed," I said. Yes, everything. Magda and I left that freezing basement and moved to an apartment in a big old townhouse up in the West Seventies, a rackety place where mysterious smart people lived, theatre types, and studiedly mournful girls who wrote poetry, and a famous black trumpet player. Success was large and loud and ludicrous. Such euphoria! And the parties, the endless string of parties, where I rubbed shoulders with living legends, all those Edmunds and Lionels and Marys, and was rubbed up against in return. In their brilliant and never quite sober company I learned a new language, one of nuance and nod, of the ambiguous smile, the insider's wink. The comrades, of course, whom I saw now as so unpolished, so gauche—*bon mot!*—I quickly put behind me. I imagined them, the jeaned and crew-cutted young militants and their attendant, solemn handmaidens in their plaid skirts and white ankle-socks, standing in a huddle on the empty sidewalk, bereft and sullen, blinking in the dust from my departing heels.

Cass Cleave put down her knife and looked at me. I shrugged again, smiling my most candid, my most winning smile. "My dear," I said, "I have turned my coat so often it has grown threadbare."

It was only then that I realized how angry I was, how angry I had been all along, ever since I had opened her letter, and before that, long before that, in the expectation of it, for I had always known it would come, from someone, sooner or later. Cass Cleave had turned her face aside now and was looking out at the street. How much did she know? Beadily I studied her. Yes, I recognized the type: driven, clever, cunning and helpless, prey to secret hungers, nameless distresses, looking for rescue in all the wrong directions. Her nails were gnawed past the quick. I shut my eyes for a moment. Could it really be that the intricate exploit that was my life, this hard-won triumph of risk and daring and mendacity, would at the end be brought to nothing by the yearnings for attention of a half-demented girl? The afternoon sunlight had angled itself down past the high roofs into the street, and something from outside kept flashing through the window into my eyes, some reflection from glass or metal. I was well on the way to being drunk. Without thinking to do it I reached out and took one of Cass Cleave's hands in both of mine and smiled my compelling smile again, showing my teeth. What a spectacle we must have been for the other lunchers in the place, the rank old roué pawing this pale girl and grinning like a horse. "Come with me," I said, gallant and jocular, "I want to show you the place where an old friend used to live." She was looking at her hand resting in mine, her head tilted to one side, with an expression of puzzlement, as if no one had ever held her hand before. I brushed my fingertips along her palm; it was warm and unexpectedly hard. When she lowered her eyes the lids, mauve-tinted, slightly glossy, were so rounded and taut they seemed almost transparent.

I looked about and the waiter came, a spry cadaver nearly as old as myself, bringing the bill, his moist fish-eye not quite looking at the girl's hand and mine where they lay together on the wine-stained tablecloth amid the empty coffee cups and the greasy glasses and the bristling ashtray. Cass Cleave had turned aside again to gaze at nothing, expressionless now. What was she thinking, what could she be thinking? Her hard hand, bird-warm, beat softly in mine, as if it contained a tiny heart of its own. Its serious weight was a sudden, shocking reminder of how much of my life was gone. I was wearing out, I, and my world as well. A wave of bitterness and anger washed over me, taking my breath away. So many of the things were blunted now that in my youth would have pierced me like . . . like what? I did not know, I had lost the thread of the thought. I let go of the girl's hand and stood up quickly, knocking over my chair, and this time she did reach out to help me, and it was as well she did, for otherwise I am sure I would have fallen down. I leaned on her arm, swearing, and beat at my dead leg furiously with my fist. The ancient waiter shuffled forward to assist me, clucking as at a misbehaving child. I shoved past him and staggered to the door. Outside, in the sun, I walked a few steps and had to halt and lean with my back against a wall. I looked up at the sky; it seemed to be throbbing, slowly, hugely. I felt dizzy, and had again that sense of displacement, of shifting and separation, that I had experienced the previous day before the mirror in the hotel bathroom, but more strongly now. I wondered without alarm if I were undergoing a heart attack, or suffering a stroke. Cass Cleave was trying to take my arm again. "It's nothing!" I cried. I vented gas from my rear end without restraint, not caring if she heard, or smelt. I was laughing, laughing and coughing, in a euphoria of drunkenness and dizziness and rage. There sleeps in me another self who at moments such as this will start awake in amazement at all that is happening, all this life, the unlikeliness of it. The girl stood before me, frowning on my disarray. I swore at her. Another flash of light struck my eyes—was it coming from inside the doorway of that church? *Ave, Deus caecans!* I fumbled and let fall my walking stick, it made a rattling as of bones. She crouched to pick it up and I would have kicked her had I not been afraid that if I did so I would lose my balance and fall headlong on the pavement. My heart was clenching like a fist. I snatched the stick from her hand and turned and poled myself off along the pavement, cursing.

Fury, fury and fear, these are the fuels that drive me, mixed in equal measure: fury at being what I am not, fear of being found out for what I am. If one day one or other of these forces should run out the violent equilibrium sustaining me will fail and I shall collapse, or fly off helplessly with farts and whistles, like a slipped balloon. Even when I was young . . . but no, no, I do not want to start remembering all that, I am sick of all that. I am done with the past; at a certain point when I look back a line is drawn stark across the view, as if a landslide had happened there. The girl was following me at a careful, fixed distance. Whenever I stopped she too would stop and turn her head away and stare at something intently. The dark dress and thonged sandals that she wore gave her an Attic look: Electra astray in the city of tombs. I pushed myself onward, and presently arrived again in the little piazza before the Carignano palace. The afternoon had woken from its lunchtime torpor. Little cars buzzed in and out of busy streets. Here was the bronze plaque on the wall I had been seeking. Three steps led up to a narrow, tall door. When I pressed the bell a voice squawked at me from the grilled mouth of a metal box on the wall and the door lock clicked. I stepped inside. Grey walls, and the musty, hot smell of an airless indoors. Cass Cleave was still crossing the street; I considered letting the front door swing shut in her face, as I had tried to let the door of the caffè knock over Carrot Head, but I relented, and held it open for her, grudgingly. Yet as we climbed the stairs I saw myself in my imagination stop and turn and take her in my irresistible grasp and rip apart her clothes to press the length of myself against her. Even her nakedness would not be enough, I would open up her flesh itself like a coat, unzip her from instep to sternum and climb bodily into her, feel her shocked heart gulp and skip, her lungs shuddering, clasp her blood-wet bones in my hands. At the top of the third flight the ferrule of my walking stick lodged itself in a crevice in the scuffed marble step and as I levered it wrathfully back and forth in the effort of freeing it I had a vision of the entire building rocking and swaying and tearing loose of its foundations and crashing forward in an avalanche of falling masonry into the astonished and cowering piazza.

Here was a door of frosted glass. I rapped on the pane with the handle of my stick. No response. I cleared my throat, Cass

Cleave cleared hers. I pointed to the name painted on the glass of the door in gold lettering. "Fino," I said, nodding. "You see? That is the family who rented him a room." We waited. I knocked again, and at last the door was opened by a diminutive, homuncular young woman wearing a drab dress like Cass Cleave's and old-fashioned spectacles with heavy black frames. She sidled forward and quickly drew the door to behind her, closing off whatever might have been glimpsed of the room, although a faint smell of something cooking did escape. She greeted us diffidently and stood looking sidelong down at our feet, incurious and still. She held her hands joined before her, moving them about each other in a slow, caressing, washing motion. I asked if we might be allowed inside to see the room where the philosopher had lived. She frowned, and her hands stopped moving. "Nietzsche," I said, loudly. "Friedrich Nietzsche!" The name sounded absurd, like a sneeze; it was swallowed in the stairwell and rang back an echo that seemed to snigger. The young woman pondered, still with her eyes on the floor. There was a small, furry mole beside her left nostril toward which my eye kept straying. She shook her head slowly. No one of that name lived here, she said. She had a strange, low, sibilant way of speaking, pausing for a second on a word and making it buzz deep in her throat, a sound like that which a cat makes when it is being stroked. "I don't mean *now*," I said, fairly bellowing. "A long time ago! He lived here. *Il grande filosofo!*" I pointed again to the name on the door, I mentioned the plaque on the wall outside. She would only keep on shaking her head, remote, unapologetic, immovable. Once she raised her eyes sideways for a second and with a flicker of interest took in Cass Cleave's naked throat and the twin pale folds of freckled flesh where the sleeveless dress pinched her at each bare armpit. The landing was a narrow, hot space, and we had to stand close together, we two tall ones and the tiny woman, swamped in each other's heat and the cooking smell that was coming more strongly now from behind the closed door. I cast about for something more to say but could think of nothing, and instead swivelled on my heel and set off in mute fury and frustration down the stairs. At the first landing I stopped and turned and saw Cass Cleave and the dwarf woman still standing up there where I had left them, neither looking at the other, both with their eyes cast down, saying nothing, simply standing, motionless as a pair of manikins.

I was in the hall, waiting inside the door, when she came down at last, stepping from stair to stair with careful deliberation, watching herself as she did so, as if descending like this were a skilled manoeuvre she had only lately learned to execute. I thought, jarringly, of Magda. Slowly the girl came to meet me, avoiding my eye, or no, not avoiding, but looking through me as though I were not there. Yet I knew she knew what I would do. I seemed to be no longer drunk; on the contrary, I felt violently sober. She stood in the circle of my arms quite still and stiff; I might have been a cascade of water falling about her but not wetting her. Her lower lip stood a little prominent of the upper, so that she seemed in permanent expectation of receiving a drop of some sacred distillate from above, yet now when I leaned my head forward I had trouble finding her mouth; when I did, I took that soft, protruding bud of flesh between my teeth. As I kissed her she did not close her eyes, and neither did I, and so we stood and stared into each other, surprised, almost aghast. I caught again from her skin that faint, flat, medicinal smell. It reminded me of something: violets, was it? Her shoulder blades flexed under my hands like hard, stiff wings, flexed, and were still. Clear as if it were being projected before my wide-open eyes I saw myself in the house on Cedar Street sitting opposite Magda at the table in the breakfast nook, feeding her the tablets, picking them up one by one from my cupped palm and dropping them into her offered mouth. It was at midnight, I could faintly hear a clock chime in the next-door house; a moth was bumping against the black and shining window. All around was silence, not a sound save of that baffled, winged thing blundering against the glass. Magda's hands rested flat before her on the table;

her fingernails were chipped and there was grime under them. How calm she was, how docile, watching me steadily, with keen interest, it might be, as I poured out the glass of water and put it into her hands. Here; drink. I had told her the tablets were a special kind of candy. They were violet-coloured. I released Cass Cleave from my embrace. Still she did not stir, but stood and looked at me, calmly attending me and the possibility of what I might do next, with Magda's very gaze.

At the hotel, when I followed her into her room she was already drawing the curtains against the glare of afternoon sunlight. Now, of course, came the last-minute faltering, and I did not want to be there. I was tired of myself and my hungers, my infantile need to clasp and squeeze and suck that the accretion of years seems only to intensify. "You realise," I said, "that I am old enough to be your great-grandfather?" I laughed. She did not answer, only unbuttoned the neck of her dress at the back and pulled it over her head, becoming for a second a hooded black beetle with clawing antenna arms. The sound of her falling underthings rustled along my nerves. "Do you know that Cranach Venus in the Beaux Arts in Brussels?" I said brightly, leaning on my stick at an angled pose. "The one in the big dark hat and rather interesting black choker?" It had struck me how like the painted woman this living one looked, the same sinuous type, with the same heavy hips and tapering limbs and somewhat costive pallor. "Cupid," I said, "hardly as high as her knee, is an angry toddler crawled all over by bees, although they always look to me, I must say, more like bluebottles. Do you know the one I mean?" She bent to turn the bed covers back, one breast, a silvered bulb, glimmering under the arc of her armpit. "Cranach," I said, "younger or elder, I cannot remember which, was a friend of Martin Luther, of all people. One wonders what the great reformer thought of those lewd ladies his chum so liked to paint." She was sitting on the bed now with her legs drawn up to her chest and her pale arms clasped about her shins. She was not looking at me, but gazed before her with a faint frown, as if she were trying to recall some elusive word or image. I leant my stick against the headboard of the bed and turned and swung myself into the windowless bathroom and locked the door.

Micturition, I find, is one of the lesser annoyances of old age; sometimes, indeed, the copious passing of water can be an almost sensual experience. My urine on this occasion smelt distinctly of grappa. I turned on the cold tap and half filled the handbasin and doused my hands, liking the water's steely coolness, its joggle and sway. Then I spent some time picking idly among her things, her salves and pastes and powders; their mingled fragrance was faintly, pleasurably repulsive. I unscrewed a cartridge of lipstick and applied the scarlet nub to the underside of my wrist, drawing a smeary mouth there, open as in a startlement of desire, and pressed my lips upon it, tasting the sticky, waxen sweetness. In the land of women I am always a traveller lately arrived. I studied myself in the mirror, the flecks of scarlet the lipstick had left on my mouth, then took a tissue and wiped them off, not without difficulty. Still I loitered. Even from within this tombal chamber I could sense the afternoon's hot pulsings all around outside. I put my ear to the door; not a sound. She would be under the covers by now, waiting for me, her leman, with her lemur eyes, waiting for me to come and devour her. I recalled the policeman standing in the kitchen the morning after Magda died. He was a short, muscular young tough fairly bursting out of his uniform, his hair shaved to within a millimetre of his bullet head, his scalp a shade of baby blue and pink. His name, improbable, and yet gruesomely appropriate, was Officer Blank. He had shaken my hand with the courteous solemnity of an opponent before the commencement of a duel, and stood now audibly breathing through his nose, his square jaw rotating around a wad of chewing gum. I had never been afforded the opportunity to study a policeman at such close quarters before, and in my hungover, tear-sodden state I was fascinated by the quantity and range of impedimenta that he carried about him, the bulky gun, clenched in its holster like a steel fist, the long black club, the handcuffs, the complicated, brick-shaped telephone, also in a sort of holster, hanging from his belt. What was most impressive, however, was his stillness, the way he just stood there, in fathomless silence, hands set on angled hips and only that jaw moving, moving. There did not seem to be anything to be said, by either of us. When I offered to make him a cup of coffee he blinked and looked askance, as if I had advanced a faintly improper suggestion. We could hear the others moving about heavy-footed upstairs. I found it peculiarly embarrassing to have to stand and listen to them like this; it was like hearing someone using the lavatory, or eavesdropping on a couple making love. Officer Blank, perhaps also feeling the indelicate awkwardness of the moment, cleared his throat and shifted the gum from one side of his mouth to the other. "My Pa went the same way," he said, nodding. "Pills." I nodded too, and frowned in sympathy, and then there was silence again, except for those noises off. I could not think how last night I had got Magda up the stairs and into bed. I remembered the leaden weight of her arm across my shoulders, and the eerily contented-sounding, burbling little sighs she kept releasing into my ear, as if she were a drunken lover trying to whisper lewd endearments. Now here she was being brought down again, this time strapped to a stretcher, with the sheet pulled over her face so tightly that I could see not only the outlines of her nose and mouth but even the protuberances of her eyes. Officer Blank said something and with surprising nimbleness stepped quickly sideways past me and went out, and a moment later, clattering over the doorstep, they were all gone, so abruptly and so thoroughly it might have been not Magda's mortal remains they were removing, but a living felon who must be hustled off without delay to secure captivity. Through the window I watched them drive away, the ambulance, and the following police car. Around me the transformed house vibrated, as if I were standing inside the dome of a great bell that a moment ago had sounded its final peal.

I came back from then to now and remembered Cass Cleave. Cautiously I pressed the door handle and opened the door and stepped out into the bedroom's tense and waiting twilight. Ah, child, woman, forgive me.

S he could not sleep. The room in the half dark was phantasmally still, like the so many sick-rooms of her childhood. It was late, long past midnight. The air in the room was heavy and hot. In the light of the single lamp beside the telephone Axel Vander lay sprawled across the disordered bed, naked and asleep, breathing through his mouth, an arm thrown up awkwardly as if he had fallen backwards trying in vain to ward off a blow that had knocked him senseless. She moved away from him and rose cautiously and stood at the foot of the bed, looking down at him. The hair on his chest was grey. She could see the sinews in his shrunken arms, the shin-bones inside the stretched, paper-white skin of his legs. His face was ashen, and there was a perfectly round spot of hectic colour printed high on each cheekbone, neat as a dyer's stamp. He was breathing so softly she wondered if he might be only feigning sleep. She saw him in her mind rearing up and catching her by the wrist, could almost feel the grip of those ancient talons on her flesh. She drew up the sheet and laid it over him and he stirred and tensed and then went slack again. She was still leaking from him, she could feel the hot stickiness between her legs. The first time, when he had come out of the bathroom at last and heaved himself on top of her, she had thought of one of those huge statues of dictators that were being pulled down all over Eastern Europe. Crash. It was quickly over. They had lain together in the shadows then, lain there all afternoon long, until the day died, and the night came on. They were like survivors, she thought, washed up on this foreign but not unfriendly shore. Between bouts of dozing he had cradled her in the crook of his old arm and told her stories about himself when he was young; she listened idly, knowing it must be all lies, or nearly all. He did not know that she knew who he really was. Would she tell him? Not yet; not yet. Flakes of ash from his cigarette fell on her breast, tiny, warm, weightless kisses. She tried to picture him at the age he had been when the newspaper photograph was taken, restless, violent, insatiable, stretching out with both hands, straining to grasp at a future that now was long ago in the past. Then he had thrown himself on her again, and this time it was different, he was all chest and churning elbows and quaking thighs, straining and heaving, until she thought she might split in two clean down the middle. He seemed so angry. Then there was the smell of almonds, and then . . . When he was done he had pushed her aside without a word and gone to sleep, but she could not follow him, for all that she was exhausted. Now she had been awake for hours. Everything was so strange, all pulled out of shape and littered with torn-up things, like a stretch of shoreline after a storm. This old, old man. All at once, as she stood there gazing down at him, he was not he, or he was he and also not. She frowned, trying to unravel it. Perhaps it was simply that he was asleep and hence not present to her even in his presence. No, that was not it, sleep was not the agent, sleep only served to hold him still, the sudden stranger, so she might concentrate on what it was of him that was not there. She heard his harsh laughter in her head and imagined his eyes snapping open, the good one fixing her, the blinded one staring wildly past her into the nothing that it saw.

She could not now remember when she had first heard of him. There had been books of his on her father's shelves, unread. As so often with the people and the things that caught her questing attention, he was first a configuration, a sort of template fitting itself to a need in her she had not known was there. The parts of the pattern assembled themselves almost casually. He had written a famous essay on a play in which her father had achieved his greatest success. She had read him on Rousseau, of whom he disapproved. There was his book on the Italian comedy. Then she saw his photograph in a newspaper, receiving an award, in Jerusalem, and had been surprised that he was still living, since she had thought he must be among the illustrious dead. Now she bought all of his books, and sat in her room above the garden in her father's house and read and read. It was winter, and the garden was a pool of dank green light where a lone bird disconsolately piped. Vander was with her in the room, a living presence, stilling the voices in her head. There was something in everything he wrote, something darkly playful, that spoke straight to her. She knew that she would find him, and now she had.

She took a cotton dress out of her bag and put it on, and despite the lightness of the material she immediately began to sweat. She wondered if she might go outside. The streets round about were quiet, she could not hear a sound except now and then when a lone car went past, its tyres making a watery hiss on the dry street. She thought of the coolness and the dark under the stone arcades. What would he think if he woke up and found her gone? Perhaps he would not care. Perhaps he thought this was all she had wanted of him, that she had written that letter and brought him to Europe just for this one day, this one night, in this hotel room that she could not afford to pay for, so that afterwards she would be able to say that she had slept with the great and notorious Axel Vander. It was not true. Yet why had she written to him, why had she brought him here? What was that thing that spoke to her out of the things he wrote? She cared nothing for Shelley's defacement, or Coleridge's dreams, or Wordsworth's suborning of nature. No; what she heard was a voice calling to her, and her alone. Cautiously, on stork's legs, she backed to the door and reached behind her and opened it, still with her eye on the sleeping figure on the bed, and went out. In the corridor she stood and listened, fancying she could still hear Axel Vander breathing. Behind her the metal-grille doors of the lift cranked themselves open, making her jump. The lift was empty. It stood there, a harshly lighted box, waiting, impassive and patient, as if it had come especially for her. She hurried away from it, looking for the stairs. It was the light in the lift that she was fleeing, it followed her, bluish-white and thin, like watered milk, and still the metal doors had not closed.

Downstairs she stood in the marble lobby with its mirrors and gilt chairs and felt suddenly helpless. How could she go out? It was late, she was naked under her dress, she was not even wearing shoes. The night porter at his station gave her a politely vacant smile and went back to checking off something in a tall, black-bound ledger open before him on the desk. He was old and bald as a baby, and moved his lips as he read down the columns of names or figures or whatever they were. She went and sat on the leather couch where she had sat that morning, yesterday morning now. The water in the fountain among the ferns had been switched off. She wondered again if the ferns were real, and thought of touching them to find out, but to do that she would have had to stand up and go forward and get down on her knees at the side of the pond. Stand, advance, kneel. It seemed, as she pictured it, as intricate and effortful as a gymnast's exercise or a complicated pass in ballet. She did not stir. Soon the silence became oppressive and made her begin to feel dizzy. She felt as if she were holding herself upright in her own hands, a frail, over-full vessel that had been given forcibly into her unwilling care. She made herself rise and walk to the porter's desk, and asked the old man for a glass of water. He nodded, or perhaps it was a little bow that he made, briefly letting his eyelids fall as he did so, and murmured something, and padded off into the shadows. He was gone for what seemed to her a long time. When he returned he was carrying the glass on a little silver tray in one hand, while over the knuckles of the other a folded white napkin was draped. He stood calmly before her, watching as she drank, swallow by long swallow. How thirsty she was! She found the old man's nearness comforting, and somehow appropriate, as if he were the necessary witness to this ritual, this raising of glass and drinking of liquid, that she was required to perform. His soft brown eyes played over her with placid interest, taking in her bare arms, her bare feet, the thinness of her dress, through which, she supposed, he would be able to see the shadow of her nipples, darkened and swollen as they were from Vander's avid lips. She drank a last, long draught of water; really, she had not known she was so thirsty. The porter, still smiling his kindly, melancholy smile, lifted the back of his hand toward her, ceremoniously offering the napkin. Draped there before her on his hand it shone with an uncanny glow, stark as neon against the surrounding velvety dark, making her think with a shiver of the light in the lift. His black uniform was greasy from age. "You do not sleep?" he said. The question had a curious intimacy, like the question a doctor might ask, or a priest, and she hardly knew how to answer. She touched the napkin to her lips, liking the roughness of the linen, its starchy, laundered smell. "The room is hot," she said, pointing to the ceiling to show him she meant the room upstairs, the bedroom, her room, where, if only the old man knew, another old man was sprawled asleep across her bed with lolling flesh and mouth agape. The porter nodded again, frowning in sympathy, in the manner of one seeking to soothe an anxious child. "*Si, si,* is hot," he said softly, with a soft little sigh, still smiling. She proffered the empty glass and the napkin and he advanced the tray to receive them. She thanked him, and he made another small bow of the head, and a dull gold lozenge of light from somewhere slid over the shiny, pitted dome of his skull. He withdrew, walking backwards, the tray with glass and napkin held before him, then turned and was gone into the darkness, making not a sound. She went back to the couch and sat down once more.

Vander. Vander. Vander. She had not been surprised at all when in the restaurant he had reached out and taken her hand. All after that had happened with the smooth, relentless inevitability of the progress in a dream. And as in a dream there was the conviction that all this had been foreordained, the room, the bed, the sliver of burning afternoon light between the curtains, the man toiling over her with a dream-torturer's intentness; it all seemed merely a set of variations on events that had already taken place, in another, more keenly wakeful, compartment of her life. Since earliest childhood, for as long as she could remember, she had been prey to hallucinations; at least, that is what people insisted they must be. To her, they were like real happenings, or memories of real happenings made immediate and vivid. This was the reason for all her confusions, all her lapses from what they called reality. It was simply that the things she saw in her head were so clear and clearly present, so matter-of-fact, that she could not distinguish them sufficiently from things that were verifiable, by the measurements the others said must apply, and verification was what they were always demanding of her, with more or less sympathy, more or less exasperation. That was why the voices spoke to her, to insist on their different version of events. None seemed to realise, the ones who spoke within her or without, what a deafening din they made, sounding all together. Against such a cacophony how could her pleas be heard? She longed to be able to prove, even if only once, incontrovertibly, not what they wanted her to know, but what she knew. In a film that she had seen when she was a child there had been a man who in what seemed a nightmare had fought and killed someone and then had woken to find himself clutching a real button that in the dream he had torn from his victim's coat. Someday she too might come back from one of her so-called hallucinations and open her palm and show them in triumph one tiny, hard, bright bit of evidence that even they could not deny.

The first time that she knew her mind was unfixably wrong was on a winter Sunday afternoon when she was six, or seven. She had been ill for as long as she could remember, but because she was so young she had not yet realised that she would not get better, only worse. That Sunday her father and her mother had taken her in the car for a drive by the sea. She had said she would not go and her father had laughed and said he knew she only wanted to stay by herself in the house so she could drink whisky and smoke cigarettes. His teasing was a kind of violence. He was in one of his smiling rages because it was Sunday and there would be no theatre performance that night and he would have to stay at home and be bored. They travelled up the coast road, taking the scenic route, as her father sourly said. He did not like to drive and so her mother drove. Along the way they stopped at places but did not get out of the car. In the front her parents sat gazing bleakly out across the sea to the islands lying humped in a grey, salt mist, while in the back she knelt on the seat and looked through the rear window at the cars going past on the road. In many of the cars there were children like her, morose, pale faces floating in the windows, glowering at her. In the silence at her back she could feel the deepening desperation of the adults. Her mother smoked without cease, lighting each new cigarette from the stub of the old one. Open the window, for God's sake, her father said. When they came to the end of the coast road her mother turned the car around and her father muttered something and the argument began. They argued in an undertone so that she should not hear; the vehemence with which they fought was all the more awful for being muffled. The short day was ending, and the undersides of the low clouds in the windscreen were tinged a shade of furnace pink. See, her father said to her in a false voice, his stage voice, breaking off for a moment from the argument and pointing, it is the colour of a coke fire! And he laughed his laugh. She turned her eyes from the louring sky and looked out to the left at the sea that came up to the grassy edge of the road. Long, undulant waves were washing slowly in, wave upon thick wave, unbreaking wrinkles, mud-coloured. She felt her flesh shrink, as a snail would shrink from being touched. A vast weight, the weight of the world itself, was pressing against her, so that she could not breathe. It was as if something frightful had happened and this was its aftermath, this scorched sky, these turbid, relentless waves, the savage murmuring in the front seat. And she was alone; that, above all. The hawser had fallen away, the prow had turned toward the open sea, and she knew that now she would never come back. Her father, sensing her distress, perhaps, touched a fingertip to her mother's shoulder to silence her and turned around in his seat and smiled frowningly and said her name, as if he were not sure that it was still she who was sitting there, his little girl so changed in an instant. That was the first time she had smelled the almond smell. Then the car was stopped at the side of the road with one wheel mounted on the verge and the doors open, and she was slumped sideways on the seat with her head leaning out and the air cool on her brow and warm stuff bubbling between her lips, and her father was kneeling before her peering anxiously into her face, asking her something. Behind him the night, a bank of brownish darkness, was coming in across the sea, and high up there were the tiny lights of an aeroplane, now ruby, now emerald. Suddenly an enormous seagull flashed past, very close, falling diagonally through the brumous air on stiff, extended wings, and for a second she thought its icy eye had fixed on her, in warning.

Her father. She saw him often when he was not there, a ghost of the living man. For instance while Vander was busy goughing and grunting at her that second time, mouth fixed wetly like a sea creature to her shoulder, Daddy had opened the door of the room and walked in, speaking. He was barefoot, and was wearing an old pair of faded blue baggy trousers of the kind that he always wore when he was on holiday. He was young, far younger than she could ever have known him, and sun-tanned, and smiling in that fierce way, showing his fine, sharp teeth, that he always did when he could not find sufficient reason to be angry. His chest was bare, and he had a white hand-towel draped around his neck. He had been shaving, there still remained a moustache and goatee of lather that gave him the look, in negative, as it were, of a dashing Elizabethan villain of the kind he so often played. He was talking to someone in a farther room, her mother, she supposed, telling her something, a joke, or a story that he had just remembered, sketching abstract diagrams on the air with the razor as he spoke, in that way that he had, always animated, always dominating, cutting and carving and moulding the world. The razor was tiny, she noticed; he must have forgotten his own and borrowed this one from her mother. Perhaps it was the razor he was talking about, perhaps it had reminded him of something that had happened on one of his tours abroad; it amused him to tell her mother of his adventures, teasing her, trying to make her jealous with talk of eager actresses and stage-door propositions. The light behind him was a glare of azure and gold, and there was a slash of purple shadow there, and a parrot-green something, a palm leaf, perhaps, that kept moving to and fro in an odd, jerking, agitated way. What caught all her attention, though, was the bead of blood, the size of a ladybird, on his lip, where he must have cut himself with the razor, without noticing. She had always been fascinated by her father's mouth; she liked to watch it moving while he spoke, liked to be kissed by it, those dry, warm lips, the upper one, where the blood was now, shaped exactly like the stylised seabirds she used to draw in her picture book as a child. She liked to feel the prickle of tiny bristles on his chin, liked to smell his laughing breath. He had stopped speaking now, and waited, listening, with a slack smile, his head lifted at an angle and his eyes bright, those lips a little parted, the bleb of blood seeping pinkly into the soap moustache. When no response came to the story or the joke he had been telling, because her mother, if it was her mother, had stopped listening, or had fallen asleep, the light went out slowly in his face, and the smile turned to a vacant frown, and, feeling the smart at last, he dabbed a finger to his lip, and looked at the blood and seemed puzzled, as if he did not know what it was, or how it had come to be there, on his finger, on his lip.

Body: that was a word she did not like, the sound of it, the bubbled *b*, the *d*'s soft thud, the nasal, whining *y*. Vander at the end had spoken something in her ear, a hoarse grunt, ugly and urgent. He could break her in his arms, crush the life out of her. She supposed she should be afraid of him. He had sucked at her breast like a child, his eyes closed and his face almost smiling.

She shivered in her thin dress; the night was turning chill at last. So silent, all around, as if the entire building were submerged in the dark deeps of a silent sea. She imagined the other people staying here, dozens of them, hundreds, maybe, all laid out in their beds like so many warm corpses, asleep, dreaming, or tossing and muttering, perhaps, or perhaps sleepless, like her, as some of them must be, surely. She pictured the couples amorously clasped in each other's arms, or lying at opposite edges of the bed, rigid with wordless fury, as so often she had seen her parents, after another of their fights. There might be someone about to die at this very moment, or someone giving birth, it was not impossible, nothing is impossible. All over the world at any instant people are dying or being born, crying out in passion or in pain. Terrifying to think of, terrifying. When she was a child she would lie awake listening to the life of the house around her winding down. Her father would come in late, after a performance, she would hear him below in the kitchen rattling the crockery, or trawling across the radio stations, the volume turned loud, making a great din, for a silent house worried him, or so he said. She would track him in her mind as he prowled from room to room, switching on all the lights, pouring himself a drink, listening to a snatch of music and abruptly turning it off: she could never hear the screech of a needle across a vinyl record without thinking of her father. Or he would talk out loud to himself, or to a phantom audience, practising dialogue, trying it at different speeds and different rhythms, or, if the play was bad, making fun of the lines, declaiming them in a booming bass voice that made her grin into the dark even though she could not make out the words, only their lugubrious cadences. He would sing, too, tunelessly; he knew only silly things, songs from when he was young, or jingles from the radio. Sometimes her mother, annoyed to be woken, or perhaps feeling sorry for him, would get out of bed and go down in her night-gown and sit with him, but never for long. For all that he said about hating silence and solitude, secretly he preferred to be alone. "Oh, Cass Cass Cassy, I'm a solitary boy," he would croon, striking a tragic pose with hands clutched to his heart. Always, last thing, he would open her door an inch or two and look in, and always she would pretend to be asleep, she was not sure why. At other times she liked to have his company, especially after she had suffered a seizure, when they would sit together, at the kitchen table, or in front of the television set with the sound turned down, not saying anything, just being together. But there were times too when she would feel shy of him, or it would be more than shyness, it would be almost revulsion, and more even than that, something for which there was no word. When he had gone on to his and her mother's room and was getting into bed she would hear the bedsprings creak, and the funny, fluting sigh he always heaved; then there would be an interval, and then she would feel a change in the atmosphere, a sort of loosening, or lapsing, that signified his consciousness slipping out of gear, and she would be left to set out on her journey into the night alone.

From far off now she heard a church bell mark the hour, a dark and leaden tolling. Three o'clock. How long had she been sitting here, on this couch? Time always became elastic after one of her attacks. And it was an attack she had suffered in Vander's arms, when her father had appeared to her, holding the razor. Probably Vander would flatter himself that it was he who had brought her to this pitch of passion, as she shook and writhed under him, her head thrown back and her teeth bared and those shaming, constricted little squeals she could not suppress coming up out of her throat. The paroxysm as always lasted no more than seconds, and when the worst of it was over she had drifted into the usual brief doze or daze, curled on her side with the joint of her thumb pressed to her front teeth, shivering a little now and then, shuddering, like a dog that has been dragged out of the sea. Vander was lying on his back beside her, asleep already, mouth jutting open and his lizard's eyelids fluttering. She knew she would not sleep. She lay motionless for a long time, afraid she might wake him, smelling the ammonia smell of their love-making, hearing the hiss and liquid rattlings of the ineffective air-conditioner that squatted behind a grille under the window. Then came the hollow sensation that was the thing she dreaded most; it was as if a huge hand had thrust itself into her irresistibly and scooped out her insides, leaving her an empty cage of bone and flaccid skin. Once she had seen Granny Cleave do that to a chicken, disembowel the bird like that, pushing her fist through the slack hole underneath and with a quick turn of her wrist bringing out the guts intact in their parcel of opalescent membrane. The old woman had shown her the glistening eggs, pale as pearls, that had been growing in the bird, a string of them, increasing in size from a gelatinous speck to one that was almost fully formed.

Smell of almonds, always the smell of almonds. Then her father in slow motion lifting her from the floor and folding her in his arms. There there. Mr. Mandelbaum has been paying a visit. *Mandel:* almond. So strange, how things strike echoes everywhere. As if . . .

The old porter appeared again out of the shadows, bearing a bucket and mop. He seemed not at all surprised to find her still here. He gave her his sweetly sad, apologetic smile. He held the mop and bucket with an air of pained fastidiousness, as if, although he had brought them, he did not quite know what they were, or what their exact use might be. She stood up, wincing as she felt her thighs peeling away from the tacky leather of the couch. Her dress at the back was damp; she hoped she had not left a sticky patch where she had been sitting. The porter said something to her, and although she did not catch what he said she smiled and nodded anyway, as if she had understood. As she was going up the stairs she paused and looked back; he was mopping the marble floor beside the pond, in long, unhurried strokes, still with that air of reluctance and vague puzzlement; he had not even taken off his jacket for the task.

She listened outside the door of the room but could hear no sound. For a moment she was convinced that the door was locked, that Vander had got up and locked it against her, had locked her out of her own room and gone back to sleep, and that she would not be able to wake him, or that if she did he would not let her in, and she would be left here, barefoot, in her stained dress, a shivering spectacle for the other guests to see when they began to get up and go down to breakfast. They would think she was drunk and had lost her key. They would think she was a whore that a dissatisfied client had thrown out of his room. Her hands had begun to shake. To her surprise but not relief, although she did not know why not relief, the doorknob turned suavely under her trembling touch. She stepped inside quickly. The bedside lamp was still burning but the bed was empty. Had he got up and gone away to his own room? Perhaps he had left altogether, had gone to his room and packed his bags and checked out. But no, she had been in the lobby all this time, so how could he have gone without her seeing him? Perhaps he had dodged out by a back way, leaving her to deal with the hotel people, leaving her to pay the bill, or bills, his own as well as hers, that she had no money to pay. But no, his clothes were still there in a heap at the foot of the bed where he had shed them, his shirt and trousers, his expensive shoes, that ugly tie. The bathroom door, white and blank, had a look of sullen admonition. She pulled off her dress and rolled it into a ball and stuffed it in the recesses of her bag. At that moment Vander came out of the bathroom. She straightened quickly, pressing a slip against her nakedness. He was naked too; he had been in the shower, drops of water glinted in the tangled bush below his belly, and the long, jagged scar on the inside of his thigh glared redly. He looked her up and down, lips pursed, one eyebrow cocked. Quickly she put on the slip, a blouse, skirt, sandals. He watched her, leaning against the door jamb, coldly smiling. "Going out?" he asked. She did not answer. He was just like any other, all supercilious bravado after the act, a little boy who has stolen a treat and is unsure he will not be punished for it, but not sorry, either. He stood there, displaying himself to her, daring her to turn aside from the sight of that gnarled leg, that crazily skewed dead eye, and all that sagging flesh, the pot belly and the shrunken acorn below and its bag suspended by an attenuated string of yellowed skin like a head of garlic on its stalk. But yes, why had she put on these clothes, where did she think she might be going? It was still the middle of the night. She had dressed only in order to be dressed; it was not the sight of his naked flesh that had made her flinch, but the consciousness of her own; not shame, but simply the being conscious. He had sat down on the side of the bed and was smiling up at her slyly, sidewise. "Venus in fig leaves," he said, writing it with a fingertip on the air, as if it were the title under a picture. He had read her mind; people always seemed to be able to read her mind. Perhaps the voices that spoke in her head spoke in theirs, too, telling them what she was thinking. Now he was buttoning his shirt and saying well, why not, yes, they should go out for a stroll. She looked up at the black shard of night showing between the curtains at the window. "For me it is still afternoon," he said. He showed her the face of his watch and for some reason laughed. "Pacific time." The watch was an ancient piece, perhaps an antique, with a scratched case and a crimson second hand in a little dial of its own; it was too small for him, a lady's watch; she did not know why it should, but it made her think of railway sidings, with abandoned carriages, their windows greyed over with grime, and poppies nodding in misty sunshine among the stones between the tracks. All right, she said, they would go for a walk. How flat and neutral and slowed down everything had become. Hard to think now of what had been happening between them on that bed only a few hours before. What had struck her, as always, was the discontinuity afterwards, the inappropriateness of everything that followed. When she was younger she had thought that in time she would surely learn to make the smooth transition between that frantic concumbence and its upright, throat clearing, eye-avoiding aftermath, just as, when she was a child in dance class, she had been taught to rise more or less gracefully from a squatting position on to the quivering tips of her toes. But this bigger trick she had never learned, and there was no one to teach it to her. Vander was leaning far out over his stiff leg, tying his shoelace, with awkward effort. She looked down at his fumbling hands and bent big head with its fright of silver hair that was all tangled and knotted at the nape and saw herself stepping forward and touching him with her hand. She blinked. She had not moved.

They went downstairs. The silence, a kind of miasma, was more oppressive than ever, weighted with the inaudible breathing of so many anonymous sleepers, and she picked her steps gingerly, as if someone might suddenly jump out and chastise her for disturbing the quiet of the place. Vander however clanged his stick deliberately against the brass handrail on the wall and at every other step brought down the heel of his shoe so hard on the edge of the marble stair she was surprised that sparks did not strike from the stone. In the lobby there was no sign of the old porter. The night, glossy and black, stood pressing itself against the glass door that at first would not open for them, but then abruptly did, shuddering, the big pane giving off a deep bell-tone: *barang!* The air outside was cool and soft and fresh, and the sky, starless, fully dark still, seemed to glisten, and she felt vertiginously as if she were looking up through a shell of crystal, invisible and immensely high. Her fingers brushed the polished leaves of the laurel bush in its pot on the pavement outside the door. Vander was already lurching away up the street. She lingered a moment, then followed. She sniffed her fingers, smelling faintly the sharp, fading leaf-stink. She caught him up and for a time they went on without speaking. The tall, unlighted buildings teetered close on either side. She tried to fit her pace to the syncopations of Vander's gait: step of good leg, stamp of bad, thump of stick. In his way he was almost graceful, stooping and swinging and throwing a shoulder back before leaning into the next long lope. She wondered what she might call him, how to address him. *Axel* was a metallic bark, and *Vander* sounded as if a final syllable had fallen off the end. A name is hard to speak. To name another is somehow to unname oneself. Is this true, she asked herself, is this really so? She pondered, feeling the cool night breathing on her face, the deep, wide stillness burring in her ears. So often the train of her thoughts carried her far beyond herself, or went off on its own way, without her. Did she think, or was she thought? She could get no steady hold on things. An idea would occur to her, some notion or theory, with all the ring of rightness about it, then its opposite would come and that too would seem right, and how was she to judge between the two, not to speak of the myriad other contrary possibilities jostling for consideration?

And anyway, Axel Vander was not his real name. She put a hand to the pocket of her blouse and felt the fountain pen. Her little gun, with its loaded chamber.

They came out into a long, cobbled piazza. A bronze horseman strode motionless above them in the dark air, with a light from somewhere gleaming on his brow. She thought of the night porter and his black book, his silver tray; she thought of the glass of water with air bubbles like tiny beads of mercury clinging to the sides inside, below the water-line; she thought of herself lifting the glass and drinking deep. The rubber tip of Vander's stick squealed on the dew-damp cobblestones. They were walking beside the arcades, each archway an identical domed vault of blackness. A dog detached itself from the shapeless mound of rags that she supposed was its slumbering master and came forward and looked at them, wagging its tail in wan hopefulness. "Who was it that betrayed me?" Vander said to her. Betrayed. She asked him why he asked; what did it matter who, after all? This he greeted with a snort. "How did you know where to go?" he said, persisting. "Why Antwerp? Why those old newspapers?" She recalled, she could not think why, a line from the dust jacket of *After Words* that a critic had written in envious emulation of Vander's style—*"all the glints and flashes of a grand and faintly shivering chandelier"*—and she could not keep from uttering a low laugh. He stared at her.

"I met," she said, "a man in a bar."

⚹

More accurately, she had been accosted by him, on what was to have been her last afternoon in Antwerp. Her father had paid for the trip; he was always happy to pay, she noticed, when it meant she would leave the country. She had come to look for Vander's past, following his trail along the shelves of public archives, libraries, university records; the farther she travelled the fainter the traces of him became, as if a broom had brushed away his tracks. There was an old man, a journalist of high reputation, and also, some said, a one-time collaborator, who she was told had known Axel Vander when they were both young, before the war. When she went to call on him, however, she learned that he had suffered a stroke and was in hospital and was not expected to live. Nevertheless she was taken to visit him. Everything was white, his hair, his long, sharp, suffering face, the robe he wore, the bed linen, the wall behind his trembling hawk's head. Nothing moved except his eyes, which fixed themselves upon her in what seemed a kind of anguished asking. It struck her that he was another ghost, his own. She sat with him for an hour, not speaking, and all the time he watched her, with angry impatience, so it seemed; far from having anything to tell her, he appeared to be waiting to hear from her something that he must know. Perhaps he was confusing her with someone else. When she saw Vander in the hotel lobby that first morning, she felt this other old man's presence behind him, saw it, almost, a shimmering shape there for an instant, a shadow made not of darkness but of cold, white light.

Now on this last day she was in one of those fake old-fashioned pubs near the cathedral, all wood and brass and pewter beer-mugs, while she waited for it to be time to take the train. It was a late afternoon in March, sombre and wet, more like mid-winter than early spring. She was sitting at a table in a cramped corner by the window, huddled in her coat, watching the trees in the square outside that now and then shook themselves in a gust of wind, shedding big silver drops of rain that shone like money as they fell. It was out there that she saw him first, the red-headed man. She did not know why she should have noticed him particularly. He was standing under the money-trees. His clothes were shabby: cracked shoes, shapeless trousers too long in the leg, and an old coat fastened so tightly with a single button at his midriff that it seemed his skinny frame must be dependent solely on this support to stay upright. He wore no hat, and seemed not to notice the rain. She watched him for a while. His hands were in his pockets, and he held his elbows pressed close into his sides, as if to aid the coat in its task of general suspension. Was he looking in her direction? An ambulance went past, with its siren howling and its blue light spinning, and she turned away, for she did not like the sight of ambulances, or their sound, and when she looked again he was gone from under the trees. A moment later, though, here he was, in the bar. He appeared from behind her, and sat down at the table next to her. He took a plastic pouch of tobacco out of his coat pocket and rolled a cigarette. She noticed the faint tremor in his hand; it was not a sign of infirmity, but rather, so she thought, the result of long hours, years, of concentration on some tiny, intricate, antique task; he might be a watchmaker, or a scribe, even; she saw him bent over his work table with gimlet or quill.

He was feigning an elaborately vague, preoccupied air, brow distractedly wrinkled and eyes fixed on nothing, and she knew that he was going to speak to her. He patted himself rapidly at hips flanks breast, frowned more deeply, pursed his lips, then with a jerky movement turned about, pretending that he had just noticed her, and mimed entreatingly the striking of a match. She said she was sorry, she had no match. "Ah, you speak English!" he cried, as if hailing a rare accomplishment. "So do I." She wondered what age he might be. Fifty? Seventy? It was impossible to tell. His face was pale as whey and so sharp it seemed it must thin to a fine straight line were he to turn it full toward her. His hair was of an almost orange shade, obviously dyed; scintillas of rain were sprinkled through it, an incongruous jewelling. He put away the cigarette, unlit. She thought she should get up now and go; she looked out at the weeping sky, the street where the daylight lingered; her train was not due to leave for hours yet. He had been eyeing Vander's book where it lay on the table before her, and now with a contortionist's rubbery agility he leaned forward and twisted his head almost upside down to read the title. "Ah," he said. "Do you know him?" She shook her head. "I do," he said. "Or I should say, I did." With long, very white fingers, like the witch's fingers in a fairytale, he turned over the book and looked at Vander's photograph on the back cover and smiled. "But he was not Axel Vander, then."

The waitress came, a brawny, blonde girl got up in a flounced blouse and a wide black skirt with a bodice, in what must be, Cass Cleave supposed, a parody of the national costume; she carried a gilt tray that she held lightly by one edge, like a weapon. The redheaded man spoke to the waitress in a language that must be Flemish, or Dutch, perhaps, and when she had nodded and gone he glanced shyly at Cass Cleave, licking a thin lower lip. She wondered unworriedly who he was or why he was speaking to her. She examined him closely, the narrow face, those white hands. He was smiling still, and nodding to himself, as at a rueful though treasured memory. Yes, he said, he had known Axel Vander. "Oh, a long time ago, a long time. In those days he was a writer for the newspapers, like"—he tapped a long, amber fingernail on the photograph—"his friend." He nodded, and his voice sank to a whisper. "Very strong opinions," he breathed, and gave a little soundless whistle. "Very extreme." She was frowning; she could not follow him. "His friend?" she said, looking at the photograph. "Is that not him?" He glanced at her sidelong and his smile became a grin of happy malice. She did not like the way he kept licking that bottom lip, the sharp, grey tip of his tongue flicking out and as quickly withdrawing. "What was his name, if he was not Axel Vander?" she asked, but he only grinned the harder, and lifted a finger and wagged it roguishly, closing his eyes and pressing his lips tight together. The bodiced Amazon reappeared, on her tray a tiny, tapered glass containing an inch of carnelian liquor, viscous, glinting. He paid from a little leather purse, counting out the coins with finical care. Cass Cleave watched him lift the glass, his bloodless lips already pursed to meet it, and drink with dainty relish. He sighed appreciatively and set down the glass and pulled his chair closer and began to tell her the story of Axel Vander, who had died, and of this other one, who lived.

⟡

High above their heads a tinny bell banged, once, twice, three times, then a quavering fourth, startling her. The gunmetal sky was turning ash-blue all up one side. She was cold now, in her thin blouse. Vander had been silent for so long she had almost forgotten he was there. She watched him stop to poke at an object on the ground with his stick. It was a white plastic bag with something soft in it, and tied at the neck with string. "A man in a bar," he said. "I see. And you happened to be reading my book. What a coincidence." He was not looking at her. "Tell me," he said, "what was the name of this mysterious man?" Max somebody, she said. "Scheindiene, Schaundeine, something like that, I cannot remember." He said he had never known anyone of that name. He was still poking at the bag, turning it this way and that. It was plump and vaguely heart-shaped, and wobbled and flopped under his proddings; the string at the neck had been knotted in a neat bow, with awful thoroughness. "He must have been speaking of someone else," he said. "He must have been mistaken." She had not told him all that the man had told her; she had kept back the most important part. Vander was frowning intently, as if the thing in the plastic bag, whatever it was, were taking all his attention. "But he knew you," she said. "He knew the dates the articles appeared. Five weeks, five issues." At last he looked at her, holding his head at a tilt, thinking, calculating. He had got the bag partly open; something dark was oozing out, a thick, dark liquid. She felt her stomach heave and settle again. "Come," he said, folding a hard hand on the tender underside of her arm above the elbow and turning her about, in the direction of the hotel, "let us go back, you are shivering." Dawn was strengthening rapidly. High cloudlets, tinged with pink. The starlings.

There was a general hesitation, and when the applause did come it was markedly restrained. I lingered for a moment longer than the clapping lasted, smiling menacingly up at the audience ranged before me in the tiered semi-circular rows of benches, my hands clamped so fiercely on the lectern edges it must have seemed to those sitting in the front rows that I was about to pick the thing up and heave it at their heads. They were offended that I had not prepared a paper especially for the occasion, but had chosen instead to read, and in a tone of tired irony at that, a chapter from *After Words,* the one, justly famous, if I may say so, on poor Nietzsche's last, calamitous days here in Turin, which the majority of them would already have read, of course. What did they expect? They should count themselves fortunate that I had agreed to address them at all. I was about to step down from the podium when Franco Bartoli shot up a hand and asked with false and nauseating sweetness if I would perhaps agree to take a question or two? I heaved a loud and pointed sigh. There was the usual interval of awkward, foot-shuffling silence, and Bartoli rose part-way in his seat and swivelled his head to cast an encouraging glance at this one or that of his tongue-tied students skulking among the audience, which was made up for the most part of middle-aged academics, instantly recognisable by the peculiar drabness of their attire. At last a young man up at the back cleared his throat and asked in an earnest mumble what was, please, Professor Vander's view on the current state of cultural criticism? I lifted my head high and back and smiled. "My view?" I said. "Very fine, from this elevation, thank you." I made a curt bow and stepped away from the lectern and went none too steadily toward my seat—I had taken more than a generous go of grappa with my morning coffee, and was feeling the effects. On all sides there were head-shakings and sarcastic laughter and even some slow handclapping. I glanced to where I expected Cass Cleave to be sitting—five minutes into my reading I had glimpsed her from the corner of my eye as she came in quickly and slipped into a seat near the door—but she was not there. The place where she should have been was occupied by a brawny Brunhilde from Göttingen with massive knees, a Nietzsche scholar, as it happened, who was glaring down on me in pop-eyed indignation at my admittedly skittish treatment of her subject's final transfiguration and collapse on the Piazza Carlo Alberto a century before to the year. Franco Bartoli, one of the slow-handclappers, was smiling at me with angry brightness. I sat down. The room had no window and the woolly air was barely breathable. I was tired, dispirited, irritated. Bartoli, rising and going forward to introduce the next speaker, paused as he passed me by and leaned down and spoke into my ear. "Very witty, Professor," he murmured with honeyed bitterness, "but not entirely original, I think." Kristina Kovacs, at the other side of the room, was squaring a sheaf of papers on her knee and looking toward Bartoli expectantly. No, no, I thought, I could not bear to listen to Kristina tease out another of her elegantly humorous conceits on the phenomenology of comic strips or the soccer star as existential hero—I do wonder sometimes why I chose to spend what I am compelled to call my professional life in that little sphere of preciosities and trivial arcana. I stood up hastily and made my way to the door like a man escaping a fire.

The corridor smelled of pencil lead, musty paper, and young bodies rich with humming hormones. A scrawny, ill-dressed person, vaguely male, a student, I presumed, leaning by an open window consuming a clandestine cigarette, gave me a defiant, surly stare. No call for truculence, pale ephebe—see, I am lighting up one myself. I heard the door of the lecture hall opening and rapid footsteps approaching behind me. It was Kristina Kovacs. She did not stop until she was almost under the lee of my chin—it was a thing I remembered about Kristina, how close she liked to stand to people, even strangers, even former casual lovers. She looked up at me with her knowing, sceptical smile, a fan of fine wrinkles opening at the outer corner of each eye. "Did you think I was next to speak?" she said, amused. "Is that why you left?" I really did wish she would not stand so near, her head tilted back and swaying infinitesimally from side to side in time to her sad, inner melody. I said that I could not have stayed another moment among that herd of earnest idiots. She laughed softly and clicked her tongue in soft reproach. She said she had enjoyed my contribution to the proceedings. "Very naughty of you, to read such a well-known piece," she said with an annoyingly merry twinkle. "Franco was furious, I am sure you saw." I scowled. Do you think, I thought of asking her, do you think the mere fact that we rolled and writhed naked in each other's arms for a few hours one afternoon long ago gives you the right to this insolent familiarity? But Kristina's gaze had turned inward. "Poor man," she said, and for a second I thought it was me that she meant, and was astonished to feel a warm something surge in response within me, with all the anxious eagerness of a dog leaping up at the sound of its master's key in the door. She put her fingers to my elbow as if in urgent supplication. "Poor creature," she said, "those letters he wrote when he was mad, speaking of the great emptiness around him." Firmly I freed my elbow from her touch; it was like being settled upon by a tremulous but insistent butterfly. I laughed. "He also informed one of his much put-upon correspondents, in what I believe is the very last of those letters, that he made his own tea, did his own shopping, and suffered from torn boots. Even Zarathustra must reckon with the dull requirements of the quotidian." She was not listening; her eyes were swimming again. "But writing to Wagner's wife," she said, "that woman, of all people, calling her Ariadne and declaring that he loved her, and then ordering that all anti-Semites should be shot . . ." She was, I saw impatiently, quite upset. In her agitation she looked suddenly old and drawn. I glanced about in desperation. The young smoker at the window was watching us with incredulous disgust, these two ancients standing together in scandalous intimacy, pawing and being pawed. Kristina linked her arm in mine and I had no choice but to turn and walk off along the corridor with her. I found faintly repelling the way she kept insisting on touching me, squeezing my arm against her side, for instance, making me feel the heat of her meagre flesh and the soft-seeming rib-cage beneath. I registered too the thinness of her arm inside its sleeve: it was as if there were no flesh there at all, just cloth and bone. At the end of the corridor, where a big window faced us, filled with a smoky white effulgence, the figure of Cass Cleave appeared and came forward, elongated and rippling in the blazing light. She faltered at the sight of the two of us advancing arm in arm. She was wearing a loose linen dress, inside which I clearly saw, as if the material had for an instant turned transparent, her lean, big-hipped, naked body. She came on, head down, looking at her feet. We met, and stopped all three. "Kristina," I said with a wave, "allow me to introduce Catherine Cleave." I watched them shake hands. There was something obscurely comical in the moment, and I had a strong urge to laugh. "Miss Cleave," I said, in a mode of lofty patronage, "is my biographer." At that I did laugh. Why had I not thought of it before? My biographer! Cass Cleave stared at me, then quickly looked away. Kristina was still holding her hand, looking her measuringly up and down, this tall, small-headed, affectingly ungainly girl. Magda, I found myself recalling, always hated shaking hands, would go to any lengths to avoid it; I wonder why? I am trying to remember her hands, to picture them; I know their shape, their feel, but I cannot see them. Is this how she will leave me at last, limb by limb, until there is nothing remaining, except my shame? "And have you seen the Shroud?" Kristina was asking of Cass Cleave. "Our famous *Sindone*." My memory snapped its fingers: *sindone,* not *signore*. Kristina set off walking again, and Cass Cleave and I turned and walked with her, me to the right and she to the left; Kristina was half a head shorter than Cass Cleave; I looked down at the little woman's lustreless hair, then up again at my girl, and grinned, and winked. My biographer. "Professor Vander has been reading to us," Kristina said, still with her head down but addressing Cass. " 'Effacement and Real Presence,' a chapter from his famous book. I was surprised," glancing up at me now, "that you did not mention the Shroud: effacement, you see." She laughed shortly. "They say it is the first self-portrait. I always think it was the Magdalene who held the cloth, not Veronica. But Magdalene was hair, is that not so?"

——Long thick brown tresses streaming like water weed in the yellow lamplight, the water sluicing from the white jug. She would kneel beside the bathtub, a votary before the sacred fount, broad shoulders bowed, her white neck bared. Feel of her big skull frail as an egg under my kneading fingers. Where? Newyorpennindianabraska. Always moving, moving westward, stepping over the chequerboard land in long, effortless strides. The cities and then the plains, then what they call the high country, with snow and pine, then the mountains, the great peaks, and then the desert, and then at last the Barbary Shore, on whose blue waters her ashes would one day briefly float, swaying——

What?

Someone asking me something.

"What?"

Cass Cleave was standing before me, peering anxiously into my face and enquiring worriedly in a voice that sounded impossibly far-off if I was all right. All right? I said of course I was. I squirmed my shoulder free of her touch. All these damned women, passing me from hand to hand! We were at the end of the corridor, by the big window. Outside, at eye level, there was the improbable ochre and burnt-siena pudding-dome of a church, the stark sun gleaming on its leads. Where was Kristina Kovacs? Somehow she had left us without my noticing. Had I dropped out of consciousness for a moment? If so, why had I not fallen down? Cass Cleave was saying something about an address, my address. I shook my head, like an old dog with water in its ears, struggling to understand. My address? My address where? "Your talk, I mean," she said, gesturing in the direction of the lecture hall, "your reading." I shook my head the more. "What are you saying?" I said. "You were there. I saw you come in." She frowned; she said no, she had arrived just now. "I saw you," I said. "You came in late. You sat at the side, by the door. I *saw* you." She tried to take my arm but I swung away from her. Stairs, and more stairs, and then a set of double emergency doors with a metal bar to open them that I could not work. Cass was beside me. She put her hand over my hand on the bar. I could feel the faint heat of her face close to mine. "I am all right," I said. "I am *all right*." The doors swung open like a bulkhead and a dazzling wash of sunlight broke over us.

✄

But the fact is, I was not all right. I said I must have something to eat. What I really wanted, of course, was another drink, many other drinks. At the first restaurant we came to I ordered that we should stop. It was on a big dusty square, Piazza Vittorio Somebody, that sloped down to the Po. We sat at a table outside, under a canvas awning, with a view across the river to wooded heights that were bluish and flat in the noonday glare. I ordered a glass of sparkling wine. As I sipped the sweetish, slightly metal-tasting fizz, clouds of tiny bubbles, cold and sharp, detonated pleasantly in my sinuses. Now and then a strong waft of warm wind would come up from the river and make the awning above us ripple and crack like the sail of a boat. Cass Cleave sat silent, looking down toward the river, a hand lifted to shade her eyes, a mauve armpit bared. "Perhaps," I said, "you really should write my biography. Put all that research to use, all that sniffing along the seams of my life that you have been so busily about." Still she said nothing, still she held her face turned aside, expressionless as a profile on a coin. It was, I was coming to see, her favourite pose; how transparent you were, my dear, after all. "You could write it in the first person," I said, "pretend that you are me. I give you full permission. I grant you the rights to my life. What do you say, *mein irisch Kind?*" Suddenly I longed to be alone, just myself and my drink. The fact is, and I am aware, in the circumstances, of the grisliness of even mentioning it, the fact is that Cass Cleave was not, as they say, or used to say, my type. I never really favoured the tall, pale, pyriform kind, although they were the very ones who always seemed to seek me out. Given the choice—which I rarely was given, because of my great bulk, naturally—I would have preferred little fat women. There sits at the centre of the by now practically leafless maze of my sensual imagination a small, squat, Buddha-like figure, pink and naked, with heavy, raspberry-tipped breasts and nicely rounded shoulders and smooth, shiny, dimpled knees, and three charming, overlapping folds of fat above each hip-bone. She has no face, this fleshy idol, only a heart-shaped blank on which my venereal fancy, attaining a certain temperature, may hastily stamp a rudimentary set of features. I do see her hair, though, very black and lustrous, parted in the middle and drawn tightly back—the only attribute, incidentally, that Magda, and only in her youth, at that, shared with my secret ideal. Where did the image of this roly-poly little idol originate? Very far back, I suspect, very far back indeed, as far, perhaps, as the birthing bed itself. Unsettling thought.

The pastel roofs of cars parked in the square were shining in the sun, gaudy and heraldic, like the banners and shields of a prostrated, ornate army. "Who is Magda?" Cass Cleave asked, frowning now, and seeming to concentrate all her attention on the traffic speeding along the embankment. "You whispered it in my ear," she said. "Magda." I saw again the room, the bed, the girl. I wondered what the experience had been like for her, poor thing. She must have felt as if she had come to a far-off country, bankrupt and pestilential, where she had been captured and set upon by an ancient beast indigenous to the place, last specimen of its species, rampant and ghastly, with its mouldering pelt and its corpse breath and its single, glaring eye. "Magda," I said, "was my wife. She died."

Lunch was brought, although I could not recall having ordered it. The waiter stopped filling my glass while it was only yet half full—red wine now, I noticed—and I snarled at him and made him fill it to the brim. When I was lifting the glass to my mouth my hand shook violently, Parkinsonially, and the wine spilled over and splashed on the tablecloth. Cass Cleave attempted to mop it up with her napkin but I smacked her hand away and told her sharply to leave it. "Do not fuss," I snapped at her. "I hate for people to fuss." I began to talk then about Hitler at Berchtesgaden. It is a little dinner table turn that I do, for my own amusement if for no other reason. Deftly I sketched a picture of the magic mountain, with its band of trolls toiling to be the first in the Führer's favour, the little smooth-haired fellows and their blonde women all calves and big, square, satin-clad buttocks, and he in the midst of them, the mountain king, dreamy and distant, exquisitely polite, calmly plotting the destruction of the world. She kept her eyes fixed on her plate. "You are wondering if I admired him?" I said. She looked at me. "I did, a little. Do. A little. My friends and I when we were young entertained the beautiful dream of a Europe cleansed and free." I took another deep draught from my glass and leaned back, smiling into her face. "I am an old leopard," I said, "my spots go all the way through."

From a nearby table a raffish-looking old fellow in a straw boater was attending us with interest, who when I caught his eye gave me the faintest little smirking nod of envy. Strange, but people never took us, Cass Cleave and me, for anything other than what we were; there must have been an aura about us, a sulphurous something that we generated, or that I generated, at least, that told them she was no daughter and I no dad. I am not sure why, but old Aschenbach's longing look had set me thinking again of Prague and Kristina Kovacs. When she came to the door of my hotel room that day I had been in bed, nursing yet another after-lunch hangover, most likely. She stood before me in something like a penitent's pose, it had a lewd effect, hands clasped at her breast and head inclined, looking up at me sideways and smiling, not bothering to say a word nor needing one from me. In those days she was famously handsome, in a smouldering, slightly bruised sort of way, and practically every man and not a few of the women at the conference we were both attending—on Molière, Kleist and *Amphitryon,* as I recall—had been trying to get her into bed, but it was to mine that she came. Why? Afterwards she said it was because she admired my mind, which made me laugh; one unhindered glimpse into that foul chamber would have sent her backing speechless out of the door, with hands uplifted, shaking her head in horror. At the time she still had a husband, in Bucharest, I believe it was, a folly of her student days. She told me about him, Istvan, or Ivan, or Igor, some such name, in that thrilling, chocolatey alto of hers, lying on her back with a hand behind her head, gazing soulfully up at the ceiling through cigarette smoke and absently touching a finger to her swollen lip where my fierce teeth had hurt it. I listened, half dozing. Such dramas! The night their apartment was searched. The day her typewriter was confiscated. The frights they had, the fights. The time when Igorstvan came home after a weekend of interrogation by the secret police, red-eyed and grey-faced, and punched her in the belly because he was angry and afraid, and after that she could not have the baby the lack of which, she said, was the tragedy of her life. "That filthy country," she hissed, her dragon-mouth smoking. "Those filthy people."

But look! here is Kristina herself, and Franco Bartoli as well, sitting with us at the table in the shade of the awning, listening to the girl, who is talking to them, and laughing, in the strangest way. How did they come to be here without my noticing? I have no recollection of them arriving, joining us, ordering these glasses of wine they are toying with. I hear Cass Cleave telling them about someone called Mandelbaum, who comes to call on her. These are the words she uses: *"He comes to call on me."* The two sit facing her, upright on their chairs, fingers fidgeting on the stems of their wine glasses, blandly frowning with widened eyes and eyebrows lifted, polite and mystified. The girl leans forward at the table, her legs twined about each other and one foot hitched behind an ankle, and speaks very rapidly, stumbling over words, winding a lock of hair around a finger, tightly round and round, and giving that strange, snuffly laugh, as if what she is telling them were the drollest thing. Mr. Mandelbaum has a smell, she is saying, a smell of almonds, that goes ahead of him and warns her that he is on his way. Then he arrives and catches her in his arms and squeezes her, and squeezes, until all the breath is squeezed out of her and she falls down. Seeing that I am attending now, or trying to, out of an alcoholic haze, she gives me a bright, desperate smile, her eyes at once burning and blurred. To my distorted sight she looks like one of those hideous folded-in cubist portraits in which the face is presented simultaneously full-on and in profile, you know the kind of thing I mean. With perfect calm and no surprise I see that she is mad. "He smells of almonds," she said, "Mr Mandelbaum." Her smile stopped as if a light in her face had been switched off and she picked up her glass—or was it mine?—in both hands and drank deeply of the dark wine, watching me above the rim. The lunch things had been cleared, and I was holding a glass of . . . what is it? Grappa again, it must be. The sun was burning the back of my neck. How was it that no one seemed to have noticed that for some time I had not been here? Where was it I had been? In Prague, yes, with Kristina Kovacs, in her salmon-coloured slip. Cass Cleave, her head back and throat throbbing, finished the last of the wine in a great gulp and set down the glass with a bang and looked at me again. Her expression had gone lopsided, as if the profile half of the portrait now had slipped a fraction. She stood up unsteadily and turned and plunged off into the dim interior of the restaurant. The awning flapped, a car roof flashed. Kristina Kovacs cleared her throat and stirred. "You say she is writing your life?" she said, doubtfully. Franco Bartoli smirked at that. "She is your biographer?" he said to me. "Ah." He palmed another smirk. "Ah, I see." With his shiny bald brow and pouting mouth and scant, soft, downy, slightly reddish beard, he has the look, little Franco, of a rare and precious domestic animal, spoilt and ill-tempered from too much coddling. The rimless spectacles perching on the bridge of his neat nose were almost invisible. I wonder why it is that I despise him so. He began to speak now, in a tone of hushed and sibilant fury, of a fashionable French scholar who had agreed to come to the conference and give a paper and then had cancelled at the last minute. "Nearly alike," I said loudly, interrupting him. "Your Frenchman. Bator, Bartoli: nearly the same." I laughed, and held my grappa glass aloft and waggled it at the waiter leaning sullenly against a vine-clad trellis. "Bator the gnome," I said. "I met him once. Nasty, brutish, and short." The place had emptied, we were the last customers. I could hear myself breathe, a low, stertorous roaring, as if there were a bellows working inside my skull, always in me a sign of incipient drunkenness. There was a watery glare on the white tablecloth, and the objects on it, knife, fork, oil bottle, pepper grinder, stood each one at an identical angle to its own shadow, looking as if they had been set there just so, like chessmen, or runes for me to read. The waiter, scowling, brought the bottle of clear poison, poured; I drank. I tried to light a cigarette and fumbled the match and scorched my fingers and swore. Bartoli and Kristina Kovacs were looking at me in an odd, not to say alarming, somehow mechanical, fashion, sitting very still, very straight, like a pair of magistrates, their hands folded before them on the table, their eyes unblinking. "I know you killed your wife,"

Franco Bartoli said. I coughed, spluttering grappa. "What?" I croaked, gagging. "What?" Kristina Kovacs patted me solicitously on the back. "He says," she said, "you dropped your knife." Sure enough, there it was, the knife, on the ground; its blade, seen there between my knees, had an evil, knowing gleam. I leaned down to pick it up. Kristina Kovacs rose, purse in hand. I made to grab her; I demanded to know where she was going, afraid suddenly to be left alone with Franco Bartoli. She directed a small, dry smile at me. "I am going to see what has become of your biographer," she said. She made her way between the tables and went into the restaurant, where Cass Cleave had gone before her. Franco Bartoli with a fingertip rolled a bread crumb back and forth slowly on the tablecloth, pensive and tense. "You know she is dying," he said, and looked at me. "Kristina, I mean." His eyes were invisible behind the sunlight flashing on the lenses of his spectacles. And at once I understood that he and Kristina Kovacs were lovers. It came to me, just like that; excess of drink often has a clairvoyant effect on me. How long had the affair been going on, I wondered? Perhaps—and somehow this was funny—perhaps it had only just begun, perhaps as recently as last night. Franco must have seen the light of realisation in my face, for he lowered his eyes quickly and began rolling another pellet of dough, more agitatedly this time. I pictured them in bed after the act, Kristina unsleeping and disconcertingly tearful, and Franco with his pot belly and his little-boy's hands, his shoes with the lifts in them tucked discreetly under the bed, making a silent rictus as he stifled yet another yawn; then, out of the dark, Kristina's awful, blurted announcement of her illness, and Franco thinking at once of the dry feel of her flesh and the brown stench she had panted out of her already failing lungs while he was bouncing up and down on her, and he would want to leap up and flee back along the trail of his discarded clothes between bed and door, and run down the hotel corridor, the stairs, along the street, out of the city itself, away! but having instead to lie there, paralysed with dismay, not daring to stir a finger for fear of bringing everything, this woman, her distress, her life and impending death, all crashing down around his unwilling ears. Then the hours of talk, all her terrors tumbling out, her anguish, using up the air in the room until he could barely breathe. Would she have told him about that afternoon with me in Prague, the drapes drawn and she crying out and my dead leg between her thighs thumping its grotesque tattoo on the mattress? She would; oh, she would. "Have a drink," I said to him, smiling almost fondly into his face. "Have a drink with me, Franco, for the sake of old times." He would say nothing, and would not lift his eyes. "I know you killed her," he said in a whisper hoarse with hate. "I know you did."

Kristina came back then, frowning. "The girl," she said, and looked at me. "I asked through the door, but she told me to go away. She sounded . . ."

There are moments, I know them well, when all goes lax and vacant suddenly, as if all the air had rushed out of things, and the people caught in the moment hesitate, feeling displaced, jostled somehow to one side of themselves. Kristina Kovacs put her purse on the table. Franco Bartoli made as if to rise from his chair but changed his mind, and for some reason looked faintly abashed. I leaned far back and peered upward, expecting something to be there, above me, but saw only the swarming air, and the edge of the awning and a tracery of leaves wreathed through with the smoke from my cigarette, and an invisible jet, very high, inscribing its gradual double chalk-mark across the zenith. That breeze again. The sun on the parked cars. The river, shining.

Cass Cleave stepped out from the dimness of the restaurant, her head down, falteringly. She stopped a moment and looked about, holding up a shielding hand and squinnying her eyes against the glare, as if this—the empty tables, the trellis of vine, the three of us looking at her—as if this were not at all where she had expected to find herself. She came forward, negotiating her way between the chairs—they might have been so many crouching animals—and stopped beside me, bracing the steepled fingers of one hand on the table and leaning forward at a teetering angle. She began to speak but her voice would not work and she laughed instead, inanely, snuffling. There was a bad scrape on her elbow beaded with blood and her dress was stained. I reached out and seized the hand she was not leaning on and tried to use it as a lever to lift myself up but could not, and fell back on the chair, and closed my eyes.

The last gift I ever gave to Magda, one of the very few things I bought for her—like most displaced persons I have a distrust of material possessions—was an ornate and absurdly expensive glass vase. I had, uncharacteristically, I suppose, remembered that this year marked the fortieth anniversary of our life together, and although her mind by now was almost gone I thought that I should mark the occasion. In the shop, a narrow box of plate-glass and angled steel on Euclid—am I alone in experiencing the peculiar and inexplicable soreness of heart that attends the purchase of a gift?—the vase had looked a fine and fetching thing, tall and slender, the pale-green glass shot through with fat coils of a clouded, sugar-coloured whiteness. However, when it had been installed in the living room for a week or two the green of the glass took on a snotlike hue, while the swirls of frozen white syrup made me feel slightly nauseous if I kept them in sight for long enough, and I came to regard it as somehow malignant, even menacing. I wanted to get rid of it, but I could see that Magda had become attached to it in all its horrid viridescence, which must, for her, have been a radiance piercing enough to strike even through the mists of her hopelessly distracted comprehension. She would sit and gaze at it for long hours, in placid quietude, and I did not have the heart to take it outside the back door and dash it to smithereens on the ground, as I was convinced I ought to do. The vase in its turn must have found me equally repulsive, or else must have felt my animosity to be unbearable, and decided to put us both out of our distress. Here is what happened; really, the oddest thing. On the day after Magda's death I was reclining on the sofa in the dimness of the lounge, awash in my new state of widowhood—the word still sounds wrong, applied to a man—with a bag of ice on my brow and a steadily diminishing bottle on the floor beside me, when a loud report, sharp and incontrovertible as a gunshot, brought me rearing up in fright, like the man-monster arching on his table when the big blue spark leaps between the conducting rods. I scrambled upright and swayed at a drunken list into the living room to investigate, thinking, in my befuddled state, of Officer Blank—remember him?—and that blunt blue pistol of his, stuffed full with live rounds. It took much fruitless peering and searching before at last I discovered what had occurred. The vase had shattered, not into fragments in the way that glass should, but into two almost equal halves, vertically, and remarkably cleanly, as if it had been sliced down the middle by an immensely swift diamond blade or a powerful, unearthly ultra-ray. As I may already have remarked, I am not of a superstitious nature—or was not, since this was before Magda's ghost had begun haunting me—and I knew that it was simply that there must have been a fault in the glass, a crack so fine as to be invisible, that had succumbed at last to an infinitesimal shift in air temperature or change of atmospheric pressure. I thought, with a pang almost of remorse, of the once-hated thing standing there, day after day, suffering my baleful glances and the hours of Magda's fond but perhaps no less assailing gaze, locked motionless in agonised struggle with the irresistible forces of the world working on it, straining to hold itself together for another hour, another minute, another few seconds, the last few, of wholeness and poise. I am thinking, of course, of Cass Cleave. For that is how it was with her, too, she was another tall, tense, fissile vessel waiting to be cloven in two.

❧

In the lavatory she had suffered one of her seizures. She did not remember falling, only the familiar, faint smell, dry and sweet, and the voices in her head suddenly starting all together to say something. The stall was cramped and dirty and when she collapsed she grazed her arm on something, although she did not feel the pain of it. Then the Kovacs woman was tapping at the door and saying her name, and she got herself up somehow and wadded a handful of tissue and scrubbed at the hem of her dress where it was stained from the filth on the floor. It was one of her worst fears that one day she would pass out in some foul place like this and not come round until someone had found her, wedged between the stool and the door with her pants around her knees. When she came out into the sun she felt fluttery and light, and the air seemed to have turned into another medium, a kind of bright, viscous fluid that both sustained and hindered her. It was always like this after an attack, the sense of everything around her being different, as though she had stepped through a looking-glass into the other, gleaming world that it contained. When Vander wrenched himself around in his chair and grabbed her hand she felt an infirm tremor run down his arm, it might have been the last of his life draining out of him, and when his head fell forward on to the table with a frightening bang she thought that he was surely dead. Her father's mother had died in his arms after he had fallen asleep holding her and even that, his mother dying, had not woken him. To be gone like that, without a sound, like slipping out of a room and turning and quietly closing the door; in her mind she saw a hand, it was hers, slowly relinquish the polished knob and her miniature, curved reflection on it shrink to a dot of darkness and disappear. To be gone.

At Vander's collapse Kristina Kovacs and Franco Bartoli sprang up at once and began to bustle about like mechanical figures, as if his fall had somehow switched on a motor and set their parts moving. Kristina Kovacs touched Bartoli on the wrist and he turned aside quickly to go, buttoning his jacket. She said nothing to him, and he nodded rapid acknowledgement of what she had not said. He muttered something in Italian: was it a prayer, perhaps, or was he cursing his bad luck in being here? He glanced at Vander where he lay slumped forward with his head on the table and his arms hanging down past his knees, and nodded again and said that, *si, certo,* he would go and fetch the car. And he went away, hurrying, with short, purposeful steps, a hand pressed flat against the side pocket of his jacket. Vander produced, as if in scornful comment, a loud, rolling belch that ended in a groan. Kristina Kovacs moved to his side, and, as Cass Cleave looked on, put her hands on his shoulders and with an effort drew him upright on his chair. He groaned again, more loudly, lolling. Kristina Kovacs spoke softly, as to a child, in a language Cass Cleave did not recognise, and then with a strange, sorrowing gesture she extended her arm all the way around his head in a sort of wrestler's hold, but tenderly, and drew him to her, until his forehead was resting against her midriff. His eyes were shut and his mouth was open, and there was a trickle of drool on his chin. Cass Cleave was sharply aware that there was something she wanted to say, or ask, but she could not think what it was, or whom she might address, and anyway here came Franco Bartoli in his little bright-red car, pulling up at the kerb.

Between the three of them they got Vander to his feet and heaved him across the pavement to the car, wheeling him forward lurchingly on his corners as if they were walking a wardrobe. Then there was the difficulty of getting him into the low front seat. He was a dead weight, yet in the midst of the struggle, as she leaned under him to support him, her neck wedged into his hot, damp armpit, Cass Cleave heard him chuckle to himself, or thought she did. Even when they had got him into the seat at last his stiff leg kept rolling out again, with comic obstinacy, until Bartoli braced it with the toe of his dainty shoe and at the last moment, like a penalty kicker in reverse, pulled his foot back smartly and slammed the door. They were about to drive away when the waiter came running with the bill they had forgotten to pay, and Bartoli, the wings of his nostrils turning white with fury, had to get out and wave the fellow's complaints aside and thrust a wad of money into his hands. At the hotel, when they were manoeuvring the drunk man up the steps, the automatic glass door kept opening wide with doltish promptness and immediately swinging shut again, as an outflung elbow or a splayed foot temporarily broke the beam of its electronic eye, while in the narrow street a line of backed-up vehicles bellowed and fumed behind Bartoli's abandoned, cowering little car. In the bedroom Franco Bartoli, with Vander's arm clamped on his neck, lost his footing and began to topple over, slowly, quakingly, and to keep themselves from falling they all three had to let go their hold on Vander, who stood swaying for a moment and then pitched forward and crashed face down on the bed with the force of a felled tree. Cass Cleave went and sat down quietly on a chair, and Bartoli stepped back, panting, and brushing his hands down the front of his jacket and hitching his lapels, like a chucker-out who has just succeeded in throwing a particularly truculent trouble-maker into the street. Kristina Kovacs had got Vander on to his back on the bed now and was taking off his shoes. Cass Cleave, trembling, stood up and went to the window and pulled the curtains closed against the daylight, not knowing why she did it, except that it seemed the necessary thing to do. Suddenly shadowed, the room took on a devotional aspect, and Vander's form supine on the bed and the two spectral people standing by him might have been, she thought, the figures at the centre of an altar-piece.

Kristina Kovacs was looking about her with interest, frowning, as if she had just realised that this was the place where she had lost something once, and were wondering if it might be here still. Franco Bartoli, anxious to be gone, plucked at her sleeve, trying to draw her toward the door. He told Cass Cleave that he would telephone later, and she nodded; she wanted them to go away now, quickly. But at the doorway Kristina Kovacs lingered, still with that distracted frown. "He should not drink," she said, as if to herself, shaking her head. "He really should not drink." Bartoli took her arm then in both his hands and pulled her after him into the hall. However, they must have stopped at the front desk on their way out, for presently, as Cass sat quietly by the bed in the room's sanctified stillness, there came a sharp tap at the door, and a very thin, elegant, elderly man in a pale, shining suit stepped inside. He was, he said, the doctor, making it sound as if there were only one doctor in all the city. He had an Eastern look. His face was swarthy, thin and fleshless, his eyes were dark but not unkind; his sparse hair was dyed black and heavily oiled, and had a fragrant smell, of sandalwood, she thought, although she was not sure she knew the smell of sandalwood. He was carrying a real doctor's bag that snapped open like the thick-lipped mouth of a fish, releasing an ancient and familiar odour. She looked as closely as she dared at the strangely radiant, pearly cloth of which his suit was made; it was less like cloth than a kind of metal, marvellously fine and soft, shining at all angles in the light of the bedside lamp. He waited while at his direction she unknotted Vander's tie and opened his shirtfront, then sat down on the side of the bed with one foot raised and resting on its toe, and listened to Vander's heart, and lifted his eyelids and shone a light into his eyes, and looked into his ears with the light, and prised open his mouth and looked in there, too. Then he took out of the depths of his bag an old-fashioned metal syringe with a glass barrel, and a small glass phial of clear liquid and held the phial upside down and inserted the needle through the rubber seal that was, she noted with interest, exactly the same colour as the inner tube of a bicycle wheel; perhaps, she thought, it was made from the same kind of rubber, and she marvelled again at how despite their seeming disparity so many things are secretly the same. The doctor was working Vander's arm up and down at the elbow like the handle of a water pump. Then there was the business with the swab of cotton that always made her shiver. She watched as the needle first made a dent in the flaccid skin and then broke through and sank smoothly at an angle into the vein. When he had put away the needle and the empty phial the doctor sat for a long moment motionless, as if it were to him and not to Vander that the calmative had been administered. Then he looked at her. "And you," he said, "you have hurt yourself?" He pointed to the scrape on her elbow. "I fell," she said. He nodded, and took her hand in his; his long, slender fingers were dry and smooth, like jointed lengths of smooth, dry wood; with his other hand he made a peculiar gesture, moving it sideways, up and back, imparting a sort of blessing, it might be. His breath smelled of tobacco and something warm and sweet. In the quiet of the room the only sound was Vander's soft and steady breathing. The doctor peered closely at the graze on her arm but then seemed to lose interest and released her hand and looked away again, thinking. She imagined where he might live. In her mind she pictured it, the big, silent, gloomy apartment, smelling like him of tobacco smoke and sandalwood and that sweetish something, with big, dark, vague furniture, and photographs in tarnished silver frames show- ing pale, solemn-faced children, his brothers and sisters, dead or scattered now, and stern-eyed elders, his father, thin like him, in a high collar, his mother as a girl, wistful and wan. How could there be so many people in the world, she wondered, so many lives? Not to mention the countless dead.

"He will sleep," the doctor said, looking askance at Vander, and then at her again, and smiled, as if it were a magic trick that he had worked. "He will sleep, and then, in the morning, he will wake."

He went away. She sat again on the chair by the bed with her hands in her lap and listened to the sounds of the day subsiding around her, a long, languishing, myriad-voiced sigh. The crack in the curtains turned from molten white to amber to a rich, arabian blue. The last time she had watched over Vander sleeping he had seemed to elude her, drifting out of himself in that strange way, but now, unconscious rather than asleep, he was more vividly pres- ent than if he had been awake; lying like that on his back, with his eyes closed, frowning, as if he were concentrating on some puzzle or problem, he somehow populated the room, making it seem there were others here besides him and her, a silent, unseen gathering. But perhaps it was not Vander who was making this effect, perhaps these were not his phantoms, but hers. She went to the window and looked out and up, and saw the moon's scurfy silver face gloating over the city.

Later, Vander woke up. At first he did not know where he was or what had happened. She told him what the doctor had said. "You are exhausted, and poisoned by alcohol. You must not drink so much." He was not listening. He ordered her to switch on more lights, and when she would not he flailed from side to side on the bed, searching the wall for the switches, but then flopped back on the pillows, groaning in anger and despair. He asked where were Bartoli and Kristina Kovacs, where had they gone to. "I told them you are my father," she said, and he lifted his head sharply and looked at her. "You are mad," he said. "And I am a fool." He demanded that she fetch him things, a glass of wine, food, cigarettes, a book to read, slurring his words, his dead eye wandering in its socket. After a while he fell asleep again. He still looked angry. She pulled the bed covers over him and went to her own room, going warily along the corridors, fearful of encountering a fellow guest, or, worse, one of the hotel staff. She thought there was someone behind every door, ready with a hand on the knob to spring out and . . . she did not know what they might spring out and do, the springing out itself would be enough.

Her room had the look of having undergone a subtle alteration: it was as if a band of intruders had come in and shifted everything around and then put it all back exactly as it had been. She changed out of her soiled skirt, and ran hot water in the bathroom and bathed her grazed elbow. She brushed her teeth, and stood for a long time motionless at the mirror, holding the toothbrush, not looking at herself. She did not know what to do. She returned to the bedroom and sat on the side of the bed and telephoned her mother and told her she was coming home. She kept her hand cupped over the mouthpiece and spoke in a whisper, as if there were someone in the room to overhear her, and her mother had to keep asking her to repeat what she had said. There were silences in which she could hear her mother's breathing. She thought of their voices flying through the darkness, over the city's roofs and then the countryside and then the high, white peaks and then other cities and then the sea and then . . . and then . . . "Your father has left me, by the way," her mother said, with a hard little laugh. "He has gone back to what he still calls home, to live with the ghost of his Mammy." She did not reply. She was wondering how telephones work. Do the wires carry the actual words, or are the words turned into signals, impulses, that are then turned back into words again? How would that be done? There must be a device in every phone to encode what is being said as it is said and to decode it again immediately at the other end. But where would it be, such a device? Would it be in the telephone itself, or in the thing she was holding, the what do you call it, the receiver? "Are you all right?" her mother said, unable to suppress a note of impatience in her voice. Was she all right? She did not know. Gently she hung up, and thought she heard the click of the connection breaking, like a tongue clicking, an instant before the line went dead. So her father had left, at last; she was glad. She waited a moment and picked up the receiver again, wondering why it should be called only the receiver, never the sender. She had not said goodbye. The line snarled softly at her, busy with reproof. Again she hung up, and waited for her mother to call back, hunched forward tensely with her arms tightly folded across her chest, gazing unblinking at the phone. But it did not ring. How could it? She had not told her mother where she was. She thought of the moon that she had looked at from the window in Vander's room, with all that space around it, that darkness.

She made her way back through the hushed, humming corridors. Vander was still asleep. She leaned over him, smelling the sick-room smell he gave off, of ash and candle wax and urine. A tiny, fish-scale glitter was visible between the not quite closed lids of his blind eye. She watched the cords in his throat stretching and straining with each breath he drew. She sat down and resumed her vigil. She was calm now, but she knew she would not sleep. She still had that sensation, that had begun after her seizure at the restaurant, of being afloat, dulled and motionless, like a fish in a stream, while everything rushed past her on all sides, the world itself and all that was in it, dense, clear and swift. What time it was when she heard the child singing she did not know, only that it was late, the middle of the night. Perhaps she had been asleep, after all, in a kind of sleep, sitting there by the bed, for certainly when she heard the child she thought that the sound had wakened her. And as sometimes when the dreamer is suddenly roused the dream vanishes, so now whatever it was that had been going through her head, dream or musings or memories, all vanished on the instant, leaving only this moment, in this room, in the lamp-light, with the old man breathing on the bed and the sound from the corridor of the child, singing. It was not one of her voices, it was outside her, outside the room, real, a thin, high, wordless crooning. She sat and listened to it for a while, unafraid. It was not so much a sound as a part of the silence, a part of the night, there and not there, like darkness, or the air itself. She went to the door and opened it cautiously. She expected to find the child standing out-side, on the very threshold, face lifted, singing to her, but no, there was nothing, and no one. She looked up and down the corridor; it was deserted. She stepped out, and the door shut itself behind her; it was all right, she had the key, Vander's key, she had it in her hand. She walked to where the corridor turned. A faint breeze came from around the turn and put its ineffectual hands against her face, her bare arms. She held back, and saw herself walk forward again. The child was a boy, or a boyish girl, perhaps, very small, a minia-ture being, more like a midget than a child, with a sharp little white face and a cap of black hair coming down on the forehead in a widow's peak. It was sitting, reclining, really, on the carpet, on the floor, outside a door that was shut, in a peculiar, twisted posture, supporting itself on one elbow. It had a sort of doll that it was playing with. Hearing her cautious step it stopped singing at once and looked up at her with a wide, solemn stare, seemingly unsurprised by her appearing like this, silently, on silent feet. Its lower lids hung a little loose of the eyes, so that from where she was standing she could see the inner edges, two narrow crescents of glistening membrane that were the same texture as the little mouth's pink, parted lips. The doll it was playing with was made of wool, a stuffed beige wool torso and beige limbs and a knobbly, bald head, all swollen and worn; the face, she saw, had no features. Losing interest in her, the child resumed its whining song and set the fat doll to a wallowing, drunken dance. She wanted to say something, but she did not think the child would understand her, whatever the language in which she spoke. So she simply stood and watched it playing, and listened to its droning song. Then the door where it was lying was opened inward suddenly, opened wide, with a suck and a gust, and although all she could see of the room was a wedge of lamplight and the leg of a chair, she had a sense of drinks and discarded clothes and smeared supper plates perched on sofa arms. A voice spoke, and was answered from farther within by a lazy laugh, and a man's shirt-sleeved arm came down and grasped the child under its shoulders and lifted it briskly up and in. The last she saw of it were its withered little legs, dangling jointlessly, like the useless nether parts of a ventriloquist's dummy as it is whisked away into the wings under its master's arm at the end of the act. She went back to Vander's room and without undressing lay down beside him on the bed and fell at last into a depthless sleep.

A clatter and crash woke them both at once. It was broad day. For the space of a held breath they lay staring at each other from pillow to pillow in baffled alarm. The crash came again. Cass Cleave rose and drew back the heavy inner curtains and opened wide the two tall panels of the window. A shutter outside had come loose from its catch and was swinging against the wall. There were white horse-tails high in the scoured sky and over the whole city an oceanic wind was pouring in luminous billows. She leaned out and hooked the shutter fast. Vander sat up, bleary and blinking, smacking gummed lips, long strands of white hair floating and flickering about his head like charged electric filaments. "You," he said, glaring at her. "Still here." She did not answer, but came and started to rearrange the bedclothes around him. He made no move to help her, would not even shift his haunches to let her pull the sheet straight. "I am sick," he said. "Was I asleep?" Still she did not answer him. With a groan he got himself out of bed and shuffled past her into the bathroom and slammed the door. The bedclothes when she pulled them back released a stronger waft of his ashy, waxen odour. From the bathroom came the sounds of retching followed by a loud moan of fury and disgust. She went to the window again. In the building opposite a man was leaning out of his window, smoking a cigarette. She could see an office behind him, with a desk and papers and office machines, all stark and shadowless under the unreal, icy glare of strip-lights in the ceiling. They regarded each other for a moment in faint, humorous desperation, like two castaways trapped on their separate islands, the deep, unfordable channel of the street running between them. She could feel the wind buffeting the building.

She was hungry, and went to the telephone to order breakfast. The voice that answered her was shrill and tinny, seeming to come up to her from a series of deeper and still deeper, echoing cisterns. She could not think what to ask for. She thought she could hear the wind rustling in the receiver. The voice from the kitchen, losing patience, said something she could not understand and the line went dead. Vander came out of the bathroom, naked and white-faced and shivering. "I'm sick," he said again, not looking at her, and made for the bed, his shoulders hunched, rubbing his palms together with squeamish vigour, like a trepidant swimmer approaching the dreaded water's edge. There were chocolate-brown moles on his back, and long grey hairs sprouting on his shoulder blades, and the loose flesh of his lop-sided rump wobbled when he walked. She had never seen anyone so huge, so naked and so defenceless. She pondered in mild amazement the mystery of time and time's damagings. Soon, in a very few years, a decade at most, surely, he would be gone, and all that he had been and was now would be no more.

He had got into bed and pulled the covers to his chin. She could see the bristles on his sunken jaw glittering like spilt grains of sand. When the knock came she turned quickly with a wild look as if whoever it was outside might be about to hurl a shoulder against the door and break it down. For a moment she thought in terror that it might be the doctor come back to make sure that she had done all he had told her to do, that Vander was resting, that he had stopped drinking, that the graze on her arm had healed, that everything was as it should be and nothing amiss. It was not the doctor, however, but a waiter, bringing the breakfast she had not ordered. It was all set out on a sort of trolley that he could wheel into the room, leaning forward over it like a billiard player and casting his hooded gaze circumspectly to right and left as he advanced. He was an elderly, bald fellow; she recognised him, she could not for the moment think from where. He glanced from her to Vander behind her in the bed and frowned: there was breakfast only for one. It was all right, she said hurriedly, lifting her hands, it would be enough, it would do. She was afraid she would scream if he said a word, a single word. She contemplated the food with something like despair, helplessly. There were eggs, and cold meats, and slices of pale, glistening cheese, and bread rolls and rusks, and miniature pots of honey and jam, and jugs of milk and hot water with tea bags and sachets of instant coffee, and a big wine glass of impossibly orange orange juice under a frilled paper lid. The waiter wheeled the table to the window and turned it about, setting it just so, aligning it to invisible markers on the floor, and looked at her, and lifted the paper crown from the orange juice glass with a strange, grave movement of his hand, like a priest lifting the white cloth from the chalice, and she recognised him. He was the night porter, the one who had fetched her the glass of water and the napkin—how was it she had not known him straight away, how could she have forgotten? Vander's trunkless head said something to him in Italian that he seemed not to hear, or chose to ignore, and he continued gazing at Cass Cleave out of his dark and melancholy eyes that were just like the doctor's eyes. She scooped a jumble of coins from her purse and gave them to him, and he made a little bow with his head, bobbing it sideways and down with a little grimace denoting gratitude, and pocketed the coins and stepped past her nimbly and went to the door and turned and bowed again and silently, silently, withdrew.

Vander was watching her, turning his head on the pillow to follow her about the room with his eyes. He bade her eat. She brought a chair and sat down before the food. She was not hungry now. She was thinking. She was excited. Her gaze gleamed. She put a tea bag in the cup and poured hot water over it. She nibbled at one of the stale-tasting rusks. "You should not bite your nails," Vander said. "Look at them." They could hear the hot wind gusting outside, and in the room everything seemed taut and thrumming, and they might have been in the cabin of a ship under full-bellied sail. "I did see you come into that lecture room," he said, sullen and accusing, not looking at her now. "It must have been your ghost." She said nothing and took a sip of tepid tea. Thinking. "You came in," he said, "and sat down, and I was talking about the inexistence of the self." Suddenly he gave a loud laugh that ended in a cough, making the bed shake. He drew his hand from under the bedclothes and held it up for her to see. "With this I wrote those articles that you found," he said. "Not a single cell survives in it from that time. Then whose hand is it?" He, I, I saw again the empty bottle on its side, the mauve pills in my palm. I closed my eyes. I listened to the wind washing over the rooftops. The girl rose and came forward and knelt beside the bed and took my hand in both of hers and brought it to her lips and kissed it. I.

∝

It was all so simple, so simple and so clear. She should have seen it from the start. The signs had been there all along, or rather, all along everything had been a sign, those high white peaks glistening in the moonlight that she had glimpsed from the train, the fat man who had almost fallen on her, the flock of pigeons at the station flying up out of shadows into the dawning sky, everything: the strange young woman at the Nietzsche house; the doctor taking her hand and making that sort of blessing over it; the child, singing. She had seen all this and yet not seen it. That was how it always was, with her, she would go along for a long time, just looking, noticing things, taking them in, but not connecting them, not recognising the connections; not understanding. It was only when the waiter had lifted the paper lid off the glass of orange juice, turning his wrist in that slow, solemn way, that at last it had come to her. It was as if a light had switched itself on in her head. Or no, no, it was as if she had been submerged in something dense and dark and suddenly had risen up and broken soundlessly through the surface into the light, the radiance. And it was all so clear, and so simple.

What was not clear was whether the signs were really signs, and meant especially for her, or if they were parts of the thing itself, the thing for which she had no name, yet; those parts, that is, that she was to be allowed to see, to notice, to register. The pattern she had suddenly discerned might be only a superficial aspect of a far deeper and infinitely more intricate order, to which she would never be allowed to penetrate. She would not mind if this were to be so. Indeed, she liked to think that there would be a level she could not reach, could never reach, a mosaic beneath the

mosaic she had uncovered. A mosaic, yes, set in the floor of a temple, and she on her knees, the priestess bound to the shrine by
immemorial, unbreakable vows. She even had her sacred sceptre,
in the form of a fountain pen, with its profane relics wrapped safe
inside it.

She did not expect to be able to understand the full meaning
and significance of what had been . . . of what had been put in
place. If she were to understand, that would mean there was no
mystery, and the mystery was essential. No, she must simply perform the rites in the way that was required. She did not doubt that
she would know the rites and the proper manner of their performance. She would be told. She would be shown. Or it might be
that she was already doing what had to be done, that she had been
doing it all along. It might be that what she did, every smallest
action, was in fact precisely what was necessary, without her
knowing it. Thinking this, she experienced a moment of such
intense—she did not know what to call it—such intense something, that it made her blench. Everything had a meaning, a function, a place in the pattern, and nothing would be lost.

She was glad when Vander in the bed fell into a doze again,
leaving her alone to think. It was to do with him, he was at the very
centre of it, he was that centre itself. Was it that she was meant to
save him? She sat looking down at his ravaged head resting in the
deep pillows as if sunk in gleaming marble. His blue-veined eyelids
were like two miniature globes of the world set into his skull,
mapped all over with the figurations of tiny, blue rivers. She felt
shivery, she was shaking, as if the searing wind blowing outside
were blowing in her, too, sweeping through empty spaces inside
her. She rose as quietly as she could and went out and went to her
room and packed her bag and brought it back to Vander's room.
She was hanging a dress in the wardrobe when she looked in the
mirror in the wardrobe door and saw that he was awake again, and
had turned his head on the pillow and was watching her. He asked
her what she was doing. She said she was unpacking. "I am going to

stay here with you, and take care of you." His gaze was listless and remote. "I dreamt of my wife," he said. "She was with me, here, in the room." He was tired, tired and ill. His brain felt molten, swollen in its bowl of bone. Perhaps he really had suffered a stroke in the street that first day with her, or at that restaurant, yesterday. What would a stroke feel like? He tried to flex his arms, to move his good leg. The covers seemed uncommonly heavy. "I think I am paralysed," he said mildly, and seemed to find the notion almost funny. "I cannot move." Cass Cleave, rearranging his pillows, paused, leaning over him, and looked into his eyes. Is that how it was to be, she asked herself, would that be all her task, simply to take care of him? She saw herself tending here, the bed a sarcophagus and his swaddled corpse topped with its living head; she saw the days rise from dawn to burning noon, then the long, slow fall to evening and the night. The head would speak, it would be the oracle, it would tell her things; she would understand; she would be given to understand; she would know. Suddenly, with an animal quickness, he reached from under the covers again and clamped his clawlike hand on her wrist. His fingers were dry and burning. She looked at the agate nails, striate, chipped. He let her go, his strength failing; his hand withdrawing under the sheet was like an animal slithering away. White weals on her wrist, and then the blood rushing back, under the slackening skin. She bent and put her mouth against his ear, saying something in a hot whisper, saying something I could not make out. Her burning breath. Saying something.

TWO

Come, my ghostly girl, plump up my pillows and sit by me here and I shall tell you a tale, a tale I had thought to think of no more until you brought it all back. It begins long, long ago, in the town of Antwerp, with a stroll along those little winding streets the name to which I gave, inevitably, was the Vander Way. The corner of the square with the plane trees was the crossing point from my world into his. When I think of that spot the weather in it is always grey, the luminous, quicksilver grey of an early northern spring, the colour for me of the past itself. On our side, the street leading up to the square was very narrow, and had to climb a slight incline, at a tilt, the left-hand pavement set higher than its counterpart on the right, giving me a giddy, toppling sensation as I walked up it, always, for some reason, on the lower level. Instead of a shifting church spire and the fragrance of hawthorn blossom I have as memory-points the three golden balls over Wassermann's pawnshop—how did they keep such a high shine, I always wondered, were they made of real gold?—and the warm, cloying aroma of vanilla from the pastry shop on the corner of the square. The big houses in the terrace on the far side, the Vander side, beyond the trees, were tall and brown and many-chimneyed; in the frost-smoke of winter mornings their upper reaches would crumble into dreamy insubstantiality, like the diaphanous edifices in the background to a Memling or a Tintoretto. They had shutters, and wrought-iron balconies, and here and there one of the tall windows would afford a glimpse of the opulent life within: a blazing chandelier, a bowl of roses on an antique table, a slender woman in silk standing with one arm folded and an elbow cupped in the palm of her hand, smoking a cigarette and looking down upon the world with an expression of lazy dissatisfaction. The Vander apartment itself was a numerous succession of high, cool rooms painted silvery white, or Greek blue, or deep, rich red. To my youthful, hungry eye the furnishings, all that brocade and ormolu and dark, gleaming wood, seemed the very epitome of taste and discreet luxury, although I suppose in reality it was just the usual high-bourgeois clutter. The Vanders did not seek to hide the fact of their wealth. Vander senior was a diamond merchant, an occupation that in a city other than ours would have seemed excitingly louche and exotic. He was very shrewd and careful behind a breezy manner. He travelled a great deal, to Amsterdam, Paris, London, and I suspect kept a mistress in more than one of those cities: he had a way of fingering his small moustache and smiling drowsily to himself that betokened a rich mental store of voluptuous images. His wife was a large, fretful woman, soft as a pigeon, big-bosomed and broad-beamed, with very round, starting eyes, of a washed-out blue that was almost colourless, and that gave her a permanent look of surprise and alarm. Everyone addressed her as Mama, even her husband. Axel treated his parents with indulgent disdain, affecting to be amused by their complacencies and pretensions. "Typical of their kind, of course," he would say, and heave a languid sigh. "I know I should hate them, but I can't." The apartment also housed a number of Vander relations, aunts and uncles, a brace of distant cousins, elderly, timid, curiously ill-defined persons, who kept out of sight as much as they could, as if fearing to risk expulsion by drawing attention to themselves. On Sunday evenings they would dispose themselves about the shad-

owy corners of the drawing room to listen with mournful earnestness as Mama Vander sang lieder to the piano accompaniment of
her husband, or sometimes an unwilling Axel. She had a lachry-
mose mezzo voice that quavered perilously on the lower notes.
She favoured the more saccharine songs of Schubert and Robert
Schumann. These recitals would leave Axel shaking with mingled
mirth and exasperation. He was a more than passable pianist.
When we were at school together he had tried to teach me one or
two easy pieces, without success. "Oh, you are hopeless," he would
say, and call me Hanswurst, and make a play of punching me in the
chest. He was right. I could not keep the tunes in my head, and my
outsized fingers—Hanswurst was right—wallowed over the keys
like two huge handfuls of raw sausages.

In those days—I am speaking now, my dear, of fifty years ago,
and more—the Vanders were for me the very ideal of what a family
should be: civilised, handsome, amused and amusing, at ease with
themselves, knowing precisely their position in the world. I see
myself moving amongst them, my face on fire with their reflected
light, like a rough youth who has been invited up from the stew of
groundlings to take part, in however small and passive a role, in
the performance of a marvellous, sophisticated, glittering comedy
of manners. If I had not exactly been spawned in an estaminet, as
the poet so prettily puts it, our place—I would never have thought
to call that low, dim warren an apartment—was the opposite of
where the Vanders grandly resided. Our family shared no candle-
lit Saturday night dinners abuzz with lively dispute and multi-
lingual jokes, enjoyed, or endured, no Sunday song recitals;
shouts, shrieks and the sound of many siblings exchanging ener-
getic blows were our weekend music. We lived an underground
life; I have a sense of something torpid, brownish, exhausted; the
smell is the smell of re-breathed air . . . But I do not intend to
oppress you with reminiscences of my family. It is not that they are
any longer an embarrassment to me—I have so many, more
recent, things to be ashamed of—but because, because, well, I do

not know. Father, mother, my older brothers and sisters, those botched prototypes along the way to producing me, and the many younger ones who were always under my feet, they have in my memory a quaint, outmoded, in some cases badly blurred, aspect, like that of the incidental figures standing about self-consciously in very old photographs, smiling worriedly and not knowing what to do with their hands. Among them I was too big, in all ways; I was the giant whose head threatened to knock a hole in their ceiling, whom they must feed and tend and humour, and encourage away from the windows lest the neighbours look in and be frightened.

I believe I would have thought better of my family, or at least more warmly, if we had been really poor, I mean ghetto poor. There was a touch of desert romance to the real shtetl people one met in the streets round about where we lived, a hint of the tent and the thorn fire and fiddle music and religious gaiety, that we entirely lacked, or had long ago suppressed. We had our own pretensions: my father too was a merchant, although it was not jewels but second-hand clothes that he dealt in. I was, of course, accepted by the Vanders; they had assimilated me; I was Axel's friend, and therefore a special case, exempt from the general distaste—I would not put it more strongly than that—with which the Vanders regarded what in my presence were referred to delicately as *your people.* Over dinner at the apartment Axel's father liked to divert the table with a routine he had developed, involving an archetypal couple, Moses and Rahel, both of which parts he would play in turn, screwing up his eyes and bowing from the shoulders and crooning and rubbing his hands, until his wife, laughing tearfully, would flap her napkin at him and cry, "For shame, Leon, for shame, you will bring a judgment on us!" It did not occur to anyone around that table, not even to me, on the few, treasured occasions when I was invited to dine there, that I should feel insulted or humiliated by what was, after all, only a piece of good-humoured mimicry. Axel too was more than anything else amused to have for a friend a member of that very race whose pernicious influence on the body politic he claimed to reprehend. I say claimed to, because I do not believe that Axel cared in any serious way about these public matters, despite his frequent and bellicose pronouncements on them. Things that did not touch him directly could not be of true, deep, thoroughgoing consequence; it was as simple as that.

He was beautiful, was Axel. Not handsome, you understand, but beautiful. He had the smooth, sculpted, slightly cruel, faintly feminine good looks of one of those French film actors of the day. He knew it, too. He was careful of his hair and his fingernails—I suspect he visited a manicurist—and dressed with the studied negligence of the true dandy. I can see him strolling by the lake in the Nachtegalenpark in Wilrijk on a Sunday morning, in old linen slacks and an open-collared white silk shirt, a cricket pullover—they were enthusiastic Anglophiles, the Vanders—thrown over his shoulders, the arms loosely knotted on his slightly concave chest, and his sunglasses pushed up into that oiled quiff, the colour of polished wheat, the moulding of which must have taken a careful five minutes' work in front of the looking-glass. His girls . . . how I envied him his girls, a long line of them, beginning in early adolescence. The bright, earnest ones in particular fell for him, but he favoured shop girls, secretaries, actresses, and the like; he was always shrewd in choosing whom to allow to view him up close. Did I resent him? Of course I did. I wanted to be him, obviously.

And yet, I despised him, too, a little. Underneath the sparkling talk, the charm, the lavish good looks, there was an entire area inside him that was vacant, vapid, entirely lacking in intellectual conviction and certainty. At moments a wary, almost a frightened, look would register in his eyes. It was the look of a limited being who knows that at any moment his limits might be reached and his narrowness revealed. He was, I am afraid, a dabbler, an opportunist of ideas, in short a dilettante, though no one, especially not I, would have dared to say so. Since I have started along this line I may as well continue: he did not have a first-rate mind, as he and so many others would claim. He was gifted; he was precocious; he could talk, in that allusive, lazy, uninterruptible way of his, but that is what it was, talk, and not much more than that. Nevertheless, great things were forecast for him, he was going to make a great noise in the world, I joined in proclaiming it myself, but I am sure that in my heart I knew better. He was a bright boy who could read fast and had a good memory; ideas, genuine thought, foundered in the shallows of his intellect. He was especially vulnerable to teasing, or anything that smacked of mockery, no matter how fond, and was constantly on the alert for slights of any kind. If in company he thought a joke that everyone was laughing at might have been made at his expense something would thicken in his face, his brow would darken, his gaze turn muddy, and he would fall upon the one who had offended him with the crushing weight and force of a school-yard bully whom a weakling has unwisely dared to cross. These flashes of vengefulness were dispiriting to witness, especially as one's urge to protest and protect sprang instinctively to the defence of Axel and not of his squirming victim. He was one of those people, the beautiful, the vivid ones, whose sense of themselves must be preserved above everything else, so that the rest of us shall not be undone, in ways we cannot quite specify. So his parents spoiled him, the poor relations flattered him, and the rest of us endured without complaint his bright disdain, content if only something of his luminence should reflect on us, and from us. I know, I know, it is not convincing, this patronising tone that I put on when speaking of him. I can still feel the envy and the bitterness, the peculiar, unassuageable, objectless yearning, the anxious and always vain scramble for self-justification, all there, boiling and muddily bubbling inside me, all still there, after so long.

I do not know, or cannot remember, or have suppressed, who it was that approached him to write those newspaper articles. It is scarcely possible that I was the go-between; although at the time I had a foot in the door of a number of papers and periodicals, the *Vlaamsche Gazet* was unlikely to have been amongst them. The paper's editorial attitude was one of noisy and confident anticipation of what it called the Day of Unity, when all the country's unnamed enemies would finally be dealt with. This Day of Unity was never defined, and a date was never put on it, but everyone knew what it would be when it came, and knew who those enemies were, too. The editor, Hendriks—I have forgotten his first name—large, overweight, glistening, with a wheezing laugh and furtive eyes, had, in the early years of that dirty decade that was now coming to a calamitous end, decided in which direction the future was headed, despite the fact that, in private, he expressed nothing but contempt for our immediate and increasingly menacing neighbour to the east. In the early hours, when work was over for the night and the presses were rolling, he would hold court for his writing staff, knuckle-duster nationalists to a man, in the Stoof, next door to the *Gazet* offices on the Nationalestraat, a fine old tavern, still going strong, I am told, although the air must surely be polluted even yet by the lingering vapours of Hendriks and his gang. There he would squat, in his special corner, banging his special pewter stein, sharing gossip and telling jokes and spitting when he laughed, his womanly bosom wobbling. It was Axel who brought me there. I suppose he was curious to see how I would fare, how I would defend myself, among that feral gathering. For the most part I was kept firmly off at the outer edge of things, where I circled, hungry as a hyena, always on the watch for an opening through which I might dart and get my head, too, into the smoking innards of the times. I would catch Axel glancing at me now and then, with that charmingly crooked half-smile of his, amused at my avidity, my glittering eagerness. My presence did nothing to tone down the rabid talk or curb Hendriks's yid jokes; it was all in fun, we were all hearty fellows here, thick of skin and merciless of purpose, and besides, to pay special consideration to those of us whose origins were . . . different, would have been really to offer insult, surely? As Hendriks was fond of repeating, his eyes skittering sideways, the issue was not Race, but Culture, our Great European Heritage. Now, isn't that so? yes? yes? the pewter stein banging, those fat bubs bobbing. And Axel would nod along with the others, and look at me sidelong again from under his pale lashes, and smile, and faintly shrug.

When those articles of his began to be published I was jealous, I will not deny it. Why had Hendriks not invited me to write for his paper, instead of Axel? I would have been far fiercer on the threat to our—their!—culture that my people were supposed to represent, if it had been asked of me. Yes, I would! I was tougher than Axel, more relentless, more daring, more vicious. I would have sold my soul, I would have sold *my people,* for one sustained moment of the public's attention, even if it was only in a rag like the *Gazet.* Why did they turn to him, to Ariel, when in me they had a more than willing Caliban? Those half-dozen articles he wrote were much too elaborated and opaque for what was required of them. But that was how it was: people like Hendriks, even brutes like him, were mesmerised by that mixture of self-esteem and false diffidence that Axel displayed, by that remote, amused, knowing air that enveloped him and into which he would retreat, like Zarathustra into his cloud, leaving only a soft laugh behind him. To me the last piece of the six that he wrote was the sharpest refinement of the insult, the blob of poison smeared on the sharp end of the series. It was cast in the form of an interview with me—with *me!*—as a typical specimen of dissatisfied intellectual youth. He wrote not only the questions but most of the answers, and freely modified the few opinions that he did allow me to express. Why did I let him do it, why did I let him put words into my mouth? Abject, abject, abject; how they rankle, these old self-betrayals. When the so-called interview appeared, and I saw our photographs accompanying it, printed side by side, I was shamefully, chokingly, unconfessably, proud, although at the same time childishly gratified that Axel's picture was a bad one—he could look quite peaky and anxious in certain lights—and his name underneath it misprinted.

For all my protests, though, I am compelled, in bitter spite of myself, to admit that he did a more successful job as a polemicist than I would have done. It was his very restraint, his scrupulousness, what one might call his insistent tact, that gave those *feuilletons* their force. I would have ranted, mocked, hurled abuse, amid shrill peals of forced Mephistophelean laughter. The poise and studied distance of Axel's style, with its high patrician burnish and flashes of covert wit—it could take two or more readings to get one of Axel's jokes—the attitude of aristocratic weariness, the sense that he was writing only because world-historical duty had dragged him to his desk and thrust the pen into his hand, these were the things that made him so effective, or would have, had he been addressing a serious audience and not the rabblement who read the *Gazet,* moving their lips as they did so. What can they have made, for instance, of his call for the *aestheticisation of national life,* or his suggestion to them that they might *escape the plight of the self by sublimation in the totalitarian ethic?* Music to their thick ears, though, simple and rousing as a marching tune, must have been his suggestion—one could hear one of Axel's studiedly otiose sighs rustling amid the words like a breeze in the grass—that nothing of consequence would be lost to the cultural and intellectual life of Europe, really, nothing at all, if certain supposedly assimilated, oriental elements were to be removed and settled somewhere far away, in the steppes of Central Asia, perhaps, or on one of Africa's more clement coasts.

Mama Vander's pill-box was the first thing I ever stole—a surprisingly intense little thrill—although of course I did not think of it as stealing, only borrowing. I saw it there, in a drape-hung anteroom in the Vander apartment, resting on the edge of a pedestal that bore a bust of Goethe, where Mama Vander had put it down in passing and forgotten it; the silver glint of it was as inviting as a wink. I pocketed it without thinking, without breaking my stride. I needed money, and quickly, for there were books I was anxious to buy while there was still time, before they were banned from the shops, or consigned to the pyre. I intended to tell Axel what I had done, after I had redeemed the box, thinking it would surely amuse him, but I never did, tell him, I mean. What kept me silent was a sense of gravity, not the gravity of my misdemeanour, but of the thing itself: the stolen object, I discovered, takes on a mysterious weight, becomes far heavier than the sum of the materials of which it is made. That little box—all it contained was a few of the sugared violet pastilles that its owner, its former owner, was addicted to—was so ponderous in my pocket it made me feel I must list to that side as I hurried away with my purloined prize. I did not delay in getting rid of it. It turned out to be a valuable piece, French, early eighteenth century; old Wassermann was reluctant to part with it, I could see, when I came back to redeem it. After that I kept it, for many years, through all manner of vicissitude and loss, and although in time it ceased to be as emblematic as once it had been, it never quite shed that unaccountable, undue weightiness. Now it has disappeared, made off stealthily without my noticing, in that mysterious way that objects have of escaping one's disregardant grasp.

That was the last time I was in the Vander apartment, the time I stole the pill-box. The theft was not the reason for my banishment; I am not sure it was ever detected, or, if it was, that I was held to be the culprit. In those days of invasion, defeat, occupation—all of which dizzying disasters came quickly to be referred to primly as *the events*—I was no longer as welcome among the Vanders as I had once been. Nothing was said, of course, but there was a constriction that occurred in the atmosphere now when I entered those spacious, overheated rooms that my heightened sensibilities could not but register. So I withdrew. The break was decorous, and went unremarked, on both sides. It is a curious thing, how even the most violently disrupted circumstances will quickly improvise and impose their own rules of mannerliness. In the early days, after it had sunk in that *les événements, de gebeurtenissen,* were irreversible and would somehow or other have to be lived with, there was a certain small smile, wry, rueful, pained, accompanied by a flicker of the eyes heavenward, that people would exchange at unwontedly difficult moments, such as when some new and seemingly capricious edict had been announced, restricting the movement or meeting of persons, or imposing yet more levies on this or that section of society, most usually that section to which I belonged. At first these measures were merely an annoyance. We suffered them, having no choice, while at the same time we strove at least to maintain the appearance of disdaining them. However, as the months went on, life in those mean little streets on the wrong side of the square became increasingly attenuated, until we seemed truly to be living on air. We had a sense of floating above ourselves, buffeted now this way, now that, the frail tethering lines jerking and straining with each new ordinance that was issued against us. We grew lighter and lighter as all that we possessed was taken from us, article by article. One week we were forbidden to ride on trams, the next to ride on bicycles. One Monday morning it was ordered that every household must hand up so many men's suits, women's dresses, children's overcoats; at noon the order was rescinded, without explanation, only to be issued again the next day. We were told we could no longer keep household pets; it was the middle of winter, and, for days, long straggles of people wound their way on foot—no trams for us, remember—along snowbound roads to the designated pound on the outskirts of the city where our dogs and cats and budgerigars were to be put down. Yet in its usual uncaring way, life went on. There was the theatre, there were concerts to go to, and lectures and public meetings to attend, and when all that was put out of bounds to us there were the cafés where we could meet and talk, and then when even talk was proscribed there was the wireless, bringing news from elsewhere, all those elsewheres, crackling along the airwaves. Music broadcasts I treasured especially; they came from Stuttgart, Hilversum, Paris, sometimes London, even, if the atmospherics were right. The music was, well, the music, but how strangely affecting it was in the intervals to hear the stir and heave of the audience as it relaxed for a minute, all those people, so far away, and yet magically here, their presence so palpable I might be sitting in their midst. Even yet I cannot hear in the concert hall the sound of that murmurously expectant concourse without being transported immediately back across half a century to the little wallpapered living room with the tasselled tablecloth and the lampshade the colour of dried skin, and the big wooden wireless set with the Bakelite knobs and the canvas grille and the single, glowing green cat's-eye pulsing and contracting, and the blurred music pouring into the room and filling it like a luminous fog. I could not but hate them, too, of course, those audiences; they seemed to my ear so at ease, so lumpenly careless of all they had and I did not, here, where all around, stealthily, the world was closing in, armed with cudgels and flaming torches.

Axel and I continued to meet, not as often as before, away from his home, away from the Stoof, and away from the shtetl people, too, needless to say. We met on neutral ground, while there still remained ground that could be called neutral. His attitude toward me, at least in the early days of *de gebeurtenissen,* was one of affability tinged with impatience, restrained exasperation. He would tap me on the wrist, not unfondly, and accuse me of being overly alarmist in the face of my plight and that of my people. "Yes yes yes," he would say, with a frowning smile, waving a hand, "I am aware of all that, I read the papers too, you know." But surely, he would go on, surely I must agree that something had to be done, that matters could not go on as they had been doing? And even if people were to be sent away somewhere, would that be so bad? They might thrive, in a climate better suited to their temperament and racial characteristics. Anyway, it would only be the trouble-makers who would go, them, and perhaps the sick, the very old, the mad, the syphilitic. They would be sent to Heligoland, to the Tatra Mountains; Hendriks had told him for a fact that only last week a thousand had been put on a ship at the Hook of Holland bound for South America. And in any case, Axel said, why was I worrying? I was safe, I was his friend. Had not our photographs appeared side by side in *De Vlaamsche Gazet*?

What could I say to him, what reply? He could not know that sense I had now when I ventured beyond our side of the square of being crouched in hiding behind myself even as I walked down one of his streets, sat in one of his cafés, listening to him tell me, with an irritated rictus, that this was just the trouble with me, with all of my people, this hysteria, this cringing and complaining, this constant, kicked-dog whining. Why had we not thought of the consequences before we infiltrated the banks and the judiciary and the government ministries until they were full to bursting with our secret, burrowing brood? It was all perfectly straightforward, perfectly obvious. Something had needed doing, as he had always insisted, and now it was being done. How could we not have seen what was coming, until it had arrived in our midst, clanking and smoking? Anyway, it would all soon be over and done with. That things were bad, and would get worse, he did not deny; most likely the last act would be bloody—"As it always," with a flash of small, square, white teeth, "is"—but when all the bodies had been dragged by the heels into the wings, how clean and free and filled with possibilities would be that emptied stage! While he was saying these things he looked me calmly in the face, shaking his head a little, with that smile, as if he were recounting to a child in simplified terms the plot of a tragedy the convolutions of which only grown-ups could properly disentangle. The possibility did not seem to occur to him that the directors and the stage managers of all this drama might end up by bringing the house down. I was embarrassed—yes, really, I was embarrassed, for myself, and for him. This, mark you, this was that same Axel Vander whose monograph on Heine which he wrote when he was seventeen had provoked more than one wise professor to mumble into his beard of the arrival in our midst of a new Hofmannsthal. What would I find to say if, one day, I were to be called upon to help him exonerate himself, when at last, slapping a hand to his forehead, he should come to his senses and see all this present foolishness and vile fantasy for what it was? He had put himself among fanatics and barbarians, the most reasonable-seeming of whom would in an instant turn a perfectly mild-mannered conversation into ranting, stamping theatrics. One quickly learned to spot in these people the signs of an incipient tirade: the reddening brow, the glazing eye, the bullish thrusting forward of the head. Women were some of the worst, adding to male fury their dash of hysteria and sexual revulsion. I was in bed one afternoon with an actress—porcelain face, bobbed hair, mouth like a scarlet insect, one of Axel's cast-offs—who halted in the middle of the act itself and lifted herself above me, her braced arms shaking from the strain and her little breasts trembling, and told me in tones of florid indignation how the previous night a *vuile jood* in a fur-collared coat had accosted her at the stage door and offered her money to come to his house and do with him what she would have realised, had she thought for a moment, was exactly the thing that she was doing now, here, in this bed, with one of the impudent fellow's pure-blooded brethren.

And yet, and yet . . . How often in my life have I said those words, *and yet*? Everything has to be qualified. The fact is, a part of me, too, was of Axel's camp. Oh, yes. Here it is, my deepest, dirtiest secret. In my heart, I too wanted to see the stage cleared, the boards swept clean, the audience cowed and aghast. It was all for love of the idea, you see, the one, dark, radiant idea. Aestheticise, aestheticise! Such was our cry. Had not our favourite philosopher decreed that human existence is only to be justified as an aesthetic phenomenon? We were sick of mere life, all that mess, confusion, weakness. All must be made over—made over or destroyed. We would have, I would have, sacrificed anything to that transfiguring fire. I whisper it: *and I still would*. The people who turned my people to ash, they were the ones I hoped would win; I regret it yet that they lost. Are you shocked? It was not those posturing brutes themselves I wanted to see victorious—for them, vulgarians to a man, if man is the word, I felt only revulsion—but the Idea that they insensately carried, like the wooden horse with its secret force of Argives. Do you see, my Cassandra? Something had been smuggled into the world, something terrible and true, which must be allowed to prevail, at whatever cost. True: yes. Never mind the necessary lies. In time they would have been dispensed with, along with the liars. Only let the Idea triumph, the great instauration begin!

How, you will ask, did I square with the terrors of everyday life these murky longings for an apocatastasis? For certainly among my people everyone was afraid, myself no less than the others. Fear is mostly a transient thing, it flashes out in the dark at the thought of death, or on the empty road at night, or in the imminence of fire or flood; the human animal is not equipped to live constantly in fear, the system cannot sustain it. Yet for the best part, the worst part, of two years, we were frightened almost all of the time. Fear burned in us unquenchably. There were periods when it was no more than a smouldering coal lodged at the base of the breast bone, then suddenly it would leap up in jagged sheets of flame, leaving behind a hot fall of cinders. These were the poles of existence for us: consuming, irresistible terror, or a sort of gluey apathy, with intervals of futile rage in between. Frenzied hope would expire into exhaustion, indifference; days that began with us crowded in hopeful excitement around a newspaper headline would see us at nightfall lolling in blank-eyed stupor like the addicts in an opium den. Headaches, stomach cramps, a constant churning in the gut, these were the body's protests at the insupportable strain of living always in fear. One suffered from an incontinence of the emotions. The slightest kindness, the slightest nod of seeming sympathy, could bring one to one's knees in grovelling appreciation. There was that gasp of gratitude we could not restrain when someone of the ones in authority over us chose to relent in the prosecution of some trivial order of the day. I heard myself doing it, that gasp, even with Axel, on those occasions, rare enough, when he would express indignation at a particularly egregious piece of petty-minded cruelty that had been ordered to be inflicted on our side of the square. His quizzical glance and silent turning away from my breathless earnests of gratefulness, however, were as jarring a rebuff as would have been an unceremonious push in the chest from someone else.

Despite all that I have said so far, I do not think harshly of him. When he died I believe I would have wept, for shock, if nothing else, were I the type to weep.

✄

I learned of his death from the newspaper, a couple of paragraphs on an inside page of the *Staandard*. Perhaps it was the way I chanced upon the item that prevented me from absorbing its contents straight away. I had been sitting on a park bench, in coat and muffler, and was about to get up and leave, the late-autumn day having turned bitterly cold, and had snapped wide the pages of the paper in outspread arms prior to folding it, when all at once the thing turned into a winged messenger and thrust Axel's name at me, alone out of all those columns of print. My first reactions were the usual ones—it must be some error, a case of mistaken identity, maybe even a practical joke—accompanied by an odd, lifting sensation in the chest, a sort of dreadful exhilaration. Giddily I read that pair of paragraphs again. They were frustratingly, scandalously and, I thought, deliberately vague. It seemed to be that he had died violently, but whether by accident or at the hands of some person or persons was not made clear. The anonymous reporter had chosen his phrases with care—tragic demise of, friends shocked at, great loss to—as if he had been advised to go cautiously in the matter, and were covertly passing on the same advice to his readers. I jumped up from the bench, rolling the paper into a wad and stuffing it guiltily into my pocket, and walked swiftly out of the park, pulling the upturned collar of my overcoat tight around my chin and resisting the urge to take to my heels and run. It was as if I were personally implicated in Axel's death, without knowing how. Before me an enormous, grape-blue cloud was nudging its way up out of the low west, like a slow, sullen thickening of nameless possibilities.

I threw away the *Staandard* and went in search of the *Gazet*. It was late afternoon, and the first newsstand I came to, on the corner of Maria-Theresialei, was the one kept by the old fellow with the goitre—good God, suddenly I see him, plain as day, in his fingerless gloves and the woollen cap with the earflaps that he always wore—who made a great fuss of retrieving for me from under a pile of grubby magazines what he claimed was the very last copy of the late edition, grumbling under his breath. I took the paper from him and skulked off like a rat with a stolen tidbit. Rounding the corner, I stopped and scanned the pages, once, twice, a third time. There was no mention of Axel. I was surprised not to be surprised.

I went next to the *Gazet* offices, to try to speak to Hendriks. I do not know what I expected of him: I had not seen or heard from him for eighteen months or more. I was kept waiting in the front office for a long time. The familiar smells, of newsprint, ink, paper dust, provoked in me an inward sob of nostalgia, distant relation, it might be, to the grief for my dead friend I supposed I was too shocked to have begun to feel yet. The girl behind the counter who took in classified advertisements pretended not to know me; we used to flirt with each other, in the old days. I turned over the already dry and brittle pages of the previous week's editions, filed in their big wooden clasps. Newsboys ran in and out, whistling. A mad old woman came in from the street and shouted something and went out again. Wind-driven scuds of wet snow were flopping against the windows. I was remembering the walking holiday Axel and I had taken together in the Ardennes before the war, and the little inn we had stumbled on one rainy night, where we sat drinking plum brandy by the light of a log fire and he told me of his plans to write a study of Coleridge's aesthetics; how enthusiastic he was, his eyes shining in the firelight; how young he looked; how young he was, and I, too. He did not live to write that book, and when, years later, I tried to write it instead—to write it for him, as it were—I could not do it either.

Hendriks would not come down, and sent one of his deputies to fob me off. I remembered the fellow's face from those late nights at the Stoof, but could not recall his name. I saw that he remembered me, too; he had the decency not to meet my eye. He was fat, like his boss, and out of breath from the stairs, and leaned against the counter, exaggeratedly gasping, with a hand pressed flat against his chest. When I demanded to know if he knew the circumstances of Axel's death he only shrugged. Everything was confused, he said, no one was certain of what had happened. I pressed him, but he only shook his head, and said again what he had said already. His petulant, brusque tone told me that the *Gazet* had no intention of being associated with this death, one among so many, after all. The girl behind the counter gazed away, tapping a pencil against her teeth, pretending not to be listening. I left, and walked dully through the streets. The snow had stopped, but a big-bellied, mauvish sky hung low over the city, promising a heavy fall later. On a street by the train station an armoured car was stopped, with a trio of teenage soldiers in outsized greatcoats sitting side by side on the front of it, dangling their legs over the edge, like three school truants paddling in a pond. And further along, by the Stadspark, three dead girls in belted, lumpy overcoats with ragged bullet holes across the front, gruesome counterparts somehow to those idling boy soldiers, were tied to the railings with placards hung about their necks on which was daubed a message I did not care to read; I thought of the dead crows, their blue-black plumage rubied with dried blood, that my grandfather long ago would string up on the fences in his cornfields to discourage their ravening fellows.

✧

I never did discover the true circumstances of Axel's death. I thought of asking his family, and went more than once and stood under the trees in the square looking up at the windows of the Vander apartment, but each time my nerve failed me. Then they moved away, or so it seemed, for on the last occasion when I skulked under their windows there was no sign of life within, no lamp burning or vase of flowers on display, only a broken roller blind, hanging down crookedly. I made enquiries of people whom Axel and I had both known, but either they would not speak to me, or claimed not to know any more about what had befallen him than I did. Extravagant rumours began to fly about. Some were too ludicrous to listen to, for example that he had committed suicide when a love affair went wrong—imagine Axel hanging himself, and over a woman! Others were slightly more plausible, but I could not believe them, either. It was said for instance that he was not dead at all, but had been rounded up by mistake with a band of communists and interned at Breendonck, from where his father was seeking to buy his release. A journalist of my acquaintance, of my former acquaintance, whom I encountered in the street late one wet night, drunk and wild-eyed, his face running with rain or tears, it was hard to tell which, grasped me by the lapels and assured me in an urgent, sobbing whisper that Axel had been caught up in a dispute among the factions surrounding the military authorities, that the affair had ended in bloodshed, and that he had been shot and his body flung into an unmarked grave. At the time all sorts of stories like that were in the air, about all sorts of people. Most amazing of all the explanations I heard of Axel's disappearance, however, was the heroic farrago, recounted to me one ice-hung morning in a café on the Groenplaats, in tones of tragic wonderment, by one of his former girlfriends, that he had been betrayed, arrested, tortured, and summarily executed for the leading part he had played in the organisation of an underground Resistance cell. She looked so sorrowful and solemn, saucer-eyed Monique, and the pink-tinged air outside was so still, so coldly lovely, that I could only nod and say nothing, trying not to laugh. Many years later, however, in Arcady, one night at a gruesome academic dinner I found myself seated opposite a withered old fellow with ash on his waistcoat and soup on his tie, a visiting savant from old Europe, of Walloon origin, who on hearing my name became greatly excited and hailed me warmly as a former colleague in arms. Holding him off with what I knew must be a horrible, temporising grin, I studied that time-ruined visage—collapsed cheek and lolling Bourbon lip, moist rheumy eye, the pallid skull smooth and domed like the cap of a giant toadstool—and tried urgently to discern in it the features of one I might once have known or at least have met in Axel's company long ago. No blank-eyed bust stirred in the shadowed gallery of my memory. And what did he think, the old fool, if he really had known Axel and now believed that I was he—that forty years had added a foot or so to his height and turned his film star's profile into that of a superannuated carthorse? The more discouragingly diffident I became the more emotional he waxed, lapsing from laughable English into execrable, macaronic French, reaching infirmly across the table and trying to clasp my crabwise retreating hand, exclaiming the while about *les beaux jours d'antan aux Pays-bas* when, shoulder to shoulder with our *amis ardents,* we wrought havoc upon the military housekeeping of the invading *sale Boche.* He would have worried me more had he not been such a caricature; nevertheless, I extricated myself as quickly as I could from his humid attentions and left the building and walked across the campus in the balmy dark, under the eucalyptus trees draped with the strenuously abradant music of crickets, wondering if I should invite the old warrior to come for a hike with me up into the hills next day and kill him. However, when I arrived at Sprague Hall next morning to hear him speak, a notice on the door informed me that due to unforeseen circumstances Professor de Becker's lecture had been cancelled. It turned out that over a shaky breakfast in the college dining room the hungover Professor had got into an altercation—on the validity of Durkheim's concept of the *conscience collective,* as I recall—with one of the faculty's many young Turks, and became so heated that he suffered an infarction and fell dead with his face on the table among the coffee cups and the bowls of muesli. I have always had the devil's luck.

For a long time I found it hard to accustom myself to the thought of Axel gone; indeed, I am not entirely accustomed to it yet. At the time it should not have been so difficult; in those perilous years the state of being alive often seemed an altogether less plausible proposition than that of being peacefully dead. In Axel's case, however, death seemed somehow . . . inappropriate. Anyone can die, of course, at any moment. The beloved child, the circus strongman, the Cranach maiden, all are sustained by the merest thread. Afterwards, though, when the first shock has worn off, we seem to discern in even the unlikeliest extinction an inevitability that had been there all along, hidden from us, the embryo of death growing steadily toward its moment of fatal parturition. This is where ghosts come from, I suppose, this phenomenon of lives unfinished before they ended. The role of revenant fitted Axel ill. He had been meant to live. Death, an early death, was something too serious, too weighty, to have befallen him. So I found myself returning again and again, with increasing speculative uncertainty, to those outlandish rumours as to what had happened to him. In particular I could not get out of my head Monique's theatrically tearful account of his involvement with the Resistance—a Resistance, by the way, of which at the time I could see little sign. Could it be true? Could what she told me be a garbled and melodramatised version of something that had really been the case, and of which the story of his having been mistakenly interned was another mangled variant? Might Axel really have been involved in some mad exploit that had turned deadly, and for which he had been picked up and had an unceremonious bullet put in the back of his head? Was it possible that I had utterly mistaken him, that in all the years I had known him he had hidden his true convictions from me? This is the trouble with the dead, that they take their secrets with them to the grave. When I tried to picture Axel huddled amid a band of bandoliered partisans in some smoke-filled cellar, poring over maps by the light of a guttering candle—"We intercept the convoy *here*"—the thing seemed preposterous, and yet I had to admit it was the kind of venture that would have fed an image he probably nursed of himself as a Byron, or a Pimpernel. I do not miss the irony for me in all of this. If, despite the comical implausibility of it, he really was an unsung hero, how piquant has been my predicament all along! I would be like the protagonist of one of those third-rate, so-called philosophical novels that were so popular in the haunted postwar years, the man who takes on the identity of a sinner all unaware that the one he is impersonating was a saint all along.

Given that possibility—I mean, that he might have been a martyr of the Resistance—given that, if nothing else, why, you will wonder, was I always so afraid of one day being unmasked? I suspect I understand it hardly any better than you do. What was it I did, after all, except adopt a dead man's name in a time of danger and mortal need? I took, or borrowed, rather, nothing except his identity, and death had already as good as deprived him of that. What has it profited me to have maintained this deception for half a century? Axel Vander's reputation in the world is of my making. It was I who clawed my way to this high place. I wrote the books, seized the prizes, flattered those who had to be flattered, struck down my rivals. What did he achieve, what legacy did he leave behind? A couple of monographs, a few not unperceptive reviews in little magazines, a handful of ill-judged poems. He was precocious, I grant him that, but you could drop the middle syllable from that word and it would better apply. And then there are those *Gazet* pieces, what about them? Although it was he who wrote them, the tarnished golden boy, they are my responsibility now. It was for his sake, in part, at least, that I hid them from the world for so long, until you, my curious cat, chanced upon them. You will not believe me, I suppose, when I say that when eventually it dawned upon my sometimes sluggish understanding that in taking on his identity I had also automatically taken on responsibility for his deeds, I made a pact with myself that in the event of being shown up as an impostor I would claim—wait for it—I would claim that it was I, and not he, who had written those damning articles, and that I had persuaded him to put his name to them because that was the only way that Hendriks would publish them in the *Gazet*! Laugh all you like, in the Elysian fields where you wander, but I have my own, peculiar code of honour. If you had exposed me to the world I would have been reviled for abandoning my people, betraying my race. It would have been said of me that in order to shed an identity of which I was ashamed, I had willingly stepped into the place left vacant by a minor monster whose poisonous opinions might one day be uncovered and attributed to me. Perhaps this is true. Yet if it was all no more, no less, than a cowardly attempt to throw off a past, and a people, of which I was ashamed, then the attempt failed. The past, my own past, the past of all the others, is still there, a secret chamber inside me, like one of those sealed rooms, behind a false wall, where a whole family might live in hiding for years. In the silence, in solitude, I close my eyes and hear them in there, the mouse-scuffles of the little ones, the grown-ups' murmurings, their sighs. How quiet they go when danger draws near. *Shush!* Something creaks. A child's wail is promptly stifled. Someone puts an ear to the wall, a cautioning finger lifted, while the others stand motionless, unbreathing, big-eyed. Knives of light come in through cracks in the plaster. Down in the courtyard engines are running, and boot-heels stamp on the cold cobbles. There are cries in the distance, shouts and cries. My eyelids lift. A breath. All gone, all of them; gone.

By the way, I had a dream, last night, or this morning, some time recently, at any rate. It has just come back to me. Shall I tell it to you? It was not properly a dream, or what I recall of it is not; it may be only a fragment of a night-long saga the rest of which I have forgotten. As is so often the case with dreams, it impresses me as highly significant even though I cannot say what it might signify. I was standing in darkness, on a high promontory; I knew it was high because of the air that wafted against my face, deep and chill, not at all pestilential. I had the sense of a precipice before me, and of a great plain below, stretching a great way off. Lightning fitfully illuminated a far horizon. Nothing happened. I was simply standing there on the brink of that dark immensity, like Dante awaiting the arrival of Virgil. Then from out of the darkness—I note the increasingly ecclesiastical sonorousness of these formulations—a great voice spoke, the voice of Yahweh himself, it might be. *Here,* it said, *here are interrèd all the Abrahams and Isaacs; here is their tomb.* That is all I remember: the darkness, the high place, the dim horizon, and that voice. And a great feeling of sorrow, too, not the sorrow of mourning or loss, but of being present at some grand and terrible, unpreventable tragedy.

No, I did not attend Axel's funeral. I knew that I would not be welcome, that my presence would be an embarrassment, possibly a danger, to the Vanders. I do not know when it took place, or where, even. I think now I should have been there to see him into the ground. It is said that those close to a person who goes missing will not find peace and an end to their grieving until they know the fate of their loved one, and, especially, the place where he, or she, is interred. I would not wish to appear fanciful, but when I look back over the years of my life, and those moments in it of great stress and suicidal urgings, I wonder if all along I may have been in a state of suspended mourning for my friend. Does this make me seem too good, too faithful? It does. But certainly there is something buried deep down in me that I do not understand and the nature of which I can only intuit. It will seem too obvious if I say that it is another self—am I not, like everyone, like you, like you especially, my protean dear, thrown together from a legion of selves?—but all the same that is the only way I can think of to describe the sensation. This separate, hidden I is prey to affects and emotions that do not touch me at all, except insofar as I am the channel through which its responses must necessarily be manifest. It will prick up its ears at the tritest, most trivial plangency; it is a sucker for the sentimental. Sunsets, the thought of a lost dog, the slushy slow movement of a symphony, any old hackneyed thing can set the funereal organ churning. I will be passing by in the street and hear a snatch of some cheap melody coming from the open window of an adolescent's bedroom and there will suddenly swell within me a huge, hot bubble of something that is as good as grief, and I will have to hurry on, head down, swallowing hard against that choking bolus of woe. A beggar will approach me, toothless and foul-smelling, and I will have an urge to open wide my arms and gather him to me and crush him against my breast in a burning, brotherly embrace, instead of which, of course, I will dodge past him, swivelling my eyes away from the spectacle of his misery and keeping my tight fists firmly plunged in my pockets. Can these splurges of unbidden and surely spurious emotion really have their source in a bereavement nearly half a century old? Did I care for Axel that much? Perhaps it is not for him alone that I am grieving, but for all my dead, congregated in a twittering underworld within me, clamouring weakly for the warm blood of life. But why should I think myself special—which amongst us has not his private Hades thronged with shades?

Yes, I should have gone to Axel's funeral, and seen him into the ground, if only to have an end of him. Even when in my heart I came at last to accept that he must truly have died, in some ancillary ventricle there still lodged a stubborn clot of doubt. I recalled the empty windows of what had been the Vander home; was there a connection between his disappearance and the family's abrupt decampment? Why had Hendriks's deputy been so evasive when I questioned him that morning at the *Gazet*? What did he know that he was not prepared to tell me? To this day I find myself wondering, with a mingled sense of unease and peculiar excitement, if after all Axel might not be dead, but living somewhere still, in hiding, for whatever reason, and going, like me, under another name, mine, perhaps, that would be a joke. Maybe back then he committed a crime none of us knew about that was so shameful that he cannot bring himself even now to step out of the shadows and confess to it. If so, it would have to have been something far more serious than that handful of *Gazet* articles, for even in senility Axel would be able to charm the world into excusing him for that peccadillo. Or is it my usurpation of his identity that has somehow prevented him, all this time, out of who knows what scruple or fear of looking a fool, from laying claim to the name, to the life, even, that is rightfully his? The possibility affords me, I admit, a certain base satisfaction. It is not entirely ungratifying to think of Axel, with all his wit, his quickness, his assurance, his good looks, languishing in obscurity these fifty years, gnawed by frustration and failure, while I strutted the world's stage, making, in all senses of the saying, a name for myself.

Oh, but I know, it is impossible. I would have heard from him, sooner or later; Axel would not have worked a vanishing act like that without coming forward to boast about it, if only to me. All the same, on occasion down the years I have experienced an eerie, crawling sensation across the back of my neck, as if I were being spied on, and quietly laughed at; as if I were being toyed with. Certainly someone did look after me that day of the deportations, although I do not insist it was Axel. It may have been Max Schaudeine, for instance, manipulating the strings from up in the flies. I am thinking of the message that came to me that snowy morning only a month or so after the announcement of Axel's death, scrawled on a scrap of paper and pushed under our front door. My mother brought it to me. We stood in the bluish snow-light by the window in my room, I in my ragged old night-shirt and she with a shawl pulled over her shoulders. Her long hair was unpinned, and I remember thinking distractedly how grey she had become without my noticing. She waited, in that silent, apprehensive way that she did everything nowadays, while I unfolded the sheet of cheap, ruled paper, torn from a school copybook, and read the terse instructions written there. The handwriting I did not recognise; it might have been that of a schoolchild, the big, square capitals pencilled hard into the paper, the grains of graphite glinting in the furrows. I was to take the noon train to Brussels that day, sitting in a certain compartment, in a certain carriage, and board the very next return train, and take the same numbered seat as on the outward journey. There was no signature. I could not think who might have sent it, nor could I say what it might portend, but, the times being so, I knew straight away that I would comply with its command. My mother was searching my face more anxiously than ever, looking for a response; I did not doubt that she had read the note before bringing it to me. It was all right, I said casually, it was from a friend, I had been expecting it. I still wonder why I lied to her. She nodded, sadly, knowing it was a lie, and shuffled off into the shadows.

I pause; I falter. My mother I rarely think of, or my father, in waking hours. It seems absurd for a man of my age even to have had parents; I am so very much older now than they were when I lost them that it might be not my parents at all that I am remembering, but my children, rather, grown to sad adulthood—the children, I hasten to say, that I never had, so far as I know. However, if mother and father are largely absent from my daytime thoughts, they do make frequent, unwilling appearances in my dreams, or at any rate at the periphery of them. There they hover, pressing close together, hesitant, uncertain, afraid, it seems, like the Vander cousins, of being seized upon and ejected, amid ridicule and general, spiteful hilarity. They are dressed in black, and my father the rag merchant wears a flowing black neck-tie, an improbably bohemian flourish. I notice they are holding hands, and my father's expression is sheepish. They are like a pair of humble guests who have turned up without costumes at a riotous and strenuously orgiastic fancy-dress party, in the steaming midst of which my sleeping self is trapped, a comatose Tiberius, unable to welcome them, invite them in, offer them hospitality, unable even to see that they are allowed to leave discreetly and with dignity. My mother has that notch in the clear space between her eyebrows that always signified her deepest, inexpressible woes. She is shy of me, and will not look at me, and keeps her eyes downcast, which makes her demeanour seem all the more desperately beseeching. My father wears his usual expression of wary amusement. He was a humorous, even a witty, man, but he made his sallies so tentatively, with such diffidence, that people rarely appreciated them, or appreciated them too late, so that in my memories of him he is always turning away with a wistful, disappointed half-smile. My parents. Did I know them at all? When they were there I think I hardly noticed them, except when they got in my light, restricting my view of the radiant future. I used piously to hope they would not have suffered, at the end, them, and the others, but since then I have learned about hope.

I took the train to Brussels, as instructed. The compartment had only one other occupant, a skinny, furtive-eyed, clerkly-looking young man in a double-breasted pin-striped suit a size or more too big for him. In looks he was unremarkable save for his nose, huge, pale, high-bridged, and pitted all over, like the stone head of a ceremonial axe. From it, the rest of his features receded, despairing of the contest. He held on his knees a small scuffed cardboard suitcase, such as conjurors keep their effects in, the lid of which he would now and then lift a little way and peer inside.

Papers? An urgent dispatch? Bars of gold bullion? Assassin's pistol? We exchanged the barest of politenesses and settled down to watch in the window the snowbound countryside opening endlessly around us its broad, slow fan. Our glances would float toward each other like amoebas, meet, and immediately flick away again. When we entered the gloom of a station and his ghostly reflection appeared in the window beside him, it would seem from the direction of his gaze that he was fixed on me intently, as if he were worried I would leap at him if he were to let fall his guard for an instant. I wondered if he might be connected with the warning note, even if perhaps he might be the one who had written it. Should I address him in some way, ask him some question, challenge him? On we rolled, through the frozen countryside, the wheels beneath us weaving their maddeningly irregular cross-rhythms, and we shifted our haunches on the dusty plush, and cleared our throats and sighed, and said nothing. Once, in the middle of nowhere, the train ground to a slow stop and stood breathing for a tormentingly long time. We peered out bleakly at the deserted snowscape. Two soldiers came to the door of the compartment and looked in at us and moved on. The Nose ran a finger around the inside of his shirt collar and gave a little puff of relief, and looked at me and ventured a queasy smile. Still I did not speak: he could be the most enthusiastic collaborationist and yet be wary of the attentions of the military. Outside, someone shouted, and with a series of clangs and wrenchings we were off again.

In Brussels I sat in the steamy station buffet and drank three glasses of schnapps in quick succession and my hands stopped trembling. When I went back out to the platform the return train was already moving, and I had to run and leap on, barking my shin badly. I limped along swaying corridors until I found the right compartment, and there he was, with his agitated eyes and his suitcase on his knees and his big nose empurpled from fear and the cold. I produced the note and he produced another just like it. I laughed. He laughed. We both laughed. It sounded as if we were gasping for breath. He knew no more than I did, he said. Someone unknown must have gone about the city in the night from door to singled-out door, delivering these forewarnings. We speculated if there might be others like us on the train, a scattered band of baffled fugitives. There must be something happening, at home, he said, and it sounded so strange, that word, home, and he gave a soundless gulp and looked away. Presently he opened his conjuror's case. He had in it sandwiches, an apple, a flask of aquavit, all of which he shared with me. We drank from the flask in turns; our comradeship could not have been sealed more solemnly had we cut our wrists and mingled our blood. By the end of the journey I was tipsy and heedlessly euphoric. On the platform we exchanged addresses, shouting above the din of trains and tannoyed announcements, shook hands fervently, vowed to meet, then turned and with a relieved straightening of shoulders went our separate ways, hurriedly, knowing we would never see each other again, unless perhaps the Angel of the Lord should pay another warning visit to our doors.

I walked home through the hushed city, hearing the snow squeal under my boots. The effect of the aquavit quickly wore off. My shin still throbbed where I had barked it that afternoon running for the train. When I got to our street it was darker than dark, not a single window lit, and all in silence, and then I knew. Three sentries with rifles were standing around a burning brazier, stamping their feet in the cold. I did not dare approach them, and crept past in the shadows, catching the sharp, hot stink of the burning coals, a consternating waft straight out of childhood. I recall the scene in expressionist terms, the brutish forms of the soldiers there, the terrible intensity of the brazier, and the street sliced clean in two by a glaring moon. Frost glittered everywhere on the pavements amid the snow, but when I trod on it I found it was not frost but broken glass. The shop windows were all shattered, their doors boarded over with fresh-cut planks; the piney fragrance of the wood was another incongruous whiff, this time of forest and mountain flank. The building where I lived, or at least where I had lived until now, was as dark and empty as all the others. The broken front door hung by a single hinge. Behind it, the hall was a square black hole giving on to another universe.

I went to a cinema. The film, as I recall, was *Jew Süss*, unless my memory, with its lamentable hunger for congruence, has substituted that title for something less apt. The audience seemed as subdued as I was, sitting back at a tilt, row after row of them, staring motionlessly, as if frozen in astonishment or fear, their faces lifted in the flickering gloom and the tips of their cigarettes glowing and fading like a swarm of fireflies, the billows of smoke in slow motion swirling up into the projector's spasmic cone of mingled light and muddied shadow. When the film was over I was the last to leave. In the street I stopped at a late-night stall and bought a paper twist of roasted chestnuts and distributed them in the pockets of my trousers, first for warmth and then for sustenance. Without thinking where I was going I made my way back to the central station, and there I spent the night on a bench in the echoing nave, like a fugitive in the sanctuary of a cathedral. I would doze off only to wake again almost immediatcly with a start of what was first fright and then a sort of slow, disbelieving amazement at all this that was happening. In the middle of the night the cold grew intense and I went into the lavatory and wrapped the sheets of a discarded newspaper—the *Gazet,* not inappropriately—around my legs under my trousers. Where had I learned all this vagabond lore? Sometime before dawn a fellow outcast tried to pick my pockets. It was an amateurish effort, and I woke at once and made a tremendous kick at him that missed. He was an old fellow with a beard. I remember his mouth, a pink, round hole sunk in tangled hair. He backed away from me cautiously, in an attitude of reproach, as if I were the aggressor, his brown-palmed hands lifted, that mouth opening and closing wordlessly. I did not sleep again, but waited for morning, when I rose stiffly and went to a workman's café and spent the last of my money on a plate of bread and sausage; I can still taste that meal. I walked the streets again. The day was clear and hard and bright, and everything rang and chimed as if the city were enclosed under a bell-jar. Frost stood in the air, a crystalline fog. Inside my stiffened boots my toes were numb. Also my barked shin was still sore, which angered me greatly. That same, hardly accountable anger was to recur often in the coming months; for the fugitive, it is the persistence of trivial afflictions that pains the most. At last, I went home. There was nowhere else to go.

I expected there would be soldiers in the street again. In daylight I would not be able to hide from them. I did not know what I would do if they should challenge me. I thought perhaps I should run at them, flailing my fists and howling, then they would shoot me and that would be an end of it. I might even get to give one of them a black eye or a smashed jaw before I fell. But the street was deserted. The brazier was no longer burning, although the clinkers were still surprisingly warm, and I stood for a while chafing my hands over them. Nothing moved, except a curtain in a shattered upstairs window, billowing in a draught. The winter sunlight made hard edges of everything, and I remembered with sudden vividness the mornings like this when I was a child setting off for school. I went into our building by the low door beside the butcher's shop, which was boarded up like all the others, and entered the courtyard with its smell of damp mortar and drains. In the vestibule there was my prohibited bicycle, and the wheelless black perambulator someone had abandoned years ago. I stood and peered up the stairwell. A great silence here, too, and an inhuman cold, and all the doors shut fast as if they would never open again. Halfway up the first flight of stairs, trite as could be, a child's shoe lay on its side, its strap torn and the button missing. On our landing the wall was scuffed where it had been rubbed and scored by years of passing shoulders, elbows, shoes; I had never taken notice of these marks before, but now they seemed as mysterious and suggestive as a set of immemorial hieroglyphs. I took out my key, but in some access of caution I paused, and put the key back in my pocket again, and knocked on the door, softly, unassumingly, as a mendicant might do, or a returning prodigal. I waited. What was I expecting? Presently I heard soft steps within approach the door and stop. Yes, you, my most assiduous reader, will recognise the moment and its image, for I have employed it in many contexts, as a mocking emblem of the human condition: two people standing on either side of a locked door, one shut out and the other listening from inside, each trying to divine the other's identity and intentions. I knocked again, more diffidently still, a mere brushing of the knuckles on the wood, and, as if this second knock were the signal, were the verification, that the one inside had been waiting for, immediately the lock clicked and the door was opened a crack and a wary, pale-lashed eye looked out at me. I mumbled something, I hardly knew what, but whatever it was it provoked a snicker from within, and the door was drawn wide open.

He was thin, remarkably thin, with a narrow, long white face and crinkled red hair. He wore a long overcoat, open, and a long, grey muffler hanging down that lent a comically doleful touch to his appearance. He was about my age, although he had the air of being somehow far older. He had a newspaper under his arm, rolled into a tight baton. He looked me up and down almost merrily, and with a large, friendly gesture invited me to step inside. I entered, but stopped just past the threshold. He stood beside me, following my gaze with interest as I looked about. I had anticipated disorder, drawers wrenched open and things thrown on the floor, but everything seemed as usual, only a little more shabby, perhaps, and a little shamefaced, under this stranger's twinkling, sceptical eye. As each moment passed, however, the place was ceasing to be real, was becoming a reproduction, as it were, skilfully done, the details all exact yet lacking all authenticity. Everything looked flat and hollow, like a stage set. I noted the flinty sunlight in the window, it might have been thrown by a powerful electric lamp set up just outside the casement. Even the smell in the air was not quite right. "The name is Schaudeine," the intruder said. "You might call me Max, if you wish. I have been having a look around." He shrugged, and smiled resignedly, showing how he made light of his responsibilities, whatever they were. I have used the word intruder, but in fact he seemed perfectly at ease, seemed at home, almost, certainly more so than I was. He sighed. There was so much to be done in these cases, he said, shaking his head, so much to be checked and listed and accounted for—really, people never thought. "When it is the whole family, that is," he said, and looked at me sidelong, and was it my fancy or did I see his eyelid twitch? Where were they, I heard myself ask, the family, where had they gone? I had been about to add, Where have they been taken to? but stopped myself in time. He made a show of considering for a moment, gnawing at his lower lip. "East?" he said at last, with lifted brows, as if I might be better expected than he to know the answer. He began to walk about the place then, looking at this and that but touching nothing. I followed after him. He stopped in the doorway of my parents' room, with his hands in the pockets of his overcoat and rocking on his heels. "Ah," he said, "the master bedroom!" Together we took in the low bed, stripped of bedclothes, with the two ghostly dents side by side in the mattress, the faded quilt folded on the foot of it, the rush-bottomed chair, the nightstand with water jug and basin. The wardrobe stood open, containing not even a hanger. The room had never been so tidy, so orderly, so empty. Schaudeine turned to me. "Did I catch your name?" he said. How polite he was, as if we were a pair of prospective tenants whose appointments to view the property had coincided by mistake, and he had taken the lead in smoothing over any awkwardnesses. "My name?" I said. "My name is Axel Vander."

I had not known what I was about to say, yet it was no surprise to hear myself say it. On the contrary, it felt entirely natural, like putting on a new suit of clothes that had been tailored expressly for me, or, rather, for my identical twin, now dead. It was thrilling, too, in a way that I could not exactly account for. Immediately I had spoken there came a breathless, tottery sensation, as if I had managed a marvellous feat of dare-devilry, as if I had leapt across a chasm, in my dazzling new raiment, or climbed to a dizzyingly high place, from which I could survey another country, one that I had heard fabulous accounts of but had never visited. Nor did I mark the disproportion of these sensations to their cause — I had merely given a false name, after all, as a petty miscreant might to an enquiring policeman. Is this what the actor experiences every night when he steps on to the stage, this weightlessness, this sudden freedom, what Goethe somewhere calls *der Fall nach oben,* accompanied by its tremor of secret, hardly containable hilarity? "Vander, eh?" Schaudeine said, and looked me up and down with redoubled interest. "That's a name I seem to know." He rubbed the palms of his slender white hands briskly against each other, producing a scraping, papery sound. "Well, we shall have to think what is to be done with you, since you seem to have been . . ." He shot me a swift, sly grin. "Since you seem to have been left behind."

I was never to find out who he was, or why he was there, or from whom he derived his authority. Nor do I know why he decided to help me. He wanted no money, which was as well, since I had none. It will seem absurd, perhaps, but I suspect he saved me, and save me he did, for no other reason than that it amused him that I had escaped seizure and deportation simply by not being at home. "What a thing, eh!" he kept saying, with his comedian's downturned grin, shaking his head as if indeed I had effected some piece of acrobatic daring. Naturally, I had not mentioned the warning note. I still wonder if it was he who wrote it, although I can offer no reasonable explanation as to why he should have done. What profit would there have been for him in an act of such selfless magnanimity? Because, again, it amused him? I have no doubt he was a scoundrel. Hard to credit he is still surviving. How did he escape the rope? They hanged lesser ones than he. Hendriks, for instance, a few years later, in the general high spirits after liberation, was strung up from a lamppost by his own belt, for not much more than writing those editorials that now suddenly everyone, in a late rush of enlightenment, realised had been treasonous. But Schaudeine, Schaudeine was not the kind to let himself be lynched.

He took me to the café on the corner of the square that Axel and I used to frequent, and treated me to a second breakfast, of coffee and rolls, saying I would need feeding up for the journey that lay ahead; I did not enquire what journey he meant. He took nothing himself, but as I ate he sat looking on with avuncular approval and pleasure, still with his rolled newspaper under his arm. I felt like a schoolboy who has been rescued from the clutches of a gang of toughs at the school gate; here I was, without bruise or bloodied nose, enjoying a grand treat generously laid on by my smiling and only slightly sinister new friend. He talked a great deal, dropping hints of powerful contacts in high places; he had access, he assured me airily, to a network of facilitators that stretched across the continent; they were friends, business associates, sympathisers—what cause it was they, and presumably he, sympathised with he did not specify—who would help me to make my way to a new life, beyond the seas, if necessary. He smiled again; this time he definitely winked; he may even have tapped a finger to the side of his nose. I nodded, reaching for another roll. I was not paying full heed. My attention was bent on something that was occurring inside me, a shift, a transformation; it was as if all the particles of which I was made up were being realigned along an entirely new axis. It is not every day one loses one's entire family at a stroke. I will not say I was not upset, or fearful for them. I did not know then that I would never see them again, that the whirlwind into which they had disappeared would release nothing of them but their dust. I took it that they had been sent away, probably to somewhere far off and uncongenial, Axel's Heligoland or Hendriks's Amazon, and I assumed that presently I too would be seized and sent to join them. I even wondered if the new life for me that Schaudeine was speaking of so glowingly might be a euphemism for my imminent arrest and transportation. Indeed, I thought, this might be exactly his job, to go about the city allaying people's fears, so that they would be prepared, however deludedly, and give no trouble, when the soldiers came, with the trucks. But even if this were to be the case I did not mind. At the moment I was too preoccupied to care. For I had been confronted with the all-excluding prospect of freedom. That was the electric possibility toward which all my bristling and crepitant particles were pointed. I was at last, I realised, a wholly free agent. Everything had been taken from me, therefore everything was to be permitted. I could do whatever I wished, follow my wildest whim. I could lie, cheat, steal, maim, murder, and justify it all. More: the necessity of justification would not arise, for the land I was entering now was a land without laws. Historians never tire of observing that one of the ways in which tyranny triumphs is by offering its helpers the freedom to fulfil their most secret and most base desires; few care to understand, however, that its victims too can be made free men. Adrift and homeless, without family or friend, unless Schaudeine should be counted a friend, I could at last become that most elusive thing, namely—namely!—myself. I sometimes surmise that this might be the real and only reason that I took on Axel's identity. If you think this a paradox you know nothing about the problematics of authenticity.

As I have already repeated—perhaps too insistently?—I am not at all given to the mystical, but I must record a curious, not to say unnerving, phenomenon from that time. In the days before I met Max Schaudeine I experienced a truly extraordinary succession of coincidences. They were trivial, as these things usually are, but no less remarkable for that. I would begin to read about a character in a novel, say, and put down the book and walk outside and encounter someone in the street of the same and not at all commonplace name. I had started to write an essay on Napoleon at Jena the morning that a letter came to me from that city, from an acquaintance who was at the university there, studying Hegel, of course. I knew two girls both of whom were called Sara; I arranged to meet one of them at a particular corner at a particular time one evening; she did not turn up, but at precisely the arranged hour I spotted the other Sara walking past on the far side of the street. What could be the explanation for these strange conjunctions? Probably no more than that I was at such a pitch of watchfulness that I fixed on things that otherwise would have passed unremarked, even unnoticed. But why in those days in particular, for was I not constantly on the watch now for the world's sly and menacing stratagems? Was it an animal presentiment of approaching danger? Were these unlikely minor events a way that kindly fate had found of delivering me a warning nudge? I do not want to think so, for if they were, then my conception of the random nature of reality is put in question, and I do not like to entertain such a possibility.

At once, then, I set foot upon the sticky web of Schaudeine's continent-wide network, and began the journey that would take me in big, unsteady, bouncing bounds to a place of refuge elsewhere. Perhaps, if I am still alive when I have done with this confession, and have energy enough left over, I shall write a full account of that time: *Katabasis, or, My Flight to Freedom*. For now, the merest sketch must suffice. Sit up and pay attention, please.

❧

The route of my escape—I do not like the word, it sounds so cloak-and-daggerish, but what else can I call it?—took me initially in a sharp diagonal across France to the south-east corner of the Bay of Biscay. It was not such hard going; there were Schaudeine's people to help me at each knot of the network along which I made my way, they offered food, shelter, forged documents, cautionary advice. I stole things, even from those who were aiding me. I became quite a skilled thief; there is an art to stealing, as there is to everything, if one's approach is pure enough, disinterested enough.

That especially is something I learned, that one must be disinterested, or at least present a credible semblance of being so, if one is to succeed in the tricky business of survival. The farther south I travelled, though, the more heartsick I became. I was not despairing, I was not even afraid, really, any more, only I could see no end to this flight I was embarked upon, and felt sometimes that this would be my life forever, just this endless journeying, and that eventually I would find myself retracing this same route from the start, seeing this same spider, and this same moonlight between the trees, over and over. I reached my lowest point on a December twilight in Hendaye, where I sat in a tenebrous bar listening to the flags flapping mournfully along the deserted sea front and realised with a sad start that it was Christmas Eve. Matters lightened next day, however—even the pendent sky lifted a little—when I met my contact in the town, a crop-haired girl in a beret and an outsized black coat whom I took for a boy until she spoke. She and her father were to drive me that night in her father's truck across the border to San Sebastián. Meantime she looked me over with a bright gleam in her dark eye—remember, I was young then, and large, and vigorous, still sound in limb and whole of sight—and brought me to her tiny room overlooking the sea, where we took off our clothes in the fish-coloured marine light, and she clambered all over me, lithe and quick as a minnow, nosing into cracks and crevices as if in search of some elusive tidbit. When we had finished, and I was finally, utterly empty, she sprang up and sat on my chest like a gymnast straddling the wooden horse, and I saw a silvery filament of my semen strung for a second between her open lips as she grinned and said in her hot, high little voice, "*Joyeux Noël, mon petit!*"

She was called, quaintly, Josette. I am ashamed to say I stole her watch, a chunky, cheap thing, but remarkably sturdy, for I have it still, and it still keeps time, of a sort. It had been given to her by one of my predecessors along this route, which probably for him too had included a detour through that bedroom above the sea

front. Josette. In manner as well as stature she was an eerie prefig-
urement of my Lady Laura, whom some weeks later, in an English
spring all sleet and spiked, wet sunlight, I met on a train travelling
up to London from the port of Southampton. I had arrived that
morning on a boat from Lisbon, a city of which I recall only the
smell of tar and the rank taste of raw olive oil, and the aluminium-
bright sheets of rain undulating across the docks at dawn when I
was leaving. At Southampton a military official of indeterminate
rank sitting behind a table had glared crossly for a long moment at
my passport, lovingly made for me by an octogenarian forger in
Liège, then with a snort of unamused laughter had snapped it shut
and dealt it to me across the table, my winning card. I was supposed to be a pilot with the Free French forces, I had a paper to
prove it. There was no heating on the train. The compartment was
crowded with army officers, and smelled of cigarette smoke and
wet wool. Lady Laura was huddled in a corner diagonally across
from me, wearing a huge coat, just like Josette's only much more
costly, and a drooping black hat with a drooping, pavonian plume.
It was hard to make out her features under all that felt and feather,
except for a pair of darkly glowing eyes, which I sensed settling
upon me now and then, speculatively. I noticed her silk-stockinged
white little feet in their expensive shoes with the strap buttoned
tightly across the instep. Her tiny hands were pale as polished bone,
and came out of the coat's wide sleeves like the claws of an animal's
skeleton peeping out of its pelt. She was hardly bigger than a child.
The soldiers, fizzing with battle fatigue, talked loudly among themselves and paid her no heed. Beads of melting sleet ran slantwise
like spit across the fogged windows. The ticket collector came, and
breathed worriedly over my ticket, and told me in a tone of awkward regret, for which I remember him with a warm spot of fondness even yet, that I was in a first class carriage and would have to
move. Before I could get my things together the coat in the corner
stirred and a hand dipped into a purse made of woven miniature
silver chains and came up with a large white bank note and wagged

it languidly back and forth in the air. The ticket collector took the money and clipped my ticket and tipped his cap and withdrew, giving me a wink as he went. From under the wing of the feathered hat those eyes, big and dark and velvety as pansies, held me briefly, without expression, and looked away.

She had been seeing one of her men off to the war. He had signed them into a hotel in Southampton the night before as Major and Mrs. Smith. "I felt quite the tart," she said, and laughed. The man was afraid he would be killed in battle, and had wept in the night and clung to her. "Honestly," she said in wonderment, "just like a baby." She was sorry now she had not said goodbye to him in London and avoided seeing him go to pieces like that. She had told me all this before we were off the train. She asked if I thought she was awful, and gave me an appraising, a testing, look. We stood in the drizzle outside the station waiting for a taxi. The crown of her hat, sprinkled all over with gemlike drops of rain, was level with the centre of my chest. "I did not think the French were made on your scale," she said. I said I was not French but she paid no heed; I would come to know well her capacity for not hearing things she considered inconvenient. For my part I was already suffering my first London headache. A taxi came. She offered to drop me at my destination but I said I had nowhere to go, which was true. She pursed her lips at that and frowned into the middle distance, thinking. We went and had a late breakfast in a hotel in Knightsbridge, which she paid for. From the dining room window we could look down on the traffic creeping through the rain. Under her overcoat she was dressed in dove-grey silk. She sipped at a cup of lemon tea and ate nothing. "They do fresh eggs here, for me," she said. "Would you like some?" And for the first time she smiled. When I had finished my food—dear me, how I could eat in those days!—she said that she would go home to sleep now, but that I must come and visit her in the afternoon. She produced another big bank note and wrote her address on it with a little silver pencil on a fine black cord. "It is a test of chivalry," she said. "If you spend it you will not know where I live." I walked around the city for hours, feeling nothing very much. There are times like that, every refugee knows them, when one seems to hang suspended, without volition, neither despairing nor hopeful, but waiting, merely, for what will come next. Daylight was already waning when I rang the bell at her tall, narrow little house in Belgravia. She came to the door in a crimson crêpe-de-chine dressing-gown and smoking a cigarette in an ebony holder, a perfect parody of the stage vamp. Her very black hair was fixed elaborately with many pearl-headed pins, and she wore a mask of clay-white make-up and crimson lipstick that gave to her delicate features an excitingly oriental cast. All these preparations had been made to welcome someone, but not me, and for the first moment after she had opened the door she looked at me in blank consternation, before remembering who I was. She led me down the hall. "Damn Southampton," she said over her shoulder, "I have caught a cold." I could see, under the make-up, the delicate pink bloom along the edges of her nostrils and in the little groove above her upper lip. Her drawing room was furnished in the chilly, angular modern style of the day: there were low steel-and-glass tables, stick-insect chairs, a chandelier of menacing crystal spikes; the walls were covered with a black woven material that kept shimmering troublingly at the side of my vision. There was the thick heat of a hothouse, but she kept complaining that she was cold. Without asking she gave me gin to drink, and sat in the corner of an uncomfortable-looking, cuboid white sofa, hugging herself and shivering delicately. "I feel terrible about Eddie, now," she said, "the poor pet." Eddie was the pseudonymous Major Smith, he of the cowardly tears. "I should not have told you those things about him. You must think me horribly unfeeling." And she looked at me from under her long and matted lashes, then dropped her gaze and bit her lip delicately in an almost-smiling travesty of contrition and remorse. The doorbell rang, adding a further theatrical touch to the proceedings. She made no move to answer it, gave no sign of having heard it, even. No doubt it was the man she had been expecting instead of me. The bell went again. We sat in silence. Calmly she considered me. My stomach, still struggling with the remains of that unaccustomedly rich breakfast, growled and rumbled. The one at the door gave the bell a last, brief, half-hearted push, and then went away. Lady Laura was running a fingertip along a seam of the sofa covering. A swatch of her hair had come loose from its pins and hung down by her ear like a shiny black seashell. In a small voice she said that perhaps we should go to bed—"even though I have only just got up."

She really was tiny; had it occurred to me I might have felt some disquiet at the ease with which I had attracted in rapid succession these two distinctly boyish little persons. When she took off her gown, under which she was conveniently naked, and lay down before me on the bed, I was nervous of putting my hands on her for fear of breaking something. Where women are concerned I have always been, as you can attest, the bull in the china shop. So many I have caused to shatter in pieces, like Meissen figurines. Even the great, glazed urn that was Magda in the end was smashed under my stamping hoofs. Lady Laura was excited by the prospect of exquisite damage. She lifted her affectingly frail knees and opened her arms and smiled up into my face with slitted eyes. "Come on," she said, in a cat's thick gurgle, "break me in two, and make a wish."

She kept me, more or less, on and off, for nigh on two years. The arrangement between us she set out clearly from the start; it was to be entirely on her terms. There was no question, for instance, of my having exclusive rights to her bed; in fact, I was to have no rights at all, worth speaking of, to anything that was hers. She already had many admirers, and went on accumulating more of them all the time. She moved in a narrow, rackety milieu where aristocratic black sheep met and mingled with the art world crowd. She had a very great deal of money from her dead father, who had been a duke, but although she was a spendthrift, she was not generous. She bought me good clothes, handmade shoes, wearable trinkets of all kinds, but they were less an adornment for me than for her, by proxy. She continued to insist on my being French—"Really, darling, *no one* comes from your country"—and introduced me everywhere as *my Frog*. I liked her, really, I did; perhaps I more than liked her. There was something unwholesome about her, something acrid, discoloured, used, that I found deeply appealing; I am remembering the stale smell of her hair, the raspy touch of her shaven legs, the deep hollows under her eyes, with their bruised, plum-brown shadows. Yet no one I have ever known, not even you, dear Cass, was as tender, as delicate, as voluptuously helpless as she was, when she chose to be. She loved, she said, my size, the improbable, impossible bulk of me, her blond, contraband brute with big square jaw and killer's paws and ridiculous, unplaceable accent.

We knew nothing about each other, I mean nothing of any consequence. She led me briefly, her slim, cool hand lying lightly in mine, into the pages of one of those smart and amusingly cruel novels which were fashionable in that era, whole shelves of which I read, to improve my English, and the echo of which, I suspect, can be detected still in the colder, primmer interiors of my lamentably heterogeneous prose style. All I saw of Laura was the brittle, bright façade she chose to present to the world at large, that undistinguished, commonplace world in which, and she was careful that I should make no mistake about it, I was as far as she was concerned just another commoner. Who knows what she saw in me, beyond the merely physical. She took me everywhere, to parties and clubs, to artists' studios, to hunt balls in huge houses, even to court, once. She knew all sorts of shady people. We went to dog races, gambling dens, to a place in the East End where cock fights were held, and where, at the end of one particularly sanguinary contest, she turned to me with a terrible, glittering smile and I saw a crescent-shaped stipple of cockerel's blood on her cheek and thought inconsequently of the bramble scratches I used to get as a child picking blackberries on my grandfather's farm. She ate too much, smoked too much, slept too late and with too many lovers. Most of all, though, she drank.

It was on a visit to her mother's house in the country that I discovered the secret of her drinking, I mean her serious, full-time dipsomania. We had motored down, as the saying went, for the weekend. It was the first time I had been shown to the Dowager Duchess, and her daughter was nervous, I could tell by the metallic brightness of her voice and the altogether too brilliant smiles she kept flashing at me as she manoeuvred her dashing little car at breakneck speed along the verdant byways of Berkshire. This hitherto unsuspected vulnerability I found affecting, and I felt protective toward her, and determined to defend her against the Dowager, who in my indignant imaginings was growing by the moment to the dimensions and ferocity of a fairy-tale dragon. She lived in grand if somewhat faded style in a stone mansion set on a hill above a tiny hamlet, from the huddled roofs of which the house's many windows averted their haughty gaze. The lady herself, like her abode, was large and stately and fascinatingly ugly. My first sight of her did nothing to contradict my expectations of fierceness and flame, for she was standing in gumboots beside a bonfire into which she was poking a mattocklike implement with scowling vigour. In greeting her daughter she consented to receive a dry kiss on the cheek. Me she took in with instant cognisance and grimly set her jaw. Beside me Laura drooped perceptibly, all her brightness dimming. I realised at once that I had been brought here as a gesture of defiance against her mother—to whom my status as semi-paid lover would have been immediately obvious—but of course the old bag had the hide of a rhino and was not in the least surprised or shocked. For a long moment we regarded each other, she and I, and for all that I was half a foot higher than her I felt that she might be about to place the heel of her rubber boot on my brow and press me without effort into the earth, like a giant tent peg. A gust of wood-smoke from the fire blew in my face and made my eyes water. I said something about the journey, commended the weather, admired the house. "Are you a German?" the Dowager said loudly, with frowning incredulity. Laura muttered something and strode off toward the house, head down and hands jammed in the pockets of her long leather car-coat.

Matters grew steadily worse as the afternoon ground on. At four o'clock tea was served in the conservatory, under the leaning fronds of a giant fern. A grandfather clock directly behind my chair clicked its tongue in large, slow, monotonous disapproval. The Dowager complained of the land girls who had been sent down from London to dig up the lawns and plant potatoes; they knew nothing of country ways, she said, and cared only for cigarettes and going to dances; she suspected them of immoral carryings-on with the village men. I nodded sympathetically and inclined my face over my teacup; the giddy urge to laugh kept bubbling up. Laura sat wordless between her mother and me in what seemed an agony of anger and violent disgust, as if she were a child being forced to endure the torment of adult company. Eventually she flung herself from her chair and slouched off, supposedly to tell the maid to bring fresh tea. She had been gone for a considerable time, and I had begun to wonder uneasily how long such an errand could take in even so large a house as this—had she fled altogether, got in the car and driven away, abandoning me here, with this hideous termagant?—when I heard from far within and high up in the house a thin, ululant cry that made my backbone tingle. I put down my cup; no doubt I had a look of alarm. The Dowager, who also had heard the scream, folded her large, mannish hands on her thigh and considered me keenly, with, I thought, a certain gratified amusement. "For how long, Mr. Vandal," she asked, "have you known my daughter?"

After a search, I found Laura upstairs, locked in a little bathroom attached to what turned out to have been the nursery. She would not open the door at first, and I had to wait, looking somewhat desperately out of a circular window at a far field with grazing cows. At last I heard the lock turning. She had a gin bottle, half empty, the neck of which she had somehow managed to break off, cutting her hand quite badly. She sat on the wooden lid of the lavatory and I knelt before her and tore my handkerchief into strips and bound the wound while she mewled and wept. The fittings in the room, the lavatory, the rust-stained bath, the handbasin, the towel rail, were all made in miniature, to a child's scale, and I had a distracting sense of grotesque disproportion; we were back in a fairy tale again, I the worried giant now, and she the tiny, hysterical princess. She was already drunk, thoroughly, comprehensively, in a way I had not seen nor drunk before. She kept alternating between clawing apologies and accusatory, hair-shaking rages, big, iridescent bubbles of saliva forming and bursting between her slack, gin-raw lips. She said it was all my fault, she should never have brought me here, what had she been thinking of, it was mad, mad, she should have known, oh, how could I ever forgive her, she was sorry, so sorry, so very sorry . . . I took her in my arms, still kneeling before her, and she twined her legs around my waist and pressed her hot temple so hard against my cheek I thought a molar might crack. She wailed in my ear and dribbled on my shoulder. If I ever loved her, it was in that moment.

She slept until evening, there in the nursery, crouched in the narrow little bed with a cushion clutched to her stomach. The Dowager, in her gumboots again, and a suit of tweed that looked as heavy as chain-mail, glanced in nonchalantly and said she must be off to attend to some pressing agricultural matter; it was apparent she had long ago become inured to her daughter's distresses. She gave me an ironical little half grin and was gone. I sat by the bed, feeling strangely at peace. The April afternoon outside was quick with running shadows and sudden sun. I listened to the life of the house going on around me, the clocks chiming the hours, one of the maids singing down in the kitchens, a delivery boy whistling, and seemed to see it all from far above, all clear and detailed, like one of those impossible distances glimpsed through an arched window in a van Eyck setpiece, the house and fields, the village, and roads winding away, and little figures standing at gaze, and then here, in the foreground, this room, the bed, the sleeping child-woman, and I, the wakeful watcher, keeping vigil. Tell me this world is not the strangest place, stranger even than what the gods would have invented, did they exist. She woke eventually and smiled at me, and sat up, plucking away a strand of hair that had caught at the corner of her mouth. She said nothing, only put out her arms, like a child asking wordlessly to be lifted from the cradle. The little bed would not accommodate us both so we lay on the floor on an old worn rug. I had never known her so mild, so attentive, so undefended. She gave off a strong sweet smell of gin. Halfway through our slow-motion love-making she squirmed out from under me and made me turn on my back, and flipped herself upside down and lay with her belly on my chest and took me into her mouth and would not let me go until I had spent myself against the burning bud of her epiglottis. Then she swivelled right way up again—such an agile girl!—and balanced the length of herself along me, a sprat riding on a shark, and for a second I saw Josette, with her bobbed hair and upturned small breasts, smiling at me in the fish-scale light of Hendaye, and something went through me, needle-sharp, that was surprisingly like pain. Laura rested her swollen face in the hollow of my shoulder. A last, thin shaft of sunlight from the window fell across her thigh, sickle-shaped. "I am all mouth, aren't I," she said with a sigh. "You, the bottle, fags, food. Weaned too early, I imagine."

I have one last memory of that weekend to record. The next day, Sunday, in the morning, when Laura and her mother were off performing some bucolic ritual—distributing bibles to the cottagers, perhaps, or administering gruel to their children—in the performance of which, it was firmly made clear, my company was not required, I took the opportunity to explore the Dowager's domain. On a short flight of uncarpeted, well-worn wooden stairs down at the back of the house, near what I supposed were the servants' quarters, I encountered a maid, whose name was Daisy, or

Dottie, a fine, strong, big-boned girl with the arms of a ploughman and a charming overlap in her front incisors, who smelled of loaves and soap, and who cheerfully allowed me to kiss her, and put my hand on her warm bodice. There had been a shower but it was stopped now, and the light was like watered silk, and the wind was blowing, and big shivery raindrops clung to the many panes of a tall window above us. I think of her often, even yet, dear Dot or Daise. I was not then the brute that I have since become. I hope that she has had a good life, and that she is living still, tended by the third or even the fourth generation. I hope too, with small confidence, that she has not altogether forgotten me. When she had freed herself from my embrace and turned aside, laughing, and tripped away up the steps, plucking up her long skirts between two fingers and two thumbs as daintily as any fine lady, I took out of my pocket a netsuke of clouded green-white jade that I had pinched from the drawing room, and, surprised at myself, went back and replaced it on the mantelpiece among its fellows.

✤

The year and I are both declining; there is a chill in the air. Yesterday I looked up and saw that overnight the tips of the corona of mountains that rings the city were fringed with snow. The little shops along the Via dei Mercanti light their lamps early. The housewives have seized the opportunity to bring out their mink coats, of which they are touchingly proud; wearing these rich furs, or being worn by them, as it often seems, they look more than ever like large, exotic, pampered pets. I am not the only one who studies the dubious charms of these matrons. There is another old codger who paces the streets of our quarter, whose eye, black and bright as a raptor's, I sometimes catch, and who will flash at me the edge of a malicious-seeming grin before turning aside to feign deep interest in a bunch of asparagus on a vegetable stall. Like me he carries a stick, but his is an elegant malacca cane with a silver handle in the shape of an animal's head, a wolf, I think; I would not be surprised if the thing conceals a sword blade. He is shorter than I am, but then practically everyone is, and has dainty, liver-spotted hands and very small feet shod in patent leather. He dresses richly in camel hair and English tweed; his shirts, from what I can see of them beneath his cashmere muffler, are custom made, of the finest cotton and silk; they were measured for a sturdier version of him, though, and his tortoise neck waggles distressingly in the rigid, upright shackle of their loose-fitting collars. His head is narrow and almost entirely fleshless, with only the thinnest integument of tobacco-coloured skin stretched tightly over the bones of the face. A slick of oiled black hair, dyed assuredly, is smeared across his pate. He is old—that is, he is about my age. He seems never to be without a cigarette perched at a graceful angle in his tapered, bony fingers. I do not know why I notice him especially, there are many of his stamp in this ambiguous city. I fear we shall become acquainted, he and I, it is surely inevitable. I can see us in the Caffè Torino or the Caval 'd Brons, stooped forehead to forehead over a pocket chess set, with our cigarettes and our thimblefuls of oily grappa, as night falls, and the snow comes down, muffling the sounds of the city.

Kristina Kovacs, poor Kristina, will be dead before the springtime.

I am not the first to have exclaimed upon the pleasures of life in wartime London. I do not mean the great, new, warm sense of communality everyone is supposed to have felt, the keeping up of peckers and of home-fires burning and all the rest of that twaddle; no, what I am thinking of is the licence, voluptuous and languid, with just a whiff of brimstone to it, that was granted to us by the permanent likelihood of imminent, indiscriminate and violent death. Living there with Lady Laura and her money was like being on an ocean liner gone out of control and helplessly adrift yet on board which all the indulgent decorums of a luxury cruise are punctiliously observed. What did it matter that up on the bridge the captain was drunk and down in the bilges the crew was frantically pumping? Despite the bombs and rumours of bombs, despite the austerities and the tiresome restrictions on everyday living, we flitted, my little lover and I, from bar to bar, from club to club, from party to party, heedless, and as happy as probably either of us was capable of being. The city was all plangent airs and melancholy graces. I am thinking of the rich, deep sheen on the casings of wooden wirelesses; of asthmatic taxis, black and square as hearses, with crosses of black tape on their headlamps; of a certain dish of quails' eggs, washed down with mugs of woody-tasting tea, eaten late at night in a strange bed in someone's flat somewhere; of loud singing in low places; of Laura's hand on my wrist as she turned laughing at some joke and caught my eye and let the laugh turn into a look of love and longing that was no less affecting for being almost entirely fake. But of all the remembered sensations of that time that I can summon up, the most immediate is that of the smell that was everywhere in the bombed-out streets when I first arrived, a glum but to me deeply stimulating mixture of cordite and old mortar and fractured sewerage pipes. The bombers were tilling London, turning over its topsoil. And I was a sort of fifth column all of my own. The authorities took a sporadic interest in me. There was an unnerving interview with some kind of policeman in plain clothes, and for a worrying couple of weeks it seemed I might be interned on some ghastly, windswept offshore island, until Laura spoke to someone she knew in military intelligence and the threat was silently dropped; I suspect a bit of discreet blackmail was involved. There were those among her more immediate circle, too, who had their suspicions of me. There was that plummy peer, Lord Somebody, large and smooth and fabulously wealthy, a picture collector, amateur jazz pianist, and one of *my people,* who would point his big pale proboscis at me like an anteater searching out its prey and venture slyly that surely there was more to me than met the eye . . . . Laura said everyone thought I was a spy; she was delighted.

I cannot say when it was exactly that I became Axel Vander, I mean when I began to think of myself as him and no longer as myself. Not when I gave his name as mine to Max Schaudeine that day when we stood together in the snow-blue light of my parents' emptied bedroom; I had no thought, then, of taking on Axel's identity, the assumption of his name alone being enough excitement for one day. Was it in Liège that freezing November twilight when the old forger with the diffident shrug of the true artist produced my—my!—passport, ready-worn, with a crease along the cover, and Axel's name under my picture? Was it when I was with Lady Laura in bed the first time and in a rush of post-coital candour was about to tell her the truth of who I really was and then smoothly, without so much as a missed breath, changed my mind? Perhaps it is not possible to identify one certain moment of decision. Do we not on countless occasions every day step effortlessly into other selves without even noticing it? The man who rises from his lover's bed is not the same man who half an hour later meets his mortal enemy. Anyway, what interests me more than when is the question why. How I worked at it, this senseless deception. I became a virtuoso of the lie, making my instrument sing so sweetly that none could doubt the veracity of its song. Such grace-notes I achieved, such cadenzas! I lied about everything, even when there was no need, even when the plain truth would have been more effective in maintaining the pretence. I made up details of my made-up life with obsessive scruple and inventiveness, building an impregnable alibi for a case that no court was ever likely to be called upon to try. Yet I am fascinated by the paradox that even as I laboured to maintain the façade, at the same time it would not have mattered to me in the slightest if someone had suddenly stepped forward with irrefutable proof of my imposture. I would have laughed in his face and owned up with a shrug. Or her face, as

the case might be. I ask what I have asked already: what did it benefit me to take on his identity? It must be, simply, that it was not so
much that I wanted to be him—although I did, I did want to be
him—but that I wanted so much more not to be me. That is to
say, I desired to escape my own individuality, the hereness of my
self, not the thereness of my world, the world of my lost, poor
people. This seems to matter much. Yet I have lived as him for so
long I can scarcely remember what it was like to be the one that I
once was . . . I pause in uncertainty, losing my way in this welter of
personal, impersonal, impersonating, pronouns. Do not imagine
I meant to perpetuate his memory, or to live the life for him of
which he had been deprived; no, nothing like that, I would not
be so loyal, so large-hearted. I would have defended him, yes, I
would have tried to protect his name, but had I been exposed
I would have slithered out of him with the ease of a secret agent
discarding his cover and stepping into another.

So many questions, so many quiddities, yet I am no further
along. The mystery remains, as always: why? If, as I believe, as I
insist, there is no essential, singular self, what is it exactly I am
supposed to have escaped by pretending to be Axel Vander? Mere
being, that insupportable medley of affects, desires, fears, tics,
twitches? To be someone else is to be one thing, and one thing
only. I think of an actor in the ancient world. He is a veteran of the
Attic drama, a spear-carrier, an old trouper. The crowd knows him
but cannot remember his name. He is never Oedipus, but once he
has played Creon. He has his mask, he has had it for years; it is his
talisman. The white clay from which it was fashioned has turned to
the shade and texture of bone. The rough felt lining has been soft-
ened by years of sweat and friction so that it fits smoothly upon the
contours of his face. Increasingly, indeed, he thinks the mask is
more like his face than his face is. At the end of a performance
when he takes it off he wonders if the other actors can see him at
all, or if he is just a head with a blank front, like the old statue of
Silenus in the marketplace the features of which the weather has

entirely worn away. He takes to wearing the mask at home, when no one is there. It is a comfort, it sustains him; he finds it wonderfully restful, it is like being asleep and yet conscious. Then one day he comes to the table wearing it. His wife makes no remark, his children stare for a moment, then shrug and go back to their accustomed bickering. He has achieved his apotheosis. Man and mask are one.

✀

Today at last he addressed me, my camel-haired doppelgänger, as I knew he would, eventually. I had stopped to gaze into the window of a butcher's shop on the Via Barbaroux. I have always been fascinated by these cheerfully shameless displays of cloven flesh and blood and bone—they are always so eerily well-lit. "A barbarous sight, signore," a voice said behind me. I turned my head and there he was, the punster, in his expensive, old-fashioned coat, leaning crookedly on his cane. He bears a marked resemblance to Stravinsky in old age. When he smiles, his wide, thin lips roll back from his teeth in an unnervingly equine fashion. We went to that little caffè behind the church in the Piazza della Consolata and drank hot chocolate spiked with grappa, for the day was bitterly cold. He tells me the place is very old, and has always been owned and run exclusively by women. N., I am interested to learn, used to come here to drink his morning coffee and read the newspapers. I said I wondered if he brought his whip with him, and my new friend chuckled, and dropped cigarette ash on his lapel. He is not a Torinese, not even Italian, but I cannot place his accent. He enquired, as everyone does, if I have been to view the Shroud. I told him I had once made an attempt to see it but had failed. He said, glancing over his shoulder and lowering his voice, that he can arrange a private viewing for me, if I wish. He might have been offering me contraband, or a woman. I let the subject drop. He told me his name but I did not catch it; sounded like Zoroaster. He is a doctor, he says. I think he knows who I am. I shall have a hard time avoiding him, from now on.

⚭

I should not have stolen Laura's money. It was too easy to be resisted, a matter of a few forged cheques and some judicious pawnings—the house in Belgravia was a jewel box stuffed with unconsidered and certainly unguarded bibelots. I felt it was my due to awaken some of this slumbering wealth. She trusted me, did Laura. Which is to say she found it inconceivable that anyone, or at least anyone she knew, would be so tasteless as to steal from her. She was quite mean—have I mentioned it?—in the way that only the very rich can be. She saved candle stubs, stopped runs in her stockings with dabs of nail polish, that kind of thing. And refused to insure her diamonds. Pity. She might have spared us both a deal of pain and expense. Expense on her part, pain on mine.

My plan was to get to America, as quickly as possible. That was where I had been aimed at all along. I was not your usual hopeful refugee from a fouled and foundering Europe. America for me was not the land of liberty, bright prospects, new beginnings. No: America was emptiness. In my image of it the country had no people anywhere, only great, stark, silent buildings, and gleaming machinery, and endless, desolate spaces. Even the name seemed a nonce-word, or an unsolvable anagram, with too many vowels in it. In America, I would not be required to be anyone, or to believe anything. No cause would clamour for my support, no ideology would require my commitment. I would be pure existence there, an affectless point moving through time, nihilism's silver bullet, penetrating clean through every obstacle, shooting holes in the flanks of every moth-eaten monument of so-called civilisation. Negative faith! That was to be the foundation of my new religion. A passionate and all-consuming belief in nothing. What I pilfered from Laura I thought of as her contribution to my Church of the Singular Soul. My due, her dues.

It was spring again when the two toughs waylaid me in the park. They were big bruisers, not as big as I am, but big enough. There are professionals in all walks of life, and after some initial fumbling they did a thorough job. It all happened wordlessly. I wonder that I did not cry out for help—there were always bobbies on the beat in those days. Curiously, I recall the incident from outside, as if I had not been part of it, but a witness, rather, a bad Samaritan hanging back in the bushes. I see myself there, walking purposefully along a path with high laurel hedges on either side. It is coming on for twilight, very nice and calm, the air smelling of grass after its first cutting of the season. I am wearing a grey, double-breasted pin-striped suit, brown brogues, a grey fedora with a black satin band, every inch the gent. I am feeling full of vigour and purpose; I had been working steadily in secret—the secrecy necessitated by the tacit rule laid down by Lady Laura that as her paid paramour I was to appear an amiable but unlettered dolt—and had finished and sent off to a pinkish New York magazine what I consider my first major piece of work, that essay, "Shelley Defaced," which you so much admired. However, here comes a harder reality in the shape of one of my two assailants, in cap and tight, shiny suit, enquiring for a match for his cigarette. I should have known. While I was fishing in my pockets, the other one came up behind me and struck me with a cosh. Yes, a cosh, the real thing. I must have sensed him coming, however, and started to turn, for the blow fell a fraction wide and struck me on, rather than behind, the ear, the spot for which I am told an experienced footpad would have been aiming. Temporarily stunned, I half fell into the arms of the fellow in front of me. There followed a brief interval of strenuous pushing and pulling as he tried to free himself and I held on, while the wielder of the cosh danced heavy-footed around us looking for the chance to hit me again. The one I was clinging on to smelled of soot, a fact, a clue, that afterwards I thought the police would be extremely interested in, but they were not; perhaps violent ambushing is, or was, a common sideline for chimney sweeps—there were so many aspects of English customs and manners of which I remained in ignorance. He breathed effortfully, and seemed more than anything else impatient with me. My ear was humming angrily where the cosh had caught me, and in a moment of suspended stillness, the three of us locked together in straining equilibrium, I saw one of my teeth falling to the ground at the end of a quivering, thin string of bloodied spittle. At length they managed to haul me off the pathway into the laurels, and knocked me down, and went to work in earnest. It is not commonly known that the eyeball is one of the toughest, most resilient muscles in the human body. You could hit it a hammer blow without bursting it, although of course it would be unlikely to function afterwards, as an eye. It was a boot-heel that did for my left orb that evening. Such a blaze of colour I saw for a second, fireworks reds and greens and celestial gold, and then a deep, soft, satin blackness settled in, that I knew would never lift. Possibly it was the same heel, with its razor-sharp metal cleat, that tore open my left inner thigh through my trousers and severed a whole ganglion of nerves.

I was found, with what I think of now as cruel but faulty aptness, by a pair of lovers, boy and girl. I recall a policeman kneeling on one knee and bending over me, his helmet cradled in the crook of his arm, enquiring politely if I could see him. This struck me as comical. The wet on my face was blood, not rain, as at first I had thought, although plainly it was not raining. The young chap who had found me stepped forward politely and asked the policeman if he and his girl might be on their way, as the girl thought she was going to be sick. My gashed leg was entirely numb, it might have been severed altogether at the hip for all I could feel of it. Presently an ambulance arrived and I was loaded in and taken away and deposited into a cavernous hospital ward in which all the other beds, twenty or thirty of them, were empty, and sinisterly waiting, their sheets turned down and blankets tucked, their pillows smooth as marble. A harassed little bulldog of a doctor came and examined me, sighing irritably the while. He bandaged my eye, and ordered me to be taken to the operating theatre, where I was inexpertly and partially anaesthetised while he sewed up my leg, and then I was trundled back to the still empty ward and left alone. In the small hours my eye became intolerably painful, but when I shouted for relief no one came. In the morning I was transferred to a private room—Laura had been on the telephone—and at the end of a week I was pronounced strong enough to be driven by ambulance into the country, to a ludicrously picturesque cottage hospital, with rose beds and a weather-vane and ivy around the windows, and white-clad nuns whose elaborate wimples looked to my drugged and pain-racked fancy like the ghosts of giant butterflies. It was here that Laura paid me her first visit.

She put her head around the door, and crept in, wincing and smiling. She was wearing, I noticed, the clinging blue-grey silk costume she had worn the day we met, or one exactly like it; she did have an instinct for the symbolic. She had brought a picnic hamper and a bottle of champagne and a pile of books for me. She looked at the books and at my bandaged eye and pulled a face. "Not very tactful," she said. "I am sorry." She touched a fingertip to the bandage; I could see her struggling to contain her curiosity. "Is it very painful, darling?" She sat on the bed, avoiding the mound of my trussed-up leg under the covers, and set the hamper between us. I opened the champagne. "My big strong man," she said. When I started to fill a glass for her she gave a little squeal and made a show of staying my hand, saying she had been for a week to a frightfully expensive place where they had thoroughly dried her out. She looked at me from under her lashes and grinned, biting her lip. "Oh, all right, then," she said, "but just the one glass, mind."

She asked if they were treating me well here, and sighed crossly and said so they should be, considering the money they were charging her. I said I had expected her to come to see me before now. "He speaks!" she cried, clapping her hands together. Then she looked serious, pouting, and began picking at the coverlet. "I would have come, of course," she said, "only you know how squeamish I am." She told me her mother had sent her love, and could not keep from smirking. I smiled too. She took my hand and squeezed it. "You are not so unhappy, then, darling, are you?" she said. "And you have forgiven me? They were not supposed to hurt you, you know, only give you a fright." I asked her who had hired them for her. She shrugged. She had knocked back three glasses of the champagne and her eyes had a faintly frantic light. We were silent for a while. She went back to teasing a thread out of the coverlet, frowning. "You took my money," she said softly, not looking at me. "You sold my things. That was very naughty." A gust of wind smacked its palm against the window, and a cherry tree outside shook its head, shedding a flurry of pink blossoms. She was still holding my hand, and now she lifted it to her lips and kissed it. "Poor love," she said, smiling sadly.

She paid all my hospital bills. I wrote to her mother, mentioning some of Laura's more bizarre bedroom predilections, and how embarrassing it would be if word of them was to find its way into the gossip columns, and a week later I received a generous cheque in the post from Berkshire, accompanied by a remarkably dignified letter of reproach from the Dowager. I redeemed one of Laura's rings from the pawnbroker's and sent it back to her. She acknowledged it with a note, saying I was very sweet, and that she was missing me already. A month later I was on the Atlantic, sailing westwards, in a convoy of ten ships, three of which were torpedoed and sunk off the islands of the Azores. On board I met a man, a Swedish functionary of the Red Cross, who promised to enquire into the whereabouts of my family. A month after my arrival in

New York he sent me the news that my father had died of malnu-
trition in a labour camp in southern Poland, where shortly afterwards my mother, no longer capable of productive work, had been
shot. Of my siblings, unfortunately, so said the Swede, no information was available.

So you see, my dear.

THREE

Those were, Cass Cleave considered, the best days of all the days, not many, not very many, that they were to spend together. She had a task, which was to take care of him. Never had she felt so free of herself. All of her energy and attention was directed toward him. She thought at first he would die, he was so listless and turned inward. She could scarcely tell the difference between his good eye and his bad, for they both seemed equally blank, although he was constantly watching her, she could sense it. If he were to die he would die; it would have been ordained. That was the word that came to her: ordained. She had an almost sanctified sense of purpose. She tended him with that equal mixture of solicitude and harshness that she remembered from the nuns who ran the hospitals where she had spent so much of her childhood. She saw herself, like them, in white, moving silently, on silent feet, carrying something. At other times she was a Christian thrown to the lions before whom the lions had knelt down in meekness; she heard the savage clamour all around her of the crowd crying out for her blood, saw the circle of blue sky above, felt the hot dust under her bare feet. And indeed, he was like some big, ailing beast, lying in his lair, panting softly in the heat, the eyelids slowly closing and slowly opening again, the yellowed gaze directed always a little to the side of her but seeing her all the same. He seldom spoke; entire days went past when she did not hear a word from him. It was May. In the mornings she would go down to the lobby and wait until no one was looking and gather up the newspapers that were set out on a big table there for the guests to read, armfuls of them, and bring them back to the room and sit on a chair at the bedside reading aloud to him, choosing items at random. Occasionally he would chuckle at a report of some absurdity, some calamity. When he was tired of listening to her he would turn his face aside and lift a hand and bat the air jadedly, waving her away. He developed a grimace, he would screw up his eyes and smack his lips disgustedly, as if he had a foul taste in his mouth. He smelled, too, no matter how thoroughly she washed him. It was a smell she recognised from long ago but could not think from where, sweetish and soft, not entirely unpleasant, a smell as of something that had died under a bush. She learned to stay out of the lavatory for a good quarter of an hour after he had used it. He said his liver must be rotting. None of this she minded.

One day the hotel manager stopped her by the fountain in the lobby and spoke to her, smiling broadly without warmth, holding his hands before his breast, the fingers splayed, like a singer in an opera. He asked her if Vander required the doctor to come again. She said no. He said the hotel was concerned. She noticed that, like the doctor's, his hair too was dyed; it looked as if it had been smeared all over with ink. At the lift she turned and he was still standing by the desk, watching her.

She liked the evenings best of all, when the daylight began to go and she could draw the curtains. Then they might be alone together in the world, not another soul existing. She would order dinner to be brought up, always something simple, an omelette or soup for him, pasta for herself. He demanded wine, of course, but she pretended not to hear, and then he swore at her. The old waiter from the first night did not appear again. She wondered if she might have imagined him; she had imagined others, often, figures who stepped out of her dreams and walked up and down in the world, real as real people. When the food was finished and she had put the tray on the floor outside in the corridor she would run a bath and lie in it for a long time. She felt so weary. The tepid water soothed her. She looked along the pallid length of herself; her skin had the dullish gleam of tarnished silver, and when she stirred, quick flashes ran along her flanks, like phosphorescence. She always left the bathroom door ajar, worrying that he would creep out of bed and get dressed and make his escape. What would she do without him? He was her vocation now.

She did not sleep. That is, she slept, but so lightly it hardly counted as sleep. She would lie beside him under the sheet, her eyes lightly closed, holding his hand if he would let her, and her mind would drift over all sorts of things, memories, imaginings, notions of the future, a possible future, with him. Sometimes she would dream, too, strange, delicate dreams such as she had never experienced before, if it could be said of dreams that they are experienced. At dawn she was always wide awake. Even though the light could not penetrate the heavy curtains she would know the sun had risen. Each night the wind died and in the morning started up again. It had a name, he told her, it was called the Föhn, pronounced *Fenn*, blowing out of season. Everyone complained of it, the waiters, the chambermaid, throwing their eyes to heaven and making a clicking noise at the back of their throats. The chambermaid she had trouble with at first. She wanted to maintain the room herself, clean the bathroom and change the bed linen and even vacuum the floors, but the maid obviously thought this a scandalous idea, not to be countenanced, and there was a tussle between them every morning over the clean towels and the clean sheets. Then Vander said something to the maid in Italian, making a threat, or offering some inducement, and there were no more arguments after that. The woman was from the south. She was short and bandy and ageless, with skin so dark it had a greenish tinge. She smelled of dishwater. Now when Vander spoke to her, after the first time, she laughed at the things he said, and probably blushed, too, only her blushes could not be seen because she was so swarthy, and made little crowing sounds of delight, waggling her head, and sometimes even threw her hands in the air and ran out of the room, squealing. Then, when she had gone and they were left alone again, he would turn a spiteful look on her before lying down on his back like a corpse and closing his eyes and pulling the sheet to his chin.

In time, out of boredom, she supposed, he began to talk to her again. It was not conversation, of course, he was not interested in anything she might say. He told her things, scraps of reminiscence, gossip about dead scholars, old jokes, fanciful tales, sitting up in bed in an old grey cardigan, red-eyed and unshaven. He spoke about his dead wife. "Magda," he said, "Magdalena," looking into the past and frowning as if in puzzlement, shaking his head. "She was a standing affront to all the things I held cheap." He chuckled, waggling his eyebrows at her, inviting her to admire his wit. He had her go out and buy packs of cards, and they played together for hours. He taught her intricate, arcane games she had never heard of. She told him she loved him and he laughed at her and said not to be a fool, but she noticed how he looked away from her quickly, showing, like a startled horse, the whites of his eyes, the yellows, rather. She said her heart was his. "Heart?" he said, throwing back his head and baring his teeth in that way that he did. "Heart? If it could think, the heart would stop beating. A great writer whom you have not read wrote that. Do not talk to me of heart." That was his way, to laugh, and pretend to be outraged, and cite quotations. Her names for him were Harlequin, and sometimes Svidrigailov. He called her Cassandra. She said if she was Cassandra then he was Agamemnon. Gagamemnon, more like, he said, and did not smile, but scowled. "Today," he told her, "today you will learn how to play piquet."

The ceaseless beating of the wind outside excited her. She felt suspended, weightless, airborne, almost. It was like being in a plane in those moments after the initial scramble into the sky when the machine is suddenly freed not only of the earth but of its own desperate effort of flight and for a minute or two pours in a sort of thrumming silence upwards smoothly through the air as if it were flying not of its own accord but had been thrown somehow. Once on a flight going somewhere she had sat beside a man, an engineer, who knew about these things, and when she said she could never understand how the engines stayed on the plane he said what was more remarkable was that the plane could hold on to the engines. She saw straight away what he meant. That was how it was with her, she was the plane and her mind was the jet engines trying to speed away from it. She was barely held together. The slightest jolt might make her fly apart into a million pieces. Everything was like that, the particles all fused together and trying to pull asunder. One instant of imbalance, one dip in the equilibrium, and it would all explode. Yes yes, the voices said eagerly, explode, all explode . . .

He did not die. At the end of a fortnight he was strong enough to get up and sit by the open window in the sun. Now he was ignoring her again. He grew restless, and paced the floor, his dead leg dragging. One day when she was out of the room for only a minute he managed to bribe the chambermaid to bring him a bottle of whisky. When she tried to take it from him he swung a fist at her, his soiled eyes glaring. But he did not drink the whisky, and he did not die.

As he got better she got worse. All the voices came back, joining all together, jostling to get at her. They said he was wicked, that he would harm her, kill her, even. At night now she fell into a kind of coma in which she could not move her limbs although her mind kept on, tumbling over and over like an electric motor gone out of control. The chambermaid told her that the Holy Shroud was to be put on public display, people from all over the world had come to the city for this rare and momentous occasion. By now Vander was well enough to go out, and she asked him if he would take her to see it. She told him how the Shroud was kept in a silver casket within an iron box inside a marble case in a black marble chapel. It had been taken to France by St. Veronica herself, who had fled the Holy Land after the Crucifixion along with Mary the Mother of God and sailed in a ship along the Mediterranean first to Cyprus and then to the coast of France and settled at last in the Languedoc. Cathars. The Knights of St. John of Jerusalem. The Revocation of the Edict of Nantes. Freemasons. The Duc d'Orléans, heir in waiting to the French throne. She had studied it all, she had made discoveries, she knew secrets. He mocked her, and said the Shroud was a fake; he said he knew about fakes. Did she really think it was the image of the crucified Christ? But he got up and got dressed. He said he felt dizzy. He said that he would probably fall over in the street, and she would have to drag him by the heels back to the hotel. He described her going along with her head down, clutching his legs like the shafts of a cart, and him behind her on the ground, his arms thrown back in the shape of a V and his jacket and his shirt pulled up and his head bumping on the pavement. He laughed, and lit a cigarette, and coughed. When they came outside, that hot wind was blowing again, making their lips dry and coating their eyelids with a fine film of grit. The city looked unreal, sprawled in the turbulent heat under acid sunlight. They walked in a murk of underwater shadow along the polished marble pavements of the Via Roma, under the tall arcades. She linked her arm tightly in his and wondered if he could feel her trembling. Crowds of people were milling in the dusty piazzas, criss-crossing back and forth about them, blank of expression or frowning vaguely, as if in the aftermath of some tremendous but impalpable event. At first they all seemed to be wandering aimlessly, but then it came to her that there must be a pattern to so much movement, and she saw it as if from above, far above, the myriad lines of people merging and melting and forming again, the design at every point shifting and yet always remaining the same, the immense complex of individuals flowing into and through itself under the guidance of secret, immutable laws, and she at the centre of it all, its unwilling, moving focus. When they entered the Duomo, Vander sat down on a bench to rest, and his stick fell to the floor with an exaggerated clatter. A blue-jawed priest was hearing confessions, sitting in full view in his open box in an attitude of angry dejection, his head inclined to catch the urgent murmurings of an old woman kneeling at his right knee. The Chapel of the Holy Shroud was shut. Why was it shut? She could not understand it. Had the maid lied to her? She hurried agitatedly here and there, asking tourists with their cameras if they knew why the chapel was shut. She could feel Vander watching her, his grin. The tourists stared at her and moved on, uneasily ignoring her pleading questions. She confronted the confessor in his box. He frowned, and spoke a sentence brusquely in a hoarse, angry whisper. She went and crouched beside Vander and squeezed his hand in hers. "It is being shown somewhere else," she said, and gnawed on a thumbnail, looking up at him.

Outside, the heat was worse than ever, the dense air drumming, making her think of a great brass gong that someone has struck. The people walking about were fewer now, most of them gone into the restaurants and hotels in search of shade and coolness. Vander again complained of feeling dizzy. His brow and upper lip were stippled with beads of sweat, and there were dark patches of damp on his jacket under the armpits and down the back. A man with carrot-coloured hair went past. He was wearing a blazer and a dirty yellow shirt and soiled running shoes; he looked, she thought, like an off-duty clown. Vander seemed to know him, and tried to say something to him, but the fellow hurried on, glancing back nervously over his shoulder.

At last they found the place where the Shroud was on display. It seemed to be in a big striped marquee set up in a grassy square between a church and a small, squat palace; when they got inside, however, they discovered that the marquee was only an elaborate entrance to the church, or to the palace, they could not tell which, but it must be in one of them that the Shroud was on show. The light under the canvas was cottony and dense, like the light in a dream. There were ticket booths, and souvenir stalls, and upright plastic display panels that lit up when this or that button was pressed and recounted the history of the Shroud. Vander began to read one of them and snorted. They went on. A stream of people pressed against them, blank-faced and vague, like the people in the piazza. Vander tried to buy entry tickets but the man in the glass booth shook his head and made a sideways chopping motion with his hand. *"Chiuso,"* he said, grimly pleased. *"Chiuso."* Vander spoke rapidly, raising his voice, but the man shook his head again, and gave a great, shoulder-rolling shrug. *"Domani,"* he said. So that was it: she had not been meant to see it. All along, she had not been meant to see it; that too was part of the pattern. Relief flowed through her, like a liquid flowing just under the skin, warm and swift as blood. She began to weep, or laugh, or both at once. With a hiccuppy sob she turned quickly and walked away from Vander, from the man in the booth. Outside the marquee she stood on the scant grass and wiped her tears, taking big, wobbly breaths. She looked about in all directions, a hand to her forehead shielding her eyes against the noonday glare. What was she searching for, what did she expect to see? She did not know. She had the impression of something huge and dreadful hovering over the city, invisible, a phantom of the air, palpitant and bright, unbearably bright, too bright to be seen.

By the time Vander had followed her back to the hotel she was in the room lying on the bed in the dimness with the curtains drawn. For a second she did not know who he was, standing in the doorway with the light of the corridor behind him. She had a vague, disembodied sensation. Had she suffered a seizure without knowing it? He came in and shut the door and crossed the room and stood beside the bed, looking down at her. She could hear his harsh breathing. He was trying to make out if she was sleeping or awake. He threw something on to the bed beside her. She sat up, and he went and opened the curtains. The light dazzled her eyes. She picked up the thing he had left on the bed. It was a cardboard tube. Inside was a reproduction of the Shroud, printed on a long narrow strip of imitation parchment. She tried to unroll it along the length of the bed but it kept snapping shut again, like a window blind; she put her sandals on one end of it and a heavy guidebook on the other to weight it down. Vander stood at the window with his back turned to her, his face lifted at an angle, as if he were searching for something in the sky, as she had searched, standing on the grass outside the marquee. She stayed still there for a long time, kneeling on the bed, studying the curiously tranquil face of the crucified Saviour. "It looks like you," she said to Vander's back. "Just like you."

There was something wrong inside her; she felt something slip and swell. She hurried into the bathroom and was sick.

⚮

She wrote in her notebook, her hand flying over the pages. *The Treaty of Vienna what year? reinstated the Savoyard Kings and gave them suzerainty over the city of. Adelaide of Susa married Otho son of Humbert the White-Handed. His hands are mottled, old. Suzerainty over. How would they not be when the rest of him is old? The child with no face. No the doll had no face. Emanuele Filiberto the Iron-Headed. White hand iron head no face. Father. I am writing down these things so you will know. It is because of you that I am here. I asked you how to live and you said not to live but only act. And laughed. I do not know what to do. All the time I feel I am falling. He will not catch me. The ancient marquisates of Ivrea and Monferrato, iron mountain does that mean, ferrous ferrous, at the foot of the iron mountains the mountains the mountains*

He asked her what she was writing, tried to read over her shoulder. He sounded like her father, the way he spoke, teasing her, making fun of her. He imitated her accent, called her his colleen, his Cathleen Ni Houlihan, his wild Irish girl. She saw her-

199

self lying down under his hand, docile as . . . as something, she did not know what. She devised ways of making him attend her. She saw herself as a puppet, with lacquered cheeks and fixed mad grin, popping up in front of him, look at me, look at me! She told him about Otho and Adelaide. He only laughed. The weeks went on, the summer burgeoned. The voices spoke to her about him, always about him, now. His hands were beautiful, she was afraid of them, those long, fine fingers. Again and again he asked her what Max Schaudeine had told her, demanding to know. She lied to him, said she knew nothing more about him than that he had written those things for the newspaper. Then he would look at her, thinking, thinking, his jaw working. He was afraid of her, she could see it. But she would not harm him. No, she would not harm him.

Harlequin.

Many years ago, in America, I found myself stalled for a couple of semesters on a high, snowy campus way out west. I was waiting to take up the first of what would prove to be a pleasingly ascending succession of posts at Arcady, and had been invited to fill the interval at Frozen Peaks, where what was to be required of me in the way of work would be happily small and the remuneration seductively large. Magda liked the place, its bleak Slavic prospects, its white birches and blue birds, and we might have stayed if I had let her have her way. We had been there a week, huddling against the cold in a rented, grey-painted wood-frame house with a swing on the porch and a big tree in the garden scrambled all over by beady-eyed squirrels, when we were invited by the President of the college to a party celebrating the end, or the beginning, of some part of the university year—for all the time I spent in the academic New World I never quite got the hang of its rituals. It was a not disagreeable occasion. The President lived in a fine old colonial house on a hill above the campus. There was an enormous log fire in the entrance hall that gave off cracks like gunshots, and we were greeted by a soft-spoken elderly negro in a white jacket and white gloves bearing silver mugs of steaming and, as I was quickly to discover, extremely strong punch. Magda and I knew no one, but it did not matter. People kept coming up and talking to us, in that breezy and yet intimate, indeed faintly suggestive, way peculiar to college people and their spouses in the more out-of-the way necks of the American wood. Polka-dotted bow ties were much in evidence, and the dresses the women were wearing that year were tight in the bosom and full in the skirts, and after the third mug of punch and a week of breathing the thin mountain air, I was overcome by the blurred sense of having stumbled into the midst of a flock of brightly plumed, cacophonous birds, the females of which all seemed plumply, pinkly available.

President Frost—how he loved his title—was a big, rangy, robust Swede with a shock of flaxen hair and an open smile and a handshake that could have cracked walnuts. He welcomed me with warm indifference and introduced me to his wife, a handsome, large-boned woman in shimmering scarlet who for some reason thought I was Russian, and remarked with an apologetic laugh that she was sure the bitty old snowfalls in this part of the world could not compare with the boreal blizzards to which I must be accustomed. She immediately took charge of Magda, whom she somewhat resembled, while the President plucked me by the sleeve and led me off into a corner of the room where, as he said, we could be out of the way of all this flapdoodle. He spoke of this and that in a practised, easy way, rocking relaxedly on his heels and looking out over the heads of his guests—we were of a height, the two of us—like a scout scanning the mountaintops, not waiting for a contribution from me, and probably not listening to himself, either. Then he paused and turned with his woodsman's lopsided grin and looked me speculatively up and down. "Let me give you a piece of advice, son," he said. "You're a fine-looking young fella, despite your war-wounds, and I don't doubt half the female students here will fall for you. But go careful, and remember: never screw a nut." We were both silent for a moment—what could I possibly have said?—and he went on looking into my face with an admonitory twinkle, then gave a great plosive laugh and, having driven a punch playfully into my shoulder, linked his arm in mine and said we should go and join the ladies.

I have been looking into Mandelbaum's Syndrome. It was not easy to find information on, for Mr. Mandelbaum is choosy, and comes to call only on a select, misfortunate few. The malady will present itself in disparate forms, which makes it difficult to identify with certainty, but there are a number of telltale signs which are constant. The seizures, presaged by their aura, most commonly a phantom odour or perfume, are characteristic, and frequently they lead the physician mistakenly to diagnose epilepsy. Schizophrenia too is a common misdiagnosis, although there are some authorities who consider the syndrome to be no more—no more!—than a rarefied form of that deplorable affliction. In Doctor Vander's opinion, Mr. Mandelbaum occupies a redoubt three-quarters of the way toward the bad end of the scale between manic depression and full-blown dementia. The patient will suffer delusions, hear voices, manifest compulsive behaviour, and will be prey to bouts of paranoia, sometimes of an extreme nature. I am quoting here. There is no cure. Palliatives have been tried, Oread, for example, and the lithium carbonate–based Empusa, and even the various Lemures and Lamia, with discouragingly poor results. The prognosis for those inflicted with the syndrome is not a promising one, although long-term statistics are scarce, since sufferers rarely survive—rarely permit themselves to survive, that is—into old or even middle age.

I knew that Cass Cleave was mad. Well, not mad, exactly, but not sane either. The very first time I spoke to her face-to-face, in the hotel lobby that spring morning, I saw straight off that she was unhinged. I did not mind. In fact, that was the very thing that drew me to her. There was her youth, of course, and her peculiar, skewed beauty—which, by the way, it took me a long time to discern—but it was the chaos and violence of her mind that fascinated me most. Hers was not a comfortable presence in which to be. By day there were the unstaunchable streams of disconnected talk punctuated with profound silences under which could be sensed the telegraph-wire fizzing of her over-stretched nerves, while in the night I would feel her lying sleepless there in that hotel bed beside me, her mind racing, mounted perilously on its waking, runaway nightmare. She was a battleground where uncontainable forces waged constant war. She was all compulsion, down to the way she gnawed her already well-gnawed nails until the quicks of them bled. I would catch her watching me from under her hair with a kind of savage surmise, like an animal watching from its covert the approach of the hunter. I knew when she was about to start hearing her voices, from the way she held her head at that peculiar tilt, still and alert and breathlessly expectant. At times I could tell the voices were so intense that I fancied I caught something of them myself, a sort of slithery din, like the noise of rain on a roof. Then the fugues began, I think I am employing the term correctly. She would fix on some tiny, concrete detail and elaborate upon it in fantastic flights of invention. In her version of the world everything was connected; she could trace the dissolution of empires to the bending of a blade of grass, with herself at the fulcrum of the process. All things attended her. The farthest-off events had a direct effect on her, or she had an effect on them. The force of her will, and all her considerable intellect, were fixed upon the necessity of keeping reality in order. This was her task, and hers alone.

She had recompense, of a sort. The affliction which darkened her mind also made it burn with a fierce, a frightening, intensity. If her brain had been right she might have been a real scholar; not a great one, probably, but a scholar all the same. There was a demented brilliancy to the way she could connect the seemingly unconnectable strands of the warp and weft of a subject and weave a shining something out of them, however quickly it might unravel in her hands. I was aware in myself of a professional disapproval, a distress, almost; had she been my student, so I fatuously told myself, I might have been able to show her how to turn her excess energies in a disciplined direction. She could not keep at a thing until it was done. Her enthusiasms were brief, her conclusions inconclusive. Worse, she had no detachment, could not divide herself from her subject—how should she, since she was the one, true subject? Thus in the thesis she had begun on Rousseau's children, and had never finished—she had brought it with her, a great wad of dog-eared foolscap, thinking to impress me—she drew a sly but unmissable comparison between the fate of those miserable babes, no sooner born than abandoned into the care of an orphanage by the philosopher and their mother, and what she saw as her own spiritually orphaned plight. And Kleist, whose last, fraught hours on earth she had attempted to chronicle in exhaustive detail, was, in her conception of him, as I quickly understood, nothing much more than a harbinger of her. She had been in and as quickly out of half a dozen academic institutions: her papa, according to her a once renowned but now broken-down actor, was financially indulgent. I wonder that she did not find her way to Arcady. However, what made her most difficult, most infuriating, to deal with, was that even in her maddest flights of fantasy there was always somewhere a hard grain of simple, sane, commonplace reality, for which she would demand, and get, acknowledgement, and then use that acknowledgement as a hook to draw one deeper into the whirlpool of her delusions. She was cunning. She could always judge—well, not always, not ultimately—how far to go, and when to stop. I can see her still, sitting cross-legged on the bed, her elbows on her knees and her head sunk between her shoulder blades and a hand thrust in her hair, talking, talking, talking, and then suddenly looking up sideways, sharply, measuring at a glance the scale of my scepticism, or exasperation, or boredom, and adjusting accordingly the intensity of her insistences.

Strangest of all the manifestations of her condition, eerier even than the seizures she was subject to, were those states of utter absence into which she would suddenly fall, without warning, and from which she was not to be roused or recalled until whatever other place it was she had been in was ready to release her. For it was absence. Although she may have seemed in those intervals like a catatonic, she would retain a quality of such vividness, such— what shall I say?—such immanence, that it was plain she was fully conscious, but, as it were, conscious somewhere else. I confess I found these lapses extremely unnerving. She would falter, and stop still as a breathing statue, and I would feel her leaving herself, as the ancients believed they could feel the soul abandoning the body of one who was dying. I too would halt, transfixed, as if I had felt the passing of a ghost, and wait for her to come back. We never spoke of any of this. I never asked where she had been, or even if she was aware of having been gone. In fact, I never mentioned any of the signs of her condition, and certainly not the condition itself, held in check as I was by a reserve that was as arbitrary and as rigid as any primitive taboo. Just as she was preserving the world, so I must preserve something in her, some last and vital shred of deco-rum, privacy, equilibrium. However, lest I present an image of myself bent low in hieratic submission at the feet of a capricious moon goddess—although they were lovely, in their way, those large, long, slender, pale feet of hers—I should say that my treat-ment of her in general was not pretty, no, not pretty at all. She was demented, and hardly more than a child, a lost poor damaged soul who trusted me, and I betrayed that trust. In defence of myself, although I do not deserve defending, I shall adduce only two arti-cles of evidence, the first of which is a product of the second. I was embarrassed. Now, there is embarrassment, and there is embar-rassment. That under which I sweated was of a kind usually expe-rienced only in those dreams in which one finds oneself caught trouserless in a public place. Do not mistake me. My shame was not that I had taken advantage of a creature who was a fraction of my age and of unsound mind. I did not care how the hotel waiters might smirk, or Franco Bartoli frown, or Kristina Kovacs offer me her sadly smiling, patronising sympathy; where lust and its easements are concerned I am and always was beyond good and evil, or at least beyond delicacy and bad taste. No. The trouble lay elsewhere. This is the second line of evidence for my defence, and the source of my embarrassment: the fact, simply, that I loved her.

I have allowed I hope a decent interval for the laughter, the jeers and the catcalls to subside. Now I must qualify this startling declaration. It was a great surprise to me, a great shock, at this late, last stage of my life, to find myself host to such a sudden and unfamiliar, if not forgotten, emotion. Inside every old man, or inside this one, anyway, there lives on an unageing youth who never had enough of love, of the Keats and moonlight variety, and who at the least encouragement and in the most unsuitable circumstances will leap out, posy in paw and glans athrob, ready to scale the ivy to the rose-hung balcony and his beloved's bedchamber. He is of a serious, a solemn, bent, this flushed and swooning Romeo; he is after more than mere gratification of the flesh. Despite the pococurantish pose to which in the matter of love I am given like all my kind—men, I mean, old or young—I approach the female body on the knees of my soul. Never, since that April evening in my earliest springtime when bad little Lili Erstenheim lifted her skirts for me in the shadows under the staircase of our apartment building and laughing seized my rigid virginity and slipped it effortlessly, like a lollipop, into the hot hollow between her skinny thighs, never, I say, have I been able to breach that holy of holies, wherever I have encountered it, without a numinous shiver. To thrust a limb of one's living flesh into the living flesh of another, how can that be other than a sacred or a sacrilegious act?

I do not say that this heightened state of reverence survives intact into the afterwards of sweat and tangled sheets and that peculiarly melancholy smell of sea-wrack and ammonia that lingers when the tide of love has ebbed. After the first time, the first two times, in the hotel room, when, half-drunk and obscurely terrified, I had thrown myself upon Cass Cleave in her bed, my mind naturally turned at once to the question of how to get rid of her. Bitter experience in my early academic life had taught me a simple but peremptory lesson, namely, that one might take a student to bed once and get away with it, but to repeat the performance is as good as giving a pledge of life-long passionate devotion, involving marriage and children, a nice big house, and dinner parties, foreign travel, a place in the country, companionship throughout a long and vigorous retirement, then tears at the graveside and a comfortable inheritance to follow. As I lay there through that long afternoon I considered carefully my little predicament. True, Cass Cleave was not the vengeful rival bent on destroying me and my reputation that I had expected; she was, I estimated, just a bright though unstable young woman who had stumbled on a great man's youthful follies, and was eager to see what profit might be made of her discovery. Perhaps merely these hours of passion in the peccant professor's arms would be enough to buy her silence? After all, I told myself, that rascal Schaudeine might not have revealed to her the real secret, that is, the secret of my, or, should I say, Axel Vander's, true identity. Yes, a kiss, a rough cuddle, a few well-fashioned endearments—*never before, my darling child, never have I known such, such . . . !*—and then I could get up from this bed and put on my hat and be gone. But I could not do it. At first, it was easy to find excuses not to have done with her just yet. I must have time, must I not, in which to worm out of her the full extent of what she knew about me? And she was disturbed in her head, remember: if I let her go now, who could say what things she might not invent to incriminate me? Even if she were only to bruit it abroad that I had taken her to bed I would be a laughingstock— is there anything more horribly funny than a lustful and infatuate old man?—and besides, I would not have been surprised if under some antique but still flourishing law of this paternalist and fervidly Catholic country the monstrous disparity in age between us were to make me guilty, in a technical sense, of rape. No, no, I must keep her beside me, under surveillance, that was the only safe and sensible strategy to adopt.

Try as I might, though, I could not hide from myself the fact, intolerably shaming to me now, that I was as gone on her as any gonadolescent on his girl. She was, I suppose, the last fire in the winter of my life. This is the part I wish I could skip. How I squirm, thinking of it. I wanted to please her. I wanted her to admire me. I wanted her to deliquesce in my arms, helpless with astonished desire and adoration. I did all the foolish things an old man does when he falls in love with a girl. I tried to seem young, naturally. I made light of my physical afflictions. Why, I even bought a bright new neck-tie. I used to entertain the happy daydream—I am blushing, blushing—of taking her to some exclusive and fabulously expensive clinic where she would be cured of her malady, where together we would banish the interloper Mr. Mandelbaum and mend her mind. In my reveries I conjured the place, a sparkling white complex cunningly designed to look like a ski lodge, clinging to an Alpine crag, with hushed corridors and an ever-smiling staff, and an open verandah where my love in her spotless smock would lie drowsing in the crystalline, pine-scented air, I on one side of her, holding her hand in mine as gently as if it were a sleeping bird, and on the other the good Herr Doktor Jungfreud, with beard and specs and tobacco pipe, smiling down upon us both benignly, working the cure already just by the kindliness of his eye. Then we would set out gloriously on our travels together. We would go everywhere, to Paris, to New York, to Zacatecoluca, to

Hy Brasail the Isle of the Blest! And I would teach her things, I would teach her everything that I had learned in a long life. For I knew, of course, that the way to her heart was through my mind. I would write at last the masterpiece that all these years, I would tell her, had been locked inside me, waiting for her to come with the key. She would be my Beatrice, my Laura, my Trilby. What times we should have—what time: for her, I would live forever. It was a splendid fantasy. However, had I harboured any real, honest, human feelings for her I would have protected her and not let her drop from my safe-keeping like a drunk man dropping a brimming glass. Even that is not quite right, I did not even have drunkenness to blame for my lack of care. It was plain inattention. The object of my true regard was not her, the so-called loved one, but myself, the one who loved, so-called. Is it not always thus? Is not love the mirror of burnished gold in which we contemplate our shining selves? Ah, see how I seek to wriggle out of my culpability: since all lovers really love themselves, I am only one among the multitude. It will not do; no, it will not do.

I am, as is surely apparent by now, a thing made up wholly of poses. In this I may not be unique, it may be thus for everyone, more or less, I do not know, nor care. What I do know is that having lived my life in the awareness, or even if only in the illusion, of being constantly watched, constantly under scrutiny, I am all frontage; stroll around to the back and all you will find is some sawdust and a few shaky struts and a mess of wiring. There is not a sincere bone in the entire body of my text. I have manufactured a voice, as once I manufactured a reputation, from material filched from others. The accent you hear is not mine, for I have no accent. I cannot believe a word out of my own mouth. I used Cass Cleave as a test of my authentic being. No, no, more than that: I seized on her to be my authenticity itself. That was what I was rooting in her for, not pleasure or youth or the last few crumbs of life's grand feast, nothing so frivolous; she was my last chance to be me.

Incidentally, I find it curious that I failed to note how much my present love-struck state resembled that phantasmagoric parody of amorousness into which poor Magda blundered at the end. She seemed to have reverted in her mind to our earliest days together. She would sit down beside me and stroke my hand, or the side of my neck, murmuring endearments. Her smile, coy yet eager, was the smile of a girl surprised by passion for the first time. Her broad forehead lost its lines, her eyes grew clear. She would follow me about the house, heaving lovelorn sighs or, worse, softly, lewdly laughing. I did not know how to deal with these grotesque displays of ardour. And anyway, in her ruined understanding she was surely embroidering the past, for certainly I had no recollection of ever having engaged with her in this kind of erotic playfulness. Perhaps she was mistaking me for someone else, my predecessor the Pole, for instance. But would that muscle-bound little tyke have submitted himself any more willingly than I would to such shows of needful and suggestive affection? Maybe it was another kind of love she was acting out. Maybe she took me for the child she had never been able to have—an early, botched abortion had left her barren—and thought I was her huge, ancient, peg-legged, Cyclopian son. Yet it was alarming how affected I could be by her when she was in this state. Once, when we were seated side by side on the couch in the lounge, where I was trying to read, and with a little moan of tenderness she laid her heavy head on my shoulder—it was noon and I had already begun the day's drinking—I suddenly burst into tears. Magda lifted her head and looked at me with what seemed pleased surprise. She put her hand up to my face and caught a single tear on her fingertip before it fell and examined it wonderingly, the plump clear bead shining there, magnifying the whorls of her skin and bearing on its brim a tiny, curved reflection of the window in front of which we were seated.

I need hardly say I shed no tears in Cass Cleave's presence. As fond an old satyr I may have been as ever stumbled in the wake of fair-limbed nymph, but I had not forfeited all my instinct for cunning and concealment. I was careful to seem to be holding her at emotional arm's length. I laughed at her, and grasped her wrist and squeezed it in my iron claw until she turned pale with pain. Yet for all the swagger and strutting before her, there must at times have been in me a faltering, a flinching, an abject, beseeching light in glance or gaze, that even she, the self-obsessed, could not but recognise and know what was betokened.

I tried, I tried to know her. I tried to see her plain and clear. I tried to put myself into her inner world, but even at those moments, all too rare, when I managed to hack my way through the thickets of fantasy and illusion inside which she was trapped I came only to an immemorial, childhood place, a region of accent-less and unemphatic prose, exclusive haunt of the third person. She would not be known; there was not a unified, singular presence there to know. She was one of those creatures—Magda was another such—who exist on a median plane between the inani-mate and the super-animate, between clay and angels. Despite any claims to the contrary I may seem to make, I am an ordinary soul. My hungers are human, my aspirations mundane. On the lip of the grave I was happy and grateful to get my hands on a girl—should I deny it? And she, what did she want, of me? At the time I thought, because it was convenient to think so, that profit was what she was after, self-advancement, a little fame, or, if fame was not for the having, notoriety at least. How I misjudged her.

When did it happen, this famous falling in love, when did I drown in that Rubicon? Impossible to say, exactly, yet I fix on a certain remembered moment which when I call it to mind pro-duces what seems the most telling, most piercing, pang of all the pangs of pain to which I am subject now. It was at the end of that term of imposed para-hospitalization in the hotel room, during which she would not let me out of her sight for more than minutes at a time. My liver had at last made a recovery of sorts from the alcoholic insults I had been piling on it for decades, and with a par-ticular vengeance since coming to the city. Not since youth had I been entirely sober for a full day at a stretch, and now, after a fortnight without a drink, I was so clear-headed that I almost felt dizzy. I registered hardly a tremor anywhere, I, who had not known a completely steady hand since early manhood. I had that heightened sense of self-awareness, that scarcely bearable feeling of being open to the world like a wound, that was last experienced in childhood, when illness seemed a chrysalis out of which one would struggle into a new and quivering, still sticky, not quite opaque version of a former, less developed, self. Everything around me was intensely sharp and clarified and almost painful to the touch, and even to the sight. That day, the day which I am remembering, it was coming on for twilight, the wind had died, the air was hot and still, and I was standing by the open window of the hotel room, re-learning how to knot my tie—extraordinary how illness can deprive one of the simplest skills—and there was traffic below in the street, and there were the sounds of people, and birds of some variety were circling slowly at an immense height, if I leaned forward and craned my neck I could glimpse them up there in the powdery, purple, late sky. I had my back turned to Cass Cleave, but her three-quarters reflection was to be seen beside me in the mirror of the wardrobe door. Something in her attitude made me pause. She was sitting on the side of the unmade bed, motionless, barefoot, her shoulders slumped, holding her shoes one in each hand and gazing before her with a look of helpless desolation that seemed to me echoed somehow, and somehow made all the more awful, by the heartless, glaring whiteness of the bed sheet where she sat and the malignant glint of the mahogany headboard beside her. I had seen this look before, it came over her always when the intolerable difficulty of being uniquely and inescapably herself brought her like this to a baffled halt in the midst of some perfectly ordinary and trivial bit of life's necessary business. For her, a pair of shoes, left and right, could be as insoluble as any conundrum with which the world might confront her. I noted with a kind of horrified tenderness the translucent white skin at her temples where her pinned-up hair was drawn back, and the shape of her knees under the light material of her frock, and the twin faint gleams of reflected window light along her shin-bones. For a moment I was dazzled by the otherness of her. Who was she, what was she, this unknowable creature, sitting there so plausibly in that deep box of mirrored space? Yet it was that very she, in all the impenetrable mysteriousness of her being entirely other, that I suddenly desired, with an intensity that made my heart constrict. I am not speaking of the flesh, I do not mean that kind of desire. What I lusted after and longed to bury myself in up to the hilt was the fact of her being her own being, of her being, for me, unreachably beyond. Do you see? Deep down it is all I have ever wanted, really, to step out of myself and clamber bodily into someone else. Everything had gone still. I dared not move; I thought that if I tried to turn I would not be able to, as if the air had turned into a solid medium in which I was stuck fast. I fancied I could hear the faint calling of those far birds. Then she bent forward with a sigh and set her shoes on the floor, one beside the other, and the movement disturbed the air and made the mirror tremble, and a watery shiver ran across the glass, and the cries of the birds became the traffic noises in the street, and she stood up, and began to say something, and then I did turn to her, the real not the mirrored she, and at my look—in that moment I must have seemed the madder of the two of us—her eyes widened, and she wavered, seeming to shrink back and at the same time to lean irresistibly into me, and I put my ape arms around her and held her with such force in my decrepit, foul embrace that she gasped, and I felt the flutter of her expelled breath against my neck, and if I had been able to speak, I do not know what I would have said.

Despite such mysteriously intense passages, when I look back to then, which is still the recent past after all, it is strange how little I can see, how little remains that is not remote, diffuse, gone small and indistinct in time's misted-over window pane. Of the three-odd months—and the hyphen, by the way, is optional—that we were together, that she was with me, or I was with her—I am not sure how to frame the thing—I retain only fragments, pitifully scarce. How did we pass the time, how fill the ordinary hours, the suspended mornings and torpid noons, the evenings that were all deserted corridors and air as dense as the shock-wave after an explosion? I see us sitting opposite each other at a table in the hotel's huge, muffled dining room, where the light falls down from the chandeliers like the light in a mortuary, and the waiters stand about in their cream jackets, fiddling with their bow ties and gloomily inspecting their fingernails. The only other regular is there, an elderly, silver-haired gentleman who lived permanently in a suite on the top floor, and had his own table in a corner by the mirrors, who makes subdued, knitting sounds with his knife and fork and at intervals will pause in eating to clear his throat delicately into a fine, white fist. These are the only sounds I hear, the clicking of the cutlery and the old man clearing his throat. We must have talked, Cass Cleave and I, or she at least must have talked to me, since she was forever talking, at table and in bed, on the streets, in trams and taxis, telling me things, but all that persists, in my ears, is a sort of deep, hollow hum, the kind of hum that lingers for a time in an auditorium after the audience has left. We did things together, she and I, visited places, museums and the like, as diligent as any pair of tourists. We went to Milan, to the Brera, to look at Mantegna's dead Christ and Bellini's Greek Madonna. We made an excursion to Genoa, and spent a pleasant afternoon there strolling in the vast cemetery of Stagione, where the air smelled faintly, sweetly, of the decaying corpses that lay under the clay and in marble vaults everywhere about, and she was fascinated by the larger than life-sized stone scenes of the domestic doings of the dead that lined the long, arcaded walkways. But even in my memories of those more memorable days, what I see of her is not her, but something far less substantial, a wavering presence that seems hardly more than the idle dream of an old man's afternoon. Is it simply because I was so old and she so young that I have kept so little of her? How could I be expected to see her clearly, peering rheumily as I must across the chasm of the years that yawned between us?

As time went on the matter that had brought her to me in the first place came up between us with less and less frequency. When I thought of it I would make a renewed effort, more or less determined, to get her to disclose the full extent of what she knew about me and my shady, not to say shrouded, past, but always without success. Why would she have told me, when she thought that my not knowing what she knew was the hold that she had over me? I admit that more than once I resorted to force in trying to extract a confession from her. I can see her still, in the hotel room, crouched in the narrow space between the bed and the wall where I had pushed her to her knees, her face, pale with pain, turned back to look up at me as I lean over her, with my horrible grin, twisting her arm past the level of her shoulder blade and threatening to break it if she will not tell me all—all, mind!—that was told to her that day in Antwerp by Schaudeine the fixer. How curiously calm she is, how solemn-seeming, despite the hurt that I am doing to her. It was, of course, a game that we were playing. By now, what mattered was not what she might know about my paltry misdeeds. Whatever I may say, all along I had been waiting for, hoping for, someone to spring out at me like this with my secret held in her hands and threatening to show it for all the world to see. What is the good of a secret, where is the power in it, if no one knows of its existence? In peril now of imminent exposure, and the disgrace, revulsion and general mockery that would inevitably follow, my attitude was one not of dread so much as a sort of jaunty fatalism. Where before I had skulked in trepidation, afraid and yet not knowing exactly what it was I feared, now I saw myself as besieged, stalwart, a roundhead suddenly become a cavalier. I felt, I confess it, quite the dashing villain.

But let me try, once more, a last time, while the mood is on me, to describe how it really was between Cass Cleave and me. I propose a series of scenes, as in a frieze, depicting a pale girl capered about by an old man, against the background of a marble cityscape. The oldster is in motley, masked and plumed, pinned all over with diamond patches, with a monstrous codpiece strapped under his belly. In each of the panels he is striking an elaborate attitude for the girl's benefit. Now he is the gay blade, hand on hip, now the demon lover, rampant, irresistible, now the unresting scholar with his taper and his book. The girl stands before him gazing upon these antics with a patient expression, forbearingly, a dreamy Columbine, waiting for him to doff the mask and motley; how eerily he reminds her of her father, playing his parts. See, here they are now, in the heights across the river, on a narrow, upwardly curving road overhung by dark trees. It is a deserted, sultry, knife-grey evening, and Franco Bartoli, that lugubrious Innamorato, has invited them to dinner. They are alighting from a taxi. She helps the old boy with his walking stick and his useless leg. She tries not to let him see her seeing the palsied shaking of his big, white-knuckled hand clamped on the handle of the stick. A waft of warm wind sways the trees, silvering the leaves; she thinks again not for the first time how the city seems to breathe, wearily, like a living, ancient thing. She takes the old man's arm and they set out across the road. For a second she sees him looming naked above her, huge and scrawny and sagging, hair wild and eyes ablaze, his old mouth open. Then she sees herself holding him; she is like the anatomically impossible Madonna in that painting they saw somewhere, cradling a giant Christ on splayed knees with no more effort than if she were dandling a babe.

The apartment building where Bartoli lives is old but instead of a front door there is a sheer pane of plate-glass that at first they take to be black and opaque. Vander flourishes his stick and presses the doorbell with the point of it. They hear the bell's nasal buzzing far off somewhere inside. They wait, blankly contemplating their own faceless shadows standing before them in the glass. In the sombre, wind-tossed air of evening she is for a moment suddenly someone else. Light floods the hall—the glass is clear, not black—

making it a stark white cell, with Franco Bartoli stepping into it. At sight of him Vander begins to breathe heavily down his nostrils, as if he had just ceased from punching someone. "Behold!" he says with a snicker. *"A shape all light . . . !"*

Nimbly the little man advanced toward them, like a clock-work toy in a toy-shop window, seeming as always to fleet along on the tips of his toes, and perkily smiling. He paused within and pressed a button in a panel on the wall and the glass door slid aside smoothly. He welcomed them with a gesture of his body that was part curtsey and part pirouette, and reached up and seized Vander's upper arm in a manly grasp, while simultaneously bending to brush his warm, dry lips over the back of Cass Cleave's hand. "Two of you!" he said. "What a good surprise." Cass Cleave had not been invited, but Vander had insisted she must come, and here she was. Bartoli shooed them ahead of him down the hall, flapping his tiny hands. He was wearing a tight little suit and a white shirt with big stiff cuffs and a tie of sky-blue, shiny stuff. Vander trailed his stick along the floor, making the rubber tip squeal on the marble tiles. Now a steel door thick enough to seal a vault confronted them. Bartoli rapped the metal with his knuckles, remarking proudly what an effort and expense it had been to have it installed. Vander was peering at him closely with a frown. "The beard!" he said now, and laughed. "You have shaved it off!" And indeed he had, revealing babyishly plump, pale cheeks and a prominent button chin with a notch in it. He blushed and lowered his eyelids bashfully, and turned aside and pressed something and the steel door opened. All inside, in contrast to the glass and marble and metal of the entrance hall, was old worn wood and thick brown drapery and uneven, creaking parquet. The lighting was low and yellowish, seeming to emanate weakly from the walls themselves, and there was a faintly unclean, elderly, old-fashioned smell. They heard voices from a farther room. They moved along a book-lined passage, picked their way across a mysteriously unlit space where unidentifiable dim objects loomed, and entered a lofty, narrow dining room crowded with large pieces of furniture, overpowering and dark. Seated at the dinner table, their faces lifted expectantly, were Kristina Kovacs, and a burly, self-consciously handsome, middle-aged man with a swept-back mane of oiled, iron-grey hair. As Vander and Cass Cleave were being led in, there entered simultaneously through an opposite door a tiny old lady swathed in black lace, whom they took to be Bartoli's mother. Fixing on Bartoli, the old woman launched at once into voluble speech, lifting a pair of trembling brown claws. Bartoli too held up his hands, shushing her, and sought to introduce the large man to Vander and Cass Cleave, but his efforts were drowned by the old woman's unstoppable cawing. Taking her by the shoulders he turned her about and gave her a firm little shove, and she tottered out of the room through the door where she had entered, still gabbling. The large man rose and reached across the table and shook hands vigorously with Vander while bending on Cass Cleave a keen, appraising glance. Bartoli was moving around the table fussily, pulling back chairs and straightening the cutlery. Vander leaned down and said something to Kristina Kovacs, and she smiled up at him and patted his hand where it rested briefly on her shoulder. Cass Cleave stood canted awkwardly with one foot crossed on the other and her hands behind her back, staring blankly into an abyss. Bartoli now was rapidly clearing an extra place for her at the table, and the grey-haired man and Kristina Kovacs had to shift their chairs, and for a moment all was confused movement and murmuring, while Vander looked on in smiling, large enjoyment. There entered then a second old woman, smaller even than the first. Her round little face was perfectly smooth, and she had a tiny, sharp, curved nose like a finch's beak. This, it turned out, was the real Signora Bartoli. She stood in the doorway and looked upon the company with an expression of placid enquiry, sweetly smiling, as if she had heard their voices and had wandered in to see who the strangers might be. Her son shouted at her to be seated; she was quite deaf. The grey-haired man was offering Cass Cleave a cigarette from a silver holder. Bartoli, having manoeuvred his mother to her place, stood beside his chair at the head of the table, beaming. Now the first old lady reappeared, bearing aloft in both frail hands a broad platter of rice. Bartoli poured the wine. The rice exuded the under-arm aroma of wild mushrooms. The tiny cook retreated to the kitchen. They sat. They ate. He said. She said.

Human occasions, how strange they are. And yet, why do I say so? What are the unstrange occasions against which I measure them? The human is all we have. And people are simple, too much so. Consider Franco Bartoli, now, perched brightly there at the head of the table, with his newly smooth jowls and his little bluish chin, indecently cleft. He is quick, he misses nothing. He can engage in one conversation while listening to another. Tonight he is safe at the centre of his little world of women, smiled upon by his happily vacant old mother and fussed over by Maria the cook, with Kristina Kovacs on his right hand and Cass Cleave opposite and me safely off at the table's other end. The grey-haired fellow too is a source of assurance for him, speaking with loud, guttural authority on a diverse range of subjects, quaffing great draughts of wine and shooting in my direction the measuring, menacing glance of a hired heavy. I have still not discovered who or what he is, and will not. His huge hands are markedly unsteady; he seems to be labouring under a suppressed, general rage. He bears a striking resemblance to the poet Montale, but when I enquire if he might perchance be a relative of the great Ligurian, he merely stares at me, frowning darkly, as if I have said something insulting. His initial flare of interest in Cass Cleave quickly fizzles out; no sooner has she begun to tell him about her latest obsession, the commedia dell'arte and its origins—Susarion and his players, the Roman circus, Plautus, pilgrim plays, and, if I heard her correctly, something about the Mohammedan invasions—than his eye wanders back speculatively in the direction of Kristina Kovacs. But Kristina too will not hold his vigorous attentions. She would have, once, but no longer. That hollowed-out look she has is more pronounced than ever, it seems that if one were to touch her with a fingertip her skin might break up and fall from her in powdered fragments. She has grown vague in manner, too. For extended periods she and Signora Bartoli will sit in silence, with the same expression, gazing at the tablecloth without seeing it, not quite smiling, not wholly here. In the midst of these marionettes Cass Cleave is speaking earnestly and fast, while trying inexpertly to smoke another of Montale's cigarettes. "The ancient *phallophori*," she is saying, staring desperately into his face, "daubed with soot and adorned with the phallus, would leap upon gourds, performing all manner of obscene acrobatics." This is really aimed at me, and I recognise it; she has been reading my books again. I smile at her sternly. Montale frowns, nodding, baffled, drinks another draught of wine. She laughs unsteadily; tears sparkle on the rims of her eyes. All stare at her, even Kristina Kovacs, even Bartoli's vague mother. Although I too am looking at her she will no longer look back at me. Now say that . . . Now say . . .

Say what? I am running out of things to say. There I am, as usual, with my glass of drink and my cigarette, smiling about me savagely, entertaining my old Caligulan dream of a world with a single neck for me to wring. My kind should be rounded up and corralled off somewhere, Madagascar, say, although I do not like the smell of cloves. Or is that Zanzibar? She wrote: *I am going to America*. The jolt, like an electric shock to the heart, as I stood there in the mild autumn light in Franco Bartoli's garden room with the scrap of paper in my trembling hand. That word, heart. I am like a stoker in the bowels of a ship, at night, on a raging sea, with only the thinnest skin of metal to save me from the black weight of waters. I look at my hand, catch sight of my old, my so old hand, and am halted. The falling flesh. Today, over our spiked coffees at the Caffè Bicerin, my new friend Dr. Zoroaster permitted me to see the numbers tattooed on his wrist. It was coy but quite deliberate, the way he turned up his hand that was holding his cigarette and let the cuff of his fine silk shirt fall back, like a stage magician pretending to show that he is hiding nothing. I made no remark, and nor did he. I was shaken, however; I still am. I have the disquieting sense that something that was dispatched to me a long time ago and went astray has suddenly turned up, something I would have been loath to take delivery of then and need even less now.

Somehow I got into an argument with the truculent Montale. Well, no, to be honest, I knew very well what I was doing. I was bored, I wanted amusement, I wanted to put on a show for Cass Cleave. The source of disagreement was some fashionable scribbler whose work Montale insisted on loudly trumpeting and whom I dismissed as a charlatan. Montale at once became heated, his face going puce under its playboy's tan. He said he believed I had not read the wretch's stuff, which was true, for all that it mattered. The rest of the table sat silent as we strove there, two moth-eaten warriors lunging and parrying with our greatswords. Franco Bartoli looked back and forth between us, his neck at each swivel seeming to grow longer and thinner, as if there were some kind of corkscrew mechanism inside it. Kristina Kovacs, her head inclined and eyes downcast, was absently rolling and unrolling a corner of her napkin under the palm of a flattened hand. Bartoli's mother, who from the first had taken Cass Cleave to be my daughter, would turn to her at each new feint of mine, and smile at her, and nod, with lips compressed and eyes widening, mutely congratulating her on her papa's fine turn of sharp-edged phrase, although I am sure she could not hear a word of what I was saying. Cass Cleave, meanwhile, was fixed on me with what I took to be an almost ecstatic intensity, her eyes alight and her fists clenched in front of her on the table, more and brighter unshed tears standing in her eyes. How I swirled and skirled for her, flashing my blade, captivated by my own ferocity and fighting skill. Franco Bartoli at last spoke up. Yes, Bartoli, that puny manling, from somewhere found the nerve to interrupt me. "Professor Vander," he said, addressing Montale and smoothly smiling, "holds that every text conceals a shameful secret, the hidden understains left behind by the author in his necessarily bad faith, and which it is the critic's task to nose out. Is that not so, Axel?" I hesitated. I considered. Montale, like his host, was smiling now, nastily, flexing his shoulders and shooting his cuffs. I took a deep, a calming breath. "I have been re-reading," I said to Franco, gazing up thoughtfully into a gloomy corner of the room, "those essays of yours on Shelley." Now, Shelley is Franco's specialty. He has got the poet wrong, of course—child of nature and champion of revolution, Apollonian prophet, drunken imbiber of the sublime, the usual Romantic claptrap—as I have tried to make him see, on more than one occasion. Self-deluding rhetoricians such as Bartoli are the monumental stonemasons of our trade. Over the buried bodies of the mighty dead they erect their marble statues, the frozen, idealised images to which I never miss the opportunity of taking a ten-pound hammer, as, for instance, now. I had squared my elbows and leaned forward to deliver the first withering blow when something . . . something happened. Grown old, the imagination, as I have been finding out, tends to play unnerving tricks. Visions that in youth or even middle age would seem no more than daydreams, mere dawdlings along the margins of fantasy, reify into what feel overwhelmingly like actual and immediate experiences. The familiar will shift and slide, will change places with things never seen before. A known face will turn into that of a stranger, a window will open on to a vista, menacing and dark, that was not there a moment ago. So it happened now. Under the dim canopy of brownish light in which I sat, attended by the silent sentinels of big black sideboards and looming bookcases, I saw the top of the table ripple and sway, and through this suddenly liquid surface something broke which seemed at first a submerged root or stump of tree. Up it came, and up, slowly, effortfully, a bloated, faceless thing with horrid head and straining shoulders and dripping chest, all hung about with fronds of water weed and wrack. There were no sounds, only the speechless shadows pressing in upon the dark-ling place, and the dark waters moving. The figure, although featureless, was facing me, and struggling, as it seemed, to frame a question, meant for me. The visitation, hallucination, whatever it was, lasted no more than a second or two, and was gone. I looked about. All was as it had been, Bartoli blackly frowning, and Montale's double clenching his fists, and Kristina Kovacs rolling the corner of her napkin, and Bartoli's mother maundering, miles away. And then, all at once, without warning, Cass Cleave gave a terrible, high, hair-raising shriek and turned her eyes up in her head and slid from her chair and with an awful clatter disappeared under the table. Now came another flash and in it I saw again the skidding lorry, the girl spinning, the blood dripping from the porcelain of her ear.

Some things, real things, seem to happen not in the world itself but in the gap between actuality and the mind's apprehending; the eye registers the event but the understanding lags. For a moment all sat still, in startled silence. It was Montale who acted first. Without rising from his chair, and despite his bulk, he turned adroitly to the side and leaned forward, below the level of the table, humping his porpoise's big back, and we heard him saying something down there in a muffled tone to the stricken girl, something to which she did not reply. Kristina Kovacs was looking at me with a peculiar, still, and, I thought, sad expression the meaning of which eludes me even now. Franco Bartoli clamped his hands on the edge of the table and pressed down hard, as if he too had seen it turn into a tub of fouled and drowning waters that he thought might be in danger of capsizing. He said something, and then hopped up and hurried away to the kitchen, and reappeared a moment later bearing in his hand a glass of water. Behind him I glimpsed Maria the ancient cook hanging back in horror, clinging to the door jamb and peeping in on the disordered scene out of one unwilling eye. Signora Bartoli sat with her palms pressed to either side of her face, like that figure on the bridge in the Munch painting, producing not a scream, however, but a curious, distressed, chirping sound, like that which a hungry or a frightened fledgling might make. Now Montale, with much grunting, straightened up from under the table with Cass Cleave draped limply across his arms, her head turned a little toward his chest and her bare arms delicately drooping. Against the muted lamplight and the large, vague shadows of the room it was a pre-Raphaelite scene: the swooning girl in the embrace of the big, square, stern-faced man, and the rest of us arrayed in a semi-circle looking on, mute and grave, constrained, it seemed, in a sort of nerveless torpor. I made to rise, but Kristina Kovacs, still with that peculiar, sorrowing look, laid a hand on mine to stay me, and rose herself instead and followed after Montale, who in turn, with Cass Cleave in his arms, and walking with the delicate, slightly pigeon-toed step that is surprisingly common among large men, was following Franco Bartoli, still holding out before him in his hands the untouched and somehow sacral glass of water. And so they processed slowly from the room. As Montale leaned sideways to manoeuvre himself through the doorway he had to lift up Cass Cleave's legs and I was afforded a fleeting sight under her dress of the undersides of her long, glimmering thighs and at the top of them a taut triangle of white cotton, and the vile old beast in me stirred itself and lifted up its questing snout. Which is worse, I wonder, that I should be capable of arousal at such a moment, or that I should feel the necessity to record the fact here? Then they were gone through the door and I was left alone with the chirping woman and the old cook's single, disconcerting and, so it seemed, greedily ogling eye.

⚮

It was a long time, and very late, before they would allow me to see her. Why I should have accepted their authority over her I do not know. I kept to my place at the table for a while, moodily smoking and drinking the dregs of the wine bottles; I suppose I was not altogether sober. The cook silently withdrew into her lair, and with the others gone Signora Bartoli grew calm again, and sat sighing and murmuring to herself, trying to pick up invisible crumbs from the table with fumbling fingertips, in that way of the old, as I know, for lately I often catch myself doing the same thing. Presently, however, she began casting alarmed, sideways glances in my direction, in an increasingly agitated fashion. I suspect it was that as the minutes moved on she was progressively forgetting what had happened, and was wondering who this mistily familiar stranger might be, or how he had come to be here, alone with her, in her own dining room, from which, as the scattered place settings seemed to attest, another group of mysterious and unruly guests had lately and precipitately fled. Then Franco Bartoli came back, all pursed and accusingly silent—had Cass Cleave come round and spilled my secrets to him?—and sat down, keeping his eyes downcast and softly clearing his throat. The moments creaked past. He would not speak, and nor would I, so that a sort of wordless contest formed itself between us in which we were both determined to prevail. I watched him narrowly, and considered firing off a fresh salvo on the topic of the Eton Atheist and his poetical works, just for the hell of it; before I could touch taper to powder, however, Montale reappeared, in quietly masterful mode, although a little unsteady on his toes, for he too had been drinking unstintingly throughout the evening. He said that Cass Cleave was asleep and should not be disturbed—remarkable, how everyone becomes a physician on these occasions—and dealt me in his turn an accusing look. He stood for a moment in heavy silence, his hands braced on the back of a chair and his bullish shoulders bunched inside his straining jacket, glaring at a plate, as though he were struggling with the urge to come round to my side of the table and take me by the scruff and chuck me out into the night— he could probably have done it, too, for I admit I was not in full possession of my strength—but Bartoli spoke to him rapidly in Italian, saying something I did not catch, and after another moment of menacing hesitation he nodded grimly and let go his grip on the chair, and, with a bow to Bartoli's mother and a parting glare at me, turned and trundled off. The silence returned. Bartoli began clearing his throat again, annoyingly. Maria the cook came in and crept around the table, stealthily gathering the dishes, giving me a wide berth. I stood up, making as much commotion as possible, and stumped out of the room, going I knew not where.

When Kristina Kovacs came to look for me I was standing in the book-lined passageway through which earlier we had entered, leaning against the shelves holding a big book up to the light and pretending to read in it. She stood before me quietly for a moment, her head bowed and hands clasped. She had taken on the distinct air of a nun, in her black dress with its white lace collar, and for a giddy moment I thought she was trying to think how to frame the news that Cass Cleave was dead. In the sallow light of the narrow passageway her skin had a sickly, moist pallor and the rims of her eyelids were inflamed. With a jolt, I was struck by the amazing fact that this woman who was here now would in a little while be here no more, would be, indeed, nowhere, that her flesh that I had intimately known would soon be falling off the bones, and in time the bones themselves would fall to dust, and then the dust itself would disappear. Always a shock, when one comes smack up against death like that, as if for the first time. I mean, one can be aware that a person is dying and yet not have acknowledged it, not have absorbed it, fully. Mortal illness, after all, is only a matter of acceleration. Who knows, I might be gone before she goes. It is a rum business. I stand amazed before the ungainsayable certainty that in a hundred years' time every creature now alive on this earth, with the exception of a few giant turtles and the odd hardy herder of yaks in the Ladakhs, will be dead. I do not necessarily deplore this arrangement—think of the crowding if it were to be otherwise. And indeed, I often feel it is not so much the passing of the present lot that should appal me as the prospect of our replacement by a fresh cast of fools and knaves, with their needs, loves, terrors, their little tragedies. Yes, the poor old world would be better rid of us entirely; leave it to the ants, I say. Meanwhile, however, here is the dying though still living Kristina Kovacs demanding my attention. "Axel," she said, "you must do something about this girl." Why, I wonder, do people always think the employment of one's first name will add irresistible weight to their pronouncements? Calmly I closed the book I had been inspecting, keeping an index finger between the pages to mark my place—it was, not that it matters, the *Hypnerotomachia Poliphili,* the London 1888 facsimile of the 1499 original, in mint condition, as the old book thief in me could not help noting with nostalgic interest—and assumed an expression of polite, perplexed enquiry. Kristina sighed. She indulges me, does Kristina, and never more than mildly chides me for my reprehensible ways. "What are you doing with her?" she said. "You can see she is sick." Sick, I expostulated, sick? "Yes," she said, "sick. And she has shown me the bruises." Bruises, bruises, what bruises? What had the child been saying about me? "Are you by any chance jealous, Kristina?" I said. The possibility had just occurred to me at that moment, I had spoken the thought before I was aware of having it. These little instances of unpremeditated insight convince me that the machines will never take over from us. Goodness, how discursive I am being today, with all this talk of insects, and machinery—whatever next? But Kristina, now, jealous . . . She gazed at me for a long moment, then turned aside with a weary, a despairing, shrug. "She wants to see you," she said.

The bedroom where they had put Cass Cleave was large and square and high-ceilinged; stepping into it was like stepping straight into the past. Occupying the centre of the room was an enormous, high, iron bed in the chilly wastes of which my girl looked like a lost Arctic explorer fast-frozen in an ice floe. An electric lamp with a brown shade was burning weakly on a low table beside her, while all around on every available surface there was set out an unnerving array of devotional prints, all of Jesus, or the Virgin Mary, or the two of them together, mother and son vying with each other in expressions of sorrow, and seeping wounds, and ever bigger and bloodier bleeding hearts. I sat down gingerly on the side of the bed; it swayed, the springs wearily protesting. Cass Cleave's eyes were closed, and her face was drawn and without colour, not unlike the many doleful faces of the Virgin and her virginal Son ranged round about, and just as unreally, as ethereally, beautiful. Only her head and hands were visible, which increased the impression of her having succumbed in the effort of trying to free herself from the frozen medium of pillowcase and sheets. I was still lugging the *Hypnerotomachia;* I laid it down now on the bed beside her and she moved a hand sideways and touched the cover, still with her eyes closed, tracing the texture of the binding with her fingertips, as if she were blind. She smiled. "Well," I said, not harshly, "what happened to you?" For a while she said nothing. I could feel her thinking. There was not a sound around us anywhere. Idly I entertained the thought that we might both have died, without noticing, and that this dim-lit chamber crowded with hearts and thorns and plaster tears was all that there would be of the next world. "The different air," Cass Cleave said, very softly. "The different smells. If you got used to that, a foreign country would not be foreign any more." I said, yes, that was true, I supposed. I looked about, and even whistled a little, softly, to myself; one can be bored no matter what the circumstances. On the wall above the bed there was a large, framed, faded photograph of a young man with longish hair, dressed in the fashion of a previous century, dark coat and high stiff collar and stock, whose slightly crossed but burning eyes stared down upon me with an expression of deep animosity and challenge. Despite the antiquity of the picture, the fellow in it bore a marked resemblance to old Signora Bartoli, whose bedroom, I surmised, this must be. Cass Cleave moved her fingers from the cover of the book and touched my hand. She was looking at me now. "I want to go to America," she said. I nodded, indulging her. "Of course you do," I said. I could have lied, I could have said I would take her to Arcady with me, but I did not. It is no matter; it was not my America she meant.

That night, what was left of it, I slept alone for the first time in months. Or did not sleep, but lay in a sort of conscious daze, rather, attended by my familiar demons. I have always been prey to night terrors— hardly surprising, I suppose—but lately they are mainly of the waking kind. When I was young my dreams were all chaos, lust and violence, now in my old age sleep is a room of quiet marvels into which I am nightly ushered. It is the ante-room of death; in it, my fears are stilled. Tonight, however, that door was locked against me, and I lay on my back under a humid sheet with my hands folded on my chest like the dead Christ in his shroud and listened to the restless world's carousings. The city seemed to be celebrating one of this festive country's many feast days, for the streets outside were loud with revellers until the early hours. Or it may have been an hallucination: at one particularly clamorous stage of the celebrations I crept to the window and looked down and saw a sort of heraldic cavalcade passing along the street, young men in doublets and striped hose carrying banners and gowned girls with elaborate headdresses mounted on prancing steeds, followed by a band of motleyed minstrels. Toward dawn the crowds, phantom or real, at last dispersed, and then the all too real garbage trucks and delivery men took over. The curtain edges were lightening when I thought I saw Cass Cleave come into the room. She sat by me in the shadows and did not speak. I tried to touch her, to feel her warmth, but my winding-sheet held me fast and I could not move a limb. What was I thinking of, to leave her in the care of others, at such a time? But then, I was not aware that it was such a time. All the same, of the many derelictions of which I have been guilty in my life, this one seems to me now the most reproachable.

I do not know what passed between Kristina Kovacs and Cass Cleave that night, while I cowered in my forsaken bed, what confidences were offered, what pledges given. Kristina has not volunteered to tell me, and I have not had the heart to ask. I harbour no resentment against her. She acted for what she thought was the best, as unwitting mischief-makers usually do. If she does know my poor secrets she likely does not care, so engrossed is she in the hard business of dying. I sit with her for hours, in the evenings especially, and often late into the night. I think that for most of the time she forgets I am there. I can sense her labouring over her pain: it is as if she is trying to hew something out of the most unmalleable material, to fashion something that is beyond her powers and her failing strength. The doctors insisted that she undergo radium treatment, the only result of which I can see is that now she is entirely bald. She refuses to wear a wig. In this shorn state she has acquired an austere, elemental beauty; her pharaonic head, held fraily aloft and faintly trembling on the delicate, fleshless column of her neck, is stark and absolute, all line and plane and angled shadow. Sometimes when I am sitting with her I stroke her head; it seems to comfort her, and she nudges against my hand, with an almost forceful insistence, like a cat. Her scalp is warm and always a little moist, and there is a vein that beats beneath it, very fast. I accused her lightly that night at Franco Bartoli's of being jealous, but I am the one who is jealous now. Whatever I may call what I felt for Cass Cleave—the word love, in my mouth, has acquired a blasphemous overtone—I know that Kristina in some way came to share it. They had only that one night together, and I am no more willing to speculate on how they spent it than I am to ask Kristina to tell me. I am prevented by a sort of prudishness, or do I mean pudency; the blaze that burns the jealous lover feels so like the heat of lust.

When in the morning I went back to Franco Bartoli's apartment he was not there, or at least did not appear, and instead Kristina received me, still in her black dinner dress, more ashen and red-rimmed than ever. She said she had not slept, but had spent the night at Cass Cleave's bedside. This seemed perfectly natural to my ears, as natural as the fact that I had, without any intention that I can now discern, packed Cass Cleave's bag and brought it with me from the hotel. I do believe that at these times our thinking is thought for us. Kristina when I handed her the bag made no comment. She led me into the dining room where we had eaten dinner the night before and bade me sit down at the table. In the spiked sunlight of morning the place had a slightly sweaty, panting atmosphere, as if the night's revels in the streets had broken in here and had only lately been quelled. Cass Cleave was right, it is the different air, the different smells, that mark a place as foreign. This room, fusty and watchful, was meant to be lived in only after dark, and the sunlight coming in at the window was scandalously bright and brash. Odd to think that for others, for Franco and his mother, for the old cook, this place was as familiar as the palms of their own hands. I have never belonged anywhere . . . I cleared my throat and enquired after Cass Cleave, diffident as a hospital visitor. Kristina was pouring coffee for me and did not lift her eyes from the cup. I could see my face reflected in the polish of the dining table, foreshortened, indistinct, the upper part of it seeming sinisterly masked. I was trying, inconsequently but with some irritation, to recall the exact distinction between the terms *gemütskrank* and *geisteskrank*. "She wishes to be alone," Kristina Kovacs said. "For a while. She has things to consider." I nodded, not seeing how else to respond. There seemed a nice point of etiquette in play here, an etiquette to which I was not party. I felt distantly a dull, dragging sense of sundering and release, as the ship must feel in the first moment of heaving away from the dockside; it was, I realise now, an initial, premonitory twinge of the coming pains of loss. "I love her, you know," I heard myself say, almost peevishly, and would have gone red all over if my ancient hide were less leathery. Now it was Kristina's turn to nod, pursing her lips. I could hear the old cook scratching about in the kitchen. "Nevertheless," I said, overly loud, sounding to my own ears like a Victorian paterfamilias reluctantly acceding to a fortune hunter's request for his homely daughter's hand, "nevertheless, I shall let her go, if that is what she wants." Kristina, still looking down, pondered my words for a moment, and then looked up at me and smiled. "Oh, Axel," she said softly, "only someone incapable of love could love so selflessly."

Later, when I saw Cass Cleave, she was in Bartoli's garden, a cramped, sunless box of stubby grass and wilting foliage wedged between two high, stuccoed walls and the blank-windowed rear of another, looming apartment house. She was sitting on a wrought-iron chair in a corner beside a blue-blossoming bush, very straight, her slender neck extended and her hands calmly folded in her lap. Her hair, I noticed, had grown appreciably longer in the months that she had been with me, and was gathered now and tied behind her head in what I believe is called a chignon. She was barefoot, and was wearing an old-fashioned white linen night-gown, lent to her by Bartoli's mother, no doubt. Placed there, all pale and russet, in front of the stained white wall, she might have been posing for a photograph, or awaiting, indeed, the arrival of the firing squad. As I approached, she looked up, her gaze not quite focused, and smiled vaguely, as if she were not sure whether I was real or only a comfortably familiar hallucination. I stood before her in the still and lifeless air, jabbing at the coarse grass with my stick. She waited, incurious, directing her blurred smile here and there. I said that I had heard that she wished to be left alone, and was unable to suppress the unexpected note of pique in my tone. I said she should know that Kristina Kovacs was ill, that she was, in fact, dying. I said that I had slept with her once, long ago, in Prague. "Yes," Cass Cleave said, "she told me." So. "And what," I asked, "did you tell her, in return?" She did not answer. I sighed. I had my little speech prepared. A livid cloud was creeping stealthily toward the sun. "You must understand," I said, "I shall have to go back to my life, and so must you go back to yours." I lightly laughed. "I have spent so much money here," I said, "my agent in Arcady, who handles my financial affairs, believes I am being blackmailed—which," with an archly frowning smile, "I am, in a way." I paced a step to right, to left, pivoting on my stick. I said that of course I loved her, but love is only an urge to isolate and be in total possession of another human being. "By loving you," I said, "I took you from the world, and now, I am giving you back. Do you see?" She listened to all this in silence, her head judiciously inclined, and now she nodded. I sighed again, impatiently. "Are you going to betray me?" I said. "Those newspaper things—will you reveal them, and betray me?" She sat quite still for a moment, then looked up with a little shiver, smiling, as if she were waking from a brief, refreshing sleep, and glanced about, in pleased surprise, it seemed, at the blue bush, and the white wall, and at me, standing before her, leaning on my stick. "We never saw the Shroud," she said. She rose from the iron chair and linked her arm in mine, and together we started back across the garden, toward the open garden window, where Kristina Kovacs stood, waiting for us, with her arms tightly folded under her bosom. "I have," Cass Cleave said softly, "something to tell you."

∞

She left the city that day. Kristina Kovacs came to the hotel to inform me of her departure—her flight—bringing Franco Bartoli with her. When I saw them in the lobby, sitting side by side on the white couch by the indoor fountain where I had caught my first, unrecognising glimpse of the girl, they looked like a pair of errant children miserably awaiting their due of punishment. A thunderstorm that had been threatening for days had broken at last and was striding about the sky in lavish fury, banging its fists together and flinging down bolt upon jovian bolt with scarce a pause. A group of guests and one or two staff were crowded in the open front doorway, watching the palls of rain sweep along the street and sending up a collective sigh of appreciation and awe at each lightning flash. "But you said you would let her go," Kristina Kovacs said, looking up at me and blinking. "I thought—" The noise of the rain from outside was louder than the splashing water in the fountain. I struck the marble floor a blow with my stick. There are times when anger is a kind of pain, whining in one's head, high-pitched and hot, like a toothache. "You thought?" I cried. "You thought? *You did not think!*" Kristina went on blinking helplessly. No, she did not know where Cass Cleave had gone to; she had given her money, a considerable sum, enough for her to travel on for weeks, for months, perhaps. I made her promise, I made her swear, to tell me at once if she should hear from her. "You do not understand," I said, shaking my head from side to side, old wounded brute. "You do not understand!" I could have broken down and wept for rage. I had walked them to the door. A crackle of lightning lit the street, the crowd said *Ahh!* Kristina Kovacs went to the reception desk to borrow an umbrella, and Franco Bartoli laid a hand solicitously on my arm. "We thought you wanted to be rid of her," he said. "We thought you would be glad." I nodded wearily and said that yes, yes, glad, I was glad, of course.

For a week I heard nothing. I seem to have done little else but pace, up and down my room, along the hotel corridors, from street to street, muttering, talking to myself and to Cass Cleave, railing at her and calling down curses on her head. In my over-heated memory, the background to that interminable interval is all rolling, rumbling noise and thunder flashes, as if the storm that broke over the city on the day of her departure had continued on, without abating, day after day, night after empty night, in sympathy somehow with the turmoil in my heart. Then at last, banal as can be, came a postcard, from Genoa, with an antique photograph on the front showing, of course, a panoramic view of the Stagione cemetery. *There is to be an eclipse of the sun,* she wrote, *do you think the world will end?* Although she had given no address I had myself taxied at once to the station and was in Genoa by noon. I swung myself off the train and walked out into the sun and set off blindly up the first street facing me. The day was foully hot and the harbour stank. Crowds, cobbles, tottering palazzi. The street, a winding gorge, narrowed and then narrowed again, and then grew narrower still, and soon I was elbowing my way through a sort of souk where enormous, blue-black men in white djellabas lounged at stalls displaying slices of fried food and spilling bags of grain and unskinned kid goats with slashed windpipes hanging up by their little black hoofs. I sat down in a café and drank a glass of anis. The fat Arab proprietor leaned comfortably on the counter picking his teeth and talked to me in demotic French about his wives and his good-for-nothing sons. It was siesta time, the shutters were coming down. A circling fan in the ceiling stirred the drooping twists of flypaper. And at that moment, in that cheerfully alien place, I knew at last that she was lost to me for good. For good: how the language mocks us. I trailed back to the station, where I had to wait a peculiarly agonising hour for the next northbound train. It was late afternoon when I returned to the hotel, exhausted and feeling obscurely ashamed. I pulled the curtains in the room and climbed into the bed that still smelled faintly, or so I fancied, of her.

As the days went on more postcards came, from Rapallo, from Santa Margherita, from the five towns of the Cinque Terre, places I had never been to and had to imagine. I followed her progress along the Ligurian coast in a big old atlas that Franco Bartoli took down for me from a high shelf in that book-lined hallway of his. By now I had left the hotel and moved in with him and his

Mama. It was a temporary arrangement, while I looked for somewhere permanent in which to set up my missing person bureau. Every afternoon Franco and I went together in his little car to the hospital on the city's industrial outskirts where Kristina Kovacs was undergoing a final, futile round of treatments. Most days we found her in a state of prostration and sleepy shock, like a survivor who has been pulled out of the rubble a week after an earthquake. Franco Bartoli was awkward in her presence, or perhaps it was only because I was there; he would sit on the metal hospital chair with his palms pressed between his knees, clearing his throat and stretching his neck up out of his too tight shirt-collar, or falling into protracted bouts of vacant staring from which he would emerge with a guilty start, casting a furtive glance at Kristina Kovacs and at me. He brought her flowers, they were a form of attempted propitiation, elaborate sprays of orchids and lilies and tuberoses that imparted an odour of the mortuary to the already faintly fetid air of the sick-room. Kristina had become touchingly dependent on him, asking him in a voice as thin as paper to do little services for her, to change the water in the vase on the window sill, to retrieve a dropped book, to ring for the nurse. The chemicals they were plying her with made her thirsty, and he would fill her water glass repeatedly and perch beside her on the bed and put an arm around her shoulders and help her to drink, and I would have to turn away and walk to the window and look out at the view of factories and shopping complexes smoking in the relentless summer heat. I brought Cass Cleave's postcards as they arrived, and Kristina had the nurses pin them on the wall beside her bed. Some days she would pass an entire visit lying motionless on her side, facing away from Franco and me, with a hand under her cheek, gazing steadily at these gaudy scenes of nude blue skies and silky seas. After we had left her Franco and I would go to a bar at the other side of an unrelievedly busy intersection, which we had to cross in zigzag fashion, perilously hurrying from one whimsical set of traffic lights to another. The bar was a nondescript place frequented by long-distance lorry drivers, solitary and haunted-eyed, and swarthy young thugs of uncertain provenance who passed the time playing the pinball machine in relentless, seething silence. As we sat there at the smeared metal counter, Franco with his coffee and me with my grappa, I would sense him trying to frame all the things that he wished to say, all the things that he felt he should be able to say, and failing every time; he was like the espresso machine behind the bar, a gleaming, big-bellied monster with countless knobs and gauges, that was forever building up a head of steam and never getting anywhere.

By the way, I do not know if it is a portent, or, if it is, what it might portend, but I have found Mama Vander's pill-box! It had slipped through a hole in the pocket of a jacket that I seldom wear and lodged in the lining. I am childishly delighted to have it back, and have been feeding it, at the rate of a tablet per visit, from Kristina Kovacs's store of pain-killers, against the day when I may need to kill my own pain, for good. Kristina will not go short: Dr. Zoroaster keeps her generously, not to say criminally, well supplied. It is he who tends her, now that she has left the hospital; they spend much time alone together, I hear them quietly talking, hour on hour, I do not know of what.

In my time at Bartoli's apartment his mother kept carefully out of my way. I felt a certain sympathy for her. It must have been distressing to be confronted anew each morning by this startling stranger, for I am certain that overnight, every night, monotonously as in a fairy-tale, the fact of my lodging there slipped through her hopelessly porous memory. Maria, the ancient cook, on the other hand, took a great shine to me, her *colosso,* and plied me coquettishly with all sorts of delicacies and sweetmeats, plates of pasta smothered in fresh truffles, and slices of *panforte* that threatened to pull out by the roots my few remaining molars, and tiny glasses of a metal-bright, thick, sweet liqueur with floating coffee beans and a wisp of ghostly blue flame trembling on the brim. She and Franco Bartoli between them had rigged up a makeshift study for me in a room at the back of the apartment looking on to the gloomy garden; here, as Franco indicated, in a tone of hushed reverence, I would be free to do my work without fear of interruption. That room became for him a hallowed place, a sanctum of intellectual sacrifice, a tabernacle of the real presence—he was, I discovered with some surprise, devoutly religious—consecrated here at the heart of his little domestic establishment. I would hear him creaking past the door on tiptoe, could almost feel him smiling in excited happiness and pride at his good fortune in having Vander the Great for a house guest. I had not known he held me in such high, such heroic, regard. No detractor ever ruffled the placid surface of my self-esteem, but an eager admirer can make me cringe for shame. I did not have the heart to tell poor Franco that my work, such as it was, had all been done, and there would be no more. Instead, I went each morning dutifully into that room, with the look of a man whose gaze is fixed unswervingly on immortality, and shut the door firmly behind me, and felt all outside it go still, waiting for the soundless roar of my mighty intellect starting up its engine. All a sham. For hours I would sit there, slumped in an uncomfortable antique chair, an elbow on the card table that served as a desk, my chin on my fist, gazing out at the place by the garden wall where Cass Cleave that last day had stood up from her chair and taken my arm and walked me off across the parched and crackling grass and told me, so calmly, smiling, with eyes cast down, as though it were the simple answer to an unanswerably complicated question, that she was going to have a child, and that it would be mine.

How is it that men are always astonished by the phenomenon of conception? It might have been understandable in primitive times, when we believed it was the wind that got women with child, but what excuse is there for us in this jadedly over-informed age? True, in the course of a long life I had slept with many women without once, so far as I was informed, impregnating a single womb. What prankster god of fertility had decreed that at the very end I should be allowed to shoot one of his potent arrows straight to its secret and palpitant home? Who would have thought that my dry old seed could still sprout? What an embarrassment! How foolish I felt! And yet, how grateful, too. I saw at once, you see, the implications, the possibilities, what I shall call the saving grace, of this absurdly wonderful happening. Let me be clear; it was not I who would be saved. For once, perhaps really for the first time, it was others I was thinking of. Growing already inside this girl was the enfolded bud of what would be a world reclaimed. Out of the unimaginably complex coils in the hollow heart of the blastula I had set swelling in her belly there had already sprung the new beginnings of my people, my lost people. It was as simple as that. My gentle mother, my melancholy father, my siblings put to summary death before they had lived, all would find their tiny share in this new life. Oh, fond old man! How could I have thought this world would allow for such redemption?

The final postcard bore a brightly tinted picture of a church on a rock in the middle of an improbably berylline bay. She sent it in a package, along with her fountain pen, of all things. *Dearest Svidrigailov—I am going to America—Your Cassandra.* She had posted it in the town of Chiavari three days previously. She must have calculated that it would take just that time, no more, no less, to reach me. I marvel at her faith in the reliability of this country's postal system, although it proved remarkably well founded, for it was a mere ten minutes later, as I was standing helplessly by the window in the garden room with the postcard in one hand and her pen in the other, trying to think what to do, that Franco Bartoli tapped at the door and put in his head warily and whispered that there was a person—*una persona*—on the telephone who wished to speak to me.

❧

Of all the traditional characters of the Italian comedy, Harlequin is at once the most individual and the most enigmatic. Who is this inexplicable being? Are his head and his heart made like our own? If an effigy were to be raised to him it must be made of rubber, for only rubber could receive the impress of his fierce and subtle spirit, created by the gods in a moment of incontrollable mirthfulness and malice. He is called by many names, and no one can say which was rightfully and originally his; many authorities maintain his name was first of all a sobriquet. He is without doubt of divine essence, if not, indeed, Mercury himself, god of twilight and the wind, the patron of thieves and panders. He is Proteus, too, now delicate, now offensive, comic or melancholic, sometimes lashed into a frenzy of madness. He is the creator of a new form of poetry, accented by gestures, punctuated by somersaults, enriched with philosophic reflections and incongruous noises. He is the first poet of acrobatics and unseemly sounds. His black half-mask completes the impression of something savage and fiendish, suggesting a cat, a satyr, an executioner. Consider how he is viewed by public opinion, and try to conceive, if you can, how he could ignore this opinion or confront it! Scarcely have the authorities assigned his dwelling, scarcely has he taken possession of it, when other men move their houses elsewhere so they no longer have to see his. Here he lives alone with his mate, whose voice is the only voice he knows and without which he would hear only groans. The day comes. A dismal signal is given. He sets out, with a black hue and a red eye. It is morning. He arrives at a public square packed with a pressing and panting crowd. He is thrown a poisoner, a parricide, a blasphemer. There is a thrilled, a terrible silence. He seizes the condemned one, stretches him on the rack, then takes and breaks him on the wheel. The head dangles down, the hair hangs on end, the mouth, gaping like a furnace, emits a bloody word, begging for death. It is finished. He steps down; he holds out his bloodstained hand; he is thrown from afar a few gold coins, which he carries away through a double row of men drawing back in horror. He returns home, sits down to table and eats, then goes to his bed and sleeps. Awaking on the morrow, he thinks not at all of what he did the day before. Is this a man? Yes. God receives him in his shrines and allows *him to pray. He is not a criminal and yet no tongue would say of him that he is virtuous, that he is honest, that he is admirable. No moral praise seems appropriate for him, since this would suppose a relation with other human beings, and he has none. He has none, this Harlequin.*

Ⅎ

So this, she saw, was where it would end. There was nowhere farther for her to go, and she was glad. She had watched from the deck of the little ferry boat the five towns receding into the evening vaguenesses of sea and sky and the humped night rising plum-blue behind the headlands, and thought how she too was disappearing, into the dark. That was how it had been all along, since she had left Turin, if not before, if not long before, a secret, gradual process of thinning and fading. The world was letting her go, as he too had let her go. She understood clearly what was happening, what must happen, so that the pattern would be complete. She had tried to explain it to Kristina Kovacs, the way everything was a part of everything else, the way it was all ordained, but Kristina had not understood. Kristina, she saw clearly, was trying to save her, as once she in turn had thought it was her task to save him. But that was not it, that was not it at all. Now they were docking, and she had a moment almost of bliss as the boat glided in silence toward the quayside, where vague figures waited, strangely still, until an old man in a seaman's cap stepped forward nimbly and caught the rope one of the sailors threw to him. The water swayed, smooth as oil, its surface running with coloured lights, peach and mauve and rose. Bats flitted in the sombre air. There were cafés and bars and little restaurants all along the quay, and, behind that, the village climbed the hillside, lamps in the windows of the houses, so many lives. There was a lamp too, or a lantern, above the door of the church that stood on its jagged promontory outlined against the darkening sky. A sailor from the ferry carried her bag all the way up to the hotel. How simply everything was happening.

She wrote again in her notebook, calm now, sitting under a lamp by the open window of her room, a moth making its tiny soft racket around the bulb and the small waves breathing below on the shingle. *Columbine is sick. The Doctor is called. Oh, save me, save me, Dottore! Columbine is going to have a baby. The Old Man is angry.* She smiled and put away the notebook and folded her arms on the table and laid her head on her arms. She felt herself slipping gradually down a dark, immense incline. That is time, she thought, time is the curve, it steepens. Everything she had ever done, her smallest acts, even in earliest infancy, had brought her to this moment, these unavoidable moments, the last. So strange, and yet so simple. She lifted her head with an effort, for she was tired, and sat for a while, listening to the drowsy noises of the night. She had gone to see the doctor, the elegant old doctor with the dyed hair. He had been kind, moving his priestly hand over her belly, sighing. She saw the numbers on his wrist and understood. He had wanted her to go into a clinic, to end it, to have it ended. "What will you do?" he had asked. "Where will you turn?" And he had looked at her for a long time. "Ah, *signorina!*"

The postcard would arrive tomorrow. She was glad she had sent him the pen along with it. She wanted him to know all that she knew.

In the bedroom in Franco Bartoli's apartment after she had collapsed that night Kristina Kovacs had got into bed beside her. So hot, there, and airless, and yet how cool Kristina's hand had felt, resting on her heart. She had slept, knowing the woman was lying awake, watching over her. She could feel Kristina's fear, it was like a living presence, a third person lying with them, veiled, silent, unappeasable. Later she woke, and Kristina had talked to her, soothingly, as if she were talking through an open window to a madwoman out on a ledge. Well, what else are you, she asked herself now, what else are you, but a madwoman, on a ledge? She smiled into the darkness outside the window. She had looked in Kristina's handbag and found a phial of sleeping pills and thought of stealing them, but did not. She knew Kristina was watching her. She wondered if that was what he had asked her to do, to watch over her, and make sure she did not take the pills, or leap from the ledge.

She opened her guidebook at random and read about Shelley's death. He had been to Livorno to see Lord Byron. The schooner was the *Ariel*. The poet, and Edward Williams, and a boy to tend the sail. Why did they give the other names, even the name of the boat, and not say what the boy's name was? They burned Shelley's body on the beach. She put the book away and rose from the chair and stood a moment motionless, listening; not a sound, anywhere, except the little waves. She went out and locked the door behind her and went as quietly as she could down the stairs and out into the night. Who was it she was afraid would hear her, try to hold her back? There was no one. The man at the desk with the grey hair and the moustache did not even lift his eyes as she went past.

The air outside was warm, and had a strong, astringent smell, like the smell of iodine. It was the sea. She could taste salt on her lips. All these vivid things, as if they knew they were the last. She walked down through the hushed streets to the harbour. She knew where she was going. On the quayside people were out strolling, not many, the last of the tourist boats had left long ago. She was aware of glances, women's, mostly. Did they know, just by looking at her? Would they remember her? The sea was invisible, just a blackness, with no horizon, as if half the world out there had fallen clean away. Tomorrow the sun's eclipse, tonight her own. There were no voices in her head any more; they had said all they had to say, had done all they had to do. She imagined them behind her, the horde of them, standing back, big-eyed, their hands over their mouths, staring in gleeful expectation, unable to credit that she was doing at last what they had been urging for so long that she must do.

She climbed the steep, cobbled hill to the church. The lantern was still burning over the stone lintel. The door was open, the doorway hung with a heavy leather curtain worn smooth along one edge by the generations of hands pushing it aside. Penny candles, a vaulted roof, stone floor, a statue of the Virgin all blues and pinks and creams, her eyes uplifted in a transport of sorrow. Such quiet. She sat in the corner of a bench. Every tiniest act, all adding up, bringing her to this. A priest came in, an elderly man, short and fat and perfectly bald. He looked at her in surprise and went out again. Father. There was a door at the side behind the altar. She rose from the bench and went forward. The door was old, its wood chill and damp to the touch, slimed by the night air. It opened, squealing on its hinges. How simply! Here was a little square stone balcony under a gaping sky, with white water snarling around the rocks far, far below. She scrambled on to the parapet, dislodging a piece of stone and grazing her knee. A night breeze pressed her skirt against her legs, so cool, so soft. She put her hands over her womb, feeling the warmth that was not hers. If only she knew the boy's name, the boy on the *Ariel*. He was drowned too. All the lost ones. Her knee smarted where she had grazed it; so insistent, everything, demanding to be noticed, to be noted. She heard someone enter the church behind her and say something, she did not understand the words. Hurry, now. She saw herself falling before she fell, falling down that quickening curve. Someone right there now, it was the priest, the old priest, she saw the light glint on his bald brow and remembered the waiter, the statue of the horseman in the dark; remembered everything. *Signorina!* She took a big breath, and for an instant was a child again, her father behind her, saying, *Jump.* Slowly, swooningly, her eyes ecstatically lifted, like the eyes of the statue of the Madonna, she leaned out into the nothing, as the priest at her back in vain reached forward his restraining hands. Time. Night. Water.

Franco Bartoli drove me in his little car all the way down to that far corner of the coast. When we got to La Spézia we buzzed hotly through the town and on to Lerici, from where I was to take a boat across the bay. It was past dinner hour when we arrived, however, and the boats had stopped running. I would have to stay the night. I chose the Hotel Shelley, to Franco's tight-lipped disapprobation; I might have lodged at the Albergo Lord Byron. Poets, you have not lived in vain. Franco offered, in a wan sort of way, to stay and keep me company, but I said no, he must go back, his *dolce mama* would be fretting. The truth is, I could not have borne his company for another minute. He departed, casting a last commiserating look at me through the windscreen as he briskly turned the car on the quayside and shot off into the gloaming. I telephoned the hotel where she had been staying a few short leagues away across that deceptively innocent-looking sea, and was told they were still searching for the body. I ate a queasy dinner and retired to my room with a bottle of whisky and one of Kristina Kovacs's most powerful bromides, and at once plunged into a series of outlandish nightmares with themes from Hokusai in his most outrageously lascivious marine mode, through which there bobbed at intervals the image of a drowned and bloated poet adrift on a burning sea. When I came out on the harbour next morning I found that the ferries would not be running until the afternoon; that eclipse was to take place presently, and it was considered bad luck to sail before it was past. I crawled back into my sour bed and slept until noon, missing the eclipse, unless a terrified, eventless dream-passage through a region of radiant murk was not a dream at all but a half-waking glimpse of solar occlusion. When at length I woke fully I was sprawled steaming in a bolt of sunlight falling unhindered and full upon me through an open window, and for a few blessed moments I did not know where I was or why I was there.

I am always angry in times of greatest stress. It is a not uncommon reaction, so Dr. Zoroaster informs me, especially in that day's circumstances. I shouted at the receptionist in my hotel, at the fellow selling tickets for the ferry, and then at a sun-blackened Charon in a jaunty peaked cap with an anchor on it who, as I was boarding the ferry at last, offered me a helping hand and almost managed to tip me off the gangplank into the sea. I was also less than civil to the polite young man who met me on the quay at the other side, an emissary from what in my mind was still Cass Cleave, the living girl. The afternoon was sunny, and quick with freshets of warm wind. The hotel clerk, let us call him Mario, a swarthy beanpole with an adam's apple that seemed to be worked by weak elastic, cowered before me as if I might be about to strike him with my stick, which I might well have done had we not been caught up in the mill of disembarkation. I demanded to hear what had happened, I must know everything, right away, now, here on the quayside, this minute, everything! Come on, I shouted into his frightened face, tell me! and I grasped him by the elbow and gave him a violent shake. When he began to speak, however, I would not listen, and instead turned him about and ordered him to take me to where it had happened. We climbed up through the village. There had been a priest, Mario was saying, he had arrived too late, the signorina had . . . He joined his hands together and mimed the act of diving. "She jumped, signore." Her body had still not been found.

After the church——there was nothing there, of course, and the priest was about his duties elsewhere and not to be seen——I went to the hotel, a small, shabby establishment, and made them show me her room. They left me there alone, closing the door on me softly. I searched through her bag, not knowing what I hoped to find. There were some soiled underclothes in a zipped side pocket, I lifted them out and examined them, these profane relics, and put the stained seams in my mouth and sucked them, to have a last savour of her familiar secretions. Then I went into the bathroom and washed them in the handbasin. The water gulped and clicked, bathing my wrists, a silvery unction. I thought of her down in the deeps of the sea, her eyes open, gazing sightlessly up at the surface swaying far above her. First I draped her silks, as clean now as I could make them, on the towel rail to dry, but thought that would not do, and stuffed them into my pocket instead. Then I returned to the basin and bathed my brow; lifting the towel away, I would not have been surprised to find the bloody image of my face imprinted on it. I went and sat at the table by the window and leafed through her notebook. Poor Columbine. On our trip to Genoa that day she had lost me briefly in the cemetery. I had wandered off up some steps to one of the latter-day sections, where the city's recently dead merchants and mafiosi are buried and the statuary is modernly pretentious. It was cool and quiet there, under the colonnades, and I tarried idly for a while, reading the inscriptions on the tombs and entertaining thoughts of the eternal. As I was about to descend again to the lower level I saw her below me, pacing a sunlit patch of gravel, and I stopped behind a pillar to observe her. She was in a state of some agitation, I could see. With her arms tightly folded and her head down, she was walking rapidly here and there in a seemingly senseless, zigzag pattern. She would stand absolutely still for a moment, as if weighing up profound alternatives, then set off abruptly at a headlong stride, only to halt again after a dozen stiff-legged paces and repeat the process, pausing, considering, and plunging off in a new direction. She kept this up for some minutes, but broke off when at last she spied me skulking behind my pillar. We stood and gazed at each other. I do not know what she was thinking. Perhaps she had thought that I had left her, finally, had just decided to disappear and abandon her here among the dead and their monuments. Strangely, or perhaps not strangely, it is the memory of moments such as this that weighs on me most heavily now, the moments, as I suppose, of her deepest desperation.

I went downstairs, her underthings a wet lump in my pocket,

and spoke to the proprietor, a handsome, grey-haired fellow with garlic on his breath. I showed him a fistful of traveller's cheques and said I should prefer it if he would forget that I had been here. He said nothing, only considered a moment and then gave the faintest of shrugs. He stood impassively looking on while I signed the cheques, leaning on his fists on the desk. From a shadowy region behind him his wife made a soundless entrance. She was a corpulent person with three chins and a suspicious eye. Mario the clerk, too, was there. A wonder the entire village did not come jostling into the doorway to have a look at me. When I had handed over the cheques I said that I wished to rest now, and asked if I might lie down in her room, the room that had been hers. Signor Albergo demurred, saying another guest was expected at any moment. I looked at him, and he relented. I went up and lay on the bed where Cass Cleave had lain. As the day waned, I thought of many things, for example that phenomenon, the existence of which I chanced upon in the course of my reading on Mr. Mandelbaum and his ways, which is known among neurologists as the anarchic hand. This remarkable and rare disorder—there are no more than half a hundred recorded cases—is the result of a peculiar form of rebellion deep within the nervous system. Otherwise normal and sound in limb, the sufferer will find himself subject to the tyranny of one or other of his hands, which seemingly on a whim and of its own volition will perform actions independent of him and often against his own best interests. At table, he will find the recalcitrant hand force-feeding him food he does not wish to eat; he will encounter someone in the street, and instead of proffering itself in salutation his hand will fly up and slap the surprised acquaintance across the face. At times the behaviour of the hand will be so obstreperous that its fellow on the other side will be called upon to quell its antics; the resulting struggle can be violent in the extreme, and end in self-lacerations and fellings to the floor. One patient even suffered repeated attempts to strangle herself, and might have succumbed had there not been others by to rush forward and tear the suicidal, or murderous, hand from her throat. What I wondered, lying on the bed that day in that utterly emptied hotel room, was whether a half of the self itself might be an anarch, bent on the destruction of the whole. For it is one thing to think of Cass Cleave willingly leaping out of the light of the world, and altogether another to entertain the possibility that even as she made away with herself, clasped in her own unbreakable embrace, one side of her was crying out in terror, like a child being borne off in the arms of a fiend.

I caught the last ferry. The young man Mario accompanied me to the quayside, I do not know why; perhaps his parents—he was the son of the proprietors, did I mention that?—wished to be sure I had left the vicinity before they cashed the boodle. Or perhaps the fact of my bereavement required a ceremonial symmetry to be observed, and having met me at the boat he must see me off on it as well. He was adamantly polite, matching his pace to mine and offering me a steadying arm as I stepped on to the swaying gang-plank. He waited on the dock, too, while the boat was pulling away, and even waved farewell. It was twilight, his white shirt had an unearthly glow. In fact, his name was not Mario, I do not know why I called him that, but Angelo; the emissaries of Heaven take the most unlikely forms. *Adio, Angelo.* With vigorous churnings the boat turned about and we glided out of the harbour and headed for the horizon where the day's last radiance lingered, trembling on the brink. I stood at the stern and took the sodden wad of under-clothes out of my pocket and dropped it into the sea, where it swirled a moment, opening like a Japanese water flower, and then was dragged down into the dark under the waves. In Lerici the shell-blue night was already falling. *She left me at the silent time* . . . I should have waited until the sea had given up her body. Yes, I should have waited.

All that long afternoon I had been dogged by the sensation of there being somehow more than one of me. When I looked in the places where she had been, or touched the things that had been hers, it was if another were looking with me, through my eyes, touching those things through my fingertips. Afterwards it came to me, with the force of certainty, that by some form of sympathetic magic I must have been anticipating, I must have been foregoing, as it were, how it would be for her father, when he came there, and took the ferry, and walked up the hill to the church, and stood in that hotel room that was so full of her not being in it. I fear that between us we destroyed her, old Thespis and I. She said one day that she loved him, and I said why would she not, since he was her father, but she shook her head, closing her eyes and wincing in that way that she sometimes did, and said no, I did not understand, that what she meant was that she was in *love* with him, and always had been. I thought it fanciful nonsense, meant to impress or shock me, and made no more remark. Late one night, after she was dead, I telephoned the number I had found among her things, and was answered on the first ring by a man's voice. He sounded unnervingly alert, as if he had been lying sleepless, waiting for someone to call, waiting for me, perhaps. I tried to say something but I was too drunk, and was weeping besides. An actor he is, or was, so she told me. I am sure we would have many things in common, he and I. After all, I am an actor too, though only an inspired amateur. The difference is that the part I play is mine alone, and may not be taken by anyone else, on or off the stage. But then, should that not also have been true of Axel Vander?

❧

There were further surprises in store for me, further shocks. One day at the card table in Franco Bartoli's garden room I was writing the opening pages of this record, using the fountain pen that she had sent to me, when the thing ran dry. I could find no ink in the house, and Franco was away. I went out, and after a tedious and listless search—the day was trying to rain, and schoolchildren were kicking leaves in the gutters—I happened at last upon a pen shop in a narrow back street down by the river. The place inside had, disquietingly, the desiccated, glue-and-wormwood smell of the schoolrooms of my childhood. The shop was so narrow that I had to insert myself sidelong between the counter and the display of writing implements and marbled notebooks on the wall opposite. The woman behind the counter, florid and disproportionately large, and dressed all in black, with painted eyebrows and a piled-up hive of lacquered hair, had something in her manner that was indefinably institutional; she might have been a hospital matron, or the wardress of an open prison, or, indeed, simply a school-mistress. She met my request with a show of stylised professionalism, holding successive bottles of ink up to her bosom for my inspection and pointing out the descriptions on their labels with a long, scarlet fingernail. When I chose a bottle, at random, she nodded approvingly, closing her eyes slowly and pursing her lips, as if I had passed a test for exceptional good taste and breeding. She asked if I had brought the pen with me, and if I would like to fill it now. This invitation, along with the schoolroom smell and the proximity enforced on us by the confined space, raised a suggestion of intimacy that was at once worrying and oddly welcome, and I felt like a small boy who had been kept back for special favours after lessons. Almost shyly I produced the pen and unscrewed the barrel, not without resistance, for there was something inside, papers of some kind, tightly wrapped around what turned out to be one of those disposable cartridges—*"Ecco, signore, una segreta!"*—and held fast with a strand of silk, which after a miniature struggle I succeeded in untying, and unfolded the scraps of paper and laid them out side by side on the glass counter and tried to hold them flat under splayed fingertips. At first, because the papers kept curling and the lights under the glass were shining through them, I could not make out the printed words. Then I saw his picture, and mine, and our names, his misspelled. The shop woman, leaning forward so that her brow was almost touching mine and I could smell the not unpleasant, soapy scent of her hair, let fall a soft, shivery sigh, as if it were a buried treasure we had unearthed there between us. Then she looked up into my face, and an expression of concern, of solicitude, even, came into her eyes, and she reached out and laid one of her hands tenderly over one of mine. So strange they are, rare, certainly, affecting, but faintly discomfiting, too, those moments when some stranger steps out of the crowd and for no reason other than simple good-heartedness offers a word of consolation, a sustaining arm. What had she seen in me to spark such sympathy? The flinch, the wild stare, the panicked feint to this side now to that, the frozen helplessness. Look at me there, caught in the headlights, speechless with surprise and pain, my last poor secrets all on show, ready to lay my head upon this woman's bombasined bosom and weep my hard heart dry.

But here is the surprising thing. The profoundest shock was not the trick Cass Cleave had played on me, nor what was here revealed, namely that all along she had been aware of who I was and was not. As I goggled at those ancient scraps of newsprint, the *Staandard* announcement of his death and the two photographs that had accompanied his travesty of an interview with me in the *Gazet,* I was thinking not of him, nor even of Cass Cleave, but of Magda. And in that moment I realised at last what I had always known without knowing, that she too had been privy to my secret. Oh, I do not say she knew for certain that I was not Axel Vander, or that the bourgeois origins I professed to despise, the indulgent parents, the grand apartment, the poor relations, were not mine but his; I do not say she knew all this in detail. Her knowledge of my duplicity ran deeper than more detail, it reached far down into my very essence. Do not ask me how she had found me out. Perhaps she met someone who had been acquainted with me before I was Axel Vander—America in those days was rife with other people's secrets—or maybe her spurned Pole had nosed out something about me and my past and had confronted her with it. Or maybe it was simply that she guessed. No matter, no matter. What I marvel at is her silence. All those years when I thought I was preserving myself through deceit, it was really she who was keeping me whole, keeping me intact, by pretending to be deceived. She was my silent guarantor of authenticity. That was what I realised, as I stood that day in the stationer's shop on the Via Bonafous and one whole wall of my life fell down and I was afforded an entire vista of the world that I had never glimpsed before.

In an access of wonderment, the wonderment of a child who has found out one of the adult world's big secrets, I had to tell someone of these discoveries. Kristina Kovacs would not do; to her, so far advanced in dying, it would all have come as no more than a distant twittering, the mere gossip of the merely living. That I should blurt out such things to Franco Bartoli was unthinkable. I might have confided in his mother, certainly my secrets would have been safe with her, no sooner heard than forgotten. However, in the end it was Dr. Zoroaster that I turned to as confidant and confessor. It was on the day that he helped me to move Kristina Kovacs into the apartment here. Yes, I have brought her to live with me, or, more accurately, to die, as she herself remarked, with one of her wry smiles that are so rare now. There had been an ambulance from the hospital, and two blue-jawed helpers in white coats, who looked more like barbers than medical attendants but were gentle all the same, had manoeuvred her up the stairs in a wheelchair and got her into bed—I have given over my bedroom to her, and fixed up a crib for myself on the couch in the other room. The Doctor had given her a sedative, and she was barely conscious, muttering to herself in a language I could not identify, her poor head lolling. Bald and shrunken, still in her white hospital gown, she had the look of a wigless eighteenth-century savant at his levee. The Doctor and I were standing together at the foot of the bed, watching her, when I heard myself starting to tell him everything. Well, no, not everything; lifelong habits of dissembling die hard. I told him how Cass Cleave had known things about me, without saying what those things were, exactly, and how when I discovered what she knew I realised at once and for the first time that my wife had known them too. He listened with calm attention, standing there in his big coat and his scarf, not looking at me but keeping his gaze bent on the by now comatose woman. The city's first snow of the season had begun to fall, and a chill breath was seeping in at the low window beside the bed, and all around us was a muffled hush. As the waning year progressively turns paler the more pronounced becomes the Assyrian swarthiness of Dr. Zoroaster's face; he has the fierce dark eye and raptor's profile of a desert monarch. One of the most striking aspects of his curious presence, at once unsettling and reassuring, is the quality of stillness he maintains. He seems to function on a principle of intermittent entropy. He will rise out of immobility and silence into movement and speech and then subside into himself again and be as if he had not stirred or spoken. At times it will take so long for him to reply to a question or formulate a remark that it will seem he is not attending to the outer world at all, but is at rest in some remote, inner sphere of enervated contemplativeness, oblivious calm. It is, I suppose, the dwelling place of one who has survived. Now he allowed an extra lengthy silence to elapse, and, since already I regretted having spoken, I was entertaining the wistful hope that he might forgo any response at all. He was lighting a cigarette with that conjuror's gestural grace which is another of his characteristics, his hands making slow hoops through which wreaths of smoke drifted and drooped, and had I not been so mesmerised watching him perform I might have registered sooner the strangeness of what it was he had begun to say. He asked if I had noticed the surprise that he had shown when I had first told him my name. "You remember?" he said. "It was a pleasant occasion. We were having coffee, at the Bicerin." I remembered, but I did not remember him being surprised; what would constitute an expression of surprise, anyway, in that mummified, regal mask that is his face? He was surprised, he said, because he had heard the name Axel Vander before, a long time ago, in altogether different circumstances and surroundings. Here he paused, a hand holding the cigarette suspended before his mouth and his eyes narrowed against the smoke, remembering. He turned slowly and walked out of the bedroom into the study, where lamplight and snowlight were joined in feeble contest. He went to the window and gazed out through its grimy panes, watching the white flakes drifting down into the street. I could feel my heart beating, a tentatively apprehensive measure, getting ready for what shocks might come. "Snow," the Doctor murmured. "Yes, snow." He had encountered the Vanders, he said, in a place in a forest, a sort of way station, while they and he were awaiting transportation elsewhere. They were a middle-aged couple, healthy still but in a state of great emotional distress. They had exchanged for food the last of a small cache of diamonds they had managed to bring with them, concealed in the linings of their clothes, and their prospects, like the prospects of all those brought to that place, were bleak. Already they had lost a son, destroyed, so they told him, by the actions of a treacherous friend. "Destroyed?" I said faintly. Or perhaps I only thought of saying it. I sat down slowly at my desk and leaned an arm on it. There are certain exhalations that sound like one's last breath. Where were they bound, the Vanders, I asked, where were they being transported to? He shrugged, without turning from the window. "East," he said.

✧

I am waiting for Franco Bartoli to come, as he comes every day, to visit Kristina Kovacs. He is growing his beard again, as if in an attempt to compensate for the loss of Kristina's hair. I think she does not always recognise him. I leave them alone together, although I suspect Franco wishes I would stay. When he has done his duty and paid his visit I invite him to sit with me for a while before he leaves; we drink a glass of wine, he sniffles a little, blows his nose and tries to talk about things, Kristina Kovacs, his work, happenings out in the great world; Cass Cleave he does not mention, no doubt to spare my feelings. I tell him again Dr. Zoroaster's curious story about the people he met in the camp in the forest, the people calling themselves Vander. I am really retelling it to myself. What am I to think? I recall Axel's father doing his Moses and Rahel routine, how persuasive a mimic he was. But if they . . . ? If Axel . . . ? What am I to think? Franco Bartoli finishes his wine and, sighing, departs. When I have heard his car drive away I put on my slouch hat, take up my stick, and, having looked in on Kristina, go out and stroll the winter streets, my daily promenade, my daily harlequinade. I think on what a gallimaufry we are, Franco and poor Kristina, the Doctor, me. The city is quiet at this time of year. The dead, though, have their voice. The air through which I move is murmurous with absences. I shall soon be one of them. Good. Why should I have life and she have none? She. She.

ACKNOWLEDGEMENTS

We set up a word . . . but not "truths," p. v, Nietzsche, *The Will to Power,* 482, translated by Walter Kaufmann and R. J. Hollingdale (New York, 1968).

"A city child . . . a fantasy born of my longing to belong," pages 46–47, is adapted from a passage in *The Future Lasts a Long Time,* by Louis Althusser, edited by Olivier Corpet and Yann Moulier Boutang, translated by Richard Veasey (London, 1993). Other themes in that book have been alluded to and employed elsewhere in the text, as have themes in the life and various works of Paul de Man.

"Of all the traditional characters . . . He has none, this Harlequin," pages 241–42, is a combined adaptation of passages from *The Italian Comedy,* by Pierre Louis Duchartre, translated by Randolph T. Weaver (New York, 1966), and *St. Petersburg Dialogues,* by Joseph de Maistre, translated by Richard A. Lebrun (Toronto, 1993).

The description in Part Two of the persecution of Jews in Belgium is not historically accurate, and is based on eyewitness accounts from Germany in *The Klemperer Diaries 1933–1945,* by Victor Klemperer (London, 2000), and from Romania in *Journal 1935–1944,* by Mihail Sebastian (Chicago, 2000).

Thanks to: Ludo Abicht, Ortwin de Graef, Fergus Martin, Hedwig Schwall.

ATHENA

In this literary thriller and sumptuously perverse love story, John Banville's narrator calls himself "Morrow." His knowledge of seventeenth-century Flemish art makes him indispensable to the baroque lowlifes who want him to authenticate some suspicious paintings. While investigating, he meets a woman who seems to have stepped out of the paintings, and who will become both his mistress and nemesis, his anguish and addiction.

Fiction/Literature/0-679-73685-9

THE BOOK OF EVIDENCE

Freddie Montgomery is a highly cultured man, a husband and father living the life of a dissolute exile on a Mediterranean island. When a debt comes due and his wife and child are held as collateral, he returns to Ireland to secure funds and commits murder. The novel unfurls his attempt to present evidence of the events that lead to the murder he committed merely because he could.

Fiction/Literature/0-375-72523-7

DOCTOR COPERNICUS

It is the sixteenth century. Princes and bishops send armies careening across Europe and order assassins into the bed chambers of their enemies. Luther's heresy convulses Germany. And in a remote corner of Poland, Copernicus, a modest canon, is practicing medicine and studying the heavens, preparing a theory that will shatter the medieval view of the universe.

Fiction/Literature/0-679-73799-5

ECLIPSE

When renowned actor Alexander Cleave was a boy living with his widowed mother and various itinerant lodgers, he saw a vivid ghost of his father. Now fifty, he has returned to his boyhood home to recover from a nervous breakdown, and finds two new lodgers, who, coupled with an onslaught of disturbing memories, compel him to confront the clutter that has become his life.

Fiction/Literature/0-375-72529-6

GHOSTS

On an unnamed island, a day boat runs aground, forcing its group of shaken travelers to wade ashore. There they encounter a reclusive art historian and his assistant. But is the meeting truly an accident? If so, why does one of the castaways appear to know the reclusive scholar, and why is the latter so afraid of him? And who is the stranger who moves among them, as omnipresent as a little god, as haunted as a fleeing murderer, observing their actions with longing, dread, and a little amusement?

Fiction/Literature/0-679-75512-8

KEPLER

Wars, witchcraft, and disease rage throughout Europe. And for this court mathematician, vexed by domestic strife, appalled by the religious upheavals that have driven him from exile to exile, and vulnerable to the whims of his eccentric patrons, astronomy is a quest for some form of divine order. For all of the mathematical precision of his exploration, though, it is a seemingly elusive quest until he makes one glorious and profoundly human discovery.

Fiction/Literature/0-679-74370-7

THE UNTOUCHABLE

Victor Maskell, formerly of British intelligence has been unmasked as a Russian agent and subjected to a disgrace that is almost a kind of death. As Maskell retraces his tortuous path from his recruitment at Cambridge to the airless upper regions of the establishment, we discover a figure of manifold doubleness: Irishman and Englishman; husband, father, and lover of men; betrayer and dupe.

Fiction/Literature/0-679-76747-9